THE HEADLESS CORPSE-MAN

A corpse was no surprise, given what I remembered. I looked it over. It had been wearing local man's clothing: boots, loose pants with a rope tie, a jacket encrusted with pockets. The jacket was pierced with a great ragged hole front and back. That could only have been made by Feather's horrible ARM weapon. This close, the head . . . I'd thought it must be under the water, but there was no head at all. There were clean white bones, and a neck vertebra cut smoothly in half.

I was hyperventilating. Dizzy. I sat down next to the skeleton so that I wouldn't fall. My empty stomach heaved. This was much worse than anything I'd imagined. I *knew* who this was . . .

◆ ◆ ◆

Beowulf Shaeffer, wandering crashlander, generally too lazy to stay out of trouble, but bright enough to think his way out once he was in . . . as long as he kept his head!

By Larry Niven
Published by Ballantine Books:

The Known Space Series:
A GIFT FROM EARTH
THE LONG *ARM* OF GIL HAMILTON
NEUTRON STAR
PROTECTOR
RINGWORLD
THE RINGWORLD ENGINEERS
TALES OF KNOWN SPACE:
  The Universe of Larry Niven
WORLD OF PTAVVS

Other Titles:
ALL THE MYRIAD WAYS
CONVERGENT SERIES
THE FLIGHT OF THE HORSE
A HOLE IN SPACE
THE INTEGRAL TREES
LIMITS
THE SMOKE RING
A WORLD OUT OF TIME
CRASHLANDER

With Steven Barnes:
THE CALIFORNIA VOODOO GAME

With David Gerrold:
THE FLYING SORCERERS

With Jerry Pournelle:
FOOTFALL
LUCIFER'S HAMMER

CRASHLANDER

Larry Niven

A Del Rey Book

BALLANTINE BOOKS • NEW YORK

Sale of this book without a front cover may be unauthorized. If this book is coverless, it may have been reported to the publisher as "unsold or destroyed" and neither the author nor the publisher may have received payment for it.

A Del Rey Book
Published by Ballantine Books

Copyright © 1994 by Larry Niven

All rights reserved under International and Pan-American Copyright Conventions. Published in the United States of America by Ballantine Books, a division of Random House, Inc., New York, and simultaneously in Canada by Random House of Canada Limited, Toronto.

"The Borderland of Sol," copyright © 1975 by the Conde Nast Publications, Inc., for *Analog*, January 1975.

"Neutron Star," copyright © 1966 by Galaxy Publishing Corp. Published in *World of If*, October 1966.

"At the Core," copyright © 1966 by Galaxy Publishing Corp. Published in *World of If*, November 1966.

"Flatlander," copyright © 1967 by Galaxy Publishing Corp. Published in *World of If*, March 1967.

"Grendel," copyright © 1968 by Larry Niven. Published by Ballantine Books, April 1968.

Library of Congress Catalog Card Number: 93-90863

ISBN 0-345-38168-8

Manufactured in the United States of America

First Edition: April 1994

10 9 8 7 6 5 4 3 2 1

For my Mother:

for all that I owe you.

✳

GHOST: ONE

We had wonderful seats ten rows back from the glass.

Two hundred feet below the ocean's surface sunlight flooded down through seaweed forests in a thousand flickering golden beams. Players swirled in shoals among the forest roots like half a hundred color-coded fighting fish.

Grandstands had been set against the city dome. Beyond the glass was the playing domain for ten color-marked teams, each team being five humans and a dolphin. Sixty players, down to fifty now, the humans using breathers and oversized fins.

The prey were local life-forms, three flattened turtles armed with hind flippers as wide as wings. Their painted shells glowed like captured suns, red, yellow, violet. The point was to move the prey through the arches, paraboloids painted in the same blazing colors. A player might pull a prey against his chest to swim with it, or hold it at arm's length and steer by the strength of his arms while the prey did the work, or even leave it swimming toward the sand during a melee, hoping a teammate could get it before it disappeared.

Sharrol was entranced. When a swarm of Entertainment Guild players carried the violet prey through the violet arch, she bellowed with the rest.

I don't understand water war. She watched the game; I watched her.

Sharrol was dressed Shashter style, a fancy cloak over a body stocking with windows in it that would serve for swimming. She was small even by flatlander standards, beginning to bulge with our second child. Strong jaw, pale skin, straight black hair: the real Sharrol. On Earth she'd worn many fantastic images, in flatlander style.

For too long fear had lurked beneath her surface emotions. Sharrol wasn't made for this world. But we'd lived beneath Fafnir's world-spanning ocean for a year and a half, we'd conceived and birthed Jeena and started a sister for her, and we'd come to see this place as our own. Gradually the fear had been etched away. I saw no sign of it now. Sharrol was at home.

Light beams danced down through the water and played over the wonderful landscape of Sharrol Janss. But I'd missed brunch. I nudged her and said, "I'm going for provisions."

She didn't turn. "Good! Handmeal, red, yes on veggies. Popcorn. Juice, any."

I left my backpurse in the seat. I glanced back when I reached the aisle. Sharrol was lovely in profile, and entirely absorbed in the game.

The stands didn't include food stalls. You had to go under the stands and all the way across the Strand, by elevated slidebridge, and into a fair-sized food court.

Or you could walk twenty yards along the glass, use a transfer booth, and save fifteen minutes.

I flicked in on the second-floor balcony. I looked over the railing at several long lines. The longest was a window for handmeals. My attention snagged on a face below.

He caught me looking.

Or not. I didn't wait to be sure. I stepped to the lone phone booth at the end of the row of transfer booths. Found a coin and dialed. I did not want this call registered on my pocket phone.

We might have had a whole lifetime, I thought. We'd been promised that, but it had been a lie. But we'd had our year and a half.

The glass at the back of the booth reflected the top of the slidestair if I held my head right. I watched while Sharrol's phone chimed six times.

She was looking past her phone, watching the game.

"Bey? What?" She showed flat in one of the walls. Her pocket phone wasn't sophisticated enough to give me a hologram.

I said, "I saw a face."

"Who?" Now she looked at me. "Not her. Tell me it's not her."

"No, of course not, but it's not good. He was my ghostwriter—"

"Bey? Your *what*?"

"Dear one, I'm short of time. Ander Smittarasheed shouldn't *be* here. I think he knew me—"

"Unlikely!"

"I was looking over a balcony. He saw just my head and shoulders, foreshortened. But maybe he doesn't know about *you*. So book a single for me at the Pequod as Persial January Hebert." It was a name I hadn't used in a while, but she knew it, and we'd stayed at the Pequod once. Furnish the room a little? Luggage? No, but— "I left my backpurse on my seat. Leave it in the room. Nothing else."

"Next?"

The man I'd seen hadn't appeared yet.

She was taking it all in, but muscles were flexing at the corners of her jaw and her eyes were wide and frightened. I asked, "How tough are you?"

Her eyes slid away, watching the game, because someone might be watching her. She said again, "Next?"

"If you can. Get Jeena. Go to Shasht. Get Outbound Enterprises to freeze you for transfer to Home, sign me in, too, and pay the extra to ship Jeena. I'll be there when I can."

Her jaw set. Sharrol was a flat phobe, and the continent Shasht wasn't just halfway round the world; it was the surface. I couldn't guess whether she was strong enough to get through this. I said, "If you can't do it, leave word—"

"When can you join us?"

"If I'm not on the same ship, go to Carlos. I'll get to you soonest."

"You'd better have one tanj of a good story for me when you do," Sharrol said, and then a head came into view, reflected in the glass. With my head still turned away I flicked off the phone, my back blocking the action, and wiggled out my pocket phone.

It was him. Square face, thin blond hair, jaw like a prey turtle, muscles rippling under the shirt. He was puffing a little. Ander was born of Earth, and he'd kept a flatlander's wild taste in dress and appearance. Today his drawstring pants were a miracle of wriggling colored lines. He wore a tunic in solid colors, green and brown with a jagged black line across chest and back. Classical cartoon characters kept peeking over the black line, chattering to each other about what they saw, then dropping back. He wore a backpurse, disappointingly drab.

He was taking his time, looking puzzled but determined, coming right at me.

So I let him see me pocket my unused phone as I turned and stepped out of the booth and right into him. I yelped. "Aghh!"

"Sorry. Beowulf, how you've changed!" He looked me over, visibly shocked, blocking me in the booth.

I shied back, wimp intimidated by a street thug, a bit offended and a bit afraid. "Sorry, man, I didn't mean to nudge you."

He stepped forward and took my hand in both of his, despite lack of encouragement, and pumped it and hung on. He bellowed over the crowd noise. "Ander Smittarasheed. We made two travelogue vids together. Beowulf, all I can say is you must have a hell of a tale to tell."

He had no doubts: he knew me. I said, "Hide. Hell of a tale to hide, Ander."

"Not anymore."

I shouted, "Yah. Right. Are you with anyone?"

"No, on my own."

"Come watch the game with me. I think there's an empty seat next to mine." There'd better be.

He was still staring. Whatever he'd known, whatever had brought him here, he hadn't expected what he was seeing.

I hugged that thought to me. He was seeing me for the

first time in twelve years. I dared to hope that Ander hadn't prepared for this meeting. There was no backup. Just him.

As we passed the booths, his hand closed on my upper arm. He might not think it *likely* that I'd dive into a transfer booth and vanish, but he wasn't risking it. He shouted, "Why a phone booth to use a pocket phone?"

And I showed myself astonished at his stupidity and bellowed, "Noise!"

Then the crowd roar drowned out any hope of conversation, we moved onto the slidebridge, and I had a few moments to think.

There's only one spaceport on We Made It, and the ships don't land every day. Some of us kids used to watch them take off and land. I'm the only one who became a pilot.

What I noticed about the tourists was muscle.

I wasn't undermuscled for a local. Some of the tourists hailed from worlds no more massive than mine, but we got Jinxians and flatlanders, too. They walked like they expected us to shy away from their moving mass. We tall, narrow, fragile crashlander men and women did as they expected, and resented it a little.

Nakamura Lines ran their ships at one Earth gravity. I had to train hard just to walk around on my own ship. Thus trained, I was a superbly muscled athlete by We Made It standards. It was still true that too many passengers looked at my albino pallor and tall, skeletal frame and saw a sickly ghoul.

I'd gotten used to that. Maybe it had left me touchy.

Visceral memory had come flooding back when Ander's hand closed on my arm like a predator's jaws. I hadn't known Ander well. I'd seen him twice in fourteen years, for periods of intense activity of a few weeks each. Now I needed a story to tell to Ander Smittarasheed; but what I remembered best was that I'd disliked him on sight.

Sharrol's seat was empty. Ander settled into it. "You really like these water wars? What guild do you favor?"

"No, Ander, it's not like that. You've seen my home-world. There's only one ocean on We Made It, and it's all one storm. Nobody swims."

"So what are we doing here?"

I had come here following a woman's whim, but Ander shouldn't know that. "I don't care who wins. I just get a kick out of watching how *good* they are."

But I'd listened to enough of Sharrol's prattling. Water war derived from a game the kzinti played on the continent, on land. In both forms the game is local to Fafnir. No offworld tourist would know of it. I need only open my mouth and let Sharrol speak.

"They all swim like dolphins, don't they? But the dol-phins can't grab the prey, they can only push the other players around, except that the Structure Team dolphin has hands. It's an option. But the rig is slowing her down; can you tell? Do you know anything about strategy? They're down to seven teams, looks like—" I saw that he was only waiting for me to stop talking. "Ander, what are you doing on Fafnir?"

"Looking for you."

"Yah, I always thought so. You're with the United Na-tions police." I need not pretend to like it.

Ander frowned. "Not . . . exactly. I'm not an ARM. I'm with Sigmund Ausfaller, and Sigmund is an ARM, but he has his own agenda. By which I mean to say I'm not here to bring you back, Beowulf."

"That's good. I don't want to go back." I didn't have my story yet, but it would not include wanting to return to Earth. "Why, then?"

"Can you tell me what happened to Feather Filip?"

"It's long and ugly."

"No problem. I'll take you to dinner."

"Thanks." It might help me, now or later, if Ander thought I was short of money. Better yet— "There's an item of great value involved, Ander. One I can't touch my-self. That, and Feather, and the way I look: they're all linked."

"Yes. Good," he said absently. "And, though he never said so to *me*, Sigmund may have wanted you to know that if you outsmarted the ARM, you did not outsmart *Sigmund*."

"I expect he did. Anything else?"

"Oh, yes. I got into this because we were talking about Pierson's puppeteers. Sigmund and I decided that you, Beowulf Shaeffer, know as much about these aliens as any ARM."

"Hah. Were you sober?"

"And then we worked out where you must be. No, not sober then, but we talked the next morning and didn't change our minds. Beowulf, how did you first learn of the puppeteers?"

"School and the holo cube. We watched a lot of travelogues when we were kids. And we hung around the spaceport, so I knew they make the General Products ships."

"And your first contact?"

"We wrote that up together. Oh, tanj, Ander! You're recording, aren't you?"

He said, "Yes," giving me an instant to object, daring me. Who was he recording *for*? Who was involved in hunting Beowulf Shaeffer? If it was Sigmund Ausfaller . . . I'd never outguessed Sigmund yet.

Ander said, "We'll pay you a consultant's fee. Ten per hour, Beowulf. Will you accept?"

"How many hours do you need?" It was generous, but my yes would be a verbal contract. I'd be his prisoner.

He waved it off. "Until midnight. Then we can renegotiate. I need the recording for Sigmund."

Ouch. "Until midnight," I said, "present time being ten to noon local."

"Your first contact with Pierson's puppeteers?"

Fifteen years flying passengers between the worlds. Then Nakamura Lines collapsed, and I was on the street . . . on We Made It, because the bankruptcy courts allowed us transport home. Two years later I was ready to accept an offer from anyone. Anyone . . .

✳
NEUTRON STAR

The *Skydiver* dropped out of hyperspace an even million miles above the neutron star. I needed a minute to place myself against the stellar background and another to find the distortion Sonya Laskin had mentioned before she died. It was to my left, an area the apparent size of the Earth's moon. I swung the ship around to face it.

Curdled stars, muddled stars, stars that had been stirred with a spoon.

The neutron star was in the center, of course, though I couldn't see it and hadn't expected to. It was only eleven miles across, and cool. A billion years had passed since BVS-1 had burned by fusion fire. Millions of years, at least, since the cataclysmic two weeks during which BVS-1 was an X-ray star, burning at a temperature of five billion degrees Kelvin. Now it showed only by its mass.

The ship began to turn by itself. I felt the pressure of the fusion drive. Without help from me, my faithful metal watchdog was putting me in a hyperbolic orbit that would take me within one mile of the neutron star's surface. Twenty-four hours to fall, twenty-four hours to rise ... and during that time something would try to kill me. As something had killed the Laskins.

The same type of autopilot, with the same program, had chosen the Laskins' orbit. It had not caused their ship to collide with the star. I could trust the autopilot. I could even change its program.

I really ought to.

How did I get myself into this hole?

8

The drive went off after ten minutes of maneuvering. My orbit was established in more ways than one. I knew what would happen if I tried to back out now.

All I'd done was walk into a drugstore to get a new battery for my lighter!

Right in the middle of the store, surrounded by three floors of sales counters, was the new 2603 Sinclair intrasystem yacht. I'd come for a battery, but I stayed to admire. It was a beautiful job, small and sleek and streamlined and blatantly different from anything that'd ever been built. I wouldn't have flown it for anything, but I had to admit it was pretty. I ducked my head through the door to look at the control panel. You never saw so many dials. When I pulled my head out, all the customers were looking in the same direction. The place had gone startlingly quiet.

I can't blame them for staring. A number of aliens were in the store, mainly shopping for souvenirs, but they were staring, too. A puppeteer is unique. Imagine a headless, three-legged centaur wearing two Cecil the Seasick Sea Serpent puppets on its arms and you'll have something like the right picture. But the arms are weaving necks, and the puppets are real heads, flat and brainless, with wide flexible lips. The brain is under a bony hump set between the bases of the necks. This puppeteer wore only its own coat of brown hair, with a mane that extended all the way up its spine to form a thick mat over the brain. I'm told that the way they wear the mane indicates their status in society, but to me it could have been anything from a dockworker to a jeweler to the president of General Products.

I watched with the rest as it came across the floor, not because I'd never seen a puppeteer but because there is something beautiful about the dainty way they move on those slender legs and tiny hooves. I watched it come straight toward me, closer and closer. It stopped a foot away, looked me over, and said, "You are Beowulf Shaeffer, former chief pilot for Nakamura Lines."

Its voice was a beautiful contralto with not a trace of accent. A puppeteer's mouths are not only the most flexible speech organs around but also the most sensitive hands. The tongues are forked and pointed; the wide, thick lips have little fingerlike knobs along the rims. Imagine a watchmaker with a sense of taste in his fingertips . . .

I cleared my throat. "That's right."

It considered me from two directions. "You would be interested in a high-paying job?"

"I'd be fascinated by a high-paying job."

"I am our equivalent of the regional president of General Products. Please come with me, and we will discuss this elsewhere."

I followed it into a displacement booth. Eyes followed me all the way. It was embarrassing being accosted in a public drugstore by a two-headed monster. Maybe the puppeteer knew it. Maybe it was testing me to see how badly I needed money.

My need was great. Eight months had passed since Nakamura Lines had folded. For some time before that I had been living very high on the hog, knowing that my back pay would cover my debts. I never saw that back pay. It was quite a crash, Nakamura Lines. Respectable middle-aged businessmen took to leaving their hotel windows without their lift belts. Me, I kept spending. If I'd started living frugally, my creditors would have done some checking . . . and I'd have ended in debtor's prison.

The puppeteer dialed thirteen fast digits with its tongue. A moment later we were elsewhere. Air puffed out when I opened the booth door, and I swallowed to pop my ears.

"We are on the roof of the General Products building." The rich contralto voice thrilled along my nerves, and I had to remind myself that it was an alien speaking, not a lovely woman. "You must examine this spacecraft while we discuss your assignment."

I stepped outside a little cautiously, but it wasn't the windy season. The roof was at ground level. That's the way we build on We Made It. Maybe it has something to do with the fifteen-hundred-mile-an-hour winds we get in summer and winter, when the planet's axis of rotation runs through its primary, Procyon. The winds are our planet's only tourist attraction, and it would be a shame to slow them down by planting skyscrapers in their path. The bare, square concrete roof was surrounded by endless square miles of desert, not like the deserts of other inhabited worlds but an utterly lifeless expanse of fine sand just crying to be planted with ornamental cactus. We've tried that. The wind blows the plants away.

The ship lay on the sand beyond the roof. It was a No. 2 General Products hull: a cylinder three hundred feet long and twenty feet through, pointed at both ends and with a slight wasp-waist constriction near the tail. For some reason it was lying on its side, with the landing shocks still folded in at the tail.

Ever notice how all ships have begun to look the same? A good ninety-five percent of today's spacecraft are built around one of the four General Products hulls. It's easier and safer to build that way, but somehow all ships end as they began: mass-produced look-alikes.

The hulls are delivered fully transparent, and you use paint where you feel like it. Most of this particular hull had been left transparent. Only the nose had been painted, around the lifesystem. There was no major reaction drive. A series of retractable attitude jets had been mounted in the sides, and the hull was pierced with smaller holes, square and round, for observational instruments. I could see them gleaming through the hull.

The puppeteer was moving toward the nose, but something made me turn toward the stern for a closer look at the landing shocks. They were bent. Behind the curved transparent hull panels some tremendous pressure had forced the metal to flow like warm wax, back and into the pointed stern.

"What did this?" I asked.

"We do not know. We wish strenuously to find out."

"What do you mean?"

"Have you heard of the neutron star BVS-1?"

I had to think a moment. "First neutron star ever found, and so far the only. Someone located it two years ago by stellar displacement."

"BVS-1 was found by the Institute of Knowledge on Jinx. We learned through a go-between that the Institute wished to explore the star. They needed a ship to do it. They had not yet sufficient money. We offered to supply them with a ship's hull, with the usual guarantees, if they would turn over to us all data they acquired through using our ship."

"Sounds fair enough." I didn't ask why they hadn't done their own exploring. Like most sentient vegetarians, puppeteers find discretion to be the *only* part of valor.

"Two humans named Peter Laskin and Sonya Laskin wished to use the ship. They intended to come within one mile of the surface in a hyperbolic orbit. At some point during their trip an unknown force apparently reached through the hull to do this to the landing shocks. The unknown force also seems to have killed the pilots."

"But that's impossible. Isn't it?"

"You see the point. Come with me." The puppeteer trotted toward the bow.

I saw the point, all right. Nothing, but nothing, can get through a General Products hull. No kind of electromagnetic energy except visible light. No kind of matter, from the smallest subatomic particle to the fastest meteor. That's what the company's advertisements claim, and the guarantee backs them up. I've never doubted it, and I've never heard of a General Products hull being damaged by a weapon or by anything else.

On the other hand, a General Products hull is as ugly as it is functional. The puppeteer-owned company could be badly hurt if it got around that something *could* get through a company hull. But I didn't see where I came in.

We rode an escalladder into the nose.

The lifesystem was in two compartments. Here the Laskins had used heat-reflective paint. In the conical control cabin the hull had been divided into windows. The relaxation room behind it was a windowless reflective silver. From the back wall of the relaxation room an access tube ran aft, opening on various instruments and the hyperdrive motors.

There were two acceleration couches in the control cabin. Both had been torn loose from their mountings and wadded into the nose like so much tissue paper, crushing the instrument panel. The backs of the crumpled couches were splashed with rust brown. Flecks of the same color were all over everything: the walls, the windows, the viewscreens. It was as if something had hit the couches from behind: something like a dozen paint-filled toy balloons striking with tremendous force.

"That's blood," I said.

"That is correct. Human circulatory fluid."

Twenty-four hours to fall.

I spent most of the first twelve hours in the relaxation room, trying to read. Nothing significant was happening, except that a few times I saw the phenomenon Sonya Laskin had mentioned in her last report. When a star went directly behind the invisible BVS-1, a halo formed. BVS-1 was heavy enough to bend light around it, displacing most stars to the sides, but when a star went directly behind the neutron star, its light was displaced to all sides at once. Result: a tiny circle which flashed once and was gone almost before the eye could catch it.

I'd known next to nothing about neutron stars the day the puppeteer picked me up. Now I was an expert. And I still had no idea what was waiting for me when I got down there.

All the matter you're ever likely to meet will be normal matter, composed of a nucleus of protons and neutrons surrounded by electrons in quantum energy states. In the heart of any star there is a second kind of matter, for there the tremendous pressure is enough to smash the electron shells. The result is degenerate matter: nuclei forced together by pressure and gravity but held apart by the mutual repulsion of the more or less continuous electron "gas" around them. The right circumstances may create a third type of matter.

Given: a burned-out white dwarf with a mass greater than 1.44 times the mass of the sun—Chandrasekhar's Limit, named for an Indian-American astronomer of the 1900s. In such a mass the electron pressure alone would not be able to hold the electrons back from the nuclei. Electrons would be forced against protons—to make neutrons. In one blazing explosion most of the star would change from a compressed mass of degenerate matter to a closely packed lump of neutrons: neutronium, theoretically the densest matter possible in this universe. Most of the remaining normal and degenerate matter would be blown away by the liberated heat.

For two weeks the star would give off X rays as its core temperature dropped from five billion degrees Kelvin to five hundred million. After that it would be a light-emitting body perhaps ten to twelve miles across: the next best thing to invisible. It was not strange that BVS-1 was the first neutron star ever found.

Neither is it strange that the Institute of Knowledge on Jinx would have spent a good deal of time and trouble looking. Until BVS-1 was found, neutronium and neutron stars were only theories. The examination of an actual neutron star could be of tremendous importance. Neutron stars might give us the key to true gravity control.

Mass of BVS-1: 1.3 times the mass of Sol, approx.

Diameter of BVS-1 (estimated): eleven miles of neutronium, covered by half a mile of degenerate matter, covered by maybe twelve feet of ordinary matter.

Nothing else was known of the tiny hidden star until the Laskins went in to look. Now the Institute knew one thing more: the star's spin.

"A mass that large can distort space by its rotation," said the puppeteer. "The Laskins' projected hyperbola was twisted across itself in such a way that we can deduce the star's period of rotation to be two minutes twenty-seven seconds."

The bar was somewhere in the General Products building. I don't know just where, and with the transfer booths it doesn't matter. I kept staring at the puppeteer bartender. Naturally only a puppeteer would be served by a puppeteer bartender, since any biped life-form would resent knowing that his drink had been made with somebody's mouth. I had already decided to get dinner somewhere else.

"I see your problem," I said. "Your sales will suffer if it gets out that something can reach through one of your hulls and smash a crew to bloody smears. But where do I come in?"

"We want to repeat the experiment of Sonya Laskin and Peter Laskin. We must find—"

"With me?"

"Yes. We must find out what it is that our hulls cannot stop. Naturally you may—"

"But I won't."

"We are prepared to offer one million stars."

I was tempted, but only for a moment. "Forget it."

"Naturally you will be allowed to build your own ship, starting with a No. 2 General Products hull."

"Thanks, but I'd like to go on living."

"You would dislike being confined. I find that We Made It has reestablished the debtor's prison. If General Products made public your accounts—"

"Now, *just* a—"

"You owe money on the close order of five hundred thousand stars. We will pay your creditors before you leave. If you return—" I had to admire the creature's honesty in not saying "When." "—we will pay you the residue. You may be asked to speak to news commentators concerning the voyage, in which case there will be more stars."

"You say I can build my own ship?"

"Naturally. This is not a voyage of exploration. We want you to return safely."

"It's a deal," I said.

After all, the puppeteer had tried to blackmail me. What happened next would be its own fault.

They built my ship in two weeks flat. They started with a No. 2 General Products hull, just like the one around the Institute of Knowledge ship, and the lifesystem was practically a duplicate of the Laskins', but there the resemblance ended. There were no instruments to observe neutron stars. Instead, there was a fusion motor big enough for a Jinx warliner. In my ship, which I now called *Skydiver*, the drive would produce thirty gees at the safety limit. There was a laser cannon big enough to punch a hole through We Made It's moon. The puppeteer wanted me to feel safe, and now I did, for I could fight and I could run. Especially I could run.

I heard the Laskins' last broadcast through half a dozen times. Their unnamed ship had dropped out of hyperspace a million miles above BVS-1. Gravity warp would have prevented their getting closer in hyperspace. While her husband was crawling through the access tube for an instrument check, Sonya Laskin had called the Institute of Knowledge. ". . . We can't see it yet, not by naked eye. But we can see where it is. Every time some star or other goes behind it, there's a little ring of light. Just a minute. Peter's ready to use the telescope . . ."

Then the star's mass had cut the hyperspatial link. It was expected, and nobody had worried—then. Later, the same effect must have stopped them from escaping from whatever attacked them into hyperspace.

When would-be rescuers found the ship, only the radar and the cameras were still running. They didn't tell us much. There had been no camera in the cabin. But the forward camera gave us, for one instant, a speed-blurred view of the neutron star. It was a featureless disk the orange color of perfect barbecue coals, if you know someone who can afford to burn wood. This object had been a neutron star a long time.

"There'll be no need to paint the ship," I told the president.

"You should not make such a trip with the walls transparent. You would go insane."

"I'm no flatlander. The mind-wrenching sight of naked space fills me with mild but waning interest. I want to know nothing's sneaking up behind me."

The day before I left, I sat alone in the General Products bar, letting the puppeteer bartender make me drinks with his mouth. He did it well. Puppeteers were scattered around the bar in twos and threes, with a couple of men for variety, but the drinking hour had not yet arrived. The place felt empty.

I was pleased with myself. My debts were all paid, not that that would matter where I was going. I would leave with not a minicredit to my name, with nothing but the ship. . .

All told, I was well out of a sticky situation. I hoped I'd like being a rich exile.

I jumped when the newcomer sat down across from me. He was a foreigner, a middle-aged man wearing an expensive night-black business suit and a snow-white asymmetrical beard. I let my face freeze and started to get up.

"Sit down, Mr. Shaeffer."

"Why?"

He told me by showing me a blue disk. An Earth government ident. I looked it over to show I was alert, not because I'd know an ersatz from the real thing.

"My name is Sigmund Ausfaller," said the government man. "I wish to say a few words concerning your assignment on behalf of General Products."

I nodded, not saying anything.

"A record of your verbal contract was sent to us as a matter of course. I noticed some peculiar things about it. Mr. Shaeffer, will you really take such a risk for only five hundred thousand stars?"

"I'm getting twice that."

"But you only keep half of it. The rest goes to pay debts. Then there are taxes . . . But never mind. What occurred to me was that a spaceship is a spaceship, and yours is very well armed and has powerful legs. An admirable fighting ship, if you were moved to sell it."

"But it isn't mine."

"There are those who would not ask. On Canyon, for example, or the Isolationist party of Wunderland."

I said nothing.

"Or you might be planning a career of piracy. A risky business, piracy, and I don't take the notion seriously."

I hadn't even thought about piracy. But I'd have to give up on Wunderland.

"What I would like to say is this, Mr. Shaeffer. A single entrepreneur, if he were sufficiently dishonest, could do terrible damage to the reputation of all human beings everywhere. Most species find it necessary to police the ethics of their own members, and we are no exception. It occurred to me that you might not take your ship to the neutron star at all, that you would take it elsewhere and sell it. The puppeteers do not make invulnerable war vessels. They are pacifists. Your *Skydiver* is unique.

"Hence, I have asked General Products to allow me to install a remote-control bomb in the *Skydiver.* Since it is inside the hull, the hull cannot protect you. I had it installed this afternoon.

"Now, notice! If you have not reported within a week, I will set off the bomb. There are several worlds within a week's hyperspace flight of here, but all recognize the dominion of Earth. If you flee, you must leave your ship within a week, so I hardly think you will land on a nonhabitable world. Clear?"

"Clear."

"If I am wrong, you may take a lie-detector test and prove it. Then you may punch me in the nose, and I will apologize handsomely."

I shook my head. He stood up, bowed, and left me sitting there cold sober.

* * *

Four films had been taken from the Laskins' cameras. In the time left to me I ran through them several times without seeing anything out of the way. If the ship had run through a gas cloud, the impact could have killed the Laskins. At perihelion they were moving at better than half the speed of light. But there would have been friction, and I saw no sign of heating in the films. If something alive had attacked them, the beast was invisible to radar and to an enormous range of light frequencies. If the attitude jets had fired accidentally—I was clutching at straws—the light showed on none of the films.

There would be savage magnetic forces near BVS-1, but that couldn't have done any damage. No such force could penetrate a General Products hull. Neither could heat, except in special bands of radiated light, bands visible to at least one of the puppeteers' alien customers. I hold adverse opinions on the General Products hull, but they all concern the dull anonymity of the design. Or maybe I resent the fact that General Products holds a near monopoly on spacecraft hulls and isn't owned by human beings. But if I'd had to trust my life to, say, the Sinclair yacht I'd seen in the drugstore, I'd have chosen jail.

Jail was one of my three choices. But I'd be there for life. Ausfaller would see to that.

Or I could run for it in the *Skydiver.* But no world within reach would have me. If I could find an undiscovered Earthlike world within a week of We Made It . . .

Fat chance. I preferred BVS-1.

I thought that flashing circle of light was getting bigger, but it flashed so seldom, I couldn't be sure. BVS-1 wouldn't show even in my telescope. I gave that up and settled for just waiting.

Waiting, I remembered a long-ago summer spent on Jinx. There were days when, unable to go outside because a dearth of clouds had spread the land with raw blue-white sunlight, we amused ourselves by filling party balloons with tap water and dropping them on the sidewalk from three stories up. They made lovely splash patterns, which dried out too fast. So we put a little ink in each balloon before filling it. Then the patterns stayed.

Sonya Laskin had been in her chair when the chairs had collapsed. Blood samples showed that it was Peter who had struck them from behind, like a water balloon dropped from a great height.

What could get through a General Products hull?

Ten hours to fall.

I unfastened the safety net and went for an inspection tour. The access tunnel was three feet wide, just right to push through in free-fall. Below me was the length of the fusion tube; to the left, the laser cannon; to the right, a set of curved side tubes leading to inspection points for the gyros, the batteries and generator, the air plant, the hyperspace shunt motors. All was in order—except me. I was clumsy. My jumps were always too short or too long. There was no room to turn at the stern end, so I had to back fifty feet to a side tube.

Six hours to go, and still I couldn't find the neutron star. Probably I would see it only for an instant, passing at better than half the speed of light. Already my speed must be enormous.

Were the stars turning blue?

Two hours to go—and I was sure they were turning blue. Was my speed that high? Then the stars behind should be red. Machinery blocked the view behind me, so I used the gyros. The ship turned with peculiar sluggishness. And the stars behind were blue, not red. All around me were blue-white stars.

Imagine light falling into a savagely steep gravitational well. It won't accelerate. Light can't move faster than light. But it can gain in energy, in frequency. The light was falling on me harder and harder as I dropped.

I told the dictaphone about it. That dictaphone was probably the best-protected item on the ship. I had already decided to earn my money by using it, just as if I expected to collect. Privately I wondered just how intense the light would get.

Skydiver had drifted back to vertical, with its axis through the neutron star, but now it faced outward. I'd thought I had the ship stopped horizontally. More clumsiness. I used the gyros. Again the ship moved mushily, until it was halfway through the swing. Then it seemed to fall automatically into place. It was as if the *Skydiver* preferred to have its axis through the neutron star.

I didn't like that.

I tried the maneuver again, and again the *Skydiver* fought back. But this time there was something else. Something was pulling at me.

So I unfastened my safety net—and fell headfirst into the nose.

The pull was light, about a tenth of a gee. It felt more like sinking through honey than falling. I climbed back into my chair, tied myself in with the net, now hanging facedown, and turned on the dictaphone. I told my story in such nit-picking detail that my hypothetical listeners could not but doubt my hypothetical sanity. "I think this is what happened to the Laskins," I finished. "If the pull increases, I'll call back."

Think? I never doubted it. This strange, gentle pull was inexplicable. Something inexplicable had killed Peter and Sonya Laskin. QED.

Around the point where the neutron star must be, the stars were like smeared dots of oil paint, smeared radially. They glared with an angry, painful light. I hung facedown in the net and tried to think.

It was an hour before I was sure. The pull was increasing. And I still had an hour to fall.

Something was pulling on me but not on the ship.

No, that was nonsense. What could reach out to me through a General Products hull? It must be the other way around. Something was pushing on the ship, pushing it off course.

If it got worse, I could use the drive to compensate. Meanwhile, the ship was being pushed *away* from BVS-1, which was fine by me.

But if I was wrong, if the ship was not somehow being pushed away from BVS-1, the rocket motor would send the *Skydiver* crashing into eleven miles of neutronium.

And why wasn't the rocket already firing? If the ship was being pushed off course, the autopilot should be fighting back. The accelerometer was in good order. It had looked fine when I had made my inspection tour down the access tube.

Could something be pushing on the ship *and* on the accelerometer but not on me? It came down to the same impossibility: something that could reach through a General Products hull.

To hell with theory, said I to myself, said I. I'm getting out of here. To the dictaphone I said, "The pull has increased dangerously. I'm going to try to alter my orbit."

Of course, once I turned the ship outward and used the rocket, I'd be adding my own acceleration to the X-force. It would be a strain, but I could stand it for a while. If I came within a mile of BVS-1, I'd end like Sonya Laskin.

She must have waited facedown in a net like mine, waited without a drive unit, waited while the pressure rose and the net cut into her flesh, waited until the net snapped and dropped her into the nose, to lie crushed and broken until the X-force tore the very chairs loose and dropped them on her.

I hit the gyros.

The gyros weren't strong enough to turn me. I tried it three times. Each time the ship rotated about fifty degrees and hung there, motionless, while the whine of the gyros went up and up. Released, the ship immediately swung back to position. I was nose down to the neutron star, and I was going to stay that way.

Half an hour to fall, and the X-force was over a gee. My sinuses were in agony. My eyes were ripe and ready to fall out. I don't know if I could have stood a cigarette, but I didn't get the chance. My pack of Fortunados had fallen out of my pocket when I had dropped into the nose. There it was, four feet beyond my fingers, proof that the X-force acted on other objects besides me. Fascinating.

I couldn't take any more. If it dropped me shrieking into the neutron star, I had to use the drive. And I did. I ran the thrust up until I was approximately in free-fall. The blood which had pooled in my extremities went back where it belonged. The gee dial registered one point two gee. I cursed it for a lying robot.

The soft pack was bobbing around in the nose, and it occurred to me that a little extra nudge on the throttle would bring it to me. I tried it. The pack drifted toward me, and I reached, and like a sentient thing it speeded up to avoid my clutching hand. I snatched at it again as it went past my ear, and again it was moving too fast. That pack was going at a hell of a clip, considering that here I was practically in free-fall. It dropped through the door to the relaxation room, still picking up speed, blurred, and vanished as it entered the access tube. Seconds later I heard a solid *thump*.

But that was *crazy*. Already the X-force was pulling blood into my face. I pulled my lighter out, held it at arm's length, and let go. It fell gently into the nose. But the pack of Fortunados had hit like I'd dropped it from a *building*.

Well.

I nudged the throttle again. The mutter of fusing hydrogen reminded me that if I tried to keep this up all the way, I might well put the General Products hull to its toughest test yet: smashing it into a neutron star at half lightspeed. I could see it now: a transparent hull containing only a few cubic inches of dwarf-star matter wedged into the tip of the nose.

At one point four gee, according to that lying gee dial, the lighter came loose and drifted toward me. I let it go. It was clearly falling when it reached the doorway. I pulled the throttle back. The loss of power jerked me violently forward, but I kept my face turned. The lighter slowed and hesitated at the entrance to the access tube. Decided to go through. I cocked my ears for the sound, then jumped as the whole ship rang like a gong.

And the accelerometer was right at the ship's center of mass. Otherwise the ship's mass would have thrown the needle off. The puppeteers were fiends for ten-decimal-point accuracy.

I favored the dictaphone with a few fast comments, then got to work reprogramming the autopilot. Luckily what I wanted was simple. The X-force was but an X-force to me, but now I knew how it behaved. I might actually live through this.

The stars were fiercely blue, warped to streaked lines near that special point. I thought I could see it now, very small and dim and red, but it might have been imagination. In twenty minutes I'd be rounding the neutron star. The drive grumbled behind me. In effective free-fall, I unfastened the safety net and pushed myself out of the chair.

A gentle push aft—and ghostly hands grasped my legs. Ten pounds of weight hung by my fingers from the back of the chair. The pressure should drop fast. I'd programmed the autopilot to reduce the thrust from two gees to zero during the next two minutes. All I had to do was be at the center of mass, in the access tube, when the thrust went to zero.

Something gripped the ship through a General Products hull. A psychokinetic life-form stranded on a sun twelve miles in diameter? But how could anything alive stand such gravity?

Something might be stranded in orbit. There is life in space: outsiders and sailseeds and maybe others we haven't found yet. For all I knew or cared, BVS-1 itself might be alive. It didn't matter. I knew what the X-force was trying to do. It was trying to pull the ship apart.

There was no pull on my fingers. I pushed aft and landed on the back wall, on bent legs. I knelt over the door, looking aft/down. When free-fall came, I pulled myself through and was in the relaxation room looking down/forward into the nose.

Gravity was changing faster than I liked. The X-force was growing as zero hour approached, while the compensating rocket thrust dropped. The X-force tended to pull the ship apart; it was two gees forward at the nose, two gees backward at the tail, and diminished to zero at the center of mass. Or so I hoped. The pack and lighter had behaved as if the force pulling them had increased for every inch they had moved sternward.

The back wall was fifteen feet away. I had to jump it with gravity changing in midair. I hit on my hands, bounced away. I'd jumped too late. The region of free-fall was moving through the ship like a wave as the thrust dropped. It had left me behind. Now the back wall was "up" to me, and so was the access tube.

Under something less than half a gee, I jumped for the access tube. For one long moment I stared into the three-foot tunnel, stopped in midair and already beginning to fall back, as I realized that there was nothing to hang on to. Then I stuck my hands in the tube and spread them against the sides. It was all I needed. I levered myself up and started to crawl.

The dictaphone was fifty feet below, utterly unreachable. If I had anything more to say to General Products, I'd have to say it in person. Maybe I'd get the chance. Because I knew what force was trying to tear the ship apart.

It was the tide.

The motor was off, and I was at the ship's midpoint. My spread-eagled position was getting uncomfortable. It was four minutes to perihelion.

Something creaked in the cabin below me. I couldn't see what it was, but I could clearly see a red point glaring among blue radial lines, like a lantern at the bottom of a well. To the sides, between the fusion tube and the tanks and other equipment, the blue stars glared at me with a light that was almost violet. I was afraid to look too long. I actually thought they might blind me.

There must have been hundreds of gravities in the cabin. I could even feel the pressure change. The air was thin at this height, one hundred fifty feet above the control room.

And now, almost suddenly, the red dot was more than a dot. My time was up. A red disk leapt up at me; the ship swung around me; I gasped and shut my eyes tight. Giants' hands gripped my arms and legs and head, gently but with great firmness, and tried to pull me in two. In that moment it came to me that Peter Laskin had died like this. He'd made the same guesses I had, and he'd tried to hide in the access tube. But he'd slipped ... as I was slipping ... From the control room came a multiple shriek of tearing metal. I tried to dig my feet into the hard tube walls. Somehow they held.

When I got my eyes open, the red dot was shrinking into nothing.

The puppeteer president insisted that I be put in a hospital for observation. I didn't fight the idea. My face and hands were flaming red, with blisters rising, and I ached as though I'd been beaten. Rest and tender loving care; that was what I wanted.

I was floating between a pair of sleeping plates, hideously uncomfortable, when the nurse came to announce a visitor. I knew who it was from her peculiar expression.

"What can get through a General Products hull?" I asked it.

"I hoped you would tell me." The president rested on its single back leg, holding a stick that gave off green incense-smelling smoke.

"And so I will. Gravity."

"Do not play with me, Beowulf Shaeffer. This matter is vital."

"I'm not playing. Does your world have a moon?"

"That information is classified." The puppeteers are cowards. Nobody knows where they come from, and nobody is likely to find out.

"Do you know what happens when a moon gets too close to its primary?"

"It falls apart."

"Why?"

"I do not know."

"Tides."

"What is a tide?"

Oho, said I to myself, said I. "I'm going to try to tell you. The Earth's moon is almost two thousand miles in diameter and does not rotate with respect to Earth. I want you to pick two rocks on the moon, one at the point nearest the Earth, one at the point farthest away."

"Very well."

"Now, isn't it obvious that if those rocks were left to themselves, they'd fall away from each other? They're in two different orbits, mind you, concentric orbits, one almost two thousand miles outside the other. Yet those rocks are forced to move at the same orbital speed."

"The one outside is moving faster."

"Good point. So there *is* a force trying to pull the moon apart. Gravity holds it together. Bring the moon close enough to Earth, and those two rocks would simply float away."

"I see. Then this 'tide' tried to pull your ship apart. It was powerful enough in the lifesystem of the Institute ship to pull the acceleration chairs out of their mounts."

"And to crush a human being. Picture it. The ship's nose was just seven miles from the center of BVS-1. The tail was three hundred feet farther out. Left to themselves, they'd have gone in completely different orbits. My head and feet tried to do the same thing when I got close enough."

"I see. Are you molting?"

"What?"

"I notice you are losing your outer integument in spots."

"Oh, *that*. I got a bad sunburn from exposure to starlight. It's not important."

Two heads stared at each other for an eyeblink. A shrug? The puppeteer said, "We have deposited the residue of your pay with the Bank of We Made It. One Sigmund Ausfaller, human, has frozen the account until your taxes are computed."

"Figures."

"If you will talk to reporters now, explaining what happened to the Institute ship, we will pay you ten thousand stars. We will pay cash so that you may use it immediately. It is urgent. There have been rumors."

"Bring 'em in." As an afterthought I added, "I can also tell them that your world is moonless. That should be good for a footnote somewhere."

"I do not understand." But two long necks had drawn back, and the puppeteer was watching me like a pair of pythons.

"You'd know what a tide was if you had a moon. You couldn't avoid it."

"Would you be interested in—"

"A million stars? I'd be fascinated. I'll even sign a contract if it states what we're hiding. How do *you* like being blackmailed for a change?"

✳
GHOST: TWO

I tried to script the story myself, of course. There was a computer program that would do it as an interview. I made lots of notes ... too many notes, because any time I tried to write text for myself, I blocked.

So I advertised for a ghost.

Ander Smittarasheed answered.

His type was familiar enough. He was a gaudy flatlander athlete, too aware of the limps and lames around him, very aware that any woman was his for the asking. It all showed in his words and body language.

Maybe I wouldn't even have hired him, but he just pushed into the situation without giving me a chance to react. Before my caution caught up, I was telling him everything ... nearly everything. He turned it into a one-act play between me and the interview program, all in one afternoon. We spent two days polishing before we filmed it. The recording sold instantly to the nets.

He could write. That in itself was amazing.

I said, "I couldn't tell you about the blackmail aspect." We weren't shouting now. The undersea dome isn't really glass; it's something that absorbs shock waves, including sound, not to mention tsunamis.

Ander Smittarasheed grinned at me patronizingly. "Did you think you were putting something over on General Products?"

"At the time. I still don't know for sure. Maybe I was crazy to think that a spacegoing species wouldn't understand tides."

"Maybe. But why would they send a human pilot to learn what they already knew?"

"Mmm . . . Ander, look at it this way. A university team sets out to investigate a cold neutron star. They make a mistake, probably without informing General Products, but they're using a GP hull. The ship comes back with the pilots dead in vividly gory fashion. General Products works out how it happened, but they'd rather not be seen as making excuses. Why not let someone of the same species solve the problem and then talk for them?"

"They seem to have had a good deal of faith in you."

I laughed as if I hadn't a care in the world. "Oh, Ander. I wonder how many times they tried it."

He thought it over. "No. They showed *Sigmund* your contract. They would have had to do *that* several times."

"Yah."

"Beowulf, Sigmund would not have participated while they killed one pilot after another."

I said, "Mad Bomber Sigmund? Ander, I never had any intention of stealing that ship." I saw his look, but I went on. "Now, that *could* imply that Sigmund is a bad judge of character. Or it could mean that he braced . . . oh, a dozen pilots, each in turn. The odds of *one of us* stealing a ship get pretty good. Remember, if each of us does our job, the hull comes back at the end of the orbit. Those things cost."

Ander's jaw set. He said, "No."

All right, no. I'd try again later. Beowulf Shaeffer is a misunderstood innocent. Sigmund Ausfaller isn't quite trustworthy. Change the subject— "Or do you mean they trusted me to write my own script? I tried that, Ander."

"You really needed help. 'First neutron star ever discovered,' " he quoted.

First *old, cold* neutron star. Good thing he'd spotted *that* embarrassment. I said, "You couldn't dive that close to a pulsar. Even a GP hull couldn't bash through the accretion disk. I've gotten better at explaining things, Ander."

I was scampering about inside my head, seeking any hole that might offer an escape.

Monitoring a citizen can be easy, or cheap, or foolproof; take your choice. Ausfaller was backing Ander with UN money. The United Nations didn't have authority outside Sol system, but Ander could be using ARM funds or equipment.

But he'd seen me on the balcony for the very first time. He'd sprinted up the slidestairs to intercept me without pausing a moment to call for backup. I'd stake our freedom on that—*their* freedom. The UN had no claim on me, but they might well extradite Carlos, or Sharrol, or the children.

So I was shaping a bribe to offer Ander, and telling myself that he wasn't too big to be killed if things broke right, and hoping that none of that showed at all while I played for time.

I asked, "What's your concern with puppeteers? They're harmless. They're cowards."

"Are cowards harmless?"

"And they're gone."

Ander smiled at me. "And you were the one who sent them. Beowulf, why would they deal with you a second time? You blackmailed them."

"They don't mind blackmail; they use it themselves. And what I thought I knew might not be true." I caught that smirk again and snapped, "All right, *what*?"

"Tides," Ander said. "We've been watching their, ah, retreat. The Pierson's puppeteers understand tides very well, Beowulf, whether or not they ever had a moon."

"*All* right." I believed him and wasn't surprised.

"By the way, that information is *absolutely* proprietary."

"Man with a secret, hah? Even so, I think they were taking a shot at me when they hired me the second time."

✳

AT THE CORE

I

I couldn't decide whether to call it a painting, a relief mural, a sculpture, or a hash, but it was the prize exhibit in the art section of the Institute of Knowledge on Jinx. The Kdatlyno must have strange eyes, I thought. My own were watering. The longer I looked at *FTLSPACE*, the more blurred it got.

I'd tentatively decided that it was *supposed* to look blurred when a set of toothy jaws clamped gently on my arm. I jumped a foot in the air. A soft, thrilling contralto voice said, "Beowulf Shaeffer, you are a spendthrift."

That voice would have made a singer's fortune. And I thought I recognized it—but it couldn't be; *that* one was on We Made It, light-years distant. I turned.

The puppeteer had released my arm. It went on: "And what do you think of Hrodenu?"

"He's ruining my eyes."

"Naturally. The Kdatlyno are blind to all but radar. *FTLSPACE* is not meant to be seen but to be touched. Run your tongue over it."

"My tongue? No, thanks." I tried running my hand over it. If you want to know what it felt like, hop a ship for Jinx; the thing's still there. I flatly refuse to describe the sensation.

The puppeteer cocked its head dubiously. "I'm sure your tongue is more sensitive. No guards are nearby."

"Forget it. You know, you sound just like the regional president of General Products on We Made It."

"It was he who sent me your dossier, Beowulf Shaeffer. No doubt we had the same English teacher. I am the regional president on Jinx, as you no doubt recognized from my mane."

Well, not quite. The auburn mop over the brain case between the two necks is supposed to show caste once you learn to discount variations of mere style. To do that, you have to be a puppeteer. Instead of admitting my ignorance, I asked, "Did that dossier say I was a spendthrift?"

"You have spent more than a million stars in the past four years."

"And loved it."

"Yes. You will shortly be in debt again. Have you thought of doing more writing? I admired your article on the neutron star BVS-1. 'The pointy bottom of a gravity well . . .' 'Blue starlight fell on me like intangible sleet . . .' Lovely."

"Thanks. It paid well, too. But I'm mainly a spaceship pilot."

"It is fortunate, our meeting here. I had thought of having you found. Do you wish a job?"

That was a loaded question. The last and only time I took a job from a puppeteer, the puppeteer blackmailed me into it, knowing it would probably kill me. It almost did. I didn't hold that against the regional president of We Made It, but to let them have another crack at me—? "I'll give you a conditional maybe. Do you have the idea I'm a professional suicide pilot?"

"Not at all. If I show details, do you agree that the information shall be confidential?"

"I do," I said formally, knowing it would commit me. A verbal contract is as binding as the tape it's recorded on.

"Good. Come." He pranced toward a transfer booth.

The transfer booth let us out somewhere in Jinx's vacuum regions. It was night. High in the sky, Sirius B was a painfully bright pinpoint casting vivid blue moonlight on a ragged lunar landscape. I looked up and didn't see Binary, Jinx's bloated orange companion planet, so we must have been in the Farside End.

But there was something hanging over us.

A No. 4 General Products hull is a transparent sphere a thousand-odd feet in diameter. No bigger ship has been built anywhere in the known galaxy. It takes a government to buy one, and they are used for colonization projects only. But this one could never have been so used; it was all machinery. Our transfer booth stood between two of the landing legs, so that the swelling flank of the ship looked down on us as an owl looks down at a mouse. An access tube ran through vacuum from the booth to the air lock.

I said, "Does General Products build complete spacecraft nowadays?"

"We are thinking of branching out. But there are problems."

From the viewpoint of the puppeteer-owned company, it must have seemed high time. General Products makes the hulls for ninety-five percent of all ships in space, mainly because nobody else knows how to build an indestructible hull. But they'd made a bad start with this ship. The only room I could see for crew, cargo, or passengers was a few cubic yards of empty space right at the bottom, just above the air lock and just big enough for a pilot.

"You'd have a hard time selling that," I said.

"True. Do you notice anything else?"

"Well . . ." The hardware that filled the transparent hull was very tightly packed. The effect was as if a race of ten-mile-tall giants had striven to achieve miniaturization. I saw no sign of access tubes; hence, there could be no in-space repairs. Four reaction motors poked their appropriately huge nostrils through the hull, angled outward from the bottom. No small attitude jets; hence, oversized gyros inside. Otherwise . . . "Most of it looks like hyperdrive motors. But that's silly. Unless you've thought of a good reason for moving moons around."

"At one time you were a commercial pilot for Nakamura Lines. How long was the run from Jinx to We Made It?"

"Twelve days if nothing broke down." Just long enough to get to know the prettiest passenger aboard, while the autopilot did everything for me but wear my uniform.

"Sirius to Procyon is a distance of four light-years. Our ship would make the trip in five minutes."

"You've lost your mind."

"No."

But that was almost a light-year per minute! I couldn't visualize it. Then suddenly I did visualize it, and my mouth fell open, for what I saw was the galaxy opening before me. We know so little beyond our own small neighborhood of the galaxy. But with a ship like that—!

"That's goddamn fast."

"As you say. But the equipment is bulky, as you note. It cost seven billion stars to build that ship, discounting centuries of research, but it will move only one man. As is, the ship is a failure. Shall we go inside?"

II

The lifesystem was two circular rooms, one above the other, with a small air lock to one side. The lower room was the control room, with banks of switches and dials and blinking lights dominated by a huge spherical mass pointer. The upper room was bare walls, transparent, through which I could see air- and food-producing equipment.

"This will be the relaxroom," said the puppeteer. "We decided to let the pilot decorate it himself."

"Why me?"

"Let me further explain the problem." The puppeteer began to pace the floor. I hunkered down against the wall and watched. Watching a puppeteer move is a pleasure. Even in Jinx's gravity the deerlike body seemed weightless, the tiny hooves tapping the floor at random. "The human sphere of colonization is some thirty light-years across, is it not?"

"Maximum. It's not exactly a sphere—"

"The puppeteer region is much smaller. The Kdatlyno sphere is half the size of yours, and the kzinti is fractionally larger. These are the important space-traveling species. We must discount the Outsiders since they do not use ships. Some spheres coincide, naturally. Travel from one sphere to another is nearly nil except for ourselves, since our sphere of influence extends to all who buy our hulls. But add all these regions, and you have a region sixty light-years across. This ship could cross it in seventy-five minutes. Allow six hours for takeoff and six for landing, assuming no traffic snarls near the world of destination, and we have a ship which can go anywhere in thirteen hours but nowhere in less than twelve, carrying one pilot and no cargo, costing seven billion stars."

"How about exploration?"

"We puppeteers have no taste for abstract knowledge. And how should we explore?" Meaning that whatever race flew the ship would gain the advantages thereby. A puppeteer wouldn't risk his necks by flying it himself. "What we need is a great deal of money and a gathering of intelligences to design something which *may* go slower but *must* be less bulky. General Products does not wish to spend so much on something that may fail. We will require the best minds of each sentient species and the richest investors. Beowulf Shaeffer, we need to attract attention."

"A publicity stunt?"

"Yes. We wish to send a pilot to the center of the galaxy and back."

"Ye . . . gods! Will it go *that* fast?"

"It would require some twenty-five days to reach the center and an equal time to return. You can see the reasoning behind—"

"It's perfect. You don't need to spell it out. Why me?"

"We wish you to make the trip and then write of it. I have a list of pilots who write. Those I have approached have been reluctant. They say that writing on the ground is safer than testing unknown ships. I follow their reasoning."

"Me, too."

"Will you go?"

"What am I offered?"

"One hundred thousand stars for the trip. Fifty thousand to write the story, in addition to what you sell it for."

"Sold."

From then on my only worry was that my new boss would find out that someone had ghostwritten that neutron star article.

Oh, I wondered at first why General Products was willing to trust me. The first time I worked for them, I tried to steal their ship for reasons which seemed good at the time. But the ship I now called *Long Shot* really wasn't worth stealing. Any potential buyer would know it was hot, and what good would it be to him? *Long Shot* could have explored a globular cluster, but her only other use was publicity.

Sending her to the Core was a masterpiece of promotion.

Look: It was twelve days from We Made It to Jinx by conventional craft, and twelve hours by *Long Shot*. What's the difference? You spent twelve years saving for the trip. But the Core! Ignoring refueling and reprovisioning problems, my old ship could have reached the galaxy's core in three hundred years. No known species had ever *seen* the Core! It hid behind layer on layer of tenuous gas and dust clouds. You can find libraries of literature on those central stars, but they all consist of generalities and educated guesses based on observation of other galaxies, like Andromeda.

Three centuries dropped to less than a month! There's something anyone can grasp. And with pictures!

The lifesystem was finished in a couple of weeks. I had them leave the control-room walls transparent and paint the relaxroom solid blue, no windows. When they finished, I had entertainment tapes and everything it takes to keep a man sane for seven weeks in a room the size of a large closet.

On the last day the puppeteer and I spoke the final ver-

sion of my contract. I had four months to reach the galaxy's
center and return. The outside cameras would run constantly; I was not to interfere with them. If the ship suffered
a mechanical failure, I could return before reaching the center; otherwise, no. There were penalties. I took a copy of
the tape to leave with a lawyer.

"There is a thing you should know," the puppeteer said
afterward. "The direction of thrust opposes the direction of
hyperdrive."

"I don't get it."

The puppeteer groped for words. "If you turned on the
reaction motors and the hyperdrive together, the flames
would precede your ship through hyperspace."

I got the picture then. Ass backward into the unknown.
With the control room at the ship's bottom, it made sense.
To a puppeteer, it made sense.

III

And I was off.

I went up under two standard gees because I like my
comfort. For twelve hours I used only the reaction motors.
It wouldn't do to be too deep in a gravity well when I used
a hyperdrive, especially an experimental one. Pilots who do
that never leave hyperspace. The relaxroom kept me enter-
tained until the bell rang. I slipped down to the control
room, netted myself down against free-fall, turned off the
motors, rubbed my hands briskly together, and turned on
the hyperdrive.

It wasn't quite as I'd expected.

I couldn't see out, of course. When the hyperdrive goes
on, it's like your blind spot expanding to take in all the
windows. It's not just that you don't see anything; you forget that there's anything to see. If there's a window between the kitchen control bank and your print of Dali's
Spain, your eye and mind will put the picture right next to
the kitchen bank, obliterating the space between. It takes
getting used to, in fact it has driven people insane, but that

wasn't what bothered me. I've spent thousands of man-hours in hyperspace. I kept my eye on the mass pointer.

The mass pointer is a big transparent sphere with a number of blue lines radiating from the center. The direction of the line is the direction of a star; its length shows the star's mass. We wouldn't need pilots if the mass pointer could be hooked into an autopilot, but it can't. Dependable as it is, accurate as it is, the mass pointer is a psionic device. It needs a mind to work it. I'd been using mass pointers for so long that those lines were like real stars.

A star came toward me, and I dodged around it. I thought that another line that didn't point *quite* straight ahead was long enough to show dangerous mass, so I dodged. That put a blue dwarf right in front of me. I shifted fast and looked for a throttle. I wanted to slow down.

Repeat, *I wanted to slow down.*

Of course there was no throttle. Part of the puppeteer research project would be designing a throttle. A long fuzzy line reached for me: a protosun ...

Put it this way: Imagine one of Earth's freeways. You must have seen pictures of them from space, a tangle of twisting concrete ribbons, empty and abandoned but never torn down. Some lie broken; others are covered with houses. People use the later rubberized ones for horseback riding. Imagine the way one of these must have looked about six o'clock on a week night in, say, 1970. Groundcars from end to end.

Now, let's take all those cars and remove the brakes. Further, let's put governors on the accelerators so that the maximum speeds are between sixty and seventy miles per hour, not all the same. Let something go wrong with all the governors at once so that the maximum speed also becomes the minimum. You'll begin to see signs of panic.

Ready? Okay. Get a radar installed in your car, paint your windshield and windows jet black, and get out on that freeway.

It was like that.

* * *

It didn't seem so bad at first. The stars kept coming at me, and I kept dodging, and after a while it settled down to a kind of routine. From experience I could tell at a glance whether a star was heavy enough and close enough to wreck me. But in Nakamura Lines I'd only had to take that glance every six hours or so. Here I didn't dare look away. As I grew tired, the near misses came closer and closer. After three hours of it I had to drop out.

The stars had a subtly unfamiliar look. With a sudden jar I realized that I was entirely out of known space. Sirius, Antares—I'd never recognize them from here; I wasn't even sure they were visible. I shook it off and called home.

"*Long Shot* calling General Products, *Long Shot* calling—"

"Beowulf Shaeffer?"

"Have I ever told you what a lovely, sexy voice you have?"

"No. Is everything going well?"

"I'm afraid not. In fact, I'm not going to make it."

A pause. "Why not?"

"I can't keep dodging these stars forever. One of them's going to get me if I keep on much longer. The ship's just too goddamn fast."

"Yes. We must design a slower ship."

"I hate to give up that good pay, but my eyes feel like peeled onions. I ache all over. I'm turning back."

"Shall I play your contract for you?"

"No. Why?"

"Your only legal reason for returning is a mechanical failure. Otherwise you forfeit twice your pay."

I said, "Mechanical failure?" There was a toolbox somewhere in the ship, with a hammer in it . . .

"I did not mention it before, since it did not seem polite, but two of the cameras are in the lifesystem. We had thought to use films of you for purposes of publicity, but—"

"I see. Tell me one thing, just one thing. When the regional president of We Made It sent you my name, did he mention that I'd discovered your planet has no moon?"

"Yes, he did mention that matter. You accepted one million stars for your silence. He naturally has a recording of the bargain."

"I see." So that's why they'd picked Beowulf Shaeffer, well-known author. "The trip'll take longer than I thought."

"You must pay a penalty for every extra day over four months. Two thousand stars per day late."

"Your voice has acquired an unpleasant grating sound. Good-bye."

I went on in. Every hour I shifted to normal space for a ten-minute coffee break. I dropped out for meals, and I dropped out for sleep. Twelve hours per ship's day I spent traveling, and twelve trying to recover. It was a losing battle.

By the end of day two I knew I wasn't going to make the four-month limit. I might do it in six months, forfeiting one hundred and twenty thousand stars, leaving me almost where I started. Serve me right for trusting a puppeteer!

Stars were all around me, shining through the floor and between the banked instruments. I sucked coffee, trying not to think. The Milky Way shone ghostly pale between my feet. The stars were thick now; they'd get thicker as I approached the Core, until finally one got me.

An idea! And about time, too.

The golden voice answered immediately. "Beowulf Shaeffer?"

"There's nobody else here, honey. Look, I've thought of something. Would you send—"

"Is one of your instruments malfunctioning, Beowulf Shaeffer?"

"No, they all work fine, as far as they go. Look—"

"Then what could you possibly have to say that would require my attention?"

"Honey, now is the time to decide. Do you want revenge, or do you want your ship back?"

A small silence. Then, "You may speak."

"I can reach the Core much faster if I first get into one of the spaces between the arms. Do we know enough about the galaxy to know where our arm ends?"

"I will send to the Institute of Knowledge to find out."

"Good."

Four hours later I was dragged from a deathlike sleep by the ringing of the hyperphone. It was not the president but some flunky. I remembered calling the puppeteer "honey" last night, tricked by my own exhaustion and that seductive voice, and wondered if I'd hurt his puppeteer feelings. "He" might be a male; a puppeteer's sex is one of his little secrets. The flunky gave me a bearing and distance for the nearest gap between stars.

It took me another day to get there. When the stars began to thin out, I could hardly believe it. I turned off the hyperdrive, and it was true. The stars were tens and hundreds of light-years apart. I could see part of the Core peeking in a bright rim above the dim flat cloud of mixed dust and stars.

IV

From then on it was better. I was safe if I glanced at the mass pointer every ten minutes or so. I could forget the rest breaks, eat meals, and do isometrics while watching the pointers. For eight hours a day I slept, but during the other sixteen I moved. The gap swept toward the Core in a narrowing curve, and I followed it.

As a voyage of exploration the trip would have been a fiasco. I saw nothing. I stayed well away from anything worth seeing. Stars and dust, anomalous wispy clusters shining in the dark of the gap, invisible indications that might have been stars—my cameras picked them up from a nice safe distance, showing tiny blobs of light. In three weeks I moved almost seventeen thousand light-years toward the Core.

The end of those three weeks was the end of the gap.

Before me was an uninteresting wash of stars backed by a wall of opaque dust clouds. I still had thirteen thousand light-years to go before I reached the center of the galaxy.

I took some pictures and moved in.

Ten-minute breaks, mealtimes that grew longer and longer for the rest they gave, sleep periods that left my eyes red and burning. The stars were thick and the dust was thicker, so that the mass pointer showed a blur of blue broken by sharp blue lines. The lines began to get less sharp. I took breaks every half hour . . .

Three days of that.

It was getting near lunchtime on the fourth day. I sat watching the mass pointer, noting the fluctuations in the blue blur which showed the changing density of the dust around me. Suddenly it faded out completely. Great! Wouldn't it be nice if the mass pointer went out on me? But the sharp starlines were still there, ten or twenty of them pointing in all directions. I went back to steering. The clock chimed to indicate a rest period. I sighed happily and dropped into normal space.

The clock showed that I had half an hour to wait for lunch. I thought about eating anyway, decided against it. The routine was all that kept me going. I wondered what the sky looked like, reflexively looked up so I wouldn't have to look down at the transparent floor. That big an expanse of hyperspace is hard even on trained eyes. I remembered I wasn't in hyperspace and looked down.

For a time I just stared. Then, without taking my eyes off the floor, I reached for the hyperphone.

"Beowulf Shaeffer?"

"No, this is Albert Einstein. I stowed away when the *Long Shot* took off, and I've decided to turn myself in for the reward."

"Giving misinformation is an implicit violation of contract. Why have you called?"

"I can see the Core."

"That is not a reason to call. It was implicit in your contract that you would see the Core."

"Damn it, don't you care? Don't you want to know what it looks like?"

"If you wish to describe it now, as a precaution against accident, I will switch you to a dictaphone. However, if your mission is not totally successful, we cannot use your recording."

I was thinking up a really searing answer when I heard the click. Great; my boss had hooked me into a dictaphone. I said one short sentence and hung up.

The Core.

Gone were the obscuring masses of dust and gas. A billion years ago they must have been swept up for fuel by the hungry, crowded stars. The Core lay before me like a great jeweled sphere. I'd expected it to be a gradual thing, a thick mass of stars thinning out into the arms. There was nothing gradual about it. A clear ball of multicolored light five or six thousand light-years across nestled in the heart of the galaxy, sharply bounded by the last of the dust clouds. I was 10,400 light-years from the center.

The red stars were the biggest and brightest. I could actually pick some of them out as individuals. The rest was a finger painting in fluorescent green and blue. But those red stars . . . they would have sent Aldebaran back to kindergarten.

It was all so *bright.* I needed the telescope to see black between the stars.

I'll *show* you how bright it was.

Is it night where you are? Step outside and look at the stars. What color are they? Antares may show red if you're near enough; in the system, so will Mars. Sirius may show bluish. But all the rest are white pinpoints. Why? Because it's *dark.* Your day vision is in color, but at night you see black and white, like a dog.

The Core suns were bright enough for color vision.

I'd pick a planet here! Not in the Core itself but right out here, with the Core on one side and on the other the dimly starred dust clouds forming their strange convoluted curtain.

Man, what a view! Imagine that flaming jeweled sphere rising in the east, hundreds of times as big as Binary shows on Jinx, but without the constant feeling Binary gives you, the fear that the orange world will fall on you, for the vast, twinkling Core is only starlight, lovely and harmless. I'd pick my world *now* and stake a claim. When the puppeteers got their drive fixed up, I'd have the finest piece of real estate in the known universe! If I could only find a habitable planet.

If only I could find it twice.

Hell, I'd be lucky to find my way *home* from here. I shifted into hyperspace and went back to work.

V

An hour and fifty minutes, one lunch break and two rest breaks, and fifty light-years later, I noticed something peculiar in the Core.

It was even clearer then, if not much bigger; I'd passed through the almost transparent wisps of the last dust cloud. Not too near the center of the sphere was a patch of white, bright enough to make the green and blue and red look dull around it. I looked for it again at the next break, and it was a little brighter. It was brighter again at the next break . . .

"Beowulf Shaeffer?"

"Yah. I—"

"Why did you use the dictaphone to call me a cowardly two-headed monster?"

"You were off the line. I *had* to use the dictaphone."

"That is sensible. Yes. We puppeteers have never understood your attitude toward a natural caution." My boss was peeved, though you couldn't tell from his voice.

"I'll go into that if you like, but it's not why I called."

"Explain, please."

"I'm all for caution. Discretion is the better part of valor and like that. You can even be good businessmen, because it's easier to survive with lots of money. But you're so damn concerned with various kinds of survival that you aren't even interested in something that isn't a threat. Nobody but a puppeteer would have turned down my offer to describe the Core."

"You forget the kzinti."

"Oh, the kzinti." Who expects rational behavior from kzinti? You whip them when they attack; you reluctantly decide not to exterminate them; you wait till they build up their strength; and when they attack, you whip 'em again. Meanwhile you sell them foodstuffs and buy their metals and employ them where you need good games theorists. It's not as if they were a real threat. They'll *always* attack before they're ready.

"The kzinti are carnivores. Where we are interested in survival, carnivores are interested in meat alone. They conquer because subject peoples can supply them with food. They cannot do menial work. Animal husbandry is alien to them. They must have slaves or be barbarians roaming the forests for meat. Why should they be interested in what you call abstract knowledge? Why should any thinking being if the knowledge has no chance of showing a profit? In practice, your description of the Core would attract only an omnivore."

"You'd make a good case if it were not for the fact that most sentient races are omnivores."

"We have thought long and hard on that."

Ye cats. I was going to have to think long and hard on *that.*

"Why did you call, Beowulf Shaeffer?"

Oh, yeah. "Look, I know you don't want to know what the Core looks like, but I see something that might represent personal danger. You have access to information I don't. May I proceed?"

"You may."

Hah! I was learning to think like a puppeteer. Was that good? I told my boss about the blazing, strangely shaped white patch in the Core. "When I turned the telescope on it, it nearly blinded me. Grade two sunglasses don't give any details at all. It's just a shapeless white patch, but so bright that the stars in front look like black dots with colored rims. I'd like to know what's causing it."

"It sounds very unusual." Pause. "Is the white color uniform? Is the brightness uniform?"

"Just a sec." I used the scope again. "The color is, but the brightness isn't. I see dimmer areas inside the patch. I think the center is fading out."

"Use the telescope to find a nova star. There ought to be several in such a large mass of stars."

I tried it. Presently I found something: a blazing disk of a peculiar blue-white color with a dimmer, somewhat smaller red disk half in front of it. That *had* to be a nova. In the core of Andromeda galaxy, and in what I'd seen of our own Core, the red stars were the biggest and brightest.

"I've found one."

"Comment."

A moment more and I saw what he meant. "It's the same color as the patch. Something like the same brightness, too. But what could make a patch of supernovas go off all at once?"

"You have studied the Core. The stars of the Core are an average of half a light-year apart. They are even closer near the center, and no dust clouds dim their brightness. When stars are that close, they shed enough light on each other to increase materially each other's temperature. Stars burn faster and age faster in the Core."

"I see that."

"Since the Core stars age faster, a much greater portion are near the supernova stage than in the arms. Also, all are hotter considering their respective ages. If a star were a few millennia from the supernova stage and a supernova exploded half a light-year away, estimate the probabilities."

"They might both blow. Then the two could set off a third, and the three might take a couple more . . ."

"Yes. Since a supernova lasts on the order of one human standard year, the chain reaction would soon die out. Your patch of light must have occurred in this way."

"That's a relief. Knowing what did it, I mean. I'll take pictures going in."

"As you say." Click.

The patch kept expanding as I went in, still with no more shape than a veil nebula, getting brighter and bigger. It hardly seemed fair, what I was doing. The light which the patch novas had taken fifty years to put out, I covered in an hour, moving down the beam at a speed which made the universe itself seem unreal. At the fourth rest period I dropped out of hyperspace, looked down through the floor while the cameras took their pictures, glanced away from the patch for a moment, and found myself blinded by tangerine afterimages. I had to put on a pair of grade one sunglasses, out of the packet of twenty which every pilot carries for working near suns during takeoff and landing.

It made me shiver to think that the patch was still nearly ten thousand light-years away. Already the radiation must have killed all life in the Core if there ever had been life there. My instruments on the hull showed radiation like a solar flare.

At the next stop I needed grade two sunglasses. Somewhat later, grade three. Then four. The patch became a great bright amoeba reaching twisting tentacles of fusion fire deep into the vitals of the Core. In hyperspace the sky was jammed bumper to bumper, so to speak, but I never thought of stopping. As the Core came closer, the patch grew like something alive, something needing ever more food. I think I knew, even then.

Night came. The control room was a blaze of light. I slept in the relaxroom to the tune of the laboring temperature control. Morning, and I was off again. The radiation meter snarled its death song, louder during each rest break. If I'd been planning to go outside, I would have dropped that plan. Radiation couldn't get through a General Products hull. Nothing else can, either, except visible light.

I spent a bad half hour trying to remember whether one of the puppeteers' customers saw X rays. I was afraid to call up and ask.

The mass pointer began to show a faint blue blur. Gases thrown outward from the patch. I had to keep changing sunglasses . . .

Sometime during the morning of the next day I stopped. There was no point in going farther.

"Beowulf Shaeffer, have you become attached to the sound of my voice? I have other work than supervising your progress."

"I would like to deliver a lecture on abstract knowledge."

"Surely it can wait until your return."

"The galaxy is exploding."

There was a strange noise. Then: "Repeat, please."

"Have I got your attention?"

"Yes."

"Good. I think I know the reason so many sentient races are omnivores. Interest in abstract knowledge is a symptom of pure curiosity. Curiosity must be a survival trait."

"Must we discuss this? Very well. You may well be right. Others have made the same suggestion, including puppeteers. But how has our species survived at all?"

"You must have some substitute for curiosity. Increased intelligence, maybe. You've been around long enough to develop it. Our hands can't compare with your mouths for tool building. If a watchmaker had taste and smell in his hands, he still wouldn't have the strength of your jaws or the delicacy of those knobs around your lips. When I want to know how old a sentient race is, I watch what he uses for hands and feet."

"Yes. Human feet are still adapting to their task of keeping you erect. You propose, then, that our intelligence has grown sufficiently to ensure our survival without depending on your hit-or-miss method of learning everything you can for the sheer pleasure of learning."

"Not quite. Our method is better. If you hadn't sent me to the Core for publicity, you'd never have known about this."

"You say the galaxy is exploding?"

"Rather, it finished exploding some nine thousand years ago. I'm wearing grade twenty sunglasses, and it's still too bright. A third of the Core is gone already. The patch is spreading at nearly the speed of light. I don't see that anything can stop it until it hits the gas clouds beyond the Core."

There was no comment. I went on. "A lot of the inside of the patch has gone out, but all of the surface is new novas. And remember, the light I'm seeing is nine thousand years old. Now, I'm going to read you a few instruments. Radiation, two hundred and ten. Cabin temperature normal, but you can hear the whine of the temperature control. The mass indicator shows nothing but a blur ahead. I'm turning back."

"Radiation two hundred and ten? How far are you from the edge of the Core?"

"About four thousand light-years, I think. I can see plumes of incandescent gas starting to form in the near side of the patch, moving toward galactic north and south. It reminds me of something. Aren't there pictures of exploding galaxies in the Institute?"

"Many. Yes, it has happened before. Beowulf Shaeffer, this is bad news. When the radiation from the Core reaches our worlds, it will sterilize them. We puppeteers will soon need considerable amounts of money. Shall I release you from your contract, paying you nothing?"

I laughed. I was too surprised even to get mad. "No."

"Surely you do not intend to enter the Core?"

"No. Look, why do you—"

"Then by the conditions of our contract, you forfeit."

"Wrong again. I'll take pictures of these instruments. When a court sees the readings on the radiation meter and the blue blur in the mass indicator, they'll *know* something's wrong with them."

"Nonsense. Under evidence drugs you will explain the readings."

"Sure. And the court will know you tried to get me to go

right to the center of that holocaust. You know what they'll say to that?"

"But how can a court of law find against a recorded contract?"

"The point is they'll want to. Maybe they'll decide that we're both lying and the instruments really did go haywire. Maybe they'll find a way to say the contract was illegal. But they'll find against you. Want to make a side bet?"

"No. You have won. Come back."

VI

The Core was a lovely multicolored jewel when it disappeared below the lens of the galaxy. I'd have liked to visit it someday, but there aren't any time machines.

I'd penetrated nearly to the Core in something like a month. I took my time coming home, going straight up along galactic north and flying above the lens where there were no stars to bother me, and still made it in two. All the way I wondered why the puppeteer had tried to cheat me at the last. *Long Shot*'s publicity would have been better than ever, yet the regional president had been willing to throw it away just to leave me broke. I couldn't ask why, because nobody was answering my hyperphone. Nothing I knew about puppeteers could tell me. I felt persecuted.

My come-hither brought me down at the base in the Farside End. Nobody was there. I took the transfer booth back to Sirius Mater, Jinx's biggest city, figuring to contact General Products, turn over the ship, and pick up my pay.

More surprises awaited me.

1) General Products had paid 150,000 stars into my account in the Bank of Jinx. A personal note stated that whether I wrote my article was solely up to me.

2) General Products has disappeared. They are selling no more spacecraft hulls. Companies with contracts have had their penalty clauses paid off. It all happened two months ago, simultaneously on all known worlds.

3) The bar I'm in is on the roof of the tallest building in

Sirius Mater, more than a mile above the streets. Even from here I can hear the stock market crashing. It started with the collapse of spacecraft companies with no hulls to build ships. Hundreds of others have followed. It takes a long time for an interstellar market to come apart at the seams, but, as with the Core novas, I don't see anything that can stop the chain reaction.

4) The secret of the indestructible General Products hull is being advertised for sale. General Products' human representatives will collect bids for one year, no bid to be less than one trillion stars. Get in on the ground floor, folks.

5) Nobody knows anything. That's what's causing most of the panic. It's been a month since a puppeteer was seen on any known world. Why did they drop so suddenly out of interstellar affairs?

I know.

In twenty thousand years a flood of radiation will wash over this region of space. Thirty thousand light-years may seem a long, safe distance, but it isn't, not with this big an explosion. I've asked. The Core explosion will make this galaxy uninhabitable to any known form of life.

Twenty thousand years *is* a long time. It's four times as long as human written history. We'll all be less than dust before things get dangerous, and I for one am not going to worry about it.

But the puppeteers are different. They're scared. They're getting out right now. Paying off their penalty clauses and buying motors and other equipment to put in their indestructible hulls will take so much money that even confiscating my puny salary would have been a step to the good. Interstellar business can go to hell; from now on the puppeteers will have no time for anything but running.

Where will they go? Well, the galaxy is surrounded by a halo of small globular clusters. The ones near the rim might be safe. Or the puppeteers may even go as far as Andromeda. They have the *Long Shot* for exploring if they come back for it, and they can build more. Outside the galaxy is space empty enough even for a puppeteer pilot, if he thinks his species is threatened.

It's a pity. This galaxy will be dull without puppeteers. Those two-headed monsters were not only the most dependable faction in interstellar business, they were like water in a wasteland of more or less humanoids. It's too bad they aren't brave, like us.

But is it?

I never heard of a puppeteer refusing to face a problem. He may merely be deciding how fast to run, but he'll never pretend the problem isn't there. Sometime within the next twenty millennia we humans will have to move a population that already numbers forty-three billion. How? To where? When *should* we start thinking about this? When the glow of the Core begins to shine through the dust clouds?

Maybe men are the cowards—at the core.

✳
GHOST: THREE

I said, "And there you were in Sirius Mater, all ready to write my story for me. I guessed then that Ausfaller must have sent you both times."

"So why did you hire me?"

"I didn't care much. The big question was, How do I tell the human race about the Core explosion? How do I make them believe? I *hoped* you were an ARM. Maybe you could do something."

Ander said, "I should have asked you then. There's supposed to be a huge black hole in there, millions of solar masses. Did you see it?"

I shook my head. "Maybe the shell of novas hid it, if it's there at all. Maybe it even caused the chain reaction. Sucking gas and dust and stars for fifteen billion years, maybe its mass passed some kind of threshold and *boom*. Maybe you'd even find it if you processed the recordings I took. They're proprietary, Ander. Get them from General Products."

"Well, but they're gone." But he had that smirk again. "Where did you go after that?"

"Earth. After the galactic core, what else could measure up?"

Ander laughed.

Five teams were fighting over two prey turtles that glowed intermittently among thrashing bodies. The crowd was standing, yelling their heads off. And Ander pulled a flat portable out of his backpurse, ten inches by ten inches by a quarter inch thick, and opened it in my lap. He tapped rapidly.

A picture stood above my lap. Five blue-white points rotated against a black background. They pulled apart, growing slowly brighter, coming toward me. Suddenly they blossomed into blue and white globes; the starscape wheeled; the spheres went murky red and began to recede. Ander tapped, and the picture froze.

Tiny suns circled four of the globes. The fifth glowed of itself, as if the continents of a world had caught fire. *Flying planets!* And nobody around us was looking at anything but the miniature war beyond the glass.

Ander said, "The puppeteers are still in known space. Receding at relativistic speeds, and they took their planets with them." He snapped his portable shut. "Five worlds all about the same size, orbiting in a pentagon around each other. Do the math yourself. You'll find that you can put a sun at the center, or not, and the orbits are stable either way. They understand tides just *fine*, Beowulf. *That's* what they hid from you."

My mind lurched. Cowards or not, peaceable or not, I could see how the traditionally paranoid ARM might react to so much sheer brute power. "What are they like? Oxygen worlds? Natural or terraformed? How—"

"Sigmund says we've dropped cameras in their path, not too close. The system goes flying by at point eight lights. We haven't learned much. Free oxygen, liquid water, fusion light sources redder than Sol, and we don't know why the odd one looks so odd. There's nothing else in the system, no asteroids, no cometary halo, just chains of spacecraft moving between the five worlds."

"Where are they going?"

"Straight north along the galactic axis."

"That's what I did, coming back from the Core. Get clear of occupied space and then turn ... turning five planets could be a bitch."

"Well, there's nothing but empty space where they're going."

"Maybe that's what they want."

Ander mulled it. "Possible. Meanwhile, we've got to guard them and keep their secret. They won't pass all that close to the Patriarchy, but that's *too* close. It's not that they can't defend themselves. It's that they're cowards."

I began to see what he meant. "Free enterprise."

"No species can control all its members."

"If some futzer published their location, you could see pirates of every shape and size."

"Yes, and reporters and news anchors likewise. Any entrepreneur with a money-making offer. Any undertrained ARM out to make a name. Whole fleets lying in wait for the puppeteer worlds to pass. Any kind of fool might cause the puppeteer government to defend themselves in some drastic fashion, with power like that," Ander said. "So we have to stop any passing ships from interfering with the fleet and guard their secret, too. Meanwhile, they haven't all left. There are business matters, loose ends being wrapped up."

"I know. I had dealings with one of their agents myself."

He perked up. "How did that come about?"

"I had a complaint about a General Products hull."

"Again?"

✳

FLATLANDER

The most beautiful girl aboard turned out to have a husband with habits so solitary that I didn't know about him until the second week. He was about five feet four and middle-aged, but he wore a hellflare tattoo on his shoulder, which meant he'd been on Kzin during the war thirty years back, which meant he'd been trained to kill adult kzinti with his bare hands, feet, elbows, knees, and whatnot. When we found out about each other, he very decently gave me a first warning and broke my arm to prove he meant it.

The arm still ached a day later, and every other woman on the *Lensman* was over two hundred years old. I drank alone. I stared glumly into the mirror behind the curving bar. The mirror stared glumly back.

"Hey. You from We Made It. What am I?"

He was two chairs down, and he was glaring. Without the beard he would have had a round, almost petulant face . . . I think. The beard, short and black and carefully shaped, made him look like a cross between Zeus and an angry bull-dog. The glare went with the beard. His square fingers wrapped a large drinking bulb in a death grip. A broad belly matched broad shoulders to make him look massive rather than fat.

Obviously he was talking to me. I asked, "What do you mean, what are you?"

"Where am I from?"

"Earth." It was obvious. The accent said Earth. So did the conservatively symmetrical beard. His breathing was unconsciously natural in the ship's standard atmosphere, and his build had been forged at one point zero gee.

"Then what am I?"

"A flatlander."

The glare heat increased. He'd obviously reached the bar way ahead of me. "A flatlander! Damn it, everywhere I go I'm a flatlander. Do you know how many hours I've spent in space?"

"No. Long enough to know how to use a drinking bulb."

"Funny. Very funny. Everywhere in human space a flatlander is a schnook who never gets above the atmosphere. Everywhere but Earth. If you're from Earth, you're a flatlander all your life. For the last fifty years I've been running about in human space, and what am I? A flatlander. Why?"

"Earthian is a clumsy term."

"What is WeMadeItian?" he demanded.

"I'm a crashlander. I wasn't born within fifty miles of Crashlanding City, but I'm a crashlander anyway."

That got a grin. I think. It was hard to tell with the beard. "Lucky you're not a pilot."

"I am. Was."

"You're kidding. They let a crashlander pilot a ship?"

"If he's good at it."

"I didn't mean to pique your ire, sir. May I introduce myself? My name's Elephant."

"Beowulf Shaeffer."

He bought me a drink. I bought him a drink. It turned out we both played gin, so we took fresh drinks to a card table . . .

When I was a kid, I used to stand out at the edge of Crashlanding Port watching the ships come in. I'd watch the mob of passengers leave the lock and move in a great clump toward customs, and I'd wonder why they seemed to have trouble navigating. A majority of the starborn would always walk in weaving lines, swaying and blinking teary eyes against the sun. I used to think it was because they came from different worlds with different gravities and different atmospheres beneath differently colored suns.

Later I learned different.

There are no windows in a passenger spacecraft. If there were, half the passengers would go insane; it takes an unusual mentality to watch the blind-spot appearance of hyperspace and still keep one's marbles. For passengers there is nothing to watch and nothing to do, and if you don't like reading sixteen hours a day, then you drink. It's best to drink in company. You get less lushed, knowing you have to keep up your side of a conversation. The ship's doc has cured more hangovers than every other operation combined, right down to manicures and haircuts.

The ship grounded at Los Angeles two days after I met Elephant. He'd made a good drinking partner. We'd been fairly matched at cards, he with his sharp card sense, I with my usual luck. From the talking we'd done, we knew almost as much about each other as anyone knows about anyone. In a way I was sorry to see him leave.

"You've got my number?"

"Yah. But like I said, I don't know just what I'll be doing." I was telling the truth. When I explore a civilized world, I like to make my own discoveries.

"Well, call me if you get a chance. I wish you'd change your mind. I'd like to show you Earth."

"I decline with thanks. Good-bye, Elephant. It's been fun."

Elephant waved and turned through the natives' door. I went on to face the smuggler baiters. The last drink was still with me, but I could cure that at the hotel. I never expected to see Elephant again.

Nine days ago I'd been on Jinx. I'd been rich. And I'd been depressed.

The money and the depression had stemmed from the same source. The puppeteers, those three-legged, two-headed professional cowards and businessmen, had lured me into taking a new type of ship all the way to the galac-

tic core, thirty thousand light-years away. The trip was for
publicity purposes, to get research money to iron out the
imperfections in the very ship I was riding.

I suppose I should have had more sense, but I never do,
and the money was good. The trouble was that the Core
had exploded by the time I got there. The Core stars had
gone off in a chain reaction of novas ten thousand years
ago, and a wave of radiation was even then (and even now)
sweeping toward known space.

In just over twenty thousand years we'll all be in deadly
danger.

You're not worried? It didn't bother me much, either. But
every puppeteer in known space vanished overnight, heading for Finagle knows what other galaxy.

I was depressed. I missed the puppeteers and hated
knowing I was responsible for their going. I had time and
money and a black melancholia to work off. And I'd always wanted to see Earth.

Earth smelled good. There was a used flavor to it, a
breathed flavor, unlike anything I've ever known. It was the
difference between spring water and distilled water. Somewhere in each breath I took were molecules breathed by
Dante, Aristotle, Shakespeare, Heinlein, Carter, and my
own ancestors. Traces of past industries lingered in the air,
sensed if not smelled: gasoline, coal fumes, tobacco and
burnt cigarette filters, diesel fumes, ale breweries. I left the
customs house with inflated lungs and a questing look.

I could have taken a transfer booth straight to the hotel.
I decided to walk a little first.

Everyone on Earth had made the same decision.

The pedwalk held a crowd such as I had never imagined.
They were all shapes and all colors, and they dressed in
strange and eldritch ways. Shifting colors assaulted the eye
and sent one reeling. On any world in human space, any
world but one, you know immediately who the natives are.
Wunderland? Asymmetrical beards mark the nobility, and
the common people are the ones who quickly step out of

their way. We Made It? The pallor of our skins in summer and winter; in spring and fall, the fact that we all race up-stairs, above the buried cities and onto the blooming desert, eager to taste sunlight while the murderous winds are at rest. Jinx? The natives are short, wide, and strong; a sweet little old lady's handshake can crush steel. Even in the Belt, within the solar system, a Belter strip haircut adorns both men and women. But Earth—!

No two looked alike. There were reds and blues and greens, yellows and oranges, plaids and stripes. I'm talking about hair, you understand, and skin. All my life I've used tannin-secretion pills for protection against ultraviolet, so that my skin color has varied from its normal pinkish-white (I'm an albino) to (under blue-white stars) tuxedo black. But I'd never known that other skin-dye pills existed. I stood rooted to the pedwalk, letting it carry me where it would, watching the incredible crowd swarm around me. They were all knees and elbows. Tomorrow I'd have bruises.

"Hey!"

The girl was four or five heads away, and short. I'd never have seen her if everyone else hadn't been short, too. Flatlanders rarely top six feet. And there was this girl, her hair a topological explosion in swirling orange and silver, her face a faint, subtle green with space-black eyebrows and lipstick, waving something and shouting at me.

Waving my wallet.

I forced my way to her until we were close enough to touch, until I could hear what she was saying above the crowd noise.

"Stupid! Where's your address? You don't even have a place for a stamp!"

"What?"

She looked startled. "Oh! You're an offworlder."

"Yah!" My voice would give out fast at this noise level.

"Well, look . . ." She shoved her way closer to me. "Look, you can't go around town with an offworlder's wallet. Next time someone picks your pocket he may not notice till you're gone."

"You picked my pocket?"

"Sure! Think I found it? Would I risk my precious hand under all those spike heels?"

"How if I call a cop?"

"Cop? Oh, a stoneface." She laughed merrily. "Learn or go under, man. There's no law against picking pockets. Look around you."

I looked around me, then looked back fast, afraid she'd disappear. Not only my cash but my Bank of Jinx draft for forty thousand stars was in that wallet. Everything I owned.

"See them all? Sixty-four million people in Los Angeles alone. Eighteen billion in the whole world. Suppose there was a law against picking pockets? How would you enforce it?" She deftly extracted the cash from my wallet and handed the wallet back. "Get yourself a new wallet, and fast. It'll have a place for your address and a window for a tenth-star stamp. Put your address in right away, and a stamp, too. Then the next guy who takes it can pull out the money and drop your wallet in the nearest mailbox—no sweat. Otherwise you lose your credit cards, your ident, everything." She stuffed two hundred-odd stars in cash between her breasts, flashing me a parting smile as she turned.

"Thanks," I called. Yes, I did. I was still bewildered, but she'd obviously stayed to help me. She could just as easily have kept wallet and all.

"No charge," she called back, and was gone.

I stopped off at the first transfer booth I saw, dropped a half star in the coin slot, and dialed Elephant.

The vestibule was intimidating.

I'd expected a vestibule. Why put a transfer booth inside your own home, where any burglar can get in just by dialing your number? Anyone who can afford the lease on a private transfer booth can also afford a vestibule with a locked door and an intercom switch.

There was a vestibule, but it was the size of a living room, furnished with massage chairs and an autovendor. There was an intercom, but it was a flat vidphone, three hundred years old, restored at perhaps a hundred times its original cost. There was a locked door; it was a double door of what looked like polished brass, with two enormous curved handles, and it stood fifteen feet high.

I'd suspected Elephant was well off, but this was too much. It occurred to me that I'd never seen him completely sober, that I had in fact turned down his offer of guidance, that a simple morning-after treatment might have wiped me from his memory. Shouldn't I just go away? I had wanted to explore Earth on my own.

But I didn't know the rules!

I stepped out of the booth and glimpsed the back wall. It was all picture window, with nothing outside—just fleecy blue sky. How peculiar, I thought, and stepped closer. And closer.

Elephant lived halfway up a cliff. A sheer mile-high cliff.

The phone rang.

On the third ear-jarring ring I answered, mainly to stop the noise. A supercilious voice asked, "Is somebody out there?"

"I'm afraid not," I said. "Does someone named Elephant live here?"

"I'll see, sir," said the voice. The screen had not lit, but I had the feeling someone had seen me quite clearly.

Seconds crawled by. I was half minded to jump back in the transfer booth and dial at random. But only half; that was the trouble. Then the screen lit, and it was Elephant. "Bey! You changed your mind!"

"Yah. You didn't tell me you were rich."

"You didn't ask."

"Well, no, of course not."

"How do you expect to learn things if you don't ask? Don't answer that. Hang on, I'll be right down. You did change your mind? You'll let me show you Earth?"

"Yes, I will. I'm scared to go out there alone."

"Why? Don't answer. Tell me in person." He hung up.

Seconds later the big bronze doors swung back with a bone-shaking boom. They just barely got out of Elephant's way. He pulled me inside, giving me no time to gape, shoved a drink in my hand, and asked why I was afraid to go outside.

I told him about the pickpocket, and he laughed. He told me about the time he tried to go outside during a We Made It summer, and I laughed, though I've heard of outworlders being blown away and to Hades doing the same thing. Amazingly, we were off again. It was just like it had been on the ship, even to the end of Elephant's anecdote. "They called me a silly flatlander, of course."

"I've been thinking about that," I said.

"About what?"

"You said you'd give a lot to do something completely original, so the next time someone called you a flatlander, you could back him into a corner and force him to listen to your story. You said it several times."

"I didn't say just that. But I would like to have some story to tell, something like your neutron star episode. If only to tell myself. The silly offworlder wouldn't know, but *I'd* know."

I nodded. I'd talked about the neutron star episode over gin cards—a habit I've developed for distracting my opponent—and Elephant had been suitably impressed.

"I've thought of a couple of things you could do," I said.

"Spill."

"One. Visit the puppeteer homeworld. Nobody's been there, but everyone knows there is one, and everyone knows how difficult it is to find. You could be the first."

"Great." He mused a moment. "Great! And the puppeteers wouldn't stop me because they're gone. Where *is* the puppeteer homeworld?"

"*I* don't know."

"What's your second idea?"

"Ask the Outsiders."

"Huh?"

"There's not a system in the galaxy that the Outsiders don't know all about. We don't know how far the puppeteer empire extended, though it was way beyond known space, but we do know about the Outsiders. They know the galaxy like the palm of their—uh … And they trade for information; it's just about the only business they do. Ask them what's the most unusual world they know of within reach."

Elephant was nodding gently. There was a glazed look in his eyes. I had not been sure he was serious about seeking some unique achievement. He was.

"The problem is," I said, "that an Outsider's idea of what is unique may not—" I stopped because Elephant was up and half running to a tridphone.

I wasn't sorry. It gave me an opportunity to gape in private.

I've been in bigger homes than Elephant's. Much bigger. I grew up in one. But I've never seen a room that soothed the eye as Elephant's living room did. It was more than a living room; it was an optical illusion, the opposite of those jittering black-and-white images they show in lectures on how we see. These clinical children of op art give the illusion of motion, but Elephant's living room gave the illusion of stillness. A physicist would have loved the soundproofing. Some interior decorator had become famous for his work here, if he hadn't been famous already, in which case he had become rich. How could tall, thin Beowulf Shaeffer fit into a chair designed to the measure of short, wide Elephant? Yet I was bonelessly limp, blissfully relaxed, using only the muscles that held a double-walled glass of an odd-tasting, strangely refreshing soft drink called Tzlotz Beer.

A glass which would not empty. Somewhere in the crystal was a tiny transfer motor connected to the bar, but the bent light in the crystal hid it. Another optical illusion, and one that must have tricked good men into acute alcoholism. I'd have to watch that.

Elephant returned. He walked as if he massed tons, as if any kzinti foolish enough to stand in his path would have a short, wide hole in him. "All done," he said. "Don

Cramer'll find the nearest Outsider ship and make my pitch for me. We should hear in a couple of days."

"Okay," said I, and asked him about the cliff. It turned out that we were in the Rocky Mountains and that he owned every square inch of the nearly vertical cliff face. Why? I remembered Earth's eighteen billion and wondered if they'd otherwise have surrounded him up, down, and sideways.

Suddenly Elephant remembered that someone named Dianna must be home by now. I followed him into the transfer booth, watched him dial eleven digits, and waited in a much smaller vestibule while Elephant used the more conventional intercom. Dianna seemed dubious about letting him in until he roared that he had a guest and she should stop fooling around.

Dianna was a small, pretty woman with skin the deep, uniform red of a Martian sky and hair like flowing quicksilver. Her irises had the same polished-silver luster. She hadn't wanted to let us in because we were both wearing our own skins, but she never mentioned it again once we were inside.

Elephant introduced me to Dianna and instantly told her he'd acted to contact the Outsiders.

"What's an Outsider?" she asked.

Elephant gestured with both hands, looked confused, turned helplessly toward me.

"They're hard to describe," I said. "Think of a cat-o'-nine-tails with a big thick handle."

"They live on cold worlds," said Elephant.

"Small, cold, airless worlds like Nereid. They pay rent to use Nereid as a base, don't they, Elephant? And they travel over most of the galaxy in big unpressurized ships with fusion drives and no hyperdrives."

"They sell information. They can tell me about the world I want to find, the most unusual planet in known space."

"They spend most of their time tracking starseeds."

Dianna broke in. "Why?"

Elephant looked at me. I looked at Elephant.

"Say!" Elephant exclaimed. "Why don't we get a fourth for bridge?"

Dianna looked thoughtful. Then she focused her silver eyes on me, examined me from head to foot, and nodded gently to herself. "Sharrol Janss. I'll call her."

While she was phoning, Elephant told me, "That's a good thought. Sharrol's got a tendency toward hero worship. She's a computer analyst at Donovan's Brains Inc. You'll like her."

"Good," I said, wondering if we were still talking about a bridge game. It struck me that I was building up a debt to Elephant. "Elephant, when you contact the Outsiders, I'd like to come along."

"Oh? Why?"

"You'll need a pilot. And I've dealt with Outsiders before."

"Okay, it's a deal."

The intercom rang from the vestibule. Dianna went to the door and came back with our fourth for bridge. "Sharrol, you know Elephant. This is Beowulf Shaeffer, from We Made It. Bey, this is—"

"You!" I said.

"You!" she said.

It was the pickpocket.

My vacation lasted just four days.

I hadn't known how long it would last, though I did know how it would end. Consequently I threw myself into it body and soul. If there was a dull moment anywhere in those four days, I slept through it, and at that I didn't get enough sleep. Elephant seemed to feel the same way. He was living life to the hilt; he must have suspected, as I did, that the Outsiders would not consider danger a factor in choosing his planet. By their own ethics they were bound not to. The days of Elephant's life might be running short.

Buried in those four days were incidents that made me wonder why Elephant was looking for a weird world. Surely Earth was the weirdest of all.

I remember when we threw in the bridge hands and decided to go out for dinner. This was more complicated than it sounds. Elephant hadn't had a chance to change to flatlander styles, and neither of us was fit to be seen in public. Dianna had cosmetics for us.

I succumbed to an odd impulse. I dressed as an albino.

They were body paints, not pills. When I finished applying them, there in the full-length mirror was my younger self. Blood-red irises, snow-white hair, white skin with a tinge of pink: the teenager who had disappeared ages ago, when I was old enough to use tannin pills. I found my mind wandering far back across the decades, to the days when I was a flatlander myself, my feet firmly beneath the ground, my head never higher than seven feet above the desert sands . . . They found me there before the mirror and pronounced me fit to be seen in public.

I remember that evening when Dianna told me she had known Elephant forever. "I was the one who named him Elephant," she bragged.

"It's a nickname?"

"Sure," said Sharrol. "His real name is Gregory Pelton."

"O-o-oh." Suddenly all came clear. Gregory Pelton is known among the stars. It is rumored that he owns the thirty-light-year-wide rough sphere called *human space*, that he earns his income by renting it out. It is rumored that General Products—the all-embracing puppeteer company, now defunct for lack of puppeteers—is a front for Gregory Pelton. It's a fact that his great-to-the-eighth-grandmother invented the transfer booth and that he is rich, rich, rich.

I asked, "Why Elephant? Why that particular nickname?"

Dianna and Sharrol looked demurely at the tablecloth.

Elephant said, "Use your imagination, Bey."

"On what? What's an elephant, some kind of animal?"

Three faces registered annoyance. I'd missed a joke.

"Tomorrow," said Elephant, "we'll show you the zoo."

There are seven transfer booths in the Zoo of Earth. That'll tell you how big it is. But you're wrong; you've forgotten the two hundred taxis on permanent duty. They're there because the booths are too far apart for walking.

We stared down at dusty, compact animals smaller than starseeds or Bandersnatchi but bigger than anything else I'd ever seen. Elephant said, "See?"

"Yah," I said, because the animals showed a compactness and a plodding invulnerability very like Elephant's. And then I found myself watching one of the animals in a muddy pool. It was using a hollow tentacle over its mouth to spray water on its back. I stared at that tentacle . . . and stared . . .

"Hey, look!" Sharrol called, pointing. "Bey's ears are turning red!"

I didn't forgive her till two that morning.

And I remember reaching over Sharrol to get a tabac stick and seeing her purse lying on her other things. I said, "How if I picked your pocket now?"

Orange and silver lips parted in a lazy smile. "I'm not wearing a pocket."

"Would it be in good taste to sneak the money out of your purse?"

"Only if you could hide it on you."

I found a small flat purse with four hundred stars in it and stuck it in my mouth.

She made me go through with it. Ever make love to a woman with a purse in your mouth? Unforgettable. Don't try it if you've got asthma.

I remember Sharrol. I remember smooth, warm blue skin, silver eyes with a wealth of expression, orange and silver hair in a swirling abstract pattern that nothing could mess up. It always sprang back. Her laugh was silver, too, when I gently extracted two handfuls of hair and tied them in a hard double knot, and when I gibbered and jumped up and down at the sight of her hair slowly untying itself like Medusa's locks. And her voice was a silver croon.

I remember the freeways.

They were the first thing that showed coming in on

Earth. If we'd landed at night, it would have been the lighted cities, but of course we came in on the day side. Why else would a world have three spaceports? There were the freeways and autostradas and autobahns, strung in an all-enclosing net across the faces of the continents.

From a few miles up you still can't see the breaks. But they're there, where girders and pavement have collapsed. Only two superhighways are still kept in good repair. They are both on the same continent: the Pennsylvania Turnpike and the Santa Monica Freeway. The rest of the network is broken chaos.

It seems there are people who collect old groundcars and race them. Some are actually renovated machines, fifty to ninety percent replaced; others are handmade reproductions. On a perfectly flat surface they'll do fifty to ninety miles per hour.

I laughed when Elephant told me about them, but actually seeing them was different.

The rodders began to appear about dawn. They gathered around one end of the Santa Monica Freeway, the end that used to join the San Diego Freeway. This end is a maze of fallen spaghetti, great curving loops of prestressed concrete that have lost their strength over the years and sagged to the ground. But you can still use the top loop to reach the starting line. We watched from above, hovering in a cab as the groundcars moved into line.

"Their dues cost more than the cars," said Elephant. "I used to drive one myself. You'd turn white as snow if I told you how much it costs to keep this stretch of freeway in repair."

"How much?"

He told me. I turned white as snow.

They were off. I was still wondering what kick they got driving an obsolete machine on flat concrete when they could be up here with us. They were off, weaving slightly, weaving more than slightly, foolishly moving at different speeds, coming perilously close to each other before sheering off—and I began to realize things.

Those automobiles had no radar.

They were being steered with a cabin wheel geared directly to four ground wheels. A mistake in steering and they'd crash into each other or into the concrete curbs. They were steered and stopped by muscle power, but whether they could turn or stop depended on how hard four rubber balloons could grip smooth concrete. If the tires lost their grip, Newton's first law would take over; the fragile metal mass would continue moving in a straight line until stopped by a concrete curb or another groundcar.

"A man could get killed in one of those."

"Not to worry," said Elephant. "Nobody does, usually."

"Usually?"

The race ended twenty minutes later at another tangle of fallen concrete. I was wet through. We landed and met some of the racers. One of them, a thin guy with tangled, glossy green hair and a bony white face with a widely grinning scarlet mouth, offered me a ride. I declined with thanks, backing slowly away and wishing for a weapon. This joker was obviously dangerously insane.

I remember flatlander food, the best in known space, and an odd, mildly alcoholic drink called Taittinger Comtes de Champagne '59. I remember invading an outworlder bar, where the four of us talked shop with a girl rock miner whose inch-wide auburn crest of hair fell clear to the small of her back. I remember flying cross-country with a lift belt and seeing nothing but city enclosing widely separated patches of food-growing land. I remember a submerged hotel off the Grand Banks of Newfoundland and a dolphin embassy off Italy, where a mixed group of dolphins and flatlanders seemed to be solving the general problem of sentient beings without hands (there are many, and we'll probably find more). It seemed more a coffee-break discussion than true business.

* * *

We were about to break up for bed on the evening of the fourth day when the tridphone rang. Don Cramer had found an Outsider.

I said, disbelieving, "You're leaving *right now*?"

"Sure!" said Elephant. "Here, take one of these pills. You won't feel sleepy till we're on our way."

A deal is a deal, and I owed Elephant plenty. I took the pill. We kissed Sharrol and Dianna good-bye, Dianna standing on a chair to reach me, Sharrol climbing me like a beanpole and wrapping her legs around my waist. I was a foot and a half taller than either of them.

Calcutta Base was in daylight. Elephant and I took the transfer booth there, to find that the *ST∞* had been shipped ahead of us.

Her full name was *Slower Than Infinity*. She had been built into a General Products No. 2 hull, a three-hundred-foot spindle with a wasp-waist constriction near the tail. I was relieved. I had been afraid Elephant might own a flashy, vulnerable dude's yacht. The two-man control room looked pretty small for a lifesystem until I noticed the bubble extension folded into the nose. The rest of the hull held a one-gee fusion drive and fuel tank, a hyperspace motor, a gravity drag, and belly-landing gear, all clearly visible through the hull, which had been left transparent.

She held fuel, food, and air. She must have been ready for days. We took off twenty minutes after arriving.

Using the fusion drive in Earth's atmosphere would have gotten us into the organ banks, in pieces. Flatlander laws are strict about air pollution. A robot rocket with huge wings lifted us to orbit, using air compressed nearly to degenerate matter as a propellant. We took off from there.

Now there was plenty of time for sleep. It took us a week at one gee just to get far enough out of the solar system's gravity well to use the hyperdrive. Somewhere in that time I removed my false coloring (it *had* been false; I'd continued to take tannin-secretion pills against Earth's sunlight), and Elephant turned his skin back to light tan and his beard and hair back to black. For four days he'd been Zeus, with marble skin, a metal-gold beard, and glowing molten-gold eyes. It had fitted him so perfectly that I hardly noticed the change.

Hyperdrive—and a long, slow three weeks. We took turns hovering over the mass indicator, though at first-quantum hyperdrive speeds we'd have seen a mass at least twelve hours before it became dangerous. I think I was the only man who knew there *was* a second quantum, a puppeteer secret. The Outsider ship was near the edge of known space, well beyond Tau Ceti.

"It was the only one around," Elephant had said. "Number fourteen."

"Fourteen? That's the same ship I dealt with before."

"Oh? Good. That should help."

Days later he asked, "How'd it happen?"

"The usual way. Number fourteen was on the other side of known space then, and she sent out an offer of information exchange. I was almost to Wunderland, and I caught the offer. When I dropped my passengers, I went back."

"Did they have anything worthwhile?"

"Yah. They'd found the *Lazy Eight II*."

The *Lazy Eight II* had been one of the old slowboats, a circular-flying wing taking colonists to Jinx. Something had gone wrong before turnover, and the ship had continued on, carrying fifty passengers in suspended animation and a crew of four, presumed dead. With a ramscoop to feed hydrogen to her fusion drive, she could accelerate forever. She was five hundred years on her way.

"I remember," said Elephant. "They couldn't reach her."

"No. But we'll know where to find her when the state of the art gets that good." Which wouldn't be soon, I thought. A hyperdrive ship not only would have to reach her but would have to carry fuel to match her speed. Her speed was barely less than a photon's, and she was more than five hundred light-years away, seventeen times the diameter of known space.

"Did you have any problems?"

"Their translator is pretty good. But we'll have to be

careful, Elephant. The thing about buying information is that you don't know what you're getting until you've got it. They couldn't just offer to sell me the present position of the *Lazy Eight II*. We'd have tracked their course by telescope until we saw the light of a fusion drive and gotten the information free."

The time came when only a small green dot glowed in the center of the mass indicator. A star would have shown as a line; no star would have shown no dot. I dropped out of hyperspace and set the deep radar to hunt out the Outsider.

The Outsider found us first.

Somewhere in the cylindrical metal pod near her center of mass, perhaps occupying it completely, was the reactionless drive. It was common knowledge that that drive was for sale and that the cost was a full trillion stars. Though nobody, and no nation now extant, could afford to pay it, the price was not exorbitant. In two or three minutes, while we were still searching, that drive had dropped the Outsider ship from above point nine lights to zero relative and pulled it alongside the *ST∞*.

One moment, nothing but stars. The next, the Outsider ship was alongside.

She was mostly empty space. I knew her population was the size of a small city, but she was much bigger because more strung out. There was the minuscule-seeming drive capsule, and there, on a pole two and a half miles long, was a light source. The rest of the ship was metal ribbons, winding in and out, swooping giddily around themselves and each other, until the ends of each tangled ribbon stopped meandering and joined the drive capsule. There were around a thousand such ribbons, and each was the width of a wide city pedwalk.

"Like a Christmas tree decoration," said Elephant. "What now, Bey?"

"They'll use the ship radio."

A few minutes of waiting, and here came a bunch of Outsiders. They looked like black cat-o'-nine-tails with grossly swollen handles. In the handles were their brains and invisible sense organs; in the whip ends, the clusters of motile root tentacles, were gas pistols. Six of them braked to a stop outside the air lock.

The radio spoke. "Welcome to Ship Fourteen. Please step outside for conveyance to our office. Take nothing on the outsides of your pressure suits."

Elephant asked, "Do we?"

I said, "Sure. The Outsiders are nothing if not honorable."

We went out. The six Outsiders offered us a tentacle each, and away we went across open space. Not fast. The thrust from the gas pistols was very low, irritatingly weak. But the Outsiders themselves were weak; an hour in the gravity of Earth's moon would have killed them.

They maneuvered us through the tangled clutter of silver ribbons, landing us on a ramp next to the looming convex wall of the drive capsule.

It wasn't quite like being lost in a giant bowl of noodles. The rigid ribbons were too far apart for that. Far above us was the light source, about as small and intense and yellowish-white as Earth's sun seen from a moon of Neptune. Shining down through the interstellar vacuum, it cast a network of sharp black shadows across all the thousand looping strands that made up the city.

Along every light-shadow borderline were the Outsiders. Just as their plantlike ancestors had done billions of years ago on some unknown world near the galactic core, the Outsiders were absorbing life energy. Their branched tails lay in shadow, their heads in sunlight, while thermoelectricity charged their biochemical batteries. Some had root tentacles dipped in shallow food dishes; the trace elements which kept them alive and growing were in suspension in liquid helium.

We stepped carefully around them, using our headlamps at lowest intensity, following one of the Outsiders toward a door in the wall ahead.

The enclosure was dark until the door closed behind us. Then the light came on. It was sourceless, the color of normal sunlight, and it illuminated a cubicle that was bare and square. The only furnishing was a transparent hemisphere with an Outsider resting inside. Presumably the hemisphere filtered out excess light going in.

"Welcome," said the room. Whatever the Outsider had said was not sonic in nature. "The air is breathable. Take off your helmets, suits, shoes, girdles, and whatnot." It was an excellent translator, with a good grasp of idiom and a pleasant baritone voice.

"Thanks," said Elephant, and we did.

"Which of you is Gregory Pelton?"

"Gronk."

The wall was not confused. "According to your agent, you want to know how to reach that planet which is most unusual inside or within five miles of the sixty-light-year-wide region you call known space. Is this correct?"

"Yes."

"We must know if you plan to go there or to send agents there. Also, do you plan a landing, a near orbit, or a distant orbit?"

"Landing."

"Are we to guard against danger to your life?"

"No." Elephant's voice was a little dry. The Outsider ship was an intimidating place.

"What kind of ship would you use?"

"The one outside."

"Do you plan colonization? Mining? Growth of food plants?"

"I plan only one visit."

"We have selected a world for you. The price will be one million stars."

"That's high," said Elephant. I whistled under my breath. It was, and it wouldn't get lower. The Outsiders never dickered.

"Sold," said Elephant.

The translator gave us a triplet set of coordinates some twenty-four light-years from Earth along galactic north. "The star you are looking for is a protosun with one planet a billion and a half miles distant. The system is moving at a point eight lights toward—" He gave a vector direction. It seemed the protosun was drawing a shallow chord through known space; it would never approach human space.

"No good," said Elephant. "No hyperdrive ship can go that fast in real space."

"You could hitch a ride," said the translator, "with us. Moor your ship to our drive capsule."

"That'll work," said Elephant. He was getting more and more uneasy; his eyes seemed to be searching the walls for the source of the voice. He would not look at the Outsider business agent in the vacuum chamber.

"Our ferry fee will be one million stars."

Elephant sputtered.

"Just a sec," I said. "I may have information to sell you."

There was a long pause. Elephant looked at me in surprise.

"You are Beowulf Shaeffer?"

"Yah. You remember me?"

"We find you in our records. Beowulf Shaeffer, we have information for you, already paid. The former regional president of General Products on Jinx wishes you to contact him. I have a transfer-booth number."

"That's late news," I said. "The puppeteers are gone. Anyway, why would that two-headed sharpie want to see me?"

"I do not have that information. I do know that not all puppeteers have left this region. Will you accept the transfer-booth number?"

"Sure."

I wrote down the eight digits as they came. A moment later Elephant was yelling just as if he were a tridee set turned on in the middle of a program. "—hell is going on here?"

"Sorry about that," said the translator.

"What happened?" I asked.

"I couldn't hear anything! Did that mon— Did the Outsider have private business with you?"

"Sort of. I'll tell you later."

The translator said, "Beowulf Shaeffer, we do not buy information. We sell information and use the proceeds to buy territory and food soil."

"You may need this information," I argued. "I'm the only man within reach who knows it."

"What of other races?"

The puppeteers might have told them, but it was worth taking a chance. "You're about to leave known space. If you don't deal with me, you may not get this information in time."

"What price do you set on this item?"

"You set the price. You've got more experience at putting values on information, and you're honorable."

"We may not be able to afford an honest price."

"The price may not exceed our ferry fee."

"Done. Speak."

I told him of the Core explosion and how I'd come to find out about it. He made me go into detail on what I'd seen: the bright patch of supernovas spreading out as my ship caught up with ancient light waves, until all the bright multicolored ball of the Core was ablaze with supernovas. "You wouldn't have known this until you got there, and then it would have been too late. You don't use faster-than-light drives."

"We knew from the puppeteers that the Core had exploded. They were not able to go into detail because they had not seen it for themselves."

"Oh. Ah, well. I think the explosion must have started at the back side of the Core from here. Otherwise it would have seemed to go much more slowly."

"Many thanks. We will waive your ferry fee. Now, there is one more item. Gregory Pelton, for an additional two hundred thousand stars we will tell you exactly what is peculiar about the planet you intend to visit."

"Can I find out for myself?"

"It is likely."

"Then I will."

Silence followed. The Outsider hadn't expected that. I said, "I'm curious. Your galaxy is rapidly becoming a death trap. What will you do now?"

"That information will cost you—"

"Forget it."

Outside, Elephant said, "Thanks."

"Forget it. I wonder what they will do."

"Maybe they can shield themselves against the radiation."

"Maybe. But they won't have any starseeds to follow."

"Do they need them?"

Finagle only knew. The starseeds followed a highly rigid migratory mating pattern out from the Core of the galaxy and into the arms, almost to the rim, before turning back down to the Core. They were doomed. As they returned to the Core, the expanding wave of radiation from the multiple novas would snuff out the species one by one. What would the Outsiders do without them? What the hell did they do *with* them? Why did they follow them? Did they need starseeds? Did starseeds need Outsiders? The Outsiders would answer these and related questions for one trillion stars apiece. Personal questions cost high with the Outsiders.

A crew was already bringing the $ST\infty$ into dock. We watched from the ramp, with crewmen sunbathing about our feet. We weren't worried. The way the Outsiders handled it, our invulnerable hull might have been made of spun sugar and sunbeams. When a spiderweb of thin strands fastened the $ST\infty$ to the wall of the drive capsule, the voice of the translator spoke in our ears and invited us to step aboard. We jumped a few hundred feet upward through the trace of artificial gravity, climbed into the air lock, and got out of our suits.

"Thanks again," said Elephant.

"Forget it again," I said magnanimously. "I owe you plenty. You've been putting me up as a houseguest on the most expensive world in known space, acting as my guide where the cost of labor is—"

"Okay okay okay. But you saved me a million stars, and don't you forget it." He whopped me on the shoulder and hurried into the control room to set up a million-star credit base for the next Outsider ship that came by.

"I won't," I called at his retreating back, and wondered what the hell I meant by that.

Much later I wondered about something else. Had Elephant planned to take me to "his" world? Or did he think to go it alone, to be the first to see it and not one of the first two? After the Outsider episode it was already too late. He couldn't throw me off the ship then.

I wished I'd thought of it in time. I never wanted to be a batman. My stake in this was to gently, tactfully keep Elephant from killing himself if it became necessary. For all his vast self-confidence, vast riches, vast generosity, and vast bulk, he was still only a flatlander and thus a little bit helpless.

We were in the expansion bubble when it happened. The bubble had inflatable seats and an inflatable table and was there for exercising and killing time, but it also supplied a fine view; the surface was perfectly transparent.

Otherwise we would have missed it.

There was no pressure against the seat of the pants, no crawling sensation in the pit of the stomach, no feel of motion. But Elephant, who was talking about a Jinxian frail he'd picked up in a Chicago bar, stopped just as she was getting ready to tear the place apart because some suicidal idiot had insulted her.

Somebody heavy was sitting down on the universe.

He came down slowly, like a fat man cautiously letting his weight down on a beach ball. From inside the bubble it looked like all the stars and nebulas around us were squeezing themselves together. The Outsiders on the ribbons outside never moved, but Elephant said something profane, and I steeled myself to look up.

The stars overhead were blue-white and blazing. Around us, they were squashed together; below, they were turning red and winking out one by one. It had taken us a week to get out of the solar system, but the Outsider ship could have done it in five hours.

The radio spoke. "Sirs, our crewmen will remove your ship from ours, after which you will be on your own. It has been a pleasure to do business with you."

A swarm of Outsider crewmen hauled us through the maze of basking ramps and left us. Presently the Outsider ship vanished like a pricked soap bubble, gone off on its own business.

In the strange starlight Elephant let out a long, shaky sigh. Some people can't take aliens. They don't find puppeteers graceful and beautiful; they find them horrifying, *wrong*. They see kzinti as slavering carnivores whose only love is fighting, which is the truth, but they don't see the rigid code of honor or the self-control which allows a kzinti ambassador to ride a human-city pedwalk without slashing out with his claws at the impertinent stabbing knees and elbows. Elephant was one of those people.

He said, "Okay," in amazed relief. They were actually gone. "I'll take the first watch, Bey."

He did not say, "Those bastards would take your heart as collateral on a tenth-star loan." He didn't see them as that close to human.

"Fine," I said, and went into the control bubble. The Fast Protosun was a week away. I'd been in a suit for hours, and there was a shower in the extension bubble.

If Elephant's weakness was aliens, mine was relativity.

The trip through hyperspace was routine. I could take the sight of the two small windows turning into blind spots, becoming areas of nothing, which seemed to draw together the objects around them. So could Elephant; he'd done some flying, though he preferred the comfort of a luxury liner. But even the best pilot occasionally has to drop back into the normal universe to get his bearings and to assure his subconscious that the stars are still there.

And each time it was changed, squashed flat. The crowded blue stars were all ahead; the sparse, dim red stars were all behind. Four hundred years ago men and women had lived for years with such a view of the universe, but it hadn't happened since the invention of hyperdrive. I'd never seen the universe look like this. It bothered me.

"No, it doesn't bug me," said Elephant when I mentioned it. We were a day out from our destination. "To me, stars are stars. But I have been worried about something. Bey, you said the Outsiders are honorable."

"They are. They've got to be. They have to be so far above suspicion that any species they deal with will remember their unimpeachable ethics a century later. You can see that, can't you? Outsiders don't show up more often than that."

"Um. Okay. Why did they try to screw that extra two hundred kilostars out of me?"

"Uh—"

"See, the goddamn problem is, what if it was a fair price? What if we *need* to know what's funny about the Fast Protosun?"

"You're right. Knowing the Outsiders, it's probably information we can use. All right, we'll nose around a little before we land. We'd have done that anyway, but now we'll do it better."

What was peculiar about the Fast Protosun?

Around lunchtime on the seventh ship's day a short green line in the sphere of the mass indicator began to extend itself. It was wide and fuzzy, just what you'd expect of a protosun. I let it reach almost to the surface of the sphere before I dropped us into normal space.

The squashed universe looked in the windows, but ahead of us was a circular darkening and blurring of the vivid blue-white stars. In the center of the circle was a dull red glow.

"Let's go into the extension bubble," said Elephant.

"Let's not."

"We'll get a better view in there." He turned the dial that would make the bubble transparent. Naturally we kept it opaque in hyperspace.

"Repeat, let's not. Think about it, Elephant. What sense does it make to use an impermeable hull, then spend most of our time outside it? Until we know what's here, we ought to retract the bubble."

He nodded his shaggy head and touched the board again. Chugging noises announced that air and water were being pulled out of the bubble. Elephant moved to a window.

"Ever see a protosun?"

"No," I said. "I don't think there are any in human space."

"That could be the peculiarity."

"It could. One thing it isn't is the speed of the thing. Outsiders spend all their time moving faster than this."

"But planets don't. Neither do stars. Bey, maybe this thing came from outside the galaxy. That would make it unusual."

It was time we made a list. I found a pad and solemnly noted speed of star, nature of star, and possible extragalactic origin of star.

"I've found our planet," said Elephant.

"Whereabouts?"

"Almost on the other side of the protosun. We can get there faster in hyperspace."

The planet was still invisibly small where Elephant brought us out. The protosun looked about the same.

A protosun is the fetus of a star: a thin mass of gas and dust, brought together by slow eddies in interstellar magnetic fields or by the presence of a Trojan point in some loose cluster of stars, which is collapsing and contracting due to gravity. I'd found material on protosuns in the ship's library, but it was all astronomical data; nobody had ever been near one for a close look. In theory the Fast Protosun must be fairly well along in its evolution, since it was glowing at the center.

"There it is," said Elephant. "Two days away at one gee."

"Good. We can do our instrument checks on the way. Strap down."

With the fusion motor pushing us smoothly along, Elephant went back to the scope, and I started checking the other instruments. One thing stood out like a beacon.

"Elephant. Have you noticed in me a tendency to use profanity for emphasis?"

"Not really. Why?"

"It's goddamn radioactive out there."

"Could you be a little more specific, sir?"

"Our suit shields would break down in three days. The extension bubble would go in twenty hours."

"Okay, add it to your list. Any idea what's causing it?"

"Not one." I made a note on my list, then went back to work. We were in no danger; the GP hull would protect us from anything but impact with something big.

"No asteroid belts," said Elephant. "Meteor density zero, as far as I can tell. No other planets."

"The interstellar gas may clean away anything small at these speeds."

"One thing's for sure, Bey. I've got my money's worth. This is a damn funny system."

"Yah. Well, we missed lunch. Shall we get dinner?"

"Philistine."

Elephant ate fast. He was back at the telescope before I was ready for coffee. Watching him move, I was again reminded of a juggernaut, but he'd never shown as much determination when I knew him on Earth. If a hungry kzinti had been standing between him and the telescope, he'd have left footprints in fur.

But the only thing that could get in his way out here was me.

"Can't get a close look at the planet," said Elephant, "but it looks polished."

"Like a billiard ball?"

"Just that. I don't see any sign of an atmosphere."

"How about blast craters?"

"Nothing."

"They should be there."

"This system's pretty clean of meteors."

"But the space around us shouldn't be. And at these speeds—"

"Uh huh. That better go on your list."

I wrote it down.

We slept on the disaster couches. In front of me were the yellow lights of the control panel; the stars glowed red through one side window, blue through the other. I stayed awake for a long time, staring through the forward window into the red darkness of the protosun. The window was opaque, but I saw the dark red blur clearly in my imagination.

The radiation held steady all through the next day. I did some more thorough checking, using temperature readings and deep radar on both sun and planet. Everywhere I looked was a new anomaly.

"This star definitely shouldn't be glowing yet. It's too spread out; the gas should be too thin for fusion."

"Is it hot enough to glow?"

"Sure. But it shouldn't be."

"Maybe the theories on protosuns are wrong."

"Then they're way wrong."

"Put it on your list."

And, an hour later:

"Elephant."

"*Another* peculiarity?"

"Yah."

From under shaggy brows Elephant's eyes plainly told me he was getting sick of peculiarities.

"According to the deep-radar shadow, this planet doesn't have any lithosphere. It's worn right down to what ought to be the magma but isn't because it's so cold out here."

"Write it down. How many entries have you got?"

"Nine."

"Is any one of them worth paying two hundred kilostars to know about beforehand?"

"The radiation, maybe, if we didn't have a GP hull."

"But," said Elephant, glaring out at the huge, dark disk, "they knew we had a GP hull. Bey, can anything get through a General Products hull?"

"Light, like a laser beam. Gravity, like tides crushing you into the nose of a ship when you get too close to a neutron star. Impact won't harm the hull, but it'll kill what's inside."

"Maybe the planet's inhabited. The more I think about it, the more sure I am it came from outside. Nothing in the galaxy could have given it this velocity. It's diving through the plane of the galaxy; it wouldn't have to push in from the rim."

"Okay. What do we do if someone shoots a laser at us?"

"We perish, I think. I had reflective paint spread around the cabin, except for the windows, but the rest of the hull is transparent."

"We can still get into hyperspace from here. And for the next twenty hours. Afterward we'll be too close to the planet."

I went right to sleep that night, being pretty tired despite the lack of exercise. Hours later I slowly realized that I was being examined. I could see it through my closed eyelids; I could feel the heat of the vast red glare, the size of the angry eye, the awful power of the mind behind it. I tried to struggle away, smacked my hand on something, and woke with a shock.

I lay there in the red darkness. The edge of the protosun peeked through a window. I could feel its hostile glare.

I said, "Elephant."

"Mngl?"

"Nothing." Morning would be soon enough.

Morning.

"Elephant, would you do me a favor?"

"Sure. You want Dianna? My right arm? Shave off my beard?"

"I'll keep Sharrol, thanks. Put on your suit, will you?"

"Sure, that makes sense. We aren't nearly uncomfortable enough just because we closed off the bubble."

"Right. And because I'm a dedicated masochist, I'm going to put my suit on this instant. Now, I hate to enjoy myself alone . . ."

"You got the wind up?"

"A little. Just enough."

"Anything for a friend. You go first."

There was just room to get our suits on one at a time. If the inner air lock door hadn't been open, there wouldn't have been that. We tried leaving our helmets thrown back, but they got in our way against the crash couches. So we taped them to the window in front of us.

I felt better that way, but Elephant clearly thought I'd flipped. "You sure you wouldn't rather eat with your helmet on?"

"I hate suit food syrup. We can reach our helmets if we get a puncture."

"*What puncture?* We're in a *General Products hull!*"

"I keep remembering that the Outsiders knew that."

"We've been through that."

"Let's go through it again. Assume they thought we might be killed anyway if we weren't prepared. Then what?"

"Gronk."

"Either they expected us to go out in suits and get killed, or they know of something that can reach through a General Products hull."

"Or both. In which case the suits do us no good at all. Bey, do you know how long it's been since a General Products hull failed?"

"I've never heard of it happening at all."

"It never has. The puppeteers offer an enormous guarantee in case one does. Something in the tens of millions if someone dies as a result."

"You're dead right. I've been stupid. Go ahead and take off your suit."

Elephant turned to look at me. "And you?"

"I'll keep mine on. Do you believe in hunches?"

"No."

"Neither do I. Except just this once."

Elephant shrugged his shaggy eyebrows and went back to his telescope. By then we were six hours out from the nameless planet and decelerating.

"I think I've found an asteroid crater," he said presently.

"Let's see." I had a look. "Yah, I think you're right. But it's damn near disappeared."

He took the telescope back. "It's round enough. Almost has to be a crater. Bey, why should it be so eroded?"

"It must be the interstellar dust. If it is, then that's why there's no atmosphere or lithosphere. But I can't see the dust being that thick, even at these speeds."

"Put it—"

"Yah." I reached for my list.

"If we find one more anomaly, I'll scream."

Half an hour later we found life.

By then we were close enough to use the gravity drag to slow us. The beautiful thing about a gravity drag is that it uses very little power. It converts a ship's momentum relative to the nearest powerful mass into heat, and all you have to do is get rid of the heat. Since the $ST\infty$'s hull would pass only various ranges of radiation corresponding to what the puppeteers' varied customers considered visible light, the shipbuilders had run a great big radiator fin out from the gravity drag. It glowed dull red behind us. And the fusion drive was off. There was no white fusion flame to hurt visibility.

Elephant had the scope at highest magnification. At first, as I peered into the eyepiece, I couldn't see what he was talking about. There was a dull white plain, all the same color except for a few blobs of blue. The blobs wouldn't have stood out except for the uniformity of the surface around them.

Then one of them moved. Very slowly, but it was moving.

"Right," I said. "Let me run a temperature check."

The surface temperature in that region was about right for helium II. And on the rest of the planet as well; the protosun wasn't putting out much energy, though it was very gung ho on radiation.

"I don't think they match any species I know."

"I can't tell," said Elephant. He had the telescope and the library screen going at the same time, with a Sirius VIII blob on the library screen. "There are twenty different species of helium life in this book, and they all look exactly alike."

"Not quite. They must have a vacuumproof integument. And you'll notice those granules in the—"

"I treasure my ignorance on this subject, Bey. Anyway, we aren't going to find any species we know on this world. Even a stage-tree seed would explode the moment it hit."

I let the subject die.

Once again Elephant ran the scope over "his" planet, this time looking for the blobby life-forms. They were fairly big for helium II life but not abnormally so. Lots of cold worlds develop life using the peculiar properties of helium II, but because it hasn't much use for complexity, it usually stays in the amoeba stage.

There was one peculiarity, which I duly noted. Every animal was on the back side of the planet with relation to the planet's course through the galaxy. They weren't afraid of protosun sunlight, but they seemed to fear interstellar dust.

"You promised to scream."

"It's not odd enough. I'll wait."

Two hours passed.

The red glow of the radiator fin became more pronounced. So did the dull uniformity of the planetary surface. The planet was a disk now beyond the front window;

if you watched it for a while, you could see it grow. Turning ship to face the planet had made no difference to the gravity drag.

"Cue Ball," said Elephant.

"No good. It's been used. Beta Lyrae I."

"Cannonball Express, then."

"Elephant, what are you doing here?"

He turned, startled. "What do you mean?"

"Look, you know by now I'm with you all the way. But I do wonder. You spent a million stars getting here, and you'd have spent two if you had to. You could be home in the Rockies with Dianna or hovering near Beta Lyrae, which is unusual enough and better scenery than this snowball. You could be sampling oddball drugs in Crashlanding or looking for Mist Demons on Plateau. Why here?"

"Because it is there."

"What the blazes is that supposed to mean?"

"Bey, once upon a time there was a guy named Miller. Six years ago he took a ramscoop-fusion drive ship and put a hyperdrive in it and set out for the edge of the universe, figuring he could get his hydrogen from space and use the fusion plant to power his hyperdrive. He's probably still going. He'll be going forever unless he hits something. Why?"

"A psychiatrist I'm not."

"He wants to be remembered. When you're dead a hundred years, what will you be remembered for?"

"I'll be the idiot who rode with Gregory Pelton, who spent two months and more than a million stars to set his ship down on a totally worthless planet."

"Gronk. All right, what about abstract knowledge? This star will be out of known space in ten years. Our only chance to explore it is right now. What—"

There was an almost silent breeze of air, and a strangling pressure in my larynx, and a stabbing pain in my ears, simultaneously. I heard the bare beginning of an alarm, but I was already reaching for my helmet. I clamped it down hard, spun the collar, and gave vent to an enormous belch at the same time that the wind went shrieking from my lungs.

There was no way to realize what was happening—and no time. But vacuum was around us, and air was spraying into my suit, frigid air. Iron spikes were being driven through my ears, but I was going to live. My lungs held a ghastly emptiness, but I would live. I turned to Elephant.

The fear of death was naked in his face. He had his helmet down, but he was having trouble with the collar. I had to force his hands away to get it fastened right. His helmet misted over, then cleared; he was getting air. Had it come in time to save his life?

I was alive. The pain was leaving my ears, and I was breathing: inhale, pause, inhale, as the pressure rose to normal.

I'd seen what had happened. Now I had time to think it through, to remember it, to play it back.

What had happened was insane.

The hull had turned to dust. Just that. All at once and nothing first, the ship's outside had disintegrated and blown away on a whispering breath of breathing air. I'd *seen* it.

And sure enough, the hull was gone. Only the innards of the ship remained. Before me, the lighted control board. A little below that, the manhole to the packed bubble and the bubble package itself. Above the board, the half disk of the mystery planet and stars. To the left, stars. To the right, Elephant, looking dazed and scared, and beyond him, stars. Behind me, the air lock, the kitchen storage block and dial board, a glimpse of the landing legs and glowing radiator fin, and stars. The $ST\infty$ was a skeleton.

Elephant shook his head, then turned on his suit radio. I heard the magnified click in my helmet.

We looked at each other, waiting. But there was nothing to say. Except, *Elephant, look! We don't have a hull no more! Isn't that remarkable?*

I sighed, turned to the control board, and began nursing the fusion drive to life. From what I could see of the ship, nothing seemed to be floating away. Whatever had been fixed to the hull must also have been fixed to other things.

"What are you doing, Bey?"

"Getting us out of here. Uh, you can scream now."

"Why? I mean, why leave?"

He'd flipped. Flatlanders are basically unstable. I got the drive pushing us at low power, turned off the gravity drag, and turned to face him. "Look, Elephant. No hull." I swept an arm around me. "None."

"But what's left of the ship is still mine?"

"Uh, yah. Sure."

"I want to land. Can you talk me out of it?"

He was serious. Completely so. "The landing legs are intact," he went on. "Our suits can keep out the radiation for three days. We could land and take off in twelve hours."

"We probably could."

"And we spent going on two months getting here."

"Right."

"I'd feel like an idiot getting this close and then turning for home. Wouldn't you?"

"I would, except for one thing. And that one thing says you're landing this ship over my unconscious body."

"All right, the hull turned to dust and blew away. What does that mean? It means we've got a faulty hull, and I'm going to sue the hind legs off General Products when we get back. But do *you* know what caused it?"

"No."

"So why do you assume it's some kind of threat?"

"Tell you what I'll do," I said. I turned the ship until it was tail down to Cannonball Express. "Now. We'll be there in three hours if you insist on landing. It's your ship, just as you say. But I'm going to try to talk you out of it."

"That's fair."

"Have you had space-pilot training?"

"Naturally."

"Did it include a history of errors course?"

"I don't think so. We got a little history of the state of the art."

"That's something. You remember that they started out with chemical fuels and that the first ship to the asteroids was built in orbit around Earth's moon?"

"Uh huh."

"This you may not have heard. There were three men in that ship, and when they were launched, it was in an orbit that took them just slightly inside the moon's orbit, then out again and away. About thirty hours after launching the men noticed that all their ports were turning opaque. A concentration of dust in their path was putting little meteor pits all through the quartz. Two of the men wanted to continue on, using instruments to finish their mission. But the third man was in command. They used their rockets and stopped themselves dead.

"Remember, materials weren't as durable in those days, and nothing they were using had been well tested. The men stopped their ship in the orbit of the moon, which by then was 230,000 miles behind them, and called base to say they'd aborted the mission."

"You remember this pretty well. How come?"

"They drilled these stories into us again and again. Everything they tried to teach us was illustrated with something from history. It stuck."

"Go on."

"They called base and told them about their windows fogging up. Somebody decided it was dust, and someone else suddenly realized they'd launched the ship through one of the moon's Trojan points."

Elephant laughed, then coughed. "Wish I hadn't breathed so much vacuum. I gather you're leading up to something."

"If the ship hadn't stopped, it would have been wrecked. The dust would have torn it apart. The moral of this story is, anything you don't understand is dangerous until you do understand it."

"Sounds paranoid."

"Maybe it does to a flatlander. You come from a planet so kind to you, so seemingly adapted to you, that you think the whole universe is your oyster. You might remember my neutron star story. I'd have been killed if I hadn't understood that tidal effect in time."

"So you would. So you think flatlanders are all fools?"

"No, Elephant. Just not paranoid enough. And I refuse to apologize."

"Who asked you?"

"I'll land with you if you can tell me what made our hull turn to dust."

Elephant crossed his arms and glared forward. I shut up and waited.

By and by he said, "Can we get home?"

"I don't know. The hyperdrive motor will work, and we can use the gravity drag to slow us down to something like normal. Physically we should be able to do it."

"Okay. Let's go. But I'll tell you this, Bey. If I were alone, I'd go down, and damn the hull."

So we turned tail and ran, under protest from Elephant. In four hours we were far enough from Cannonball Express's gravity well to enter hyperspace.

I turned on the hyperdrive, gasped, and turned it off just as fast as I could. We sat there shaking, and Elephant said, "We can inflate the bubble."

"But can we get in?"

"It doesn't have an air lock."

We worked it, though. There was a pressure-control dial in the cabin, and we set it for zero; the electromagnetic field that folded the bubble would now inflate it without pressure. We went inside, pressurized it, and took off our helmets.

"We're out of the radiation field," said Elephant. "I looked."

"Good." You can go pretty far in even a couple of seconds of hyperdrive. "Now, there's one thing I've got to know. Can you take that again?"

Elephant shuddered. "Can you?"

"I think so. I can do all the navigating if I have to."

"Anything you can take, I can take."

"Can you take it and stay sane?"

"Yes."

"Then we can trade off. But if you change your mind, let me know that instant. A lot of good men have left their marbles in the Blind Spot, and all they had were a couple of windows."

"I believe you. Indeed I do, sir. How do we work it?"

"We'll have to chart a course through the least dense part of space. The nearest inhabited world is Kzin. I hate to risk asking help from the kzinti, but we may have to."

"Tell you what, Bey. Let's at least try to reach Jinx. I want to use that number of yours to give the puppeteers hell."

"Sure. We can always turn off to something closer."

I spent an hour or so working out a course. When I'd finished, I was pretty sure we could navigate it without either of us having to leave the bubble more than once every twenty-four hours to look at the mass indicator. We threw fingers for who got the first watch, and I lost.

We put on our suits and depressurized the bubble. As I crawled through the manhole, I saw Elephant opaqueing the bubble wall.

I squeezed into the crash couch, all alone among the stars. They were blue ahead and red behind when I finished turning the ship. I couldn't find the protosun.

More than half the view was empty space. I found myself looking thoughtfully at the air lock. It was behind and to the left, a metal oblong standing alone at the edge of the deck, with both doors tightly closed. The inner door had slammed when the pressure dropped, and now the air lock mechanisms guarded the pressure inside against the vacuum outside in both directions. Nobody inside to use the air, but how do you explain that to a pressure sensor?

I was procrastinating. The ship was aimed; I clenched my teeth and sent the ship into hyperspace.

The Blind Spot, they call it. It fits.

There are ways to find the blind spot in your eye. Close one eye, put two dots on a piece of paper, and bring the paper toward you, focusing on one of the dots. If you hold the paper just right, the other dot will suddenly vanish.

Let a ship enter hyperspace with the windows transparent, and the windows will seem to vanish. So will the space enclosing them. Objects on either side stretch and draw closer together to fill the missing space. If you look long enough, the Blind Spot starts to spread; the walls and the things against the walls draw even closer to the missing space until they are engulfed.

It's all in your mind, they tell me. So?

I turned the key, and half my view was Blind Spot. The control board stretched and flowed. The mass-indicator sphere tried to wrap itself around me. I reached for it, and my hands were distorted, too. With considerable effort I put them back at my sides and got a grip on myself.

There was one fuzzy green line in the plastic distortion that had been a mass indicator. It was behind and to the side. The ship could fly itself until Elephant's turn came. I fumbled my way to the manhole and crawled through.

Hyperspace was only half the problem.

It was a big problem. Every twenty-four hours one of us had to go out there, see if there were any dangerous masses around, drop back to normal space to take a fix and adjust course. I found myself getting unbearably tense during the few hours before each turn. So did Elephant. At these times we didn't dare talk to each other.

On my third trip I had the bad sense to look up—and went more than blind. Looking up, there was nothing at all in my field of vision, nothing but the Blind Spot.

It was more than blindness. A blind man, a man whose eyes have lost their function, at least remembers what things looked like. A man whose optic brain center has been damaged doesn't. I could remember what I'd come out here for—to find out if there were masses near enough to harm us—but I couldn't remember how to do it. I touched a curved glass surface and knew that this was the machine that would tell me, if only I knew its secret.

Eventually my neck got sore, so I moved my head. That brought my eyes back into existence.

When we got the bubble pressurized, Elephant said, "Where were you? You've been gone half an hour."

"And lucky at that. When you go out there, don't look up."

"Oh."

That was the other half of the problem. Elephant and I had stopped communicating. He was not interested in saying anything, and he was not interested in anything I had to say.

It took me a good week to figure out why. Then I braced him with it.

"Elephant, there's a word missing from our language."

He looked up from the reading screen. If there hadn't been a reading screen in the bubble, I don't think we'd have made it. "More than one word," he said. "Things have been pretty silent."

"One word. You're so afraid of using that word, you're afraid to talk at all."

"So tell me."

"Coward."

Elephant wrinkled his brows, then snapped off the screen. "All right, Bey, we'll talk about it. First of all, you said it, I didn't. Right?"

"Right. Have you been thinking it?"

"No. I've been thinking euphemisms like 'overcautious' and 'reluctance to risk bodily harm.' But since we're on the subject, why were you so eager to turn back?"

"I was scared." I let that word soak into him, then went on. "The people who trained me made certain that I'd be scared in certain situations. With all due respect, Elephant, I've had more training for space than you have. I think your wanting to land was the result of ignorance."

Elephant sighed. "I think it would have been safe to land. You don't. We're not going to get anywhere arguing about it, are we?"

We weren't. One of us was right, one wrong. And if I

was wrong, then a pretty good friendship had gone out the air lock.

It was a silent trip.

We came out of hyperspace near the two Sirius suns. But that wasn't the end of it, because we still faced a universe squashed by relativity. It took us almost two weeks to brake ourselves. The gravity drag's radiator fin glowed orange-white for most of that time. I have no idea how many times we circled around through hyperspace for another run through the system.

Finally we were moving in on Jinx with the fusion drive.

I broke a silence of hours. "Now what, Elephant?"

"As soon as we get in range, I'm going to call that number of yours."

"Then?"

"Drop you off at Sirius Mater with enough money to get you home. I'd take it kindly if you'd use my house as your own until I come back from Cannonball Express. I'll buy a ship here and go back."

"You don't want me along."

"With all due respect, Bey, I don't. I'm going to land. Wouldn't you feel like a damn fool if you died then?"

"I've spent about three months in a small extension bubble because of that silly planet. If you conquered it alone, I would feel like a damn fool."

Elephant looked excruciatingly unhappy. He started to speak, caught his breath—

If ever I picked the right time to shut a man up, that was it.

"Hold it. Let's call the puppeteers first. Plenty of time to decide."

Elephant nodded. In a moment he'd have told me he didn't want me along because I was overcautious. Instead, he picked up the ship phone.

Jinx was a banded Easter egg ahead of us. To the side was Binary, the primary to which Jinx is a moon. We should be close enough to talk ... and the puppeteers' transfer-booth number would also be their phone number.

Elephant dialed.

A sweet contralto voice answered. There was no picture, but I could tell: no woman's voice is quite that good. The puppeteer said, "Eight eight three two six seven seven oh."

"My General Products hull just failed." Elephant was wasting no time at all.

"I beg your pardon?"

"My name is Gregory Pelton. Twelve years ago I bought a No. 2 hull from General Products. A month and a half ago it failed. We've spent the intervening time limping home. May I speak to a puppeteer?"

The screen came on. Two flat, brainless heads looked out at us. "This is quite serious," said the puppeteer. "Naturally we will pay the indemnity in full. Would you mind detailing the circumstances?"

Elephant didn't mind at all. He was quite vehement. It was a pleasure to listen to him. The puppeteer's silly expressions never wavered, but he was blinking rapidly when Elephant finished.

"I see," he said. "Our apologies are insufficient, of course, but you will understand that it was a natural mistake. We did not think that antimatter was available anywhere in the galaxy, especially in such quantity."

It was as if he'd screamed. I could hear that word echoing from side to side in my skull.

Elephant's booming voice was curiously soft. "Antimatter?"

"Of course. We have no excuse, of course, but you should have realized it at once. Interstellar gas of normal matter had polished the planet's surface with minuscule explosions, had raised the temperature of the protosun beyond any rational estimate, and was causing a truly incredible radiation hazard. Did you not even wonder about these things? You knew that the system was from beyond the galaxy. Humans are supposed to be highly curious, are they not?"

"The hull," said Elephant.

"A General Products hull is an artificially generated molecule with interatomic bonds artificially strengthened by a small power plant. The strengthened molecular bonds are proof against any kind of impact and heat into the hundreds of thousands of degrees. But when enough of the atoms had been obliterated by antimatter explosions, the molecule naturally fell apart."

Elephant nodded. I wondered if his voice was gone for good.

"When may we expect you to collect your indemnity? I gather no human was killed; this is fortunate, since our funds are low."

Elephant turned off the phone. He gulped once or twice, then turned to look me in the eye. I think it took all his strength, and if I'd waited for him to speak, I don't know what he would have said.

"I gloat," I said. "I gloat. I was right; you were wrong. If we'd landed on your forsaken planet, we'd have gone up in pure light. At this time it gives me great pleasure to say, I Told You So."

He smiled weakly. "You told me so."

"Oh, I did, I did. Time after time I said, Don't Go Near That Haunted Planet! It's Worth Your Life And Your Soul, I said. There Have Been Signs in the Heavens, I said, To Warn Us from This Place—"

"All right, don't overdo it, you bastard. You were dead right all the way. Let's leave it at that."

"Okay. But there's one thing I want you to remember."

"If you don't understand it, it's dangerous."

"That's the one thing I want you to remember besides I Told You So."

And that should have ended it.

But it doesn't. Elephant's going back. He's got a little flag with a UN insignia, about two feet by two feet, with spring wires to make it look like it's flapping in the breeze, and a solid rocket in the handle so it'll go straight when the flag is furled. He's going to drop it on the antimatter planet from a great height, as great as I can talk him into.

It should make quite a bang.

And I'm going along. I've got a solidly mounted tridee camera and a contract with the biggest broadcasting company in known space. *This* time I've got a reason for going!

✳
GHOST: FOUR

"But he never went back," I said.

"It happens I know why," Ander said, and then the crowd drowned us out. Administration and Structure swirled together; Entertainment saw a chance and arrowed into the dance behind its dolphin. The depleted fourth team, Police, hung back in a nervous arc. All the teams looked to be milling without purpose, and from listening to Sharrol I could guess why.

So I said, "Prey submerged." The last of the prey turtles must have escaped into the sand. For the next few minutes I watched the game with a concentration that would have surprised Sharrol.

This was the story I was telling Ander: If I hadn't been led here by a woman, *why was I here*? I must love the game! "There! Yellow prey!" I shouted as sand stirred. An instant later the glowing mock turtle emerged outside the melee and flapped clownishly toward safety. A Police swimmer dove to capture it, his dolphin keeping station to block for him, and everyone converged too late: he was swimming like mad, and so was the prey; he was through the yellow arch at the point of a great angry cloud—

And that was the end. I bellowed over the crowd's roar: "Dinner!"

"Oh?"

"I missed brunch. I'm starving."

I didn't want to fight the crowds trying to leave. We crossed the slidebridge instead, this time in comparative quiet. The booths lined below us were whirlpools in a surging sea of escapees.

Ander's hand was above my elbow, companionably. I was a prisoner, and that was hard to ignore. Make conversation? I asked, "Did you know there's an ice age going on Earth?"

"Sure."

"Well, I never even wondered. I did wonder why Cuba wasn't much hotter than Nome."

Ander said, "The whole planet's a web of superconductor cable. We had to restart the Gulf Stream five hundred years ago, and it just went from there. Nome imports heat; Cuba imports cold. Even so, Earth would be pretty cold if we weren't getting so much power from the orbiting satellites."

"Uh huh. What are you going to do when the ice age turns off?"

"Move." Ander grinned. "Where did you go after the antimatter system?"

"I moved in with Sharrol in Nome."

He looked at me. "You? Settled down like a Grog on a rock?"

Maybe he had the right to sneer. Ander and I had toured singles nodes together on two worlds, blowing off steam after marathon work sessions. I held my temper and said, "You can spend a lifetime seeing Earth."

"Where do you want to eat?"

I said, "The Pequod Grill is good." Good and expensive, and an offworlder would have heard of it. Just the place a destitute B. Shaeffer might pick if someone else was paying. And nobody would ask me where Sharrol was.

We had almost reached the transfer booths. Just to pull Ander's chain, I turned suddenly into the phone booth to see if I could break his grip.

He pulled me back effortlessly. "What?"

"I thought I'd phone and see if the Grill's full up," I said, and remembered. I couldn't use my pocket phone. It was in the wrong name.

"I'll do it." He used a card. It took him ten seconds to get a reservation. There are mistakes you don't pay for.

We pushed into a transfer booth. He said, "So there you were, nesting—"

I said, "It was love, stet? We weren't lockstepped . . . well, we were, a little. I didn't know any women on Earth. Sharrol had some playmates, but a lot of the men she knew were moaning and clutching themselves." I grinned, remembering. "Rasheed. 'Lockstepped, sure, but you can't mean *me!*' with a great dramatic wave of his arms, like he could have been joking. There were some couples we played with, but not so much of that, either, after a while. We talked about having children. Then we looked into it."

Ander said, "You?" I wasn't sure how to read his expression. A little disgust, a little pity.

I dialed the Pequod.

We flicked in on the roof, under a rolling curve of green-black water. The daylight was fading. Ander led off toward the restaurant twelve floors down. He seemed to be familiar with the Pequod. Might even be registered here.

Test that. "I need to visit a 'cycler, Ander. Long day."

"Me, too," he said. "This way."

In the 'cycler he maneuvered himself between me and the door, and I let him. Amusing scenarios came to mind: If I needed a booth, he could watch the door, but what if *he* needed a booth? Not that it mattered. I didn't want to escape, not until I could *know* I was loose. I wanted to speak of lost treasure.

But I *needed* to know how much he already knew. Why was I here? Who had come with me? How? How was I surviving? I waited in the hope that he might speak of those things, and of Carlos Wu's autodoc, too.

So we didn't talk much until we were settled at a table, with drinks. Ander wasn't interested in local cuisine. He ordered beef: no imagination. I found crew snapper on the menu, billed as an order for two. Heh heh.

I asked, "What happened to Greg Pelton's expedition?"

Ander said, "Antimatter planet. The more he thought about it, the more he needed to know. He kept expanding his plans until some government gnome took notice. After that it just inflated. Government projects can do that. Everyone wants in; they always think there's infinite money, and suddenly it's gone from science fiction to fantasy.

"I don't even know if Pelton's still involved. The UN has probes in the system. Meanwhile the current plan calls for a base on the planet."

I laughed. "Oh, *sure!*"

He grinned at me. "Set on a metal dish in stasis, inside a roller sphere also in stasis. It *is* antimatter, after all."

He wasn't making it up. He was *too* amused. "Civil servants love making plans. You can't get caught in a mistake if you're only making plans, and it can pay your salary for life. And I shouldn't have heard that much, Beowulf, nor should you. If a terrorist knew where to find infinite masses of antimatter, things could get sticky."

"And that is why you weren't asked to ghostwrite the tour guide," I surmised.

Ander smiled. He said, "Back to work. You've met Outsiders. Would you consider them a threat?"

"No."

He waited. I said, "They're fragile. Superfluid helium metabolism and no real skeleton, I think. Anyplace we consider interesting, they die. But never mind that, Ander—"

"They've got the *technology* to take accelerations that would reduce you or me to a film of neutrons."

"Not the point. Can you tell me why they honor contracts? They've got ships to run away from *any* obligation. I think it must be built into their brains, Ander. They honor contracts, and they keep their promises. They're trustworthy."

He nodded, in no way dissatisfied. "Grogs? Are they dangerous?"

"Tanj straight they're dangerous."

He laughed. "Well, *finally!* Kzinti?"

"Sure."

"Puppeteers. Where are they going?"

"Anywhere they want to." He kept looking, so I said, "Clouds of Magellan? That's not the interesting question. The Outsiders can boost a ship or a planet to near lightspeed. Can the puppeteers do that, too? Or will they have to summon Outsiders to change their course?"

"And stop."

"Yeah. I'd say they have the Outsider drive. They bought it or they built it."

"Or they've got a research project that'll get it for them."

"I . . . futz." Hire Outsiders to push five planets up to four-fifths of lightspeed, then try to figure out how to slow them down. Was that as risky as it sounded? I began to believe it wasn't. *There was nothing dangerous in the path of the puppeteer fleet.* They had thousands of years to solve the puzzle.

Ander asked again: "Are the puppeteers a threat?"

He had generated in me a mulish urge to defend them. "They honor their contracts."

"They're manipulative bastards, Beowulf. You know that."

"So are the ARMs. Your people have been in my face since I reached Earth. Do you know what Sharrol and I had to go through to have children?"

"The Fertility Board turned you down, of course."

"Yah."

"What did you do?"

"Sharrol used to play with a Carlos Wu. Carlos had an open birthright. So we worked something out. Then I went traveling."

He was, from the look of him, learning far more about Beowulf Shaeffer than he had ever wanted to. He tried to stick to what he knew. "Traveling. Any contact at all with Pierson's puppeteers during that period?"

"No."

"Other aliens? Aliens the puppeteers dealt with?"

That made me smile. "I'm a celebrity among the Kdatlyno . . ."

✳ GRENDEL

There were the sounds of a passenger starship.

You learn those sounds, and you don't forget, even after four years. They are never loud enough to distract, except during takeoff, and most are too low to hear anyway, but you don't forget, and you wake knowing where you are.

There were the sensations of being alone.

A sleeper field is not a straight no-gee field; there's an imbalance that keeps you more or less centered so you don't float out the edge and fall to the floor. When your field holds two, you set two imbalances for the distance you want, and somehow you feel that in your muscles. You touch from time to time, you and your love, twisting in sleep. There are rustlings and the sounds of breathing.

Nobody had touched me this night. Nothing breathed here but me. I was dead center in the sleeping field. I woke knowing I was alone, in a tiny sleeping cabin of the *Argos*, bound from Down to Gummidgy.

And where was Sharrol?

Sharrol was on Earth. She couldn't travel; some people can't take space. That was half our problem, but it did narrow it down, and if I wanted her, I need only go to Earth and hunt her up in a transfer-booth directory.

I didn't want to find her. Not now. Our bargain had been clear, and also inevitable; and there are advantages to sleeping alone. I'll think of them in a moment.

I found the field control switch. The sleeper field collapsed, letting me down easy. I climbed into a navy-blue

107

falling jumper, moving carefully in the narrow sleeping cabin, statted my hair, and went out.

Margo hailed me in the hall, looking refreshingly trim and lovely in a clinging pilot's uniform. Her long, dark hair streamed behind her, rippling, as if underwater or in free-fall. "You're just in time. I was about to wake everyone up."

"It's only nine-thirty. You want to get lynched?"

She laughed. "I'll tell them it was your idea. No, I'm serious, Bey. A month ago a starseed went through the Gummidgy system. I'm going to drop the ship out a light-month away and let everybody watch."

"Oh. That'll be nice," I said, trying for enthusiasm. "I've never seen a starseed set sail."

"I'll give you time to grab a good seat."

"Right. Thanks." I waved and went on, marveling at myself. Since when have I had to work up enthusiasm? For anything?

Margo was Captain M. Tellefsen, in charge of getting the *Argos* to Gummidgy sometime this evening. We'd spent many of her off-duty hours talking shop, since the *Argos* resembled the liners I used to fly seven years ago, before my boss, Nakamura Lines, collapsed. Margo was a bright girl, as good a spacer as I'd been once. Her salary must have been good, too. That free-fall effect is the most difficult trick a hairdresser can attempt. No machine can imitate it.

Expensive tastes . . . I wondered why she'd left Earth. By flatlander standards she was lovely enough to make a fast fortune on tridee.

Maybe she just liked space. Many do. Their eyes hold a dreamy, distant look, a look I'd caught once in Margo's green eyes.

This early the lounge held only six passengers out of the twenty-eight. One was a big biped alien, a Kdatlyno touch sculptor named Lloobee. The chairs were too short for him. He sat on a table, with his great flat feet brushing the floor, his huge arms resting on horn-capped knees.

The other nonhumans aboard would have to stay in their

rooms. Rooms 14-16-18 were joined and half-full of water, occupied by a dolphin. His name was Pszzzz, or Bra-a-ack, or some such impolite sound. Human ears couldn't catch the ultrasonic overtones of that name, nor could a human throat pronounce it, so he answered to Moby Dick. He was on his way to Wunderland, the *Argos*'s next stop. Then there were two sessile grogs in 22 and a flock of jumpin' jeepers in 24, with the connecting door open so the Grogs could get at the jumpin' jeepers, which were their food supply. Lloobee, the Kdatlyno touch sculptor, had room 20.

I found Emil at the bar. He raised a thumb in greeting, dialed me a Bloody Marriage, and waited in silence for my first sip. The drink tasted good, though I'd been thinking in terms of tuna and eggs.

The other four passengers, eating breakfast at a nearby table, all wore the false glow of health one carries out of an autodoc tank. Probably they'd been curing hangovers. But Emil always looked healthy, and he couldn't get drunk no matter how hard he tried. He was a Jinxian, short and wide and bull-strong, a top-flight computer programmer with an intuitive knack for asking the right questions when everyone else has been asking the wrong ones and blowing expensive circuits in their iron idiots.

"So," he said.

"So," I responded. "I'll do you a favor. Let's go sit by the window."

He looked puzzled but went.

The *Argos* lounge had one picture window. It was turned off in hyperspace, so that it looked like part of the wall, but we found it from memory and sat down. Emil asked, "What's the favor?"

"This is it. Now we've got the best seats in the house. In a few minutes everyone will be fighting for a view because Margo's stopping the ship to show us a starseed setting sail."

"Oh? Okay, I owe you one."

"We're even. You bought me a drink."

Emil looked puzzled, and I realized I'd put an edge in

my voice. As if I didn't want anyone owing me favors. Which I didn't. But it was no excuse for being a boor.

I dialed a breakfast to go with the drink: tuna fillet, eggs Florentine, and double-strength tea. The kitchen had finished delivering it when Margo spoke over the intercom, as follows: "Ladies and gentlemen and other guests, we are dropping out some distance from CY Aquarii so that you may watch a starseed which set sail in the system of Gummidgy last month. I will raise the lounge screen in ten minutes." Click.

In moments we were surrounded. The Kdatlyno sculptor squeezed in next to me, spiked knees hunched up against the lack of room, the silver tip of the horn on his elbow imperiling my eggs. Emil smiled with one side of his mouth, and I made a face. But it was justice. I'd chosen the seats myself.

The window went on. Silence fell.

Everyone who could move was crowded around the lounge window. The Kdatlyno's horned elbow pinned a fold of my sleeve to the table. I let it lie. I wasn't planning to move, and Kdatlyno are supposed to be touchy.

There were stars. Brighter than stars seen through atmosphere, but you get used to that. I looked for CY Aquarii and found a glaring white eye.

We watched it grow.

Margo was giving us a slow telescopic expansion. The bright dot grew to a disk bright enough to make your eyes water, and then no brighter. The eyes on a ship's hull won't transmit more than a certain amount of light. The disk swelled to fill the window, and now dark areas showed beneath the surface, splitting and disappearing and changing shape and size, growing darker and clearer as they rode the shock wave toward space. The core of CY Aquarii exploded every eighty-nine minutes. Each time the star grew whiter and brighter, while shock waves rode the explosion to the surface. Men and instruments watched to learn about stars.

The view swung. A curved edge of space showed, with

curling hydrogen flames tracing arcs bigger than some suns. The star slid out of sight, and a dully glowing dot came into view. Still the view expanded, until we saw an egg-shaped object in dead center of the window.

"The starseed," said Margo via intercom. There was cool authority in her public-speaking voice. "This one appears to be returning to the galactic core, having presumably left its fertilized egg near the tip of this galactic arm. When the egg hatches, the infant starseed will make its own way home across fifty thousand light-years of space . . ."

The starseed was moving fast, straight at the sensing eye, with an immediacy that jarred strangely against Margo's dry lecture voice. Suddenly I knew what she'd done. She'd placed us directly in the path of the starseed. If this one was typical of its brethren, it would be moving at about point eight lights. The starseed's light image was moving only one-fifth faster than the starseed itself, and both were coming toward us. Margo had set it up so that we watched it five times as fast as it actually happened.

Quite a showman, Margo.

". . . believe that at least some eggs are launched straight outward, toward the Clouds of Magellan or toward the globular clusters or toward Andromeda. Thus, the starseeds could colonize other galaxies and could also prevent a population explosion in this galaxy." There were pinpoints of blue light around the starseed now: newsmen from Down, come to Gummidgy to cover the event, darting about in fusion ships. "This specimen is over a mile in thickness and about a mile and a half in length . . ."

Suddenly it hit me.

Whatinhell was the Kdatlyno watching? With nothing resembling eyes, with only his radar sense to give form to his surroundings, he was seeing nothing but a blank wall!

I turned. Lloobee was watching me.

Naturally. Lloobee was an artist, subsidized by his own world government, selling his touch sculptures to humans and kzinti so that his species would acquire interstellar money. Finagle knew they didn't have much else to sell—

yet. They'd been propertyless slaves before we took their world from the kzinti, but now they were building industries.

He didn't look like an artist. He looked like a monster. That brown dragon skin would have stopped a knife. Curved silver-tipped horns marked his knees and elbows, and his huge hands, human in design, nonetheless showed eight retractile claws at the knuckles. No silver there. They were filed sharp and then buffed to a polished glow. The hands were strangler's hands, not sculptor's hands. His arms were huge even in proportion to his ten-foot height. They brushed his knees when he stood up.

But his face gave the true nightmare touch. Eyeless, noseless, marked only by a gash of a mouth and by a goggle-shaped region above it where the skin was stretched drumhead taut. That tympanum was turned toward me. Lloobee was memorizing my face.

I turned back as the starseed began to unfold.

It seemed to take forever. The big egg fluttered; its surface grew dull and crinkly and began to expand. It was rounding the sun now, lighted on one side, black on the other. It grew still bigger, became lopsided ... and slowly, slowly the sail came free. It streamed away like a comet's tail, and then it filled, a silver parachute with four threadlike shrouds pointing at the sun. Where the shrouds met was a tiny knob.

This is how they travel. A starseed spends most of its time folded into a compact egg shape, falling through the galaxy on its own momentum. But inevitably there come times when it must change course. Then the sail unfolds, a silver mirror thinner than the paint on a cheap car but thousands of miles across. A cross-shaped thickening in the material of the sail is the living body of the starseed itself. In the knob that hangs from the shrouds is more living matter. There are the muscles to control the shrouds and set the attitude of the sail, and there is the egg, fertilized at the Core, launched near the galactic rim.

The sail came free, and nobody breathed. The sail expanded, filled the screen, and swung toward us. A blue-white point crossed in front of it, a newsman's ship, a candle so tiny as to be barely visible. Now the sail was fully inflated by the light from behind, belling outward, crimped along one side for attitude control.

The intercom said, "And that's it, ladies and gentlemen and other guests. We will make one short hyperspace hop into the system of Gummidgy and will proceed from there in normal space. We will be landing in sixteen hours."

There was a collective sigh. The Kdatlyno sculptor took his horn out of my sleeve and stood up, improbably erect.

And what would his next work be like? I thought of human faces set in expressions of sheer wonder and grinning incredulity, muscles bunched and backs arched forward for a better view of a flat wall. Had Lloobee known of the starseed in advance? I thought he had.

Most of the spectators were drifting away, though the starseed still showed. My tea was icy. We'd been watching for nearly an hour, though it felt like ten minutes.

Emil said, "How are you doing with Captain Tellefsen?"

I looked blank.

"You called her Margo a while back."

"Oh, that. I'm not really trying, Emil. What would she see in a crashlander?"

"That girl must have hurt you pretty bad."

"What girl?"

"It shows through your skull, Bey. None of my business, though." He looked me up and down, and I had the uncomfortable feeling that my skull really was transparent. "What would she see? She'd see a crashlander, yes. Height seven feet, weight one sixty pounds—close enough? White hair, eyes blood-red. Skin darkened with tannin pills, just like the rest of us. But you must take more tannin pills than anybody."

"I do. Not, as you said, that it's any of your business."

"Was it a secret?"

I had to grin at that. How do you hide the fact that you're an albino? "No, but it's half my problem. Do you know that the Fertility Board of Earth won't accept albinos as potential fathers?"

"Earth is hardly the place to raise children, anyway. Once a flatlander, always a flatlander."

"I fell in love with a flatlander."

"Sorry."

"She loved me, too. Still does, I hope. But she couldn't leave Earth."

"A lot of flatlanders can't stand space. Some of them never know it. Did you want children?"

"Yah."

In silent sympathy Emil dialed two Bloody Marriages. In silent thanks I raised the bulb in toast and drank.

It was as neat a cleft stick as had ever caught man and woman. Sharrol couldn't leave Earth. On Earth she was born, on Earth she would die, and on Earth she would have her children.

But Earth wouldn't let me have children. No matter that forty percent of We Made It is albino. No matter that albinism can be cured by a simple supply of tannin pills, which anyone but a full-blooded Maori has to take anyway if he's visiting a world with a brighter than average star. Earth has to restrict its population, to keep it down to a comfortable eighteen billion. To a flatlander that's comfortable. So . . . prevent the useless ones from having children—the liabilities, such as paranoia prones, mental deficients, criminals, uglies, and Beowulf Shaeffer.

Emil said, "Shouldn't we be in hyperspace by now?"

"Up to the captain," I told him.

Most of the passengers who had watched the starseed were now at tables. Sleeping cubicles induce claustrophobia. Bridge games were forming, reading screens were being folded out of the walls, drinks were being served. I reached for my Bloody Marriage and found, to my amazement, that it was too heavy to pick up.

Then I fainted.

* * *

I woke up thinking, *It wasn't that strong!*

And everyone else was waking, too.

Something had knocked us all out at once. Which might mean the ship had an unconscious captain! I left the lounge at full speed, which was a wobbly walk.

The control-room door was open, which is bad practice. I reached to close it and changed my mind because the lock and doorknob were gone, replaced by a smooth hole nine inches across.

Margo drooped in her chair. I patted her cheeks until she stirred.

"What happened?" she wanted to know.

"We all went to sleep together. My guess is gas. Stun guns don't work across a vacuum."

"Oh!" It was a gasp of outrage. She'd spotted the gaping hole in her control board, as smooth and rounded as the hole in the door. The gap where the hyperwave radio ought to be.

"Right," I said. "We've been boarded, and we can't tell anyone about it. Now what?"

"That hole . . ." She touched the rounded metal with her fingertips.

"Slaver disintegrator, I think. A digging tool. It projects a beam that suppresses the charge on the electron, so that matter tears itself apart. If that's what it was, we'll find the dust in the air filters."

"There was a ship," said Margo. "A big one. I noticed it just after I ended the show. By then it was inside the mass limit. I couldn't go into hyperspace until it left."

"I wonder how they found us." I thought of some other good questions but let them pass. One I let out. "What's missing? We'd better check."

"*That's* what I don't understand. We aren't carrying anything salable! Valuable, yes. Instruments for the base. But hardly black-market stuff." She stood up. "I'll have to go through the cargo hold."

"Waste of time. Where's the cargo mass meter on this hulk?"

"Oh, of course." She found it somewhere among the

dials. "No change. Nothing missing there, unless they replaced whatever they took with equivalent masses."

"Why, so we wouldn't know they were here? Nuts."

"Then they didn't take anything."

"Or they took personal luggage. The lifesystem mass meter won't tell us. Passengers move around so. You'd think they'd have the courtesy to stay put just in case some pirates should—ung."

"What?"

I tasted the idea and found it reasonable. More. "Ten to one Lloobee's missing."

"Who?"

"Our famous, valuable Kdatlyno sculptor. The third Kdatlyno in history to leave his home planet."

"One of the ET passengers?"

Oh, brother. I left, running.

Because Lloobee was the perfect theft. As a well-known alien artist who had been under the protection of Earth, the ransom he could command was huge. As a hostage his value would be equal. No special equipment would be needed; Lloobee could breathe Earth-normal air. His body could even use certain human food proteins and certain gaseous human anesthetics.

Lloobee wasn't in the lounge. And his cabin was empty.

With Lloobee missing and with the hyperwave smashed, the *Argos* proceeded to Gummidgy at normal speed. Normal speed was top speed; there are few good reasons to dawdle in space. It took us six hours in hyperdrive to reach the edge of CY Aquarii's gravity well. From there we had to proceed on reaction drive and gravity drag.

Margo called Gummidgy with a com laser as soon as we were out of hyperspace. By the time we landed, the news would be ten hours old. We would land at three in the morning, ship's time, and at roughly noon Gummidgy time.

Most of us, including me, went to our cabins to get some sleep. An hour before planetfall I was back in the lounge, watching us come in.

Emil didn't want to watch. He wanted to talk.

"Have you heard? The kidnappers called the base a couple of hours ago."

"What'd they have to say?"

"They want ten million stars and a contract before they turn the Kdatlyno loose. They also—" Emil was outraged at their effrontery. "—reminded the base that Kdatlyno don't eat what humans eat. And they don't have any Kdat foodstuffs!"

"They must be crazy. Where would the base get ten million stars in time?"

"Oh, that's not the problem. If the base doesn't have funds, they can borrow money from the hunting parties, I'm sure. There's a group down there with their own private yacht. It's the contract that bothers me."

Gummidgy was blue on blue under a broken layer of white, with a diminutive moon showing behind an arc of horizon. Very Earthlike but with none of the signs that mark Earth: no yellow glow of sprawling cities on the dark side, no tracery of broken freeways across the day. A nice-looking world, from up here. Unspoiled. No transfer booths, no good nightclubs, no tridee except old tapes and those only on one channel. Unspoiled.

With only half my mind working on conversation, I said, "Be glad we've got contracts. Otherwise we might get him back dead."

"Obviously you don't know much about Kdatlyno."

"Obviously." I was nettled.

"They'll do it, you know. They'll pay the kidnappers ten million stars to give Lloobee back, and they'll tape an immunity contract, too. Total immunity for the kidnappers. No reprisals, no publicity. Do you know what the Kdatlyno will think about that?"

"They'll be glad to have their second-best sculptor back."

"Best."

"Hrodenu is the best."

"It doesn't matter. What they'll think is, they'll wonder

why we haven't taken revenge for the insult to Lloobee. They'll wonder what we're doing about getting revenge. And when they finally realize we aren't doing anything at all . . ."

"Go on."

"They'll blame the whole human race. You know what the kzinti will think?"

"Who cares what the kzinti think?"

He snorted. Great. Now he had me pegged as a chauvinist.

"Why don't you drop it?" I suggested. "We can't do anything about it. It's up to the base MPs."

"It's up to nobody. The base MPs don't have ships."

Right about then I should have accidentally bitten my tongue off. I didn't have that much sense. I never do. Instead I said, "They don't need ships. Whoever took Lloobee has to land somewhere."

"The message came in on hyperwave. Whoever sent it is circling outside the system's gravity well."

"Whoever sent it may well be." I was showing off. "But whoever took Lloobee landed. A Kdatlyno needs lots of room, room he can feel. He sends out a supersonic whistle—one tone—all his life, and when the echoes hit the tympanum above his mouth, he knows what's around him. On a liner he can feel corridors leading all around the ship. He can sense the access tubes behind walls and the rooms and closets behind doors. Nothing smaller than a liner is big enough for him. You don't seriously suggest that the kidnappers borrowed a liner for the job, do you?"

"I apologize. You do seem to know something about Kdatlyno."

"I accept your apology. Now, the kidnappers have definitely landed. Where?"

"Have to be some rock. Gummidgy's the only planet-sized body in the system. Look down there."

I looked out the window. One of Gummidgy's oceans was passing beneath us. The biggest ocean Gummidgy had, it covered a third of the planet.

"Circle Sea. Round as a ten-star piece. A whale of a big asteroid must have hit there when Gummidgy was passing through the system. Stopped it cold, or almost. All the other rocks in the system are close enough to the star to be half-molten."

"Okay. Could they have built their own space station? Or borrowed one? Doubtful. So they must have landed on Gummidgy," I concluded happily, and waited for the applause.

Emil was slowly nodding his head, up, down, up, down. Suddenly he stood up. "Let's ask Captain Tellefsen."

"Hold it! Ask her what?"

"Ask her how big the ship was. She saw it, didn't she? She'll know whether it was a liner."

"Sit down. Let's wait till we're aground, then tell the MPs. Let them ask Margo."

"What for?"

Belatedly, I was getting cautious. "Just take my word for it, will you. Assume I'm a genius."

He gave me a peculiar look, but he did sit down.

Later, after we landed, we favored the police with our suggestions. They'd already asked Margo about the ship. It was a hell of a lot smaller than the *Argos* . . . about the size of a big yacht.

"They aren't trying," Emil said as we emerged from city hall.

"You can't blame them," I told him. "Suppose we knew exactly where Lloobee was. Suppose that. Then what? Should we charge in with lasers blazing and risk Lloobee catching a stray beam?"

"Yes, we should. That's the way Kdatlyno think."

"I know, but it's not the way I think."

I couldn't see Emil's face, which was bent in thought two feet below eye level. But his words came slowly, as if he had picked them with care. "We could find the ship that brought him down. You can't hide a spaceship landing. The gravity drag makes waves on a spaceport indicator."

"Granted."

"He could be right here in the base. So many ships go in and out."

"Most of the base ships don't have hyperdrive."

"Good. Then we can find them wherever they landed." He looked up. "What are we waiting for? Let's go look at the spaceport records!"

It was a waste of time, but there was no talking him out of it. I tagged along.

The timing was a problem.

From where the kidnapping took place, any ship in known space would take six hours to reach the breakout point. If it tried to go farther in hyperspace, CY Aquarii's gee well would drop it permanently into the Blind Spot.

From breakout it had taken us ten hours to reach Gummidgy. That was at five-gee acceleration, fusion drive and gravity drag, with four gees compensated by the internal gee field. CY Aquarii was a hot star, and if Gummidgy hadn't been near the edge of the system, it would have been boiling rock. Now, the fastest ship I'd ever heard of could make twenty gees . . .

"Which would take it here in five hours," said Emil. "Total of eleven. A one-gee ship would—"

"Would take too long. Lloobee would go crazy. They must know *something* about Kdatlyno. In fact, I'll bet they're lying about not having Kdatlyno food."

"Maybe. Okay, assume they're at least as fast as the *Argos*. That gives us five hours to play in. Hmmm . . . ?"

"Nineteen ships." On the timetable they were listed according to class. I crossed out fifteen that didn't have hyperdrive, crossed out the *Argos* itself to leave three. Crossed out the *Pregnant Banana* because it was a cargo job, flown by computer, ten gee with no internal compensating fields. Crossed out the *Golden Voyage*, a passenger ship smaller than the *Argos*, with a one-gee drive.

"That's nice," said Emil. "*Drunkard's Walk*. Say! Remember the hunting party I told you about, with their own yacht?"

"Yah. I know that name."

"Well, that's the yacht. *Drunkard's Walk. What* did you say?"

"The owner of the yacht. Larchmont Bellamy. I met him once, at Elephant's house."

"Go on."

By then it was too late to bite my tongue, though I didn't know it yet. "Not much to tell. Elephant's a friend of mine, a flatlander. He's got friends all over known space. I walked in at lush hour one afternoon, and Bellamy was there, with a woman named . . . here she is, Tanya Wilson. She's in the same hunting party. She's Bellamy's age."

"What's Bellamy like?"

"He's three hundred years old, no kidding. He was wearing a checkerboard skin-dye job and a shocking-pink Belter crest. He talked well. Old jokes, but he told them well, and he had some new ones, too."

"Would he kidnap a Kdatlyno?"

I had to think about that. "He might. He's no xenophobe; aliens don't make him nervous, but he doesn't like them. I remember him telling us that we ought to wipe out the kzinti for good and all. He doesn't need money, though."

"Would he do it for kicks?"

Bellamy. Pink bushy eyebrows over deep eyes. A mimic's voice, a deadpan way of telling a story, deadpan delivery of a punch line. I'd wondered at the time if that was a put-on. In three hundred years you hear the same joke so many times, tell the same story so many ways, change your politics again and again to match a changing universe . . . Was he deadpan because he didn't care anymore? How much boredom can you meet in three hundred years?

How many times can you change your morals without losing them all? Bellamy was born before a certain Jinxian biological laboratory produced boosterspice. He reached maturity when the organ banks were the only key to long life, when a criminal's life wasn't worth a paper star. He was at draft age when the kzinti were the only known extrasolar civilization and a fearful alien threat. Now civilization included humans and nine known alien life-forms, and criminal rehabilitation accounted for half of all published work in biochemistry and psychotherapy.

What *would* Bellamy's morals say about Lloobee? If he wouldn't kidnap a Kdatlyno, would he "steal" one?

"You make your own guess there. I don't know Bellamy that well."

"Well, it's worth checking." Jilson bent over the timetables. "Mist Demons, he landed a third of the way around the planet! Oh, well. Let's go rent a car."

"Hah?"

"We'll need a car." He saw he'd left me behind. "To get to their camp. To find out if they rescued Lloobee. You know, the Kdatlyno touch sculptor who—"

"I get the picture. Good-bye and good luck. If they ask who sent you, for Finagle's sake don't mention me."

"That won't work," Emil said firmly. "Bellamy won't talk to me. He doesn't know me."

"Apparently I didn't make it clear. I'll try again. If we knew who the kidnappers were, *which we don't,* we still couldn't charge in with lasers blazing."

But he was shaking his head, left, right, left, right. "It's different now. These men have reputations to protect, don't they? What would happen to those reputations if all human space knew they'd kidnapped a Kdatlyno?"

"You're not thinking. Even if everyone on Gummidgy knew the truth, the pirates would simply change the contract. A secrecy clause enforced by monetary penalty."

Emil slapped the table, and the walls echoed. "Are we just going to sit here while they rob us? You're a hell of a man to wear a hero's name!"

"Look, you're taking this too personally—huh?"

"A hero's name! Beowulf! He must be turning over in his barrow about now."

"Who's Beowulf?"

Emil stood up, putting us eye to eye, so that I could see

his utter disgust. "Beowulf was the first epic hero in English literature. He killed monsters bare-handed, and he did it to help people who didn't even belong to his own country. And you—" He turned away. "I'm going after Bellamy."

I sat there for what seemed a long time. Any time seems long when you need to make a decision but can't. It probably wasn't more than a minute.

But Emil wasn't in sight when I ran outside.

I shouted at the man who'd loaned us the timetables. "Hey! Where do you go to rent a car?"

"Public rentals. Dial fourteen in the transfer booth, then walk a block east."

So the base did have transfer booths. I found one, paid my coin, and dialed.

Getting to public rentals gave me my first chance to look at the base. There wasn't much to see. Buildings, half of them semipermanent; the base was only four years old. Apartment buildings, laboratories, a nursery school. Overhead, the actinic pinpoint of CY Aquarii hit the weather dome and was diffused into a wide, soft white glow. There were few people about, and all of them were tanned the same shade of black for protection against the savage, invisible ultraviolet outside. Most of them had goggles hung around their necks.

That much I saw while running a block at top speed.

He was getting into a car when I came panting up. He said, "Change your mind?"

"No, but ... hoo! ... you're going to change yours. Whew! The mood you're in, you'll fly straight into ... Bellamy's camp and ... tell him he's a lousy pirate. Hyooph! Then if you're wrong, he'll ... punch you in the nose ... and if you're right, he'll either ... laugh at you or have you ... killed."

Emil climbed into the car. "If you're going to argue, get in and argue there."

I got in. I had some of my breath back. "Will you get it

through your thick head? You've got your life to lose and nothing to gain. I told you why."

"I've got to try, don't I? Fasten your crash web."

I fastened my crash web. Its strands were thin as coarse thread and not much stronger, but they had saved lives. Any sharp pull on the crash web would activate the crash field, which would enfold the pilot and protect him from impact.

"If you've still got to look for the kidnappers," I said, "why not do it here? There's a good chance Lloobee's somewhere on the base."

"Nuts," said Emil. He turned on the lift units, and we took off. "Bellamy's yacht is the only ship that fits."

"There's another ship that fits. The *Argos*."

"Put your goggles on. We're about to go through the weather dome. What about the *Argos*?"

"Think it through. There had to be someone aboard in the first place to plant the gas bomb that knocked us out. Why shouldn't that same person have hidden Lloobee somewhere, gagged or unconscious, until the *Argos* could land?"

"Finagle's gonads! He could still be on the *Argos*! No, he couldn't; they searched the *Argos*." Emil glared at nothing. At that moment we went through the weather dome. CY Aquarii, which had been a soft white patch, became for an instant a tiny bright point of agony. Then a spot on each lens of my goggles turned black and covered the sun.

"We'll have to check it out later," said Emil. "But we can call city hall now and tell them one of the kidnappers was on the *Argos*."

But we couldn't. Where the car radio should have been was a square hole.

Emil smote his forehead. With his Jinxian strength it's a wonder he survived. "I forgot. Car radios won't work on Gummidgy. You have to use a ship's com laser and bounce the beam off one of the orbital stations."

"Do we have a com laser?"

"Do you see one? Maybe in ten years someone'll think

of putting com lasers in cars. Well, we'll have to do it later."

"That's silly. Let's do it now."

"First we check on Bellamy."

"I'm not going."

Emil just grinned.

He was right. It had been a futile comment. I had three choices:

Fighting a Jinxian.

Getting out and walking home. But we must have gone a mile up already, and the base was far behind.

Visiting Bellamy, who was an old friend, and looking around unobtrusively while we were there. Actually, it would have been rude not to go. Actually, it would have been silly not to at least drop by and say hello while we were on the same planet.

Actually, I rationalize a lot.

"Do one thing for me," I said. "Let me do all the talking. You can be the strong, silent type who smiles a lot."

"Okay. What are you going to tell him?"

"The truth. Not the whole truth, but some of it."

The four-hour trip passed quickly. We found cards and a score pad in a glove compartment. The car blasted quietly and smoothly through a Mach four wall of air, rising once to clear a magnificent range of young mountains.

"Can you fly a car?"

I looked up from my cards. "Of course." Most people can. Every world has its wilderness areas, and it's not worthwhile to spread transfer booths all through a forest, especially one that doesn't see twenty tourists in a year. When you're tired of civilization, the only way to travel is to transfer to the edge of a planetary park and then rent a car.

"That's good," said Emil, "in case I get put out of action."

"Now it's your turn to cheer me up."

Emil cocked his head at me. "If it's any help, I think I know how Bellamy's group found the *Argos*."

"Go on."

"It was the starseed. A lot of people must have known about it, including Margo. Maybe she told someone that she was stopping the ship so the passengers could get a look."

"Not much help. She had a lot of space to stop in."

"Did she? Think about it. First, Bellamy'd have no trouble at all figuring when she'd reach the Gummidgy system."

"Right." There's only one speed in hyperdrive.

"That means Margo would have to stop on a certain spherical surface to catch the light image of the starseed setting sail. Furthermore, in order to watch it happen in an hour, she had to be right in front of the starseed. That pinpoints her exactly."

"There'd be a margin of error."

Emil shrugged. "Half a light-hour on a side. All Bellamy had to do was wait in the right place. He had an hour to maneuver."

"Bravo," I said. There were things I didn't want him to know yet. "He could have done it that way, all right. I'd like to mention just one thing."

"Go ahead."

"You keep saying 'Bellamy did this' and 'Bellamy did that.' We don't know he's guilty yet, and I'll thank you to remember it. Remember that he's a friend of a friend and don't start treating him like a criminal until you know he is one."

"All right," Emil said, but he didn't like it. *He* knew Bellamy was a kidnapper. He was going to get us both killed if he didn't watch his mouth.

At the last minute I got a break. It was only a bit of misinterpretation on Emil's part, but one does not refuse a gift from the gods.

We'd crossed six or seven hundred kilometers of veldt: blue-green grass with herds grazing at wide intervals. The herds left a clear path, for the grass (or whatever; we hadn't seen it close up) changed color when cropped. Now we were coming up on a forest, but not the gloomy green type of forest native to human space. It was a riot of color: patches of scarlet, green, magenta, yellow. The yellow patches were polka-dotted with deep purple.

Just this side of the forest was the hunting camp. Like a nudist at a tailors' convention, it leapt to the eye, flagrantly alien against the blue-green veldt. A bulbous plastic camp tent the size of a mansion dominated the scene, creases marring its translucent surface to show where it was partitioned into rooms. A diminutive figure sat outside the door, its head turning to follow our sonic boom. The yacht was some distance away.

The yacht was a gaily decorated playboy's space boat with a brilliant orange paint job and garish markings in colors that clashed. Some of the markings seemed to mean something. Bellamy, one year ago, hadn't struck me as the type to own such a boat. Yet there it stood, on three wide landing legs with paddle-shaped feet, its sharp nose pointed up at us.

It looked ridiculous. The hull was too thick and the legs were too wide, so that the big businesslike attitude jets in the nose became a comedian's nostrils. On a slender needle with razor-sharp swept-back airfoils that paint job might have passed. But it made the compact, finless *Drunkard's Walk* look like a clown.

The camp swept under us while we were still moving at Mach two. Emil tilted the car into a wide curve, slowing and dropping. As we turned toward the camp for the second time, he said, "Bellamy's taking precious little pains to hide himself. Oh, oh."

"What?"

"The yacht. It's not big enough. The ship Captain Tellefsen described was twice that size."

A gift from the gods. "I hadn't noticed," I said. "You're right. Well, that lets Bellamy out."

"Go ahead. Tell me I'm an idiot."

"No need. Why should I gloat over one stupid mistake? I'd have had to make the trip anyway, sometime."

Emil sighed. "I suppose that means you'll have to see Bellamy before we go back."

"Finagle's sake, Emil! We're here, aren't we? Oh, one thing. Let's not tell Bellamy why we came. He might be offended."

"And he might decide I'm a dolt. Correctly. Don't worry, I won't tell him."

The "grass" covering the veldt turned out to be knee-high ferns, dry and brittle enough to crackle under our socks. Dark blue-green near the tips of the plants gave way to lighter coloring on the stalks. Small wonder the herbivores had left a trail. Small wonder if we'd seen carnivores treading that easy path.

The goggled figure in front of the camp tent was cleaning a mercy rifle. By the time we were out of the car, he had closed it up and loaded it with inch-long slivers of anesthetic chemical. I'd seen such guns before. The slivers could be fired individually or in one-second bursts of twenty, and they dissolved instantly in anything that resembled blood. One type of sliver would usually fit all the lifeforms on a given world.

The man didn't bother to get up as we approached. Nor did he put down the gun. "Hi," he said cheerfully. "What can I do for you?"

"We'd like—"

"Beowulf Shaeffer?"

"Yah. Larch Bellamy?"

Now he got up. "Can't recognize anybody on this crazy world. Goggles covering half your face, everybody the same color—you have to go stark naked to be recognized, and then only the women know you. Whatinhell are you doing on Gummidgy, Bey?"

"I'll tell you later. Larch, this is Emil Horne. Emil, meet Larchmont Bellamy."

"Pleasure," said Bellamy, grinning as if indeed it were.

Then his grin tried to break into laughter, and he smothered it. "Let's go inside and swallow something wet."

"What was funny?"

"Don't be offended, Mr. Horne. You and Bey do make an odd pair. I was thinking that the two of you are like a medium-sized beach ball standing next to a baseball bat. How did you meet?"

"On the ship," said Emil.

The camp tent had a collapsible revolving door to hold the pressure. Inside, the tent was almost luxurious, though it was all foldaway stuff. Chairs and sofas were soft, cushiony fabric surfaces, holding their shape through insulated static charges. Tables were memory plastic. Probably they compressed into small cubes for storage aboard ship. Light came from glow strips in the fabric of the pressurized tent. The bar was a floating portable. It came to meet us at the door, took our orders, and passed out drinks.

"All right," Bellamy said, sprawling in an armchair. When he relaxed, he relaxed totally, like a cat. Or a tiger. "Bey, how did you come to Gummidgy? And where's Sharrol?"

"She can't travel in space."

"Oh? I didn't know. That can happen to anyone." But his eyes questioned.

"She wanted children. Did you know that? She's always wanted children."

He took in my red eyes and white hair. "I . . . see. So you broke up."

"For the time being."

His eyes questioned.

That's not emphatic enough. There was something about Bellamy . . . He had a lean body and a lean face, with a straight, sharp-edged nose and prominent cheekbones, all setting off the dark eyes in their deep pits beneath black shaggy brows.

But there was more to it than eyes. You can't tell a man's age by looking at his photo, not if he takes boosterspice. But you can tell, to some extent, by watching him in motion. Older men know where they're going before they start to move. They don't dither, they don't waste energy, they don't trip over their feet, and they don't bump into things.

Bellamy was old. There was a power in him, and his eyes *questioned*.

I shrugged. "We used the best answer we had, Larch. He was a friend of ours, and his name was Carlos Wu. You've heard of him?"

"Mathematician, isn't he?"

"Yah. Also playwright and composer. The Fertility Board gave him an unlimited breeding license when he was eighteen."

"*That* young?"

"He's a genius. As I say, he was a good friend of ours. Liked to talk about space; he had the flatland phobia, like Sharrol. Well, Sharrol and I made our decision, and then we went to him for help. He agreed.

"So Sharrol's married him on a two-year contract. In two years I'll go back and marry her, and we'll raise our family."

"I'll be damned."

I'd been angry about it for too long, with nobody to be angry at. I flared up. "Well, what would *you* have done?"

"Found another woman. But I'm a dirty old man, and you're young and naive. Suppose Wu tried to keep her."

"He won't. He's a friend; I told you. Besides, he's got more women than ten of him could handle with that license of his."

"So you left."

"I had to. I couldn't stand it."

He was looking at me with something like awe. "I can't remember ever being in love that hard. Bey, you're overdue for a drunk, and you're surrounded by friends. Shall we switch to something stronger than beer?"

"It's a good offer, but no, thanks. I didn't mean to cry on your shoulder. I've had my drunk. A week on Wunderland, drinking Vurguuz."

"Finagle's ears! Vurguuz?"

"I said to myself, Why mess around with half measures? said I. So—"

"What does it taste like?"

"Like a hand grenade with a minted sugar casing. Like you better have a chaser ready."

Silence threatened to settle. No wonder, the way I'd killed the conversation by spilling my personal problems all over everything. I said, "So as long as I had to do some traveling, I thought I'd do some people some favors. That's why I'm here."

"What kind of favors?"

"Well, a friend of mine happens to be an ET taxidermist. It's a complicated profession. I told him I'd get him some information on Gummidgy animals and Gummidgy biochemistry. Now that the planet's open to hunters, sooner or later people like you are going to be carting in perforated alien bodies."

Bellamy frowned. "I wish I could help," he said, "but I don't kill the animals I hunt. I just shoot them full of anesthetic so they'll hold still while I photo them. The same goes for the rest of us."

"I see."

"Otherwise I'd offer to take you along one day."

"Yah. I'll do my own research, then. Thanks for the thought."

Then, being a good host, Bellamy proceeded to work Emil into the conversation. Emil was far from being the strong, silent type who smiles a lot; in fact, we were soon learning all about the latest advances in computer technology. But he kept his word and did not mention why we had come.

I was grateful.

The afternoon passed swiftly. Dinnertime arrived early. Most of the people on Gummidgy accommodate to the eighteen-hour day by having two meals: brunch and dinner. We accepted Bellamy's invitation.

With dinner arrived a dedicated hunter named Warren,

who insisted on showing us photos of everything he'd caught since his arrival. That day he'd shot a graceful animal like a white greyhound, "but even faster," he said; a monkeylike being with a cupped hand for throwing rocks; and a flower.

"A flower?"

"See those tooth marks on my boot? I had to shoot it to get it to let go. No real sport in it, but as long as I'd already shot the damn thing . . ."

His only resemblance to Bellamy was this: He carried the same indefinable air of age. Now I was sure it had nothing to do with appearance. Perhaps it was a matter of individuality. Bellamy and Warren were individuals. They didn't push it, they didn't have to demonstrate it, but neither were they following anybody's lead.

Warren left after dinner. Going to see how the others were doing, he said; they must be hot on the trail of something or they'd have been back to eat. Not wanting to wear out our welcome, we said our good-byes and left, too. It was near sunset when we emerged from the camp tent.

"Let me drive," I said.

Emil raised his brows at me but moved around to the passenger seat.

He did more than raise his brows when he saw what I was doing.

I set the autopilot to take us back to the base and let the car fly itself until we were below the horizon. We were a mile up by then and a goodly distance away. Whereupon I canceled the course, dipped the car nearly to ground level, and swung back toward the forest. I flew almost at treetop level, staying well below the speed of sound.

"Tell me again," I said, "about Beowulf the hero."

"What kind of game are you playing now?"

"You thought the size of the *Drunkard's Walk* cleared Bellamy, didn't you?"

"It does. It's much too small to be Captain Tellefsen's pirate."

"So it is. But we already know there was a pirate on board the *Argos*."

"Right."

"Let's assume it's Margo."

"The *captain*?"

"Why not?"

I'll say this for him, he got it all in one gulp. Margo to release the gas. Margo to tell Bellamy where to meet the *Argos* and to hold the ship in one place long enough to be met. Margo to lie about the size of Bellamy's ship.

And me to keep Emil in the dark until now, so he wouldn't blow his lines when he met Bellamy.

He gulped, and then he said, "It fits. But I'd swear Bellamy's innocent."

"Except for one thing. He didn't invite me to go hunting with him."

A yellow patch of forest streamed away beneath us. The purple polka dots we'd seen from high up turned out to be huge blossoms several feet across, serviced by birds the size of storks. Then we were over scarlet puffballs that shook in the wind of our passage. I kept us low and slow. A car motor is silent, but a sonic boom would make us more than conspicuous.

"That's your evidence against him? He didn't want you hunting with him?"

"And he gave lousy reasons."

"You said he hated ETs. He's a flatlander. To some flatlanders we'd both look like ETs."

"Maybe. But the *Drunkard's Walk* is still the only ship that could have landed Lloobee, and Margo's still our best bet as the kidnapper on the *Argos*. Maybe the pirates *could* have found the *Argos* by guess and hope, but they'd have a damn sight better chance with Margo working with them."

Emil glared out through the windshield. "Were you thinking this all the time we were in the camp?"

"Not until he turned down the chance to take me hunting. Then I was pretty sure."

"You make a first-class liar."

I didn't know how to deny it, so I said nothing. Nonetheless, Emil was wrong. If I'd spilled my personal problems in Bellamy's lap, if I'd accepted his hospitality, professed friendship, drunk his liquor, laughed at his jokes and made him laugh at mine, it was not an act. Bellamy made you like him, and he made you want him to like you. And Emil would never understand that in my eyes Bellamy had done nothing seriously wrong.

Six years earlier I'd tried to steal a full-sized spacecraft, fitted more or less for war, from a group of Pierson's puppeteers. I'd been stopped before the plan had gotten started, but so what? The puppeteers had been blackmailing me, but again, so what? Who says the aliens of known space have to think we're perfect? *We* know we're not. Ask us!

"I'm sorry," said Emil. "Excuse my mouth. I got you into this practically over your dead body, and now, when you do your best to help out, I jump on you. I'm an ungrateful ..." And what he said then about his anatomic makeup probably wasn't true. He was married, after all. He concluded, "You're the boss. Now what?"

"Depends. We don't have any evidence yet."

"You really think Bellamy's the one?"

"I really do."

"He could be holding Lloobee anywhere. Hundreds of miles away."

"We'll never find him thinking that way. He wasn't in the camp tent. Even Bellamy wouldn't have that much nerve. If he'd been in the ship, we'd have seen the air lock open—"

"Closed."

"Open. Lloobee couldn't sense anything through a ship's hull. In a closed ship that size he'd go nuts."

"Okay."

"We know one thing that might be helpful. Bellamy's got a disintegrator."

"He does?"

"The holes in the *Argos*. You didn't see them, did you?"

"No. You think he might have dug himself a hideout?"

"Yah. Bellamy isn't the type to let a tool like that go to waste. If he's got a slaver disintegrator, he'll use it. It's a fine digging tool. A big roomy cave would take you an hour, and even the dust would be blown hundreds of miles. Disintegrator dust is nearly monatomic."

"How are you planning to find this cave?"

"Let's see if the car has a deep-radar attachment."

It didn't. Rent-a-cars usually do on worlds where there are swampy areas. So now we knew Gummidgy wasn't swampy. Everything on the dash had its uses, and not one of them was sonar.

"We'll have to make a sight search," said Emil. "How close are we to Bellamy's camp?"

"About thirty miles."

"Well, there's a chance they won't see us." Emil sat forward in his chair, hands gripping his knees. His smile was thin and tight. Obviously he had something. "Take us up to ten miles. Don't cross sonic speed until we've got lots of room."

"What can we see from ten miles up?"

"Assume I'm a genius."

That served me right. I took the car up without quibbling.

Ten miles down was the wandering line of the forest border, sharply demarcated from the veldt. At this height all the magnificent colors of Gummidgy vegetation blurred into a rich brown.

"Do you see it?"

"No."

"Look for two nearly parallel lines," said Emil. "A little lighter than the rest of the forest."

"I still don't see it."

"It shows on the veldt, too."

"Nope. Hah! Got it." Crossing the rich brown of the forest was a strip of faintly lighter, faintly more uniform brown. "Hard to see, though. What is it?"

"Dust. Blown for hundreds of miles, just like you said. Some of it settled on the tops of the trees."

So dim was the path that it kept flickering in and out of the visible. But it was straight, with edges that slowly converged. It crossed the veldt, too, in a strip of faintly dimmed blue-green. Before its edges met, the path faded out, but one could extend those edges in the mind's eye.

I let the car fall.

Unless we were building dream castles, Lloobee's cave must be at the intersection.

When we got too low, the dust path disappeared in the colors of forest and veldt. Bellamy's hypothetical cave was half a mile into the forest. I couldn't land there for reasons involving too many big plants and too many pirates. I dropped the car in a curve of the forest.

Emil had been fumbling in the back. Now he pressed something into my hand and said, "Here, take this." To my amazement I found myself holding a sonic stunner.

"That's illegal!" I whispered furiously.

"Why are you whispering? Kidnapping Kdatlyno is illegal, too. We may be glad we've got these before we're finished."

"But where did you get police stunners?"

"Let's say some criminal slipped them into my luggage. And if you'll look at the butts, you'll see they aren't police stunners."

They'd started life as police stunners, but they weren't anymore. The butts were hand-carved from big cultured emeralds. Expensive. Dueling pistols?

Sure, dueling pistols. Lose a duel with one of these and you'd lose nothing but face. I hear most Jinxians would rather lose an arm, permanently. They were not illegal—on Jinx.

"Remember," said Emil, "they only knock a man out for ten minutes."

"I can run a long way in ten minutes."

Emil looked me over rather carefully. "You've changed.

You could have driven me straight back to base, and I'd never have been the wiser."

"I never thought of that."

"Bah."

"Would you believe I've decided to be an epic hero? Whatever that is."

Emil shrugged and moved into the forest. I followed.

I wasn't about to explain my motives to Emil. He'd put me in an unpleasant situation, and if he wanted to worry about my backing out, let him worry.

Back out? I couldn't. It was too late.

There had been a time when I knew nothing about Lloobee's kidnappers. I might suspect Margo, but I had no evidence.

Later, I could suspect Bellamy. But I had no proof.

But Emil had pressured me into confronting Bellamy, and Bellamy had been pressured into putting on an act. If I quit now, Bellamy would continue to think I was a fool.

And when Bellamy confronted Margo, Margo would continue to think I was a fool. That would hurt. To have Margo and Bellamy both thinking that I had been twice an idiot . . .

It wasn't Bellamy's fault, except that he had voluntarily kidnapped a valuable Kdatlyno sculptor. It was partly my fault and mostly Emil's. I might be able to leave Margo out of this. But Bellamy would have to pay for my mistakes.

And why shouldn't he? It was *his* antisocial act.

The vegetation was incredibly lush, infinitely varied. Its chemistry was not that of terrain life, but the chemical it used for photosynthesis was similar to chlorophyll. For billions of years the plants of Gummidgy had had oversupplies of ultraviolet light. The result was life in plenty, a profusion of fungi and animals and parasites. On every branch of the magenta trees was an orchid thing, a sessile beast waiting for its dinner to fly by. The air was full of life: birdforms, insectforms, and a constant rain of dust and spores and feathery seeds and bits of leaf and bird dung. The soil was dry and spongy and rich, and the air was rich with oxygen and alien smells. Somewhere in the spectrum of odors were valuable undiscovered perfumes.

Once we saw a flower thing like the one in Warren's photo. I found a dry branch and stuck it down the thing's blossom and pulled back half a branch.

Again, four feet of snake flew by. Emil stunned it. It had two small fins near the head end, and its hind end was a huge, leathery delta wing. Its mouth was two-thirds back along the body.

With typical abruptness, the flowering magenta trees gave way to a field of scarlet tubing. No branches, no leaves; just interlocking cables, three feet thick, moving restlessly over each other like too many snakes in a pit. They were four or five deep. Maybe they were all one single plant or animal; we never did see a head or a tail. And we'd never have kept our footing if we'd tried to cross.

We circled the area, staying in the magenta trees because we were getting too close to where the hypothetical cave ought to be. That brought us to a small round hill surmounted by a tree that was mostly wandering roots. We started around the hill, and Emil gripped my arm.

I saw it. A cave mouth, small and round, in the base of the hill. And leaning against the dirt slope of the hill was a woman with a mercy gun.

"All *right*!" I whispered. "Come on, let's get out of here!" I pulled at Emil's arm and turned toward freedom.

It was like trying to stop a warship from taking off. Emil was gone, running silently toward the cave with his gun held ready, leaving me with numb fingers and a deep appreciation of Finagle's first law. I swallowed a groan and started after him.

On flat ground I can beat any Jinxian who ever ran the short sprint. My legs were twice the length of Emil's. But Emil moved like a wraith through the alien vegetation, while I kept getting tangled up. My long legs and arms stuck out too much, and I couldn't catch him.

It was such a crying pity. Because we had it! We had it all, or all we were going to get. The guarded cave was our

proof. Bellamy and his hunter friends were the kidnappers.
That knowledge would be a powerful bargaining point in
our negotiations for the return of Lloobee, despite what I'd
told Emil. All we had to do now was get back to base and
tell somebody.

But I couldn't catch Emil!

I couldn't even keep up with him.

A bare area fronted the cave, a triangular patch of ground
bounded by two thick, sprawling roots belonging to the
treelike thing on the hill. I'd lost sight of Emil; when I saw
him again, he was running for the cave at full speed, and
the woman with the gun was faceup in the dirt. Emil
reached the darkness at the mouth of the cave and disappeared within.

And as he vanished into the dark, he was unmistakably
falling.

Well, now they had Emil. With blazing lasers . . . ! Proof
wasn't enough. He'd decided to bring back Lloobee himself. Now we'd have to negotiate for the two of them.

Would we? Bellamy was back at the hunting camp.
When he found out his men had Emil, he'd know I was
somewhere around. But whoever was in the cave might
think Emil was alone. In which case they might kill him
right now.

I settled my back against the tree. As a kind of afterthought I focused the dueling pistol on the woman and
fired. I'd have to do that every ten minutes to keep her
quiet.

Eventually someone would be coming out to see why she
hadn't stopped Emil.

I didn't dare try to enter the cave. Be it man or booby
trap, whatever had stopped Emil would stop me.

Too bad the dueling pistols didn't have more power. The
craftsmen who had carved their emerald butts had scaled
them down because, after all, they would be used only to
prove a point. It would take a shopful of tools to readjust
them, because readjusting them to their former power

would violate Jinxian law. Real police stunners will knock a man out for twelve hours or more.

I was sitting there waiting for someone to come out when I felt the prickly numbness of a stunner.

The sensations came separately. First, a pull in my ankles. Then, in the calves of my legs. Then, something rough and crumbly sliding under me. Separate sensations, just above the threshold of consciousness, penetrating the numbness. A sliding bump! bump! against the back of my head. Gritty sensation in the backs of my hands, arms trailing above and behind my head.

Conclusion, arrived at after long thought: I was being dragged.

I was limp as a noodle and nearly as numb. It was all over. Nobody had walked innocently out of the cave. Instead, the man in there with Lloobee had looked out with a heat sensor, then used his sonic on anything that might possibly be the temperature of a man.

Things turned dark. I thought I was unconscious, but no, I'd been dragged into the cave.

"That's a relief," said Bellamy. Unmistakably, Bellamy.

"Bastard," said a woman's voice. It seemed familiar: rich and fruity, with a flatlander accent that was not quite true. Misplaced in time, probably. A dialect doesn't stay the same forever.

My eyes fell open.

Bellamy stood over me, looking down with no expression. Tanya Wilson sat some distance away, looking sullenly in my direction. The man named Warren, standing behind her, carefully did something to her scalp, and she winced.

"There," said Warren, "you go back to the camp. If anyone asks—"

"I was scratched by a flower bird," said Tanya. "The rest of you are out hunting. Will you please assume I've got a mind."

"Don't be so damn touchy. Larch, you'd better tie them up, hadn't you?"

"You do it if you like. It's not necessary. They'll be out for hours."

Oh, really?

Tanya Wilson got up and went to the cave mouth. Before leaving, she pulled a cord hanging at the side. Warren, who had followed her, pulled it again after she was gone.

The cord was attached to what looked like a police stunner, the same model as Emil's guns. The stunner was mounted on a board, and the board was fixed in place over the mouth of the cave, aimed downward. A booby trap. So easy.

The numbness was gone. My problem was the opposite: It was all I could do to keep from moving. I was stretched full-length on a rocky floor with my heels a foot higher than my nose and my arms straight above my head. If I so much as clenched a fist . . .

"I wonder," Bellamy said, "what made him turn against me."

"Who? Shaeffer?"

I could see four in the cave. Bellamy was standing over me; Warren was nearer the cave mouth. The two others were near the back, near a line of plastic crates. One was a man I'd never seen. The other—huge and frightening in the semidark, a monster from man's dimmest past, when demons and supernatural beings walked the homeworld— was Lloobee. They sat silently facing each other, as if each were waiting for something.

"Yes," said Bellamy. "Beowulf Shaeffer. He seemed such a nice guy. Why would he go to so much effort to get me in trouble?"

"You forget, Larch." Warren spoke with patient understanding. "They are the good guys; we are the bad guys. A simple sense of law and order—"

"Too much law and order around, Warren. There are no more frontiers. We sit in our one small area of the universe called known space, sixty light-years across, and we rot. Too much security. Everyone wants security."

"That's Shaeffer's motive. He was backing up law and order."

"I don't think so. Bey's not the type."

"What type is he?"

"Lazy. A survival type, but lazy. He doesn't start to use his brain until he's in obvious, overt trouble. But he's got pride."

"Could the other one have talked him into it?"

"I suppose so."

There was an uncomfortable silence.

"Well," said Warren, "it's too bad. What'll we do with them?"

Bellamy looked unhappily down at me. He couldn't see my eyes behind the goggles, not in the dim cave light. "They could be found half-eaten. By one of those big hopping things, say. The ones that prey on the gray plains herbivores."

"The carnivore that did it would be poisoned. It would have to be found nearby."

"Right." Bellamy pondered. "It's vital that there be no evidence against us. If we tried to square a murder rap in the contract, they'd chivvy our price down to nothing. You were bright to use the sonic. A mercy needle would have left chemicals."

A small, sharp rock was pressing against the side of my neck. It itched. If I was planning to leap to my feet from this ridiculous position, I couldn't delay too long. Sooner or later I'd reach to scratch. Sooner or later Bellamy or Warren would notice the butts of Emil's altered police stunners and know them for what they were.

"First we need a plains carnivore," said Warren. "Do you think we can starve it into—"

Lloobee leapt.

He was five yards from the man who was guarding him at the back of the cave. The man fired instantly, and then he screamed and tried to dodge. The Kdatlyno slammed into him and knocked him sliding across the floor.

I didn't see any more. I was running. I heard panicky

shouting and then Bellamy's roar: "Relax, you idiot. He was unconscious before he left the ground." And Warren's, "Relax, hell! Where's Shaeffer?"

I barely remembered to pull the trigger cord on Bellamy's booby trap. The cave entrance was long and low, sloping upward. I took it at a crouching run. Behind me was more confusion. Could the first man through have pulled the trigger cord *again*? That would give me time I needed.

Outside the cave I turned sharp right. The winding, half-exposed roof was almost Emil's height. I went over it like a spider monkey and then under it, hiding under its protective bulk.

CY Aquarii was directly behind me, minutes from sunset. Its white light threw a sharp black shadow along the side of the root.

I started crawling uphill, staying in the shadow. Two sets of pelting footsteps followed me from the other side of the root.

Voices came from below, barely audible. They didn't sound like a search in progress. Why not? I looked back and saw no pursuit. Halfway up the hill I slid out of my blue falling jumper, tucked it as far under the root as it would go, and went on, thinking kindly thoughts about tannin pills. Now I'd be all but invisible if I stayed in the shadows. All but my white hair.

Why had Lloobee made that grandstand play? It was as if he'd read my mind. He must have known there was no chance of escape for him. But I'd have had no chance without his diversion. Had he known I was conscious?

Could Kdatlyno read minds?

At the top of the hill I stopped in a cleft between two huge roots. The magenta tree seemed much too small to need all that root area, but the sunlight was rich, and maybe the soil was poor. And the roots would hide me.

But where were my pursuers?

I knew they needed me. They couldn't dispose of Emil until they had me. Granted that they could find me as soon as it got dark; I'd stand out like a beacon on a heat sensor. But suppose I reached the car first?

The car!

Sure, that was it. While I was crouching somewhere or taking a tangled trail that would keep me hidden at all times, Bellamy or one of his men was taking the shortest, straightest route to my car. To move it before I could reach it.

I pounded my head to get it working. No use. I was stymied. The cave? I'd find guns in there, hunting guns. The anesthetic slivers probably wouldn't work on human beings, but they might be poisonous—and they would certainly hurt. But no, I couldn't attack the cave. There'd be no way around the booby trap.

But there'd be someone in there to turn the booby trap on and off and to guard Lloobee. Another on the way to the car; that made two.

The third would have found some high point, chosen days previously for its view of the surroundings. He'd be waiting now for a glimpse of my snow-white hair. I couldn't break and run for the car.

Maybe.

And maybe the third man had been the first to come charging after me. And maybe he'd snatched at the trigger cord as he passed to turn off a police stunner that was already off. And maybe he'd run through the beam.

Maybe.

But if anyone reached the car, I was cooked.

I spun it over and over while handfuls of needed seconds passed me by. There was no other way to figure it. Tanya was back at camp. A second man was in the cave; a third was on the way to the car. The fourth either was waiting for me to show myself or he wasn't. I had to risk it.

I came out from under the roots, running.

I'm good at sprinting, not so good at a long-distance run. The edge of the forest was half a mile away. I was walking when I got there and blowing like a city-sized air pump. There was no sign of anyone and no sign of the car. I stood just within the forest, sucking wind, nerving myself to run out into the fern grass.

Then Bellamy emerged to my left. He dogtrotted fearlessly out onto the veldt, into the fern grass, and stood looking around. One of Emil's sonics dangled from one hand. He must have known by then that it was only a dueling pistol, but it was the only sonic he had.

He saw something to his right, something hidden from me by a curve of forest. He turned and trotted toward it.

I followed as best I could. Multicolored things kept tripping me, and I didn't dare step out into the fern grass. Bellamy was going to get there first . . .

He was examining the car when I found him. The car was right out in the open, tens of yards from any cover. Any second now he'd get in and take off.

What was he waiting for? Me?

I knelt behind a magenta bush, dithering. Bellamy was peering into the backseat. He wanted to know just what we'd planned before he made his move. Every two seconds his head would pop up for a long, slow look around.

A black dot in the distance caught my eye. It took me a moment to realize that it was in the plastic goggles, blotting out the dot of actinic sunlight. The sun was right on the horizon.

Bellamy was opening the trunk.

. . . The sun.

I started circling. The magenta bushes offered some cover, and I used it all. Bellamy's eyes maintained their steady sweep, but they hadn't found me yet.

Abruptly he slammed the trunk, circled the car to get in.

I was where I wanted to be. My long shadow pointed straight at the car. I charged.

He looked up as I started. He looked straight at me, and then his eyes swept the curve of forest, taking their time. He bent to get into the car, and then he saw me. But his gun hand was in the car, and I was close enough. The dots on his goggles had covered more than CY Aquarii. They'd covered my approach.

My shoulder knocked him spinning away from the car, and I heard a metal *tick*. He got up fast, empty-handed. No gun. He'd dropped it. I turned to look in the car, fully expecting to find it on the floor or on the seat. It was nowhere to be seen. I looked back in time to duck, and his other hand caught me and knocked me away. I rolled with it and came to my feet.

He was standing in a relaxed boxer stance between me and the car.

"I'm going to break you, Bey."

"So you can't find the gun, either."

"I don't need it. Any normal ten-year-old could break you in two."

"Then come on." I dropped into boxer stance, thanking Finagle that he didn't know karate or ju-whatsis or any of the other illegal killing methods. Hundreds of years had passed since the usual laws against carrying a concealed weapon were extended to cover special fighting methods, but Bellamy had had hundreds of years to learn. I'd come up lucky.

He came toward me, moving lightly and confidently, a flatlander in prime condition. He must have felt perfectly safe. What could he have to fear from an attenuated weakling, a man born and raised in We Made It's point six gee? He grinned when he was almost in range, and I hit him in the mouth.

My range was longer than his.

He danced back, and I danced forward and hit him in the nose before he got his guard up. He'd have to get used to the extra reach of my arms. But his guard was up now, and I saw no point in punching his forearms.

"You're a praying mantis," he said. "An insect. Overspecialized." And he moved in.

I moved back, punching lightly, staying out of his reach. He'd have to get used to that, too. His legs were too short. If he tried to move forward as fast as I could backpedal, he wouldn't be able to keep his guard up.

He tried anyway. I caught him one below the ribs, and

his head jerked up in surprise. I wasn't hurting him much
. . . but he'd been expecting love pats. Four years in Earth's
one point oh gee had put muscle on me, muscle that didn't
show along my long bones. He tried crowding me, and I
caught him twice in the right eye. He tried keeping his
guard intact, and that was suicide because he couldn't reach
me at all.

I caught that eye a third time. He bellowed, lowered his
head, and charged.

I ran like a thief.

I'd led him in a half circle. He never had a chance to
catch me. He reached the car just as I slammed the door in
his face and locked it.

By the time he reached the left-hand door, I had that
locked, too, and all the windows up. He was banging a rock
on a window when I turned on the lift units and departed
the field of battle.

He'd have to get used to my methods of fighting, too.

As I took the car up, I saw him running back toward the
hunting camp.

No radio. No com laser. The base was a third of the way
around the planet, and I'd have to go myself.

I set the autopilot to take me a thousand miles north of
the base, flying low. Bellamy was bound to come after me
with a car, and I didn't want to be found.

Come to that, did he have a car? I hadn't seen one.

Maybe he'd use— But that didn't bear thinking about, so
I didn't.

A glove compartment held a small bar. Emil and I hadn't
depleted it much on the way out. I ordered something simple and sat sipping it.

The forest disappeared behind me. I watched the endless
plain of fern grass whipping underneath. Mach four is drifting with the breeze if you're a spaceman, but try it in a car
with the altitude set for fifty yards. It wasn't frightening; it
was hypnotic.

The sun had been setting. Now it stayed just where it

was, on the horizon, a little to my left. The ground was a
blur; the sky was a frozen sphere. It was as if time had
stopped.

I thought of Margo.

What an actress she would have made! The confusion
she'd shown after the kidnapping. She hadn't remembered
the cargo mass meter; oh, no! She hadn't even known
Lloobee was one of her passengers! Sure she hadn't.

She'd taken me for a fool.

I had no wish to harm her. When I told the MPs about
Bellamy, she would not be mentioned. But she'd know that
I knew.

I wondered what had brought her into this.

Come to that, what had brought Bellamy? He couldn't
need the money that badly. Simple kicks? Had he wanted to
strike at human-alien relationships? The races of known
space are vastly richer for the interstellar trade. But
Bellamy had lived through at least three human-kzinti wars;
he'd read of things that looked like Lloobee in his children's books.

He was a man displaced in time. I remembered the way
he'd said "stark naked." I'd used a nudist's license myself
on Earth, not because I believed the incredible claims for
nudism's health-giving properties but because I was with
friends who did. Come to that, I was nude now. (Would I
have to buy a license when I reached the base?) But
Bellamy had laughed when he'd said it. Nudism was funny.

I remembered the archaisms in his speech.

Bellamy. He'd done nothing seriously wrong, not until he
had decided to kill Emil and me. We could have been
friends. Now it was too late. I finished my drink and crumpled the cup; it evaporated.

A black streak on my goggles at the edge of my right
eye.

. . . Much too late. The black blotch of Bellamy's fusion
flame was far to the north, passing me. He'd done it. He'd
brought the *Drunkard's Walk*.

Had he seen me?

The ship curved around toward the sun, slowed, and stopped in my path. It came down my throat. I swerved; Bellamy swerved to meet me.

He flashed by overhead, and my car, moving at Mach four, bucked under the lash of the sonic boom. The crash field gripped me for an instant, then went off.

He turned and came from behind.

Slam! And he was disappearing into the blue and green and orange sunset. What was he playing at? He must know that one touch of fusion flame would finish me.

He could end me any time he pleased. The *Drunkard's Walk* was moving at twice my speed, and Bellamy moved it about like an extension of his fingers. He was playing with me.

Again he turned, and again the hypersonic boom slapped me down. The blur of veldt came up at me, then receded. Another such might slap me into the fern grass at Mach four.

He wasn't playing. He was trying to force me to land. My corpse was to carry no evidence of murder.

Slam! And again the black blotch shrank against the sunset.

It was no playboy's yacht he was flying. Such an expensive toy would have been long and slender, with a superfluous needle nose and low maneuverability due to its heavy angular movement. The *Drunkard's Walk* was short, with big attitude jets showing like nostrils in the stubby nose. I should have known when I saw the landing legs. Big and wide and heavy, folded now into the hull, but when they were down, they were comically splayfooted, with a wide reach to hold the ship on almost any terrain.

The playboy's flashy paint job was indirection only. The ship . . .

The ship made a wide loop ahead of me and came slashing back.

I pulled back hard on the wheel.

The blood left my head, and then the crash field took hold. I was in a cushioned shell, and the crash field held my shape

like an exoskeleton. As I curved up to meet him, Bellamy
came down my throat.

Give him a taste of his own medicine!

If I hadn't been half-loaded, I'd never have done it.

A crash now was the last thing Bellamy wanted. It would
leave evidence not only on the car but on the *Drunkard's
Walk*. But space pilots crack up more cars. They can't get
used to the idea that in the atmosphere of a planet Mach
four is *fast*. He must have been doing Mach eight himself.

He pulled up too late.

I smashed into the ship's flank at a low angle. Without
the crash field I'd have been hamburger. As it was, I
blacked out instantly.

I woke in the midst of a flaming maelstrom, gripped in
a vise that wouldn't let me breathe, with agony tearing at
my hands. The car was diving out of the sky at four times
sonic speed, with its aerodynamic stability smashed to hell.
I could feel the terrific deceleration in my inner ear.

I tried to use the controls. Not that they would have
worked; the ship was obviously stone dead. But I tried it
anyway, and then the pain came. My hands had been outside the crash field, naturally; how else could I control the
car? Half the joints had been dislocated in the crash.

The ground came up, rotating. I tried to pull my hands
back, but deceleration pulled me hard against the crash
web, and the crash field held. I was embedded in glass.

I hit.

The car was on its nose in high fern grass. All the plastic
windows had become flying shards, including the windshield; they littered the car. The windshield frame was
crushed and bent. I hung from the crash web, unable to unfasten it with my crippled hands, unable to move even if I
were free.

And I watched the *Drunkard's Walk*, its fusion drive off,
floating down ahead of me on its gravity drag.

I didn't notice the anomaly then. I was dazed, and I saw
what I expected to see: a spaceship landing. Bellamy? He

didn't see it, either, but he would have if he'd looked to the side when he came down the landing ladder.

He came down the ladder with his eyes fixed on mine and Emil's sonic in his hand. He stepped out into the fern grass, walked over to the car, and peered in through the bent windshield frame.

"Come on out."

"I can't use my hands."

"So much the better." Bellamy rested the sonic on the rim of the frame and pointed it at my face. With his other hand he reached in to unfasten the crash web and pull me out by the arm. "Walk," he said. "Or be dragged."

I could walk, barely. I could keep walking because he kept prodding the small of my back with the gun.

"You've helped me, you know. You had a car crash," he said. "You and Jilson. Then some predators found you."

It sounded reasonable. I kept walking.

We were halfway to the ship when I saw it. The anomaly. I said, "Bellamy, what's holding your ship up?"

He prodded me. "Walk."

"Your gyros. That's what's holding the ship up."

He prodded me without answering. I walked. Any moment now he'd see . . .

"What the—" He'd seen it. He stared in pure amazement, and then he ran. I stuck out a foot to trip him, lost my balance, and fell on my face. Bellamy passed me without a glance.

One of the landing legs wasn't down. I'd smashed it into the hull. He hadn't seen it on the indicators, so I must have smashed the sensors, too. The odd thing was that we'd both missed it, though it was the leg facing us.

The *Drunkard's Walk* stood on two legs, wildly unbalanced, like a ballet dancer halfway through a leap. Only her gyros held her monstrous mass against gravity. Somewhere in her belly they must be spinning faster and faster . . . I could hear the whine now, high-pitched, rising . . .

Bellamy reached the ladder and started up. He'd have to use the steering jets now, and quickly. With steering jets that size, the gyros—which served more or less the same purpose—must be small, little more than an afterthought.

Now was my chance!

I struggled to my feet and staggered a few steps. Bellamy looked down, then ignored me. He'd take care of me when he had time. Where could I go? Where could I hide on this flat plain?

Some chance. I stopped walking.

Bellamy had almost reached the air lock when the ship screamed like a wounded god.

The gyros had taken too much punishment. That metal scream must have been the death agony of the mountings. Bellamy stopped. He looked down, and the ground was too far. He looked up, and there was no time. Then he turned and looked at me.

I read his mind then, though I'm no telepath.

Bey! What'll I DO?

I had no answer for him. The ship screamed, and I hit the dirt. Well, I didn't hit it; I allowed myself to collapse. I was on the way down when Bellamy looked at me, and in the next instant the *Drunkard's Walk* spun end for end, shrieking.

The nose gouged a narrow furrow in the soil, but the landing legs came down hard, dug deep, and held. Bellamy sailed high over my head, and I lost him in the sky. The ship poised, braced against her landing legs, taking spin from her dying flywheels. Then she jumped.

The landing legs acted like springs, hurling her somersaulting into the air. She landed and jumped again, screaming, tumbling, like a wounded jackrabbit trying to flee the hunter. I wanted to cry. I'd done it; I was guilty; no ship should be killed like this.

Somewhere in her belly the gyroscope flywheels were coming to rest in a tangle of torn metal.

The ship landed and rolled. Bouncing. Rolling. I watched as she receded, and finally the *Drunkard's Walk* came to rest, dead, far across the blue-green veldt.

I stood up and started walking.

I passed Bellamy on the way. If you'd like to imagine what he looked like, go right ahead.

It was nearly dark when I reached the ship.

What I saw was a ship on its side, with one landing leg up. It's hard to damage hullmetal, especially at the low subsonic speeds the *Drunkard's Walk* was making when she did all that jumping. I found the air lock and climbed in.

The lifesystem was a scrambled mess. Parts of it, the most rugged parts, were almost intact, but thin partitions between sections showed ragged, gaping holes. The flywheel must have passed here.

The autodoc was near the back. It looked intact, and I needed it badly to take the pain from my hands and put them back together. I'd as soon have stepped into a Bandersnatch's mouth. You can get the willies thinking about all the things that can go wrong with a 'doc.

The bouncing flywheel hadn't reached the control cone.

Things lighted up when I turned on the communications board. I had to manipulate switches with the heel of my hand. I turned on everything that looked like it had something to do with communications, rolled all the volume knobs to maximum between my palms, and let it go at that, making no attempt to aim a com laser, talk into anything, or tap out code. If anything was working on that board— and something was delivering power, even if the machinery to use it was damaged—then the base would get just the impression I wanted them to have. Someone was trying to communicate with broken equipment.

So I settled myself in the control cone and smoked. Using my toes was less painful than trying to hold a cigarette in my fingers. I remembered how shocked Sharrol had been the first time she saw me with a cigarette between my toes. Flatlanders are less than limber.

Eventually someone came.

I picked up the open bulb of glass that Margo had called a snifter and held it before me, watching the play of light in the red-brown fluid. It was a pleasure to use my hands.

Twelve hours ago they had been useless, swollen, and blackening—like things long dead.

"To the hero's return," said Margo. Her green eyes sparkled. She raised the snifter in a toast and drank.

"I've been in a 'doc the past twelve hours," I said. "Fill me in. Are we going to get Lloobee back?"

"Lloobee and your friend, too." Satisfaction was rich in her voice; she was almost purring. "The kidnappers settled for a contract of amnesty and antipublicity, with a penalty of ten thousand stars to the man who causes their names to be published anywhere in known space. Penalty to apply to every man, woman, and child on Gummidgy—you and me included. They insisted we list the names. Did you know there are half a million people on Gummidgy?"

"That's a big contract."

"But they never made a tenth star. They were lucky to get what they did. With their ship wrecked, they're trapped here. Lloobee and your friend should be arriving any minute."

"And Bellamy's death should satisfy Kdatlyno honor."

"Mm hm." She nodded, happy, relaxed. What an actress she could have been! How nice it would have been to play along . . .

"I didn't kill him deliberately," I said.

"You told me."

"That leaves us only one loose end."

She looked up over the snifter. "What's that?"

"Persuading Emil to leave you out of it."

She dropped the snifter. It hit the indoor grass rug and rolled under the coffee table while Margo stared at me as at a stranger. Finally she said, "You're hard to read. How long have you known?"

"Practically since your friends took Lloobee. But we weren't sure until we knew Bellamy really had him. You'd lied about his ship."

"I see." Her voice was flat, and the sparkle in her eyes was a long forgotten thing. "Emil Horne knows. Who else?"

"Just me. And Emil owes me one. Two, really."

"Well," she said. "Well." And she went to pick up the snifter. Right then, the rest of it fell into place.

"You're old."

"You're hard to fool, Bey."

"I've never seen you move like that before. It's funny; I can tell a man's age within a few decades, but I can't tell a woman's. Why don't you move like that all the time?"

She laughed. "And have everyone know I'm a crone? Not likely. So I hesitate when I move, and I knock against things occasionally, and catch my heel on rugs ... Every woman learns to do that, usually long after she's learned not to. Too much poise is a giveaway." She stood with her feet apart, hands on her hips, challenging. Now her poise was tremendous, a shocking, glowing dignity. Perhaps she had been an actress, so long ago that her most devoted admirers had died or forgotten her. "So I'm old. Well?"

"Well, now I know why you joined the kidnappers. You and Bellamy and the rest; you all think alike. No persuasion needed."

She shook her head in mock sadness. "How you simplify. Do you really think that everyone over two hundred and fifty is identical under the skull?

"Piet Lindstrom disliked the idea from the beginning, but he needed the money. He's been off boosterspice for years. Warren's loved hunting all his life. He hadn't hunted a civilized animal since the kzinti wars. Tanya was in love with Larch. She'll probably try to kill you."

"And you?"

"Larch would have gone ahead without me. Anything could have happened. So I saw to it that I was flying Lloobee's ship, and I declared myself in."

She was so damn vivid. I'd thought she was beautiful before, but now, with the little-girl mannerisms gone, she *glowed*.

I thought of the brandy.

"You loved him, too," I said.

"I'm his mother."

That jolted me to my toes. "The brandy," I said. "What was in the brandy?"

"Something I developed long ago. Hormones, hypnotics . . . a love potion. You're going to love me. Two years from now I'll abandon you like an empty beer bulb. You won't be able to live without me." Her smile was cruel and cold. "A fitting revenge."

"Finagle help me!" I hadn't drunk the brandy, of course, but what the hell . . . Then it penetrated. *Two years.* "You know about Sharrol?"

"Yes."

"I didn't drink the brandy."

"There's nothing in it but alcohol."

We grinned at each other across the length of the couch. Then the ghost was between us, and I said, "What about Bellamy?"

"Larch took his chances. He knew what he was doing."

"I can't understand that." I couldn't understand why she didn't hate me. Worse, all my questions were sure to be the wrong ones. I picked one that might be right and asked, "What *was* he doing?"

"Dying. He'd run out of things to do. He'd have taken greater and greater chances until one of them killed him. One day I'll reach the same point. Maybe I'll know it in time."

"What will you do then?"

"Don't ask me," she said with finality. I never did again.

"And what will you do now?"

"I have an idea," she said carefully, watching me. "Sharrol Janss is bearing children on Earth for you to raise. I can't have children myself. My ovaries have long since run out of ova. But is there any reason why we shouldn't spend two years together?"

"I can't think of any. But what would you get out of it?"

"I've never known a crashlander."

"And you're curious."

"Yes. Don't be offended."

"I'm not. Your flattery has turned my head." After all, there were two years to fill, and Margo was lovely.

I was alone on Jinx two years later, waiting for the next ship to Earth. As it turned out, Lloobee's latest works were there, too, on loan to the Institute of Knowledge. To the Institute I went, to see what my protégé had produced.

Seeing them was a shock.

That was the first shock: that they should make sense when seen. Touch sculpture is to be felt: it has no meaning otherwise. But these were busts and statuettes. Someone had even advised Lloobee on color.

I looked closer.

First: a group of human statuettes, some seated, some standing, all staring with great intensity at a flat pane of clear glass.

Second: a pair of heads. Human, humane, handsome, noble as all hell, but child's play to recognize nonetheless. I touched them, and they felt like warm human faces. My face and Emil's.

Third and last: a group of four, a woman and three men. They showed a definite kinship with the ape and a second admixture of what must have been demon blood. Yet they were quite recognizable. Three felt like human faces, though somehow . . . repellent. But the fourth felt horribly dead.

The kidnappers had neglected to include Lloobee in their contract. And Lloobee has been talking to newsmen, telling them all about how his latest works had come to be.

✳

GHOST: FIVE

"Can I ghost that story for you?" Ander asked. "Might be money in it."

"Old news. Everyone's seen Lloobee's version," I said, thinking that my story, even edited, could call too much attention to Margo. Lloobee hadn't known of Margo's involvement in the kidnapping, and I hadn't told Ander. I watched him, wondering if he knew.

"I've never turned on to a . . . mature woman," he said. "What's it like? Why did you break up?"

I shrugged. "It was supposed to be temporary. It stayed that way . . . didn't have to, just did. Ander, it boggles me a little, too, Margo contracting for a two-year date the way I used to angle for a hot weekend. Aliens scare you; do you ever worry about elderly humans?"

"No."

"They've learned too much. They don't like change. If they could stop civilization in its tracks, they would."

He didn't exactly think that over; he disliked the taste, so he spit it out. "I always figure, if you can't lick 'em, join 'em. So I've decided to get older. Beowulf, General Products gave you a number—"

"I take it as being for my use only."

His eyes narrowed, but he let it slide. "But you could use it if we needed to know something."

"I might ask a properly phrased question. Ander Smittarasheed, I am out of the aliens business."

Again he let it slide. "After Margo, where?"

"Earth. I had a hell of a time getting back."

"Did you go back for Sharrol Janss?"

I stared. "Of *course*, for Sharrol and the children."

"Carlos Wu's children!"

I stood up, knowing it was a mistake, and so what? "I'm leaving. If you want to apologize, my phone is—"

"Beowulf Shaeffer, I just can't see you losing your head over a woman."

I lost my breath. It was as if he'd punched me in the belly. I sat down, but my vision was still graying. Ander watched in amazement. When my eyes would focus again, he asked, "What was that about?"

"Not now." I couldn't breathe.

He sighed. He tapped at the menu board. A squeezebulb popped up, and he handed it across. I found my hand massaging my throat, removed it, took the bulb, and drank. Brandy and soda. Just right.

He watched me drink again. "Stet. Sigmund told me how you got back to Sol system."

"He might possibly have left something out."

"Go ahead."

THE BORDERLAND OF SOL

Three months on Jinx, marooned.

I played tourist for the first couple of months. I never saw the high-pressure regions around the ocean because the only way down would have been with a safari of hunting tanks. But I traveled the habitable lands on either side of the sea, the East Band civilized, the West Band a developing frontier. I wandered the East End in a vacuum suit, toured the distilleries and other vacuum industries, and stared up into the orange vastness of Primary, Jinx's big twin brother.

I spent most of the second month between the Institute of Knowledge and the Camelot Hotel. Tourism had palled.

For me that's unusual. I'm a born tourist. But—

Jinx's one point seven eight gravities put an unreasonable restriction on elegance and ingenuity in architectural design. The buildings in the habitable bands all look alike: squat and massive.

The East and West Ends, the vacuum regions, aren't that different from any industrialized moon. I never developed much of an interest in touring factories.

As for the ocean shorelines, the only vehicles that go there go to hunt Bandersnatchi. The Bandersnatchi are freaks: enormous, intelligent white slugs the size of mountains. They hunt the tanks. There are rigid restrictions to the equipment the tanks can carry, covenants established between men and Bandersnatchi, so that the Bandersnatchi win about forty percent of the duels. I wanted no part of that.

And all my touring had to be done in three times the gravity of my homeworld.

I spent the third month in Sirius Mater, and most of that in the Camelot Hotel, which has gravity generators in most of the rooms. When I went out, I rode a floating contour couch. I passed like an invalid among the Jinxians, who were amused. Or was that my imagination?

I was in a hall of the Institute of Knowledge when I came on Carlos Wu running his fingertips over a Kdatlyno touch sculpture.

A dark, slender man with narrow shoulders and straight black hair, Carlos was lithe as a monkey in any normal gravity, but on Jinx he used a travel couch exactly like mine. He studied the busts with his head tilted to one side. And I studied the familiar back, sure it couldn't be him.

"Carlos, aren't you supposed to be on Earth?"

He jumped. But when the couch spun around, he was grinning. "Bey! I might say the same for you."

I admitted it. "I was headed for Earth, but when all those ships started disappearing around Sol system, the captain changed his mind and steered for Sirius. Nothing any of the passengers could do about it. What about you? How are Sharrol and the kids?"

"Sharrol's fine, the kids are fine, and they're all waiting for you to come home." His fingers were still trailing over the Lloobee touch sculpture called *Heroes*, feeling the warm, fleshy textures. *Heroes* was a most unusual touch sculpture; there were visual as well as textural effects. Carlos studied the two human busts, then said, "That's *your* face, isn't it?"

"Yah."

"Not that you ever looked that good in your life. How did a Kdatlyno come to pick Beowulf Shaeffer as a classic hero? Was it your name? And who's the other guy?"

"I'll tell you about it sometime. Carlos, what are you doing *here*?"

"I . . . left Earth a couple of weeks after Louis was

born." He was embarrassed. Why? "I haven't been off Earth in ten years. I needed the break."

But he'd left just before I was supposed to get home. And ... hadn't someone once said that Carlos Wu had a touch of the flatland phobia? I began to understand what was wrong. "Carlos, you did Sharrol and me a valuable favor."

He laughed without looking at me. "Men have killed other men for such favors. I thought it was ... tactful ... to be gone when you came home."

Now I knew. Carlos was here because the Fertility Board on Earth would not favor me with a parenthood license.

You can't really blame the Board for using any excuse at all to reduce the number of producing parents. I am an albino. Sharrol and I wanted each other, but we both wanted children, and Sharrol can't leave Earth. She has the flatland phobia, the fear of strange air and altered days and changed gravity and black sky beneath her feet.

The only solution we'd found had been to ask a good friend to help.

Carlos Wu is a registered genius with an incredible resistance to disease and injury. He carries an unlimited parenthood license, one of sixty-odd among Earth's eighteen billion people. He gets similar offers every week ... but he is a good friend, and he'd agreed. In the last two years Sharrol and Carlos had had two children, who were now waiting on Earth for me to become their father.

I felt only gratitude for what he'd done for us. "I forgive you your odd ideas on tact," I said magnanimously. "Now. As long as we're stuck on Jinx, may I show you around? I've met some interesting people."

"You always do." He hesitated, then, "I'm not actually stuck on Jinx. I've been offered a ride home. I may be able to get you in on it."

"Oh, really? I didn't think there were any ships going to Sol system these days. Or leaving."

"This ship belongs to a government man. Ever heard of a Sigmund Ausfaller?"

"That sounds vaguely ... Wait! Stop! The last time I saw Sigmund Ausfaller, he had just put a bomb aboard my ship!"

Carlos blinked at me. "You're kidding."

"I'm not."

"Sigmund Ausfaller is in the Bureau of Alien Affairs. Bombing spacecraft isn't one of his functions."

"Maybe he was off duty," I said viciously.

"Well, it doesn't really sound like you'd want to share a spacecraft cabin with him. Maybe—"

But I'd thought of something else, and now there just wasn't any way out of it. "No, let's meet him. Where do we find him?"

"The bar of the Camelot," said Carlos.

Reclining luxuriously on our travel couches, we slid on air cushions through Sirius Mater. The orange trees that lined the walks were foreshortened by gravity; their trunks were thick cones, and the oranges on the branches were not much bigger than Ping-Pong balls.

Their world had altered them, even as our worlds have altered you and me. And underground civilization and point six gravities have made of me a pale stick figure of a man, tall and attenuated. The Jinxians we passed were short and wide, designed like bricks, men and women both. Among them the occasional offworlder seemed as shockingly different as a Kdatlyno or a Pierson's puppeteer.

And so we came to the Camelot.

The Camelot is a low, two-story structure that sprawls like a cubistic octopus across several acres of downtown Sirius Mater. Most offworlders stay here for the gravity control in the rooms and corridors and for access to the Institute of Knowledge, the finest museum and research complex in human space.

The Camelot Bar carries one Earth gravity throughout. We left our travel couches in the vestibule and walked in like men. Jinxians were walking in like bouncing rubber bricks, with big happy grins on their wide faces. Jinxians love low gravity. A good many migrate to other worlds.

We spotted Ausfaller easily: a rounded, moon-faced flatlander with thick, dark wavy hair and a thin black mustache. He stood as we approached. "Beowulf Shaeffer!" he beamed. "How good to see you again! I believe it has been eight years or thereabouts. How have you been?"

"I lived," I told him.

Carlos rubbed his hands together briskly. "Sigmund! Why did you bomb Bey's ship?"

Ausfaller blinked in surprise. "Did he tell you it was his ship? It wasn't. He was thinking of stealing it. I reasoned that he would not steal a ship with a hidden time bomb aboard."

"But how did you come into it?" Carlos slid into the booth beside him. "You're not police. You're in the Extremely Foreign Relations Bureau."

"The ship belonged to General Products Corporation, which is owned by Pierson's puppeteers, not human beings."

Carlos turned on me. "Bey! Shame on you."

"Damn it! They were trying to blackmail me into a suicide mission! And Ausfaller let them get away with it! And that's the least convincing exhibition of tact I've ever seen!"

"Good thing they soundproof these booths," said Carlos. "Let's order."

Soundproofing field or not, people were staring. I sat down. When our drinks came, I drank deeply. Why had I mentioned the bomb at all?

Ausfaller was saying, "Well, Carlos, have you changed your mind about coming with me?"

"Yes, if I can take a friend."

Ausfaller frowned and looked at me. "You wish to reach Earth, too?"

I'd made up my mind. "I don't think so. In fact, I'd like to talk you out of taking Carlos."

Carlos said, "Hey!"

I overrode him. "Ausfaller, do you know who Carlos *is*? He had an unlimited parenthood license at the age of eighteen. Eighteen! I don't mind you risking your own life; in fact, I love the idea. But his?"

"It's not that big a risk!" Carlos snapped.

"Yah? What has Ausfaller got that eight other ships didn't have?"

"Two things," Ausfaller said patiently. "One is that we will be incoming. Six of the eight ships that vanished were *leaving* Sol system. If there are pirates around Sol, they must find it much easier to locate an outgoing ship."

"They caught two incoming. Two ships, fifty crew members and passengers, gone. Poof!"

"They would not take me so easily," Ausfaller boasted. "The *Hobo Kelly* is deceptive. It seems to be a cargo and passenger ship, but it is a warship, armed and capable of thirty gees acceleration. In normal space we can run from anything we can't fight. We are assuming pirates, are we not? Pirates would insist on robbing a ship before they destroy it."

I was intrigued. "Why? Why a disguised warship? Are you *hoping* you'll be attacked?"

"If there are actually pirates, yes, I hope to be attacked. But not when entering Sol system. We plan a substitution. A quite ordinary cargo craft will land on Earth, take on cargo of some value, and depart for Wunderland on a straight-line course. My ship will replace it before it has passed through the asteroids. So you see, there is no risk of losing Mr. Wu's precious genes."

Palms flat to the table, arms straight, Carlos stood looming over us. "Diffidently I raise the point that they are my futzy genes and I'll do what I futzy please with them! Bey, I've already had my share of children, and yours, too!"

"Peace, Carlos. I didn't mean to step on any of your inalienable rights." I turned to Ausfaller. "I still don't see why these disappearing ships should interest the Extremely Foreign Relations Bureau."

"There were alien passengers aboard some of the ships."

"Oh."

"And we have wondered if the pirates themselves are aliens. Certainly they have a technique not known to humanity. Of six outgoing ships, five vanished after reporting that they were about to enter hyperdrive."

I whistled. "They can precipitate a ship out of hyperdrive? That's impossible. Isn't it? Carlos?"

Carlos's mouth twisted. "Not if it's being done. But I don't understand the principle. If the ships were just disappearing, that'd be different. Any ship does that if it goes too deep into a gravity well on hyperdrive."

"Then ... maybe it isn't pirates at all. Carlos, could there be living beings in hyperspace, actually eating the ships?"

"For all of me, there could. I don't know everything, Bey, contrary to popular opinion." But after a minute he shook his head. "I don't buy it. I might buy an uncharted mass on the fringes of Sol system. Ships that came too near in hyperdrive would disappear."

"No," said Ausfaller. "No single mass could have caused all of the disappearances. Charter or not, a planet is bounded by gravity and inertia. We ran computer simulations. It would have taken at least three large masses, all unknown, all moving into heavy trade routes simultaneously."

"How large? Mars size or better?"

"So you have been thinking about this, too."

Carlos smiled. "Yah. It may sound impossible, but it isn't. It's only improbable. There are unbelievable amounts of garbage out there beyond Neptune. Four known planets and endless chunks of ice and stone and nickel-iron."

"Still, it is most improbable."

Carlos nodded. A silence fell.

I was still thinking about monsters in hyperspace. The lovely thing about that hypothesis was that you couldn't even estimate a probability. We knew too little.

Humanity has been using hyperdrive for almost four hundred years now. Few ships have disappeared in that time, except during wars. Now eight ships in ten months, all around Sol system.

Suppose one hyperspace beast had discovered ships in this region, say during one of the Man-Kzin Wars? He'd gone to get his friends. Now they were preying around Sol system. The flow of ships around Sol is greater than that around any three colony stars. But if more monsters came, they'd surely have to move on to the other colonies.

I couldn't imagine a defense against such things. We might have to give up interstellar travel.

Ausfaller said, "I would be glad if you would change your mind and come with us, Mr. Shaeffer."

"Um? Are you sure you want me on the same ship with you?"

"Oh, emphatically! How else may I be sure that you have not hidden a bomb aboard?" Ausfaller laughed. "Also, we can use a qualified pilot. Finally, I would like the chance to pick your brain, Beowulf Shaeffer. You have an odd facility for doing my job for me."

"What do you mean by that?"

"General Products used blackmail in persuading you to do a close orbit around a neutron star. You learned something about their homeworld—we still do not know what it was—and blackmailed them back. We know that blackmail contracts are a normal part of puppeteer business practice. You earned their respect. You have dealt with them since. You have dealt also with Outsiders without friction. But it was your handling of the Lloobee kidnapping that I found impressive."

Carlos was sitting at attention. I hadn't had a chance to tell him about that one yet. I grinned and said, "I'm proud of that myself."

"Well, you should be. You did more than retrieve known space's top Kdatlyno touch sculptor: you did it with honor, killing one of their number and leaving Lloobee free to pursue the others with publicity. Otherwise the Kdatlyno would have been annoyed."

Helping Sigmund Ausfaller had been the farthest thing

from my thoughts for these past eight years, yet suddenly I felt damn good. Maybe it was the way Carlos was listening. It takes a lot to impress Carlos Wu.

Carlos said, "If you thought it was pirates, you'd come along, wouldn't you, Bey? After all, they probably can't *find* incoming ships."

"Sure."

"And you don't really believe in hyperspace monsters."

I hedged. "Not if I hear a better explanation. The thing is, I'm not sure I believe in supertechnological pirates, either. What about those wandering masses?"

Carlos pursed his lips, said, "All right. The solar system has a good number of planets—at least a dozen so far discovered, four of them outside the major singularity around Sol."

"And not including Pluto?"

"No, we think of Pluto as a loose moon of Neptune. It runs *Neptune, Persephone, Caïna, Antenora, Ptolemea,* in order of distance from the sun. And the orbits aren't flat to the plane of the system. Persephone is tilted at 120 degrees to the system and retrograde. If they find another planet out there, they'll call it *Judecca*."

"Why?"

"Hell. The four innermost divisions of Dante's hell. They form a great ice plain with sinners frozen into it."

"Stick to the point," said Ausfaller.

"Start with the cometary halo," Carlos told me. "It's very thin: about one comet per spherical volume of the Earth's orbit. Mass is denser going inward: a few planets, some inner comets, some chunks of ice and rock, all in skewed orbits and still spread pretty thin. Inside Neptune there are lots of planets and asteroids and more flattening of orbits to conform with Sol's rotation. Outside Neptune space is vast and empty. There *could* be uncharted planets. Singularities to swallow ships."

Ausfaller was indignant. "But for three to move into main trade lanes simultaneously?"

"It's not impossible, Sigmund."

"The probability—"

"Infinitesimal, right. Bey, it's damn near impossible. Any sane man would assume pirates."

It had been a long time since I had seen Sharrol. I was sorely tempted. "Ausfaller, have you traced the sale of any of the loot? Have you gotten any ransom notes?" *Convince me!*

Ausfaller threw back his head and laughed.

"What's funny?"

"We have hundreds of ransom notes. Any mental deficient can write a ransom note, and these disappearances have had a good deal of publicity. The demands were all fakes. I wish one or another had been genuine. A son of the Patriarch of Kzin was aboard *Wayfarer* when she disappeared. As for loot—hmm. There has been a fall in the black market prices of boosterspice and gem woods. Otherwise—" He shrugged. "There has been no sign of the Barr originals or the Midas Rock or any of the more conspicuous treasures aboard the missing ships."

"Then you don't know one way or another."

"No. Will you go with us?"

"I haven't decided yet. When are you leaving?"

They'd be taking off tomorrow morning from the East End. That gave me time to make up my mind.

After dinner I went back to my room, feeling depressed. Carlos was going, that was clear enough. Hardly my fault . . . but he was here on Jinx because he'd done me and Sharrol a large favor. If he was killed going home . . .

A tape from Sharrol was waiting in my room. There were pictures of the children, Tanya and Louis, and shots of the apartment she'd found us in the Twin Peaks arcology, and much more.

I ran through it three times. Then I called Ausfaller's room. It had been just too futzy long.

I circled Jinx once on the way out. I've always done that, even back when I was flying for Nakamura Lines, and no passenger has ever objected.

Jinx is the close moon of a gas giant planet more massive then Jupiter and smaller than Jupiter because its core has been compressed to degenerate matter. A billion years ago Jinx and Primary were even closer, before tidal drag moved them apart. This same tidal force had earlier locked Jinx's rotation to Primary and forced the moon into an egg shape, a prolate spheroid. When the moon moved outward, its shape became more nearly spherical, but the cold rock surface resisted change.

That is why the ocean of Jinx rings its waist, beneath an atmosphere too compressed and too hot to breathe, whereas the points nearest to and farthest from Primary, the East and West Ends, actually rise out of the atmosphere.

From space Jinx looks like God's Own Easter Egg: the Ends bone white tinged with yellow, then the brighter glare from rings of glittering ice fields at the limits of the atmosphere, then the varying blues of an Earthlike world, increasingly overlaid with the white frosting of cloud as the eyes move inward, until the waist of the planet/moon is girdled with pure white. The ocean never shows at all.

I took us once around and out.

Sirius has its own share of floating miscellaneous matter cluttering the path to interstellar space. I stayed at the controls for most of five days for that reason and because I wanted to get the feel of an unfamiliar ship.

Hobo Kelly was a belly-landing job, three hundred feet long, of triangular cross section. Beneath an uptilted, forward-thrusting nose were big clamshell doors for cargo. She had adequate belly jets, and a much larger fusion motor at the tail, and a line of windows indicating cabins. Certainly she looked harmless enough, and certainly there was deception involved. The cabin should have held forty or fifty, but there was room only for four. The rest of what should have been cabin space was only windows with holograph projections in them.

The drive ran sure and smooth up to a maximum at ten gravities: not a lot for a ship designed to haul massive cargo. The cabin gravity held without putting out more than a fraction of its power. When Jinx and Primary were invisible against the stars, when Sirius was so distant that I could look directly at it, I turned to the hidden control panel Ausfaller had unlocked for me. Ausfaller woke up, found me doing that, and began showing me which did what.

He had a big X-ray laser and some smaller laser cannon set for different frequencies. He had four self-guided fusion bombs. He had a telescope so good that the ostensible ship's telescope was only a finder for it. He had deep radar.

And none of it showed beyond the discolored hull.

Ausfaller was armed for Bandersnatchi. I felt mixed emotions. It seemed we could fight anything and run from it, too. But what kind of enemy was he expecting?

All through those four weeks in hyperdrive, while we drove through the Blind Spot at three days to the light-year, the topic of the ship eaters reared its disturbing head.

Oh, we spoke of other things: of music and art and of the latest techniques in animation, the computer programs that let you make your own holo flicks almost for lunch money. We told stories. I told Carlos why the Kdatlyno Lloobee had made busts of me and Emil Horne. I spoke of the only time the Pierson's puppeteers had ever paid off the guarantee on a General Products hull, after the supposedly indestructible hull had been destroyed by antimatter. Ausfaller had some good ones . . . a lot more stories than he was allowed to tell, I gathered, from the way he had to search his memory every time.

But we kept coming back to the ship eaters.

"It boils down to three possibilities," I decided. "Kzinti, puppeteers, and humans."

Carlos guffawed. "Puppeteers? Puppeteers wouldn't have the guts!"

"I threw them in because they might have some interest in manipulating the interstellar stock market. Look, our hypothetical pirates have set up an embargo, cutting Sol system off from the outside world. The puppeteers have the capital to take advantage of what that does to the market. And they need money. For their migration."

"The puppeteers are philosophical cowards."

"That's right. They wouldn't risk robbing the ships or coming anywhere near them. Suppose they can make them disappear from a distance?"

Carlos wasn't laughing now. "That's easier than dropping them out of hyperspace to rob them. It wouldn't take more than a great big gravity generator . . . and we've never known the limits of puppeteer technology."

Ausfaller asked, "You think this is possible?"

"Just barely. The same goes for the kzinti. The kzinti are ferocious enough. Trouble is, if we ever learned they were preying on our ships, we'd raise pluperfect hell. The kzinti know that, and they know we can beat them. Took them long enough, but they learned."

"So you think it's humans," said Carlos.

"Yah. If it's pirates."

The piracy theory still looked shaky. Spectrum telescopes had not even found concentrations of ship's metals in the space where they have vanished. Would pirates steal the whole ship? If the hyperdrive motor was still intact after the attack, the rifled ship could be launched into infinity, but could pirates count on that happening eight times out of eight?

And none of the missing ships had called for help via hyperwave.

I'd never believed pirates. Space pirates have existed, but they died without successors. Intercepting a spacecraft was too difficult. They couldn't make it pay.

Ships fly themselves in hyperdrive. All a pilot need do is watch for green radial lines in the mass sensor. But he has to do that frequently, because the mass sensor is a psionic device; it must be watched by a mind, not another machine.

As the narrow green line that marked Sol grew longer, I became abnormally conscious of the debris around Sol system. I spent the last twelve hours of the flight at the controls, chain-smoking with my feet. I should add that I do that normally when I want both hands free, but now I did it to annoy Ausfaller. I'd seen the way his eyes bugged the first time he saw me take a drag from a cigarette between my toes. Flatlanders are less than limber.

Carlos and Ausfaller shared the control room with me as we penetrated Sol's cometary halo. They were relieved to be nearing the end of a long trip. I was nervous. "Carlos, just how large a mass would it take to make us disappear?"

"Planet size, Mars and up. Beyond that it depends on how close you get and how dense it is. If it's dense enough, it can be less massive and still flip you out of the universe. But you'd see it in the mass sensor."

"Only for an instant . . . and not then, if it's turned off. What if someone turned on a giant gravity generator as we went past?"

"For what? They couldn't rob the ship. Where's their profit?"

"Stocks."

But Ausfaller was shaking his head. "The expense of such an operation would be enormous. No group of pirates would have enough additional capital on hand to make it worthwhile. Of the puppeteers I might believe it."

Hell, he was right. No human that wealthy would need to turn pirate.

The long green line marking Sol was almost touching the surface of the mass sensor. I said, "Breakout in ten minutes."

And the ship lurched savagely.

"Strap down!" I yelled, and glanced at the hyperdrive monitors. The motor was drawing no power, and the rest of the dials were going bananas.

I activated the windows. I'd kept them turned off in hyperspace lest my flatlander passengers go mad watching the Blind Spot. The screens came on, and I saw stars. We were in normal space.

"Futz! They got us anyway." Carlos sounded neither frightened nor angry, but awed.

As I raised the hidden panel Ausfaller cried, "Wait!" I

ignored him. I threw the red switch, and *Hobo Kelly* lurched again as her belly blew off.

Ausfaller began cursing in some dead flatlander language.

Now two-thirds of *Hobo Kelly* receded, slowly turning. What was left must show as what she was: a No. 2 General Products hull, puppeteer-built, a slender transparent spear three hundred feet long and twenty feet wide, with instruments of war clustered along what was now her belly. Screens that had been blank came to life. And I lit the main drive and ran it up to full power.

Ausfaller spoke in rage and venom. "Shaeffer, you idiot, you coward! We run without knowing what we run from. Now they know exactly what we are. What chance that they will follow us now? This ship was built for a specific purpose, and you have ruined it!"

"I've freed your special instruments," I pointed out. "Why don't you see what you can find?" Meanwhile I could get us the futz out of here.

Ausfaller became very busy. I watched what he was getting on screens at my side of the control panel. Was anything chasing us? They'd find us hard to catch and harder to digest. They could hardly have been expecting a General Products hull. Since the puppeteers stopped making them, the price of used GP hulls has gone out of sight.

There *were* ships out there. Ausfaller got a close-up of them: three space tugs of the Belter type, shaped like thick saucers, equipped with oversized drives and powerful electromagnetic generators. Belters use them to tug nickel-iron asteroids to where somebody wants the ore. With those heavy drives they could probably catch us, but would they have adequate cabin gravity?

They weren't trying. They seemed to be neither following nor fleeing. And they looked harmless enough.

But Ausfaller was doing a job on them with his other instruments. I approved. *Hobo Kelly* had looked peaceful enough a moment ago. Now her belly bristled with weaponry. The tugs could be equally deceptive.

From behind me Carlos asked, "Bey? What happened?"

"How the futz would I know?"

"What do the instruments show?"

He must mean the hyperdrive complex. A couple of the indicators had gone wild; five more were dead. I said so. "And the drive's drawing no power at all. I've never heard of anything like this. Carlos, it's *still* theoretically impossible."

"I'm . . . not so sure of that. I want to look at the drive."

"The access tubes don't have cabin gravity."

Ausfaller had abandoned the receding tugs. He'd found what looked to be a large comet, a ball of frozen gases a good distance to the side. I watched as he ran the deep radar over it. No fleet of robber ships lurked behind it.

I asked, "Did you deep-radar the tugs?"

"Of course. We can examine the tapes in detail later. I saw nothing. And nothing has attacked us since we left hyperspace."

I'd been driving us in a random direction. Now I turned us toward Sol, the brightest star in the heavens. Those lost ten minutes in hyperspace would add about three days to our voyage.

"If there was an enemy, you frightened him away. Shaeffer, this mission and this ship have cost my department an enormous sum, and we have learned nothing at all."

"Not quite nothing," said Carlos. "I still want to see the hyperdrive motor. Bey, would you run us down to one gee?"

"Yah. But . . . miracles make me nervous, Carlos."

"Join the club."

We crawled along an access tube just a little bigger than a big man's shoulders, between the hyperdrive motor housing and the surrounding fuel tankage. Carlos reached an inspection window. He looked in. He started to laugh.

I inquired as to what was so futzy funny.

Still chortling, Carlos moved on. I crawled after him and looked in.

There was no hyperdrive motor in the hyperdrive motor housing.

I went in through a repair hatch and stood in the cylindrical housing, looking about me. Nothing. Not even an exit hole. The superconducting cables and the mounts for the motor had been sheared so cleanly that the cut ends looked like little mirrors.

Ausfaller insisted on seeing for himself. Carlos and I waited in the control room. For a while Carlos kept bursting into fits of giggles. Then he got a dreamy, faraway look that was even more annoying.

I wondered what was going on in his head and reached the uncomfortable conclusion that I could never know. Some years ago I took IQ tests, hoping to get a parenthood license that way. I am not a genius.

I knew only that Carlos had thought of something I hadn't, and he wasn't telling, and I was too proud to ask.

Ausfaller had no pride. He came back looking like he'd seen a ghost. "Gone! Where could it go? How could it happen?"

"That I can answer," Carlos said happily. "It takes an extremely high gravity gradient. The motor hit that, wrapped space around itself, and took off at some higher level of hyperdrive, one we can't reach. By now it could be well on its way to the edge of the universe."

I said, "You're sure, huh? An hour ago there wasn't a theory to cover any of this."

"Well, I'm sure our motor's gone. Beyond that it gets a little hazy. But this is one well-established model of what happens when a ship hits a singularity. At a lower gravity gradient the motor would take the whole ship with it, then strew atoms of the ship along its path till there was nothing left but the hyperdrive field itself."

"Ugh."

Now Carlos burned with the love of an idea. "Sigmund,

I want to use your hyperwave. I could still be wrong, but there are things we can check."

"If we are still within the singularity of some mass, the hyperwave will destroy itself."

"Yah. I think it's worth the risk."

We'd dropped out, or been knocked out, ten minutes short of the singularity around Sol. That added up to sixteen light-hours of normal space, plus almost five light-hours from the edge of the singularity inward to Earth. Fortunately, hyperwave is instantaneous, and every civilized system keeps a hyperwave relay station just outside the singularity. Southworth Station would relay our message inward by laser, get the return message the same way, and pass it on to us ten hours later.

We turned on the hyperwave, and nothing exploded.

Ausfaller made his own call first, to Ceres, to get the registry of the tugs we'd spotted. Afterward Carlos called Elephant's computer setup in New York, using a code number Elephant doesn't give to many people. "I'll pay him back later. Maybe with a story to go with it," he gloated.

I listened as Carlos outlined his needs. He wanted full records on a meteorite that had touched down in Tunguska, Siberia, USSR, Earth, in 1908 A.D. He wanted a reprise on three models of the origin of the universe or lack of same: the big bang, the cyclic universe, and the steady state universe. He wanted data on collapsars. He wanted names, career outlines, and addresses for the best known students of gravitational phenomena in Sol system. He was smiling when he clicked off.

I said, "You got me. I haven't the remotest idea what you're after."

Still smiling, Carlos got up and went to his cabin to catch some sleep.

I turned off the main thrust motor entirely. When we were deep in Sol system, we could decelerate at thirty gravities. Meanwhile we were carrying a hefty velocity picked up on our way out of Sirius system.

Ausfaller stayed in the control room. Maybe his motive was the same as mine. No police ships out here. We could still be attacked.

He spent the time going through his pictures of the three mining tugs. We didn't talk, but I watched.

The tugs seemed ordinary enough. Telescopic photos showed no suspicious breaks in the hulls, no hatches for guns. In the deep-radar scan they showed like ghosts: we could pick out the massive force-field rings, the hollow, equally massive drive tubes, the lesser densities of fuel tank and life-support system. There were no gaps or shadows that shouldn't have been there.

By and by Ausfaller said, "Do you know what *Hobo Kelly* was worth?"

I said I could make a close estimate.

"It was worth my career. I thought to destroy a pirate fleet with *Hobo Kelly*. But my pilot fled. Fled! What have I now, to show for my expensive Trojan horse?"

I suppressed the obvious answer, along with the plea that my first responsibility was Carlos's life. Ausfaller wouldn't buy that. Instead, "Carlos has something. I know him. He knows how it happened."

"Can you get it out of him?"

"I don't know." I could put it to Carlos that we'd be safer if we knew what was out to get us. But Carlos was a flatlander. It would color his attitudes.

"So," said Ausfaller. "We have only the unavailable knowledge in Carlos's skull."

A weapon beyond human technology had knocked me out of hyperspace. I'd run. Of *course* I'd run. Staying in the neighborhood would have been insane, said I to myself, said I. But, unreasonably, I still felt bad about it.

To Ausfaller I said, "What about the mining tugs? I can't understand what they're doing out here. In the Belt they use them to move nickel-iron asteroids to industrial sites."

"It is the same here. Most of what they find is useless—stony masses or balls of ice—but what little metal there is, is valuable. They must have it for building."

"For building what? What kind of people would live here? You might as well set up shop in interstellar space!"

"Precisely. There are no tourists, but there are research groups here where space is flat and empty and temperatures are near absolute zero. I know that the Quicksilver Group was established here to study hyperspace phenomena. We do not understand hyperspace, even yet. Remember that we did not invent the hyperdrive; we bought it from an alien race. Then there is a gene-tailoring laboratory trying to develop a kind of tree that will grow on comets."

"You're kidding."

"But they are serious. A photosynthetic plant to use the chemicals present in all comets . . . it would be very valuable. The whole cometary halo could be seeded with oxygen-producing plants—" Ausfaller stopped abruptly, then, "Never mind. But all these groups need building materials. It is cheaper to build out here than to ship everything from Earth or the Belt. The presence of tugs is not suspicious."

"But there was nothing else around us. Nothing at all."

Ausfaller nodded.

When Carlos came to join us many hours later, blinking sleep out of his eyes, I asked him, "Carlos, could the tugs have had anything to do with your theory?"

"I don't see how. I've got half an idea, and half an hour from now I could look like a half-wit. The theory I want isn't even in fashion anymore. Now that we know what the quasars are, everyone seems to like the steady state hypothesis. You know how that works: the tension in completely empty space produces more hydrogen atoms, forever. The universe has no beginning and no end." He looked stubborn. "But if I'm right, then I know where the ships went to after being robbed. That's more than anyone else knows."

Ausfaller jumped on him. "Where are they? Are the passengers alive?"

"I'm sorry, Sigmund. They're all dead. There won't even be bodies to bury."

"What is it? What are we fighting?"

"A gravitational effect. A sharp warping of space. A planet wouldn't do that, and a battery of cabin gravity generators wouldn't do it; they couldn't produce that sharply bounded a field."

"A collapsar," Ausfaller suggested.

Carlos grinned at him. "That would do it, but there are other problems. A collapsar can't even form at less than around five solar masses. You'd think someone would have noticed something that big, this close to Sol."

"Then *what*?"

Carlos shook his head. We would wait.

The relay from Southworth Station gave us registration for three space tugs, used and of varying ages, all three purchased two years ago from IntraBelt Mining by the Sixth Congregational Church of Rodney.

"Rodney?"

But Carlos and Ausfaller were both chortling. "Belters do that sometimes," Carlos told me. "It's a way of saying it's nobody's business who's buying the ships."

"That's pretty funny, all right, but we still don't know who owns them."

"They may be honest Belters. They may not."

Hard on the heels of the first call came the data Carlos had asked for, playing directly into the shipboard computer. Carlos called up a list of names and phone numbers: Sol system's preeminent students of gravity and its effects, listed in alphabetical order.

An address caught my attention:

Julian Forward, #1192326 Southworth Station.

A hyperwave relay tag. He was out *here*, somewhere in the enormous gap between Neptune's orbit and the cometary belt, out here where the hyperwave relay could function. I looked for more Southworth Station numbers. They were there:

Launcelot Starkey, #1844719 Southworth Station.

Jill Luciano, #1844719 Southworth Station.

Mariana Wilton, #1844719 Southworth Station.

"These people," said Ausfaller. "You wish to discuss your theory with one of them?"

"That's right. Sigmund, isn't 1844719 the tag for the Quicksilver Group?"

"I think so. I also think that they are not within our reach now that our hyperdrive is gone. The Quicksilver Group was established in distant orbit around Antenora, which is now on the other side of the sun. Carlos, has it occurred to you that one of these people may have built the ship-eating device?"

"What? . . . You're right. It would take someone who knew something about gravity. But I'd say the Quicksilver Group was beyond suspicion. With upwards of ten thousand people at work, how could anyone hide anything?"

"What about this Julian Forward?"

"Forward. Yah. I've always wanted to meet him."

"You know of him? Who is he?"

"He used to be with the Institute of Knowledge on Jinx. I haven't heard of him in years. He did some work on the gravity waves from the galactic core . . . work that turned out to be wrong. Sigmund, let's give him a call."

"And ask him what?"

"Why . . . ?" Then Carlos remembered the situation. "Oh. You think he might— Yah."

"How well do you know this man?"

"I know him by reputation. He's quite famous. I don't see how such a man could go in for mass murder."

"Earlier you said that we were looking for a man skilled in the study of gravitational phenomena."

"Granted."

Ausfaller sucked at his lower lip. Then, "Perhaps we can do no more than talk to him. He could be on the other side of the sun and still head a pirate fleet."

"No. That he could not."

"Think again," said Ausfaller. "We are outside the singularity of Sol. A pirate fleet would surely include hyperdrive ships."

"If Julian Forward is the ship eater, he'll have to be nearby. The, uh, device won't move in hyperspace."

I said, "Carlos, what we don't know can kill us. Will you quit playing games." But he was smiling, shaking his head. Futz. "All right, we can still check on Forward. Call him up and ask where he is! Is he likely to know you by reputation?"

"Sure. I'm famous, too."

"Okay. If he's close enough, we might even beg him for a ride home. The way things stand we'll be at the mercy of any hyperdrive ship for as long as we're out here."

"I hope we are attacked," said Ausfaller. "We can outfight—"

"But we can't outrun. They can dodge; we can't."

"Peace, you two. First things first." Carlos sat down at the hyperwave controls and tapped out a number.

Suddenly Ausfaller said, "Can you contrive to keep my name out of this exchange? If necessary you can be the ship's owner."

Carlos looked around in surprise. Before he could answer, the screen lit. I saw ash-blond hair cut in a Belter crest over a lean white face and an impersonal smile.

"Forward Station. Good evening."

"Good evening. This is Carlos Wu of Earth calling long distance. May I speak to Dr. Julian Forward, please?"

"I'll see if he's available." The screen went on HOLD.

In the interval Carlos burst out: "What kind of game are *you* playing now? How can I explain owning an armed, disguised warship?"

But I began to see what Ausfaller was getting at. I said, "You'd want to avoid explaining that, whatever the truth was. Maybe he won't ask. I—" I shut up because we were facing Forward.

Julian Forward was a Jinxian, short and wide, with arms as thick as legs and legs as thick as pillars. His skin was almost as black as his hair: a Sirius suntan, probably maintained by sunlights. He perched on the edge of a massage chair. "Carlos Wu!" he said with flattering enthusiasm.

"Are you the same Carlos Wu who solved the Sealeyham Limits problem?"

Carlos said he was. They went into a discussion of mathematics, a possible application of Carlos's solution to another limits problem, I gathered. I glanced at Ausfaller—not obtrusively, because for Forward he wasn't supposed to exist—and saw him pensively studying his side view of Forward.

"Well," Forward said, "what can I do for you?"

"Julian Forward, meet Beowulf Shaeffer," said Carlos. I bowed. "Bey was giving me a lift home when our hyperdrive motor disappeared."

"Disappeared?"

I butted in for verisimilitude. "Disappeared, futzy right. The hyperdrive motor casing is empty. The motor supports are sheared off. We're stuck out here with no hyperdrive and no idea how it happened."

"Almost true," Carlos said happily. "Dr. Forward, I do have some ideas as to what happened here. I'd like to discuss them with you."

"Where are you now?"

I pulled our position and velocity from the computer and flashed them to Forward Station. I wasn't sure it was a good idea, but Ausfaller had time to stop me, and he didn't.

"Fine," said Forward's image. "It looks like you can get here a lot faster than you can get to Earth. Forward Station is ahead of you, within twenty a.u. of your position. You can wait here for the next ferry. Better than going on in a crippled ship."

"Good! We'll work out a course and let you know when to expect us."

"I welcome the chance to meet Carlos Wu." Forward gave us his own coordinates and rang off.

Carlos turned. "All right, Bey. Now *you* own an armed and disguised warship. *You* figure out where you got it."

"We've got worse problems than that. Forward Station is exactly where the ship eater ought to be."

He nodded. But he was amused.

"So what's our next move? We can't run from hyperdrive ships. Not now. Is Forward likely to try to kill us?"

"If we don't reach Forward Station on schedule, he might send ships after us. We know too much. We've told him so," said Carlos. "The hyperdrive motor disappeared completely. I know half a dozen people who could figure out how it happened, knowing just that." He smiled suddenly. "That's assuming Forward's the ship eater. We don't know that. I think we have a splendid chance to find out one way or the other."

"How? Just walk in?"

Ausfaller was nodding approvingly. "Dr. Forward expects you and Carlos to enter his web unsuspecting, leaving an empty ship. I think we can prepare a few surprises for him. For example, he may not have guessed that this is a General Products hull. And I will be aboard to fight."

True. Only antimatter could harm a GP hull . . . though things could go through it, like light and gravity and shock waves. "So you'll be in the indestructible hull," I said, "and we'll be helpless in the base. Very clever. I'd rather run for it myself. But then, you have your career to consider."

"I will not deny it. But there are ways in which I can prepare you."

Behind Ausfaller's cabin, behind what looked like an unbroken wall, was a room the size of a walk-in closet. Ausfaller seemed quite proud of it. He didn't show us everything in there, but I saw enough to cost me what remained of my first impression of Ausfaller. This man did not have the soul of a pudgy bureaucrat.

Behind a glass panel he kept a couple of dozen special-purpose weapons. A row of four clamps held three identical hand weapons, disposable rocket launchers for a fat slug that Ausfaller billed as a tiny atomic bomb. The fourth clamp was empty. There were laser rifles and pistols, a shotgun of peculiar design with four inches of recoil shock absorber, throwing knives, an Olympic target pistol with a sculpted grip and room for just one .22 bullet.

I wondered what he was doing with a hobbyist's touch-sculpting setup. Maybe he could make sculptures to drive a human or an alien mad. Maybe something less subtle: maybe they'd explode at the touch of the right fingerprints.

He had a compact automated tailor's shop. "I'm going to make you some new suits," he said. When Carlos asked why, he said, "You can keep secrets? So can I."

He asked us for our preference in styles. I played it straight, asking for a falling jumper in green and silver with lots of pockets. It wasn't the best I've ever owned, but it fit.

"I didn't ask for buttons," I told him.

"I hope you don't mind. Carlos, you will have buttons, too."

Carlos chose a fiery red tunic with a green and gold dragon coiling across the back. The buttons carried his family monogram. Ausfaller stood before us, examining us in our new finery, with approval.

"Now, watch," he said. "Here I stand before you, un-armed."

"Right."

"*Sure* you are."

Ausfaller grinned. He took the top and bottom buttons between his fingers and tugged hard. They came off. The material between them ripped open as if a thread had been strung between them.

Holding the buttons as if to keep an invisible thread taut, he moved them to either side of a crudely done plastic touch sculpture. The sculpture fell apart.

"Sinclair molecule chain. It will cut through any normal matter if you pull hard enough. You must be very careful. It will cut your fingers so easily that you will hardly notice they are gone. Notice that the buttons are large to give an easy grip." He laid the buttons carefully on a table and set a heavy weight between them. "This third button down is a sonic grenade. Ten feet away it will kill. Thirty feet away it will stun."

I said, "Don't demonstrate."

"You may want to practice throwing dummy buttons at

a target. This second button is Power Pill, the commercial stimulant. Break the button and take half when you need it. The entire dose may stop your heart."

"I never heard of Power Pill. How does it work on crashlanders?"

He was taken aback. "I don't know. Perhaps you had better restrict yourself to a quarter dose."

"Or avoid it entirely," I said.

"There is one more thing I will not demonstrate. Feel the material of your garments. You feel three layers of material? The middle layer is a nearly perfect mirror. It will reflect even X rays. Now you can repel a laser blast for at least the first second. The collar unrolls to a hood."

Carlos was nodding in satisfaction.

I guess it's true: all flatlanders think that way.

For a billion and a half years humanity's ancestors had evolved to the conditions of one world: Earth. A flatlander grows up in an environment peculiarly suited to him. Instinctively he sees the whole universe the same way.

We know better, we who were born on other worlds. On We Made It there are the hellish winds of summer and winter. On Jinx, the gravity. On Plateau, the all-encircling cliff edge and a drop of forty miles into unbearable heat and pressure. On Down, the red sunlight and plants that will not grow without help from ultraviolet lamps.

But flatlanders think the universe was made for their benefit. To them, danger is unreal.

"Earplugs," said Ausfaller, holding up a handful of soft plastic cylinders.

We inserted them. Ausfaller said, "Can you hear me?"

"Sure." "Yah." They didn't block our hearing at all.

"Transmitter and hearing aid with sonic padding between. If you are blasted with sound, as by an explosion or a sonic stunner, the hearing aid will stop transmitting. If you go suddenly deaf, you will know you are under attack."

To me, Ausfaller's elaborate precautions only spoke of what we might be walking into. I said nothing. If we ran for it, our chances were even worse.

* * *

Back to the control room, where Ausfaller set up a relay to the Bureau of Alien Affairs on Earth. He gave them a condensed version of what had happened to us, plus some cautious speculation. He invited Carlos to read his theories into the record.

Carlos declined. "I could still be wrong. Give me a chance to do some studying."

Ausfaller went grumpily to his bunk. He had been up too long, and it showed.

Carlos shook his head as Ausfaller disappeared into his cabin. "Paranoia. In his job I guess he has to be paranoid."

"You could use some of that yourself."

He didn't hear me. "Imagine suspecting an interstellar celebrity of being a space pirate!"

"He's in the right place at the right time."

"Hey, Bey, forget what I said. The, uh, ship-eating device has to be in the right place, but the pirates don't. They can just leave it loose and use hyperdrive ships to commute to their base."

That was something to keep in mind. Compared to the inner system, this volume within the cometary halo was enormous, but to hyperdrive ships it was all one neighborhood. I said, "Then why are we visiting Forward?"

"I still want to check my ideas with him. More than that: he probably knows the head ship eater without knowing it's him. Probably we both know him. It took something of a cosmologist to find the device and recognize it. Whoever it is, he has to have made something of a name for himself."

"Find?"

Carlos grinned at me. "Never mind. Have you thought of anyone you'd like to use that magic wire on?"

"I've been making a list. You're at the top."

"Well, watch it. Sigmund knows you've got it, even if nobody else does."

"He's second."

"How long till we reach Forward Station?"

I'd been rechecking our course. We were decelerating at

thirty gravities and veering to one side. "Twenty hours and a few minutes," I said.

"Good. I'll get a chance to do some studying." He began calling up data from the computer.

I asked permission to read over his shoulder. He gave it.

Bastard. He reads twice as fast as I do. I tried to skim to get some idea of what he was after.

Collapsars: three known. The nearest was one component of a double in Cygnus, more than a hundred light-years away. Expeditions had gone there to drop probes.

The theory of the black hole wasn't new to me, though the math was over my head. If a star is massive enough, then after it has burned its nuclear fuel and started to cool, no possible internal force can hold it from collapsing inward past its own Swartzchild radius. At that point the escape velocity from the star becomes greater than lightspeed, and beyond that deponent sayeth not, because nothing can leave the star, not information, not matter, not radiation. Nothing—except gravity.

Such a collapsed star can be expected to weigh five solar masses or more; otherwise its collapse would stop at the neutron star stage. Afterward it can only grow bigger and more massive.

There wasn't the slightest chance of finding anything that massive out here at the edge of the solar system. If such a thing were anywhere near, the sun would have been in orbit around it.

The Siberia meteorite must have been weird enough, to be remembered for nine hundred years. It had knocked down trees over thousands of square miles, yet trees near the touchdown point were left standing. No part of the meteorite itself had ever been found. Nobody had seen it hit. In 1908, Tunguska, Siberia, must have been as sparsely settled as the Earth's moon is today.

"Carlos, what does all this have to do with anything?"

"Does Holmes tell Watson?"

I had real trouble following the cosmology. Physics verged on philosophy here, or vice versa. Basically the big bang theory—which pictures the universe as exploding from a single point mass, like a titanic bomb—was in competition with the steady state universe, which has been going on forever and will continue to do so. The cyclic universe is a succession of big bangs followed by contractions. There are variants on all of them.

When the quasars were first discovered, they seemed to date from an earlier stage in the evolution of the universe, which, by the steady state hypothesis, would not be evolving at all. The steady state went out of fashion. Then, a century ago, Hilbury had solved the mystery of the quasars. Meanwhile one of the implications of the big bang had not panned out. That was where the math got beyond me.

There was some discussion of whether the universe was open or closed in four-space, but Carlos turned it off. "Okay," he said with satisfaction.

"What?"

"I could be right. Insufficient data. I'll have to see what Forward thinks."

"I hope you both choke. I'm going to sleep."

Out here in the broad borderland between Sol system and interstellar space, Julian Forward had found a stony mass the size of a middling asteroid. From a distance it seemed untouched by technology: a lopsided spheroid, rough-surfaced and dirty white. Closer in, flecks of metal and bright paint showed like randomly placed jewels. Air locks, windows, projecting antennae, and things less identifiable. A lighted disk with something projecting from the center: a long metal arm with half a dozen ball joints in it and a cup on the end. I studied that one, trying to guess what it might be . . . and gave up.

I brought *Hobo Kelly* to rest a fair distance away. To Ausfaller I said, "You'll stay aboard?"

"Of course. I will do nothing to disabuse Dr. Forward of the notion that the ship is empty."

We crossed to Forward Station on an open taxi: two seats, a fuel tank, and a rocket motor. Once I turned to ask

Carlos something and asked instead, "Carlos? Are you all right?"

His face was white and strained. "I'll make it."

"Did you try closing your eyes?"

"It was worse. Futz, I made it this far on hypnosis. Bey, it's so *empty*."

"Hang on. We're almost there."

The blond Belter was outside one of the air locks in a skintight suit and a bubble helmet. He used a flashlight to flag us down. We moored our taxi to a spur of rock—the gravity was almost nil—and went inside.

"I'm Harry Moskowitz," the Belter said. "They call me Angel. Dr. Forward is waiting in the laboratory."

The interior of the asteroid was a network of straight cylindrical corridors, laser-drilled, pressurized, and lined with cool blue light strips. We weighed a few pounds near the surface, less in the deep interior. Angel moved in a fashion new to me: a flat jump from the floor that took him far down the corridor to brush the ceiling, push back to the floor, and jump again. Three jumps and he'd wait, not hiding his amusement at our attempts to catch up.

"Doctor Forward asked me to give you a tour," he told us.

I said, "You seem to have a lot more corridor than you need. Why didn't you cluster all the rooms together?"

"This rock was a mine once upon a time. The miners drilled these passages. They left big hollows wherever they found air-bearing rock or ice pockets. All we had to do was wall them off."

That explained why there was so much corridor between the doors and why the chambers we saw were so big. Some rooms were storage areas, Angel said; not worth opening. Others were tool rooms, life-support systems, a garden, a fair-sized computer, a sizable fusion plant. A mess room built to hold thirty actually held about ten, all men, who looked at us curiously before they went back to eating. A hangar, bigger than need be and open to the sky, housed taxis and powered suits with specialized tools and three identical circular cradles, all empty.

I gambled. Carefully casual, I asked, "You use mining tugs?"

Angel didn't hesitate. "Sure. We can ship water and metals up from the inner system, but it's cheaper to hunt them down ourselves. In an emergency the tugs could probably get us back to the inner system."

We moved back into the tunnels. Angel said, "Speaking of ships, I don't think I've ever seen one like yours. Were those *bombs* lined up along the ventral surface?"

"Some of them," I said.

Carlos laughed. "Bey won't tell me how he got it."

"Pick, pick, pick. All right, I *stole* it. I don't think anyone is going to complain."

Angel, frankly curious before, was frankly fascinated as I told the story of how I had been hired to fly a cargo ship in the Wunderland system. "I didn't much like the looks of the guy who hired me, but what do I know about Wunderlanders? Besides, I needed the money." I told of my surprise at the proportions of the ship: the solid wall behind the cabin, the passenger section that was only holographs in blind portholes. By then I was already afraid that if I tried to back out, I'd be made to disappear.

But when I learned my destination, I got really worried. "It was in the Serpent Stream—you know, the crescent of asteroids in Wunderland system? It's common knowledge that the Free Wunderland Conspiracy is *all through* those rocks. When they gave me my course, I just took off and aimed for Sirius."

"Strange they left you with a working hyperdrive."

"Man, they *didn't*. They'd ripped out the relays. I had to fix them myself. It's lucky I looked, because they had the relays wired to a little bomb under the control chair." I stopped, then, "Maybe I fixed it wrong. You heard what happened? My hyperdrive motor just plain vanished. It must have set off some explosive bolts, because the belly of the ship blew off. It was a dummy. What's left looks to be a pocket bomber."

"That's what I thought."

"I guess I'll have to turn it in to the goldskin cops when we reach the inner system. Pity."

Carlos was smiling and shaking his head. He covered by saying, "It only goes to prove that you *can* run away from your problems."

The next tunnel ended in a great hemispherical chamber lidded by a bulging transparent dome. A man-thick pillar rose through the rock floor to a seal in the center of the dome. Above the seal, gleaming against night and stars, a multijointed metal arm reached out blindly into space. The arm ended in what might have been a tremendous iron puppy dish.

Forward was in a horseshoe-shaped control console near the pillar. I hardly noticed him. I'd seen this arm-and-bucket thing before, coming in from space, but I hadn't grasped its *size*.

Forward caught me gaping. "The Grabber," he said.

He approached us in a bouncing walk, comical but effective. "Pleased to meet you, Carlos Wu. Beowulf Shaeffer." His handshake was not crippling, because he was being careful. He had a wide, engaging smile. "The Grabber is our main exhibit here. After the Grabber there's nothing to see."

I asked, "What does it do?"

Carlos laughed. "It's beautiful! Why does it have to do anything?"

Forward acknowledged the compliment. "I've been thinking of entering it in a junk-sculpture show. What it does is manipulate large, dense masses. The cradle at the end of the arm is a complex of electromagnets. I can actually vibrate masses in there to produce polarized gravity waves."

Six massive arcs of girder divided the dome into pie sections. Now I noticed that they and the seal at their center gleamed like mirrors. They were reinforced by stasis fields.

More bracing for the Grabber? I tried to imagine forces that would require such strength.

"What do you vibrate in there? A megaton of lead?"

"Lead sheathed in soft iron was our test mass. But that was three years ago. I haven't worked with the Grabber lately, but we had some satisfactory runs with a sphere of neutronium enclosed in a stasis field. Ten billion metric tons."

I said, "What's the point?"

From Carlos I got a dirty look. Forward seemed to think it was a wholly reasonable question. "Communication, for one thing. There must be intelligent species all through the galaxy, most of them too far away for our ships. Gravity waves are probably the best way to reach them."

"Gravity waves travel at lightspeed, don't they? Wouldn't hyperwave be better?"

"We can't count on their having it. Who but the Outsiders would think to do their experimenting this far from a sun? If we want to reach beings who haven't dealt with the Outsiders, we'll have to use gravity waves ... once we know how."

Angel offered us chairs and refreshments. By the time we were settled, I was already out of it; Forward and Carlos were talking plasma physics, metaphysics, and what are our old friends doing? I gathered that they had large numbers of mutual acquaintances. And Carlos was probing for the whereabouts of cosmologists specializing in gravity physics.

A few were in the Quicksilver Group. Others were among the colony worlds, especially on Jinx, trying to get the Institute of Knowledge to finance various projects, such as more expeditions to the collapsar in Cygnus.

"Are you still with the Institute, Doctor?"

Forward shook his head. "They stopped backing me. Not enough results. But I can continue to use this station, which is Institute property. One day they'll sell it, and we'll have to move."

"I was wondering why they sent you here in the first place," said Carlos. "Sirius has an adequate cometary belt."

"But Sol is the only system with any kind of civilization this far from its sun. And I can count on better men to work with. Sol system has always had its fair share of cosmologists."

"I thought you might have come to solve an old mystery. The Tunguska meteorite. You've heard of it, of course."

Forward laughed. "Of course. Who hasn't? I don't think we'll ever know just what it was that hit Siberia that night. It may have been a chunk of antimatter. I'm told that there is antimatter in known space."

"If it was, we'll never prove it," Carlos admitted.

"Shall we discuss your problem?" Forward seemed to remember my existence. "Shaeffer, what does a professional pilot think when his hyperdrive motor disappears?"

"He gets very upset."

"Any theories?"

I decided not to mention pirates. I wanted to see if Forward would mention them first. "Nobody seems to like my theory," I said, and I sketched out the argument for monsters in hyperspace.

Forward heard me out politely. Then, "I'll give you this; it'd be hard to disprove. Do you buy it?"

"I'm afraid to. I almost got myself killed once, looking for space monsters when I should have been looking for natural causes."

"Why would the hyperspace monsters eat only your motor?"

"Um ... futz. I pass."

"What do you think, Carlos? Natural phenomena or space monsters?"

"Pirates," said Carlos.

"How are they going about it?"

"Well, this business of a hyperdrive motor disappearing and leaving the ship behind—that's brand new. I'd think it would take a sharp gravity gradient with a tidal effect as strong as that of a neutron star or a black hole."

"You won't find anything like that anywhere in human space."

"I know." Carlos looked frustrated. That had to be faked. Earlier he'd behaved as if he already had an answer.

Forward said, "I don't think a black hole would have that effect, anyway. If it did, you'd never know it, because the ship would disappear down the black hole."

"What about a powerful gravity generator?"

"Hmmm." Forward thought about it, then shook his massive head. "You're talking about a surface gravity in the millions. Any gravity generator I've ever heard of would collapse itself at that level. Let's see, with a frame supported by stasis fields ... no. The frame would hold, and the rest of the machinery would flow like water."

"You don't leave much of my theory."

"Sorry."

Carlos ended a short pause by asking, "How do you think the universe started?"

Forward looked puzzled at the change of subject.

And I began to get uneasy.

Given all that I don't know about cosmology, I do know attitudes and tones of voice. Carlos was giving out broad hints, trying to lead Forward to his own conclusion. Black holes, pirates, the Tunguska meteorite, the origin of the universe—he was offering them as clues. And Forward was not responding correctly.

He was saying, "Ask a priest. Me, I lean toward the big bang. The steady state always seemed so futile."

"I like the big bang, too," said Carlos.

There was something else to worry about. Those mining tugs: they almost had to belong to Forward Station. How would Ausfaller react when three familiar spacecraft came cruising into his space?

How did I want him to react? Forward Station would make a dandy pirate base. Permeated by laser-drilled corridors distributed almost at random ... could there be two networks of corridors, connected only at the surface? How would we know?

Suddenly I didn't want to know. I wanted to go home. If only Carlos would stay off the touchy subjects—

But he was speculating about the ship eater again. "That ten billion metric tons of neutronium, now, that you were using for a test mass. That wouldn't be big enough or dense enough to give us enough of a gravity gradient."

"It might, right near the surface." Forward grinned and held his hands close together. "It was about that big."

"And that's as dense as matter gets in this universe. Too bad."

"True, but . . . have you ever heard of quantum black holes?"

"Yah."

Forward stood up briskly. "Wrong answer."

I rolled out of my web chair, trying to brace myself for a jump, while my fingers fumbled for the third button on my jumper. It was no good. I hadn't practiced in this gravity.

Forward was in midleap. He slapped Carlos alongside the head as he went past. He caught me at the peak of his jump and took me with him via an iron grip on my wrist.

I had no leverage, but I kicked at him. He didn't even try to stop me. It was like fighting a mountain. He gathered my wrists in one hand and towed me away.

Forward was busy. He sat within the horseshoe of his control console, talking. The backs of three disembodied heads showed above the console's edge.

Evidently there was a laser phone in the console. I could hear parts of what Forward was saying. He was ordering the pilots of the three mining tugs to destroy *Hobo Kelly*. He didn't seem to know about Ausfaller yet.

Forward was busy, but Angel was studying us thoughtfully, or unhappily, or both. Well he might. We could disappear, but what messages might we have sent earlier?

I couldn't do anything constructive with Angel watching me. And I couldn't count on Carlos.

I couldn't see Carlos. Forward and Angel had tied us to

opposite sides of the central pillar, beneath the Grabber. Carlos hadn't made a sound since then. He might be dying from that tremendous slap across the head.

I tested the line around my wrists. Metal mesh of some kind, cool to the touch . . . and it was tight.

Forward turned a switch. The heads vanished. It was a moment before he spoke.

"You've put me in a very bad position."

And Carlos answered. "I think you put yourself there."

"That may be. You should not have let me guess what you knew."

Carlos said, "Sorry, Bey."

He sounded healthy. Good. "That's all right," I said. "But what's all the excitement about? What has Forward *got*?"

"I think he's got the Tunguska meteorite."

"No. That I do not." Forward stood and faced us. "I will admit that I came here to search for the Tunguska meteorite. I spent several years trying to trace its trajectory after it left Earth. Perhaps it *was* a quantum black hole. Perhaps not. The Institute cut off my funds without warning just as I had found a real quantum black hole, the first in history."

I said, "That doesn't tell me a lot."

"Patience, Mr. Shaeffer. You know that a black hole may form from the collapse of a massive star? Good. And you know that it takes a body of at least five solar masses. It may mass as much as a galaxy—or as much as the universe. There is some evidence that the universe is an infalling black hole. But at less than five solar masses the collapse would stop at the neutron star stage."

"I follow you."

"In all the history of the universe there has been one moment at which smaller black holes might have formed. That moment was the explosion of the monoblock, the cosmic egg that once contained all the matter in the universe. In the ferocity of that explosion there must have been loci of unimaginable pressure. Black holes could have formed of mass down to two point two times ten to the minus fifth grams, one point six times ten to the minus twenty-fifth angstrom in radius."

"Of course you'd never detect anything that small," said Carlos. He seemed almost cheerful. I wondered why . . . and then I knew. He'd been right about the way the ships were disappearing. It must compensate him for being tied to a pillar.

"But," said Forward, "black holes of all sizes could have formed in that explosion, and should have. In more than seven hundred years of searching no quantum black hole has ever been found. Most cosmologists have given up on them, and on the big bang, too."

Carlos said, "Of course there was the Tunguska meteorite. It could have been a black hole of, oh, asteroidal mass—"

"—and roughly molecular size. But the tide would have pulled down trees as it went past—"

"—and the black hole would have gone right through the Earth and headed back into space a few tons heavier. Eight hundred years ago there was actually a search for the exit point. With that they could have charted a course—"

"Exactly. But I had to give up that approach," said Forward. "I was using a new method when the Institute, ah, severed our relationship."

They must both be mad, I thought. Carlos was tied to a pillar and Forward was about to kill him, yet they were both behaving like members of a very exclusive club . . . to which I did not belong.

Carlos was interested. "How'd you work it?"

"You know that it is possible for an asteroid to capture a quantum black hole? In its interior? For instance, at a mass of ten to the twelfth kilograms—a billion metric tons," he added for my benefit, "a black hole would be only one point five times ten to the minus fifth angstroms across. Smaller than an atom. In a slow pass through an asteroid it might absorb a few billions of atoms, enough to slow it into an orbit. Thereafter it might orbit within the asteroid for eons, absorbing very little mass on each pass."

"So?"

"If I chance on an asteroid more massive than it ought to be, and if I contrive to move it, and some of the mass stays behind . . ."

"You'd have to search a lot of asteroids. Why do it out here? Why not the asteroid belt? Oh, of course. You can use hyperdrive out here."

"Exactly. We could search a score of masses in a day, using very little fuel."

"Hey. If it was big enough to eat a spacecraft, why didn't it eat the asteroid you found it in?"

"It wasn't that big," said Forward. "The black hole I found was exactly as I have described it. I enlarged it. I towed it home and ran it into my neutronium sphere. *Then* it was large enough to absorb an asteroid. Now it is quite a massive object. Ten to the twentieth power kilograms, the mass of one of the larger asteroids, and a radius of just under ten to the minus fifth centimeters."

There was satisfaction in Forward's voice. In Carlos's there was suddenly nothing but contempt. "You accomplished all that, and then you used it to rob ships and bury the evidence. Is that what's going to happen to us? Down the rabbit hole?"

"To another universe, perhaps. Where does a black hole lead?"

I wondered about that myself.

Angel had taken Forward's place at the control console. He had fastened the seat belt, something I had not seen Forward do, and was dividing his attention between the instruments and the conversation.

"I'm still wondering how you move it," said Carlos. Then, "Uh! The tugs!"

Forward stared, then guffawed. "You didn't guess that? But of course the black hole can hold a charge. I played the exhaust from an old ion drive reaction motor into it for nearly a month. Now it holds an enormous charge. The tugs can pull it well enough. I wish I had more of them. Soon I will."

"Just a minute," I said. I'd grasped one crucial fact as it had gone past my head. "The tugs aren't armed? All they do is pull the black hole?"

"That's right." Forward looked at me curiously.

"And the black hole is invisible."

"Yes. We tug it into the path of a spacecraft. If the craft comes near enough, it will precipitate into normal space. We guide the black hole through its drive to cripple it, board and rob it at our leisure. Then a slower pass with the quantum black hole, and the ship simply disappears."

"Just one last question," said Carlos. "Why?"

I had a better question.

Just what was Ausfaller going to do when three familiar spacecraft came near? They carried no armaments at all. Their only weapon was invisible.

And it would eat a General Products hull without noticing.

Would Ausfaller fire on unarmed ships?

We'd know too soon. Up there, near the edge of the dome, I had spotted three tiny lights in a tight cluster.

Angel had seen it, too. He activated the phone. Phantom heads appeared, one, two, three.

I turned back to Forward and was startled at the brooding hate in his expression.

"Fortune's child," he said to Carlos. "Natural aristocrat. Certified superman. Why would *you* ever consider stealing anything? Women beg you to give them children, in person if possible, by mail if not! Earth's resources exist to keep you healthy, not that you need them!"

"This may startle you," said Carlos, "but there are people who see *you* as a superman."

"We bred for strength, we Jinxians. At what cost to other factors? Our lives are short, even with the aid of boosterspice. Longer if we live outside Jinx's gravity. But the people of other worlds think we're funny. The women . . . never mind." He brooded, then said it anyway. "A woman of Earth once told me she would rather go to bed with a tunneling machine. She didn't trust my strength. What woman would?"

The three bright dots had nearly reached the center of the dome. I saw nothing between them. I hadn't expected to. Angel was still talking to the pilots.

Up from the edge of the dome came something I didn't want anyone to notice. I said, "Is that your excuse for mass murder, Forward? Lack of women?"

"I need give you no excuses at all, Shaeffer. My world will thank me for what I've done. Earth has swallowed the lion's share of the interstellar trade for too long."

"They'll thank you, huh? You're going to tell them?"

"I—"

"Julian!" That was Angel calling. He'd seen it . . . no, he hadn't. One of the tug captains had.

Forward left us abruptly. He consulted with Angel in low tones, then turned back. "Carlos! Did you leave your ship on automatic? Or is there someone else aboard?"

"I'm not required to say," said Carlos.

"I could—no. In a minute it will not matter."

Angel said, "Julian, look what he's doing."

"Yes. Very clever. Only a human pilot would think of that."

Ausfaller had maneuvered the *Hobo Kelly* between us and the tugs. If the tugs fired a conventional weapon, they'd blast the dome and kill us all.

The tugs came on.

"He still does not know what he is fighting," Forward said with some satisfaction.

True, and it would cost him. Three unarmed tugs were coming down Ausfaller's throat, carrying a weapon so slow that the tugs could throw it at him, let it absorb *Hobo Kelly*, and pick it up again long before it was a danger to us.

From my viewpoint *Hobo Kelly* was a bright point with three dimmer, more distant points around it. Forward and Angel were getting a better view through the phone. And they weren't watching us at all.

I began trying to kick off my shoes. They were soft ship slippers, ankle-high, and they resisted.

I kicked the left foot free just as one of the tugs flared with ruby light.

"He did it!" Carlos didn't know whether to be jubilant or horrified. "He fired on unarmed ships!"

Forward gestured peremptorily. Angel slid out of his seat. Forward slid in and fastened the thick seat belt. Neither had spoken a word.

A second ship burned fiercely red, then expanded in a pink cloud.

The third ship was fleeing.

Forward worked the controls. "I have it in the mass indicator," he rasped. "We have but one chance."

So did I. I peeled the other slipper off with my toes. Over our heads the jointed arm of the Grabber began to swing . . . and I suddenly realized what they were talking about.

Now there was little to see beyond the dome. The swinging Grabber, and the light of *Hobo Kelly*'s drive, and the two tumbling wrecks, all against a background of fixed stars. Suddenly one of the tugs winked blue-white and was gone. Not even a dust cloud was left behind.

Ausfaller must have seen it. He was turning, fleeing. Then it was as if an invisible hand had picked up *Hobo Kelly* and thrown her away. The fusion light streaked off to one side and set beyond the dome's edge.

With two tugs destroyed and the third fleeing, the black hole was falling free, aimed straight down our throats.

Now there was nothing to see but the delicate motions of the Grabber. Angel stood behind Forward's chair, his knuckles white with his grip on the chair's back.

My few pounds of weight went away and left me in free-fall. Tides again. The invisible thing was more massive than this asteroid beneath me. The Grabber swung a meter more to one side . . . and something struck it a mighty blow.

The floor surged away from beneath me, left me head

down above the Grabber. The huge soft-iron puppy dish
came at me; the jointed metal arm collapsed like a spring.
It slowed, stopped.

"You got it!" Angel crowed like a rooster, and slapped at
the back of the chair, holding himself down with his other
hand. He turned a gloating look on us, turned back just as
suddenly. "The ship! It's getting away!"

"No." Forward was bent over the console. "I see him.
Good, he is coming back, straight toward us. This time
there will be no tugs to warn the pilot."

The Grabber swung ponderously toward the point where
I'd seen *Hobo Kelly* disappear. It moved centimeters at a
time, pulling a massive invisible weight.

And Ausfaller was coming back to rescue us. He'd be a
sitting duck unless—

I reached up with my toes, groping for the first and
fourth buttons on my falling jumper.

The weaponry in my wonderful suit hadn't helped me
against Jinxian strength and speed. But flatlanders are less
than limber, and so are Jinxians. Forward had tied my
hands and left it at that.

I wrapped two sets of toes around the buttons and
tugged.

My legs were bent pretzel-fashion. I had no leverage. But
the first button tore loose, and then the thread. Another invisible weapon to battle Forward's portable bottomless hole.

The thread pulled the fourth button loose. I brought my
feet down to where they belonged, keeping the thread taut,
and pushed backward. I felt the Sinclair molecule chain
sinking into the pillar.

The Grabber was still swinging.

When the thread was through the pillar, I could bring it
up in back of me and try to cut my bonds. More likely I'd
cut my wrists and bleed to death, but I had to try. I wondered if I could do anything before Forward launched the
black hole.

A cold breeze caressed my feet.

I looked down. Thick fog boiled out around the pillar.

Some very cold gas must be spraying through the hair-fine crack.

I kept pushing. More fog formed. The cold was numbing. I felt the jerk as the magic thread cut through. Now the wrists—

Liquid helium?

Forward had moored us to the main superconducting power cable.

That was probably a mistake. I pulled my feet forward carefully, steadily, feeling the thread bite through on the return cut.

The Grabber had stopped swinging. Now it moved on its arm like a blind, questing worm as Forward made fine adjustments. Angel was beginning to show the strain of holding himself upside down.

My feet jerked slightly. I was through. My feet were terribly cold, almost without sensation. I let the buttons go, left them floating up toward the dome, and kicked back hard with my heels.

Something shifted. I kicked again.

Thunder and lightning flared around my feet.

I jerked my knees up to my chin. The lightning crackled and flashed white light into the billowing fog. Angel and Forward turned in astonishment. I laughed at them, letting them see it. Yes, gentlemen, I did it on purpose.

The lightning stopped. In the sudden silence Forward was screaming, "—know what you've *done*?"

There was a grinding *crunch*, a shuddering against my back. I looked up.

A piece had been bitten out of the Grabber.

I was upside down and getting heavier. Angel suddenly pivoted around his grip on Forward's chair. He hung above the dome, above the sky. He screamed.

My legs gripped the pillar hard. I felt Carlos's feet fumbling for a foothold and heard Carlos's laughter.

Near the edge of the dome a spear of light was rising. *Hobo Kelly*'s drive, decelerating, growing larger. Otherwise the sky was clear and empty. And a piece of the dome disappeared with a snapping sound.

Angel screamed and dropped. Just above the dome he seemed to flare with blue light.

He was gone.

Air roared out through the dome—and more was disappearing into something that had been invisible. Now it showed as a blue pinpoint drifting toward the floor. Forward had turned to watch it fall.

Loose objects fell across the chamber, looped around the pinpoint at meteor speed, or fell into it with bursts of light. Every atom of my body felt the pull of the thing, the urge to die in an infinite fall. Now we hung side by side from a horizontal pillar. I noted with approval that Carlos's mouth was wide open, like mine, to clear his lungs so that they wouldn't burst when the air was gone.

Daggers in my ears and sinuses, pressure in my gut.

Forward turned back to the controls. He moved one knob hard over. Then he opened the seat belt and stepped out and up and fell.

Light flared. He was gone.

The lightning-colored pinpoint drifted to the floor and into it. Above the increasing roar of air I could hear the grumbling of rock being pulverized, dwindling as the black hole settled toward the center of the asteroid.

The air was deadly thin but not gone. My lungs thought they were gasping vacuum. But my blood was not boiling. I'd have known it.

So I gasped and kept gasping. It was all I had attention for. Black spots flickered before my eyes, but I was still gasping and alive when Ausfaller reached us, carrying a clear plastic package and an enormous handgun.

He came in fast, on a rocket backpack. Even as he decelerated, he was looking around for something to shoot. He returned in a loop of fire. He studied us through his faceplate, possibly wondering if we were dead.

He flipped the plastic package open. It was a thin sack

with a zipper and a small tank attached. He had to dig for a torch to cut our bonds. He freed Carlos first, helped him into the sack. Carlos bled from the nose and ears. He was barely mobile. So was I, but Ausfaller got me into the sack with Carlos and zipped it up. Air hissed in around us.

I wondered what came next. As an inflated sphere the rescue bag was too big for the tunnels. Ausfaller had thought of that. He fired at the dome, blasted a gaping hole in it, and flew us out on the rocket backpack.

Hobo Kelly was grounded nearby. I saw that the rescue bag wouldn't fit the air lock, either, and Ausfaller confirmed my worst fear. He signaled us by opening his mouth wide. Then he zipped open the rescue bag and half carried us into the air lock while the air was still roaring out of our lungs.

When there was air again, Carlos whispered, "Please don't do that anymore."

"It should not be necessary anymore." Ausfaller smiled. "Whatever it was you did, well done. I have two well-equipped autodocs to repair you. While you are healing, I will see about recovering the treasures within the asteroid."

Carlos held up a hand, but no sound came. He looked like something risen from the dead: blood running from nose and ears, mouth wide open, one feeble hand raised against gravity.

"One thing," Ausfaller said briskly. "I saw many dead men; I saw no living ones. How many were there? Am I likely to meet opposition while searching?"

"Forget it," Carlos croaked. "Get us out of here. Now."

Ausfaller frowned. "What—"

"No time. Get us out."

Ausfaller tasted something sour. "Very well. First the autodocs." He turned, but Carlos's strengthless hand stopped him.

"Futz, no. I want to see this," Carlos whispered.

Again Ausfaller gave in. He trotted off to the control room. Carlos tottered after him. I tottered after them both, wiping blood from my nose, feeling half-dead myself. But

I'd half guessed what Carlos expected, and I didn't want to miss it.

We strapped down. Ausfaller fired the main thruster. The rock surged away.

"Far enough," Carlos whispered presently. "Turn us around."

Ausfaller took care of that. Then, "What are we looking for?"

"You'll know."

"Carlos, was I right to fire on the tugs?"

"Oh, yes."

"Good. I was worried. Then Forward was the ship eater?"

"Yah."

"I did not see him when I came for you. Where is he?"

Ausfaller was annoyed when Carlos laughed and more annoyed when I joined him. It hurt my throat. "Even so, he saved our lives," I said. "He must have turned up the air pressure just before he jumped. I wonder why he did that."

"Wanted to be remembered," said Carlos. "Nobody else knew what he'd done. *Ahh—*"

I looked just as part of the asteroid collapsed into itself, leaving a deep crater.

"It moves slower at apogee. Picks up more matter," said Carlos.

"What *are* you talking about?"

"Later, Sigmund. When my throat grows back."

"Forward had a hole in his pocket," I said helpfully. "He—"

The other side of the asteroid collapsed. For a moment lightning seemed to flare in there.

Then the whole dirty snowball was growing smaller.

I thought of something Carlos had probably missed. "Sigmund, has this ship got automatic sunscreens?"

"Of *course* we've got—"

There was a universe-eating flash of light before the screen went black. When the screen cleared, there was nothing to see but stars.

✳
GHOST: SIX

"Sigmund Ausfaller killed three miners without a thought," I said.

"He was right, though."

"That weapons shop he built aboard *Hobo Kelly*: he was in love with it. No sane man toys with such things."

"Saved your life."

"He was wearing an asymmetrical beard when I first saw him. He's too short and stocky to pass for a Wunderlander. I've wondered about that for twelve years."

"None of my business, nor yours," Ander said. "Maybe someone was supposed to take him for a gullible tourist, or a fool, or a crazy."

"He's not to be trusted, Ander."

Ander laughed suddenly. Stared me in the face and laughed harder. "That's it! He needed to look crazy. He needed to look crazy enough to plant a bomb aboard a crashlander's ship!"

All I had for answer was a wordless snarl. Tanj, he could even be right.

Our dinners arrived, and Ander's chuckle died. He stared at what was on my plate. Crew snapper is a sea creature as big as a short man's leg, with rows of fins down each side and a jaw built to crush bones. It took up most of the table. It was hideous.

"Have some," I said. "It's an order for two."

We ate in silence for a bit. Ander's eyes kept straying to the crew snapper. He wouldn't touch it. He wouldn't speak of it. Presently he said, "For the record, any further contact with Pierson's puppeteers?"

I said, "Ander, this was an amazing expenditure just so you can hear Beowulf Shaeffer's barroom description of a species that no longer deals with any known world."

Ander Smittarasheed nodded. "What if I say I talked Sigmund Ausfaller out of a free vacation?"

"Maybe, if I didn't know you were recording."

He was losing patience. "Any further contact—"

"None. I've seen enough kzinti to last me. Don't they scare the ARM anymore?"

Ander Smittarasheed said, "You wouldn't remember the old Soviet Union? They used a technical term that translates as 'neutral.' 'Neutral' was any nation that could not conceivably damage the Soviet Union. Puppeteers think like that. If you can hurt them, you have to be rendered neutral."

"Better keep an eye on the planets they'll be passing on their way to nowhere."

"They'll be in range of some Patriarchy worlds, including at least three slave species. After that they're out of known space."

"And the Core explosion is twenty thousand years away. They'll have to turn first. Plenty of time."

"Yah—"

"Ander?" I set down my hashi. "Never mind."

"What?"

"They're moving at near lightspeed through normal space? Everything comes on as gamma rays at that velocity! Those planets are repelling gamma rays that'll make the Core explosion look sickly!"

He stared. "But. They could have built ... whatever ... built it and never ... If they can shield planets against gamma rays, they didn't need to go!"

I felt a grin pulling my lips way-y-y back. Ander had lost his aplomb. I wondered, "What are they running from, then? What are they up to?"

"Maybe it's not dependable, this shield. No, that's stupid," he said. I dug into my fish, letting him run on. "So . . . what *are* they running from?"

I said, enjoying myself, "Consider this. Puppeteers don't like hyperdrive. Humans do. Kzinti do. By the time their traveling worlds reach the Clouds of Magellan, we'll have been there for thousands of years. After all, the Core explosion is coming for *us*, too."

"We wondered if they didn't like the kzinti for neighbors," Ander said. "Or humans. Or all of us together. Known space seems to be packed with sapient species. Maybe the rest of the universe isn't like that."

"They could even be running from their own reputation, but they're not, Ander. They're going too slowly. They'd find all of us waiting, every species that uses hyperdrive, or else something tougher that ate us. And they're not going to where territory is cheap."

"Cheap?"

"Well, they've got their own planets, but even Outsiders pay rent when they use somebody's sunlight. The Clouds will be packed with refugee species and locals, too. If . . . Ander, I can't see why they would want the Clouds of Magellan at all. They could find something closer. Something in the plane of the galaxy, for the shielding effect, maybe a spherical cluster. Did I mention I was out of the aliens business?"

He scowled. "Yah, and settled down forever, except you weren't. What happened?"

I thought it through before I spoke. Here was my tale, and whatever Ander could check had better be the truth.

"We ran," I said. "Bad mistake, but I still don't know what I could have done differently. Puppeteers don't come into it. Or . . . well, I got money from them years ago. I thought the ARM couldn't trace that."

Of course the ARM had, and it wasn't much. But General Products had indemnified Elephant for his hull, and Elephant had given that to me when we were ready to flee Earth. They wouldn't trace *that*.

Ander said, "Beowulf, what if they've got a low-thrust

drive big enough for a planet? The Outsiders could boost
them up to speed. They'd use their own drive to turn and
then stop over the next two hundred thousand years."

I thought it over. "They wouldn't have to depend on anyone else, then. Yah. Puppeteers wouldn't trust Outsiders for
their species survival."

"Do you think Outsiders trust puppeteers?"

Nobody knew very much about Outsiders. "Ander?
There's a place where there's no Outsiders."

"What are you thinking? Close to a sun?"

"Outsiders and starseeds. We only guess at the relationship, but the best guess is they'll try to rescue the starseeds.
Stet?"

"Stet. Maybe *they'll* make for the Clouds of Magellan."

"The shock wave will drive the starseeds ahead of it,
wherever they're going. There won't be Outsiders near the
Core. Ander, there won't be *anybody* near the Core."

"What?"

I was trying to picture it. Worlds in flight— "Drive up
along the galactic pole, then turn toward the hub. In ten
thousand years they'd meet the shock wave from the Core
explosion. I saw it, Ander. A shell of exploding suns, fairly
tight, fairly narrow. They'd be through it in another five
thousand years. The Outsiders are gone. All the sapient species are gone, too, dead or fled or hopelessly mutated and
still mutating. Thousands of worlds would have been
sterilized—maybe millions—but they'd still be covered
with free oxygen and organic sludge and maybe even deep-
sea life. All ready for easy terraforming. That's it. They're
headed for the Core."

He said, "Well." And thought again and said, "At least
it's different."

"Is this what you came for?"

"Beowulf, I believe I can tell Sigmund it was worth the
trip. Now, will you tell me what happened to Feather Filip
and Carlos Wu?"

"Yah. And Carlos Wu's autodoc?"

He shrugged it off. "Feather Filip vanished from the

same time and locale as you and Carlos Wu and Sharrol Janss. I'm supposed to find out who's dead."

It wasn't a slip of the tongue. He put the question that brutally quite deliberately. Maybe it got him what he wanted, because the blood was draining out of my face again. I found my hand at my throat, massaging.

I said, "Nobody should have to eat with you, Ander."

He looked at the monster on my plate and again wouldn't give me the satisfaction. "Who's dead?"

Me! I said, "At least Carlos. You want it from the beginning?"

"Why not?"

✳
PROCRUSTES

Asleep, my mind plays it all back in fragments and dreams. From time to time a block of nerves wakes:

That's some kind of ARM weapon! Move it move it too late blam. *My head rolls loose on black sand. Bones shattered, ribs and spine. Fear worse than the agony. Agony fading* and I'm gone.

Legs try to kick. Nothing moves. Again, harder, *move! No go. The 'doc floats nicely on the lift plate, but its mass is resisting me. Push! Voice behind me, I turn, she's holding some kind of tube.* Blam. *My head bounces on sand. Agony flaring, sensation fading. Try to hang on, stay lucid . . . but everything turns mellow.*

My balance swings wildly around my inner ear. *Where's the planet's axis? Fafnir doesn't have polar caps. The ancient lander is flying itself. Carlos looks worried, but Feather's having the time of her life.*

Sprawled across the planet's face, a hurricane flattened along one edge. Under the vast cloud fingerprint, a ruddy snake divides the blue of a world-girdling ocean. A long, narrow continent runs almost pole to pole.

The lander reenters over featureless ocean. Nothing down there seems to be looking at us. I'm taking us down fast. Larger islands have low, flat buildings on them. Pick a little one. Hover while flame digs the lamplighter pit wider and deeper, until the lander sinks into the hole with inches to spare. Plan A is right on track.

I remember how Plan A ended. The Surgery program senses my distress and turns me off.

I'm in Carlos Wu's 'doc, in the intensive care cavity. The Surgery program prods my brain, running me through my memories, maintaining the patterns lest they fuzz out to nothing while my brain and body heal.

I must be terribly damaged.

Waking was sudden. My eyes popped open, and I was on my back, my nose two inches from glass. Sunlight glared through scattered clouds. Display lights glowed above my eyebrows. I felt fine, charged with energy.

Ye gods, how long had I slept? All those dreams . . . dream memories.

I tried to move. I was shrink-wrapped in elastic. I wiggled my arm up across my chest, with considerable effort, and up to the displays. It took me a few seconds to figure them out.

Biomass tank: nearly empty. *Treatment:* pages of data, horrifying . . . terminated, successful. *Date:* Ohmygod. Four months! I was out for four months and eleven days!

I typed, *Open:*

The dark, glass lid retracted, sunlight flared, and I shut my eyes tight. After a while I pulled myself over the rim of the intensive care cavity and rolled out.

My balance was all wrong. I landed like a lumpy sack, on sand, and managed not to yell or swear. Who might hear? Sat up, squinting painfully, and looked around.

I was still on the island.

It was weathered coral, nearly symmetrical, with a central peak. The air was sparkling clear, and the ocean went on forever, with another pair of tiny islands just touching the horizon.

I was stark naked and white as a bone, in the glare of a yellow-white dwarf sun. The air was salty and thick with organic life, sea life.

Where was everybody?

I tried to stand, wobbled, gave it up, and crawled around into the shadow of the 'doc. I still felt an amazing sense of well-being, as if I could solve anything the universe could throw at me.

During moments of half wakefulness I'd somehow worked out where I must be. Here it stood, half coffin and half chemical lab, massive and abandoned on the narrow black sand beach. A vulnerable place to leave such a valuable thing, but this was where I'd last seen it, ready to be loaded into the boat.

Sunlight could damage me in minutes, kill me in hours, but Carlos Wu's wonderful 'doc was no ordinary mall autodoctor. It was state of the art, smarter than me in some respects. It would cure anything the sun could do to me.

I pulled myself to my feet and took a few steps. Ouch! The coral cut my feet. The 'doc could cure that, too, but it hurt.

Standing, I could see most of the island. The center bulged up like a volcano. Fafnir coral builds a flat island with a shallow cone rising at the center, a housing for a symbiote, the lamplighter. I'd hovered the lander above the cone while belly jets scorched out the lamplighter nest until it was big enough to hold the lander.

Just me and the 'doc and a dead island. I'd have to live in the 'doc. Come out at night, like a vampire. My chance of being found must be poor if no passing boat had found me in these past four-plus months.

I climbed. The coral cut my hands and feet and knees. From the cone I'd be able to see the whole island.

The pit was two hundred feet across. The bottom was black and smooth and seven or eight feet below me. Feather had set the lander to melt itself down slowly, radiating not much heat over many hours. Several inches of rainwater now covered the slag, and something sprawled in the muck.

It might be a man . . . a tall man, possibly raised in low gravity. Too tall to be Carlos. Or Sharrol, or Feather, and who was left?

I jumped down. Landed clumsily on the smooth slag and splashed full length in the water. Picked myself up, unhurt.

My toes could feel an oblong texture, lines and ridges, the shapes within the lander that wouldn't melt. Police could determine what this thing had been if they ever looked; but why would they look?

The water felt good on my ruined feet. And on my skin. I was already burned. Albinos can't take yellow dwarf sunlight.

A corpse was no surprise, given what I remembered. I looked it over. It had been wearing local clothing for a man: boots, loose pants with a rope tie, a jacket encrusted with pockets. The jacket was pierced with a great ragged hole front and back. That could only have been made by Feather's horrible ARM weapon. This close, the head . . . I'd thought it must be under the water, but there was no head at all. There were clean white bones, and a neck vertebra cut smoothly in half.

I was hyperventilating. Dizzy. I sat down next to the skeleton so that I wouldn't fall.

These long bones looked more than four months dead. Years, decades . . . wait, now. We'd scorched the nest, but there would be lamplighter soldiers left outside. They would have swarmed down and stripped the bones.

I found I was trying to push my back through a wall of fused coral. My empty stomach heaved. This was much worse than anything I'd imagined. I *knew* who this was.

Sunlight burned my back. My eyes were going wonky in the glare. Time was not on my side: I was going to be much sicker much quicker than I liked.

I made myself pull the boots loose, shook the bones out, and put them on. They were too big.

The jacket was a sailor's survival jacket, local style. The shoulders looked padded: shoulder floats. The front and sides had been all pockets, well stuffed, but front and back had been torn to confetti.

I stripped it off him and began searching pockets.

No wallet, no ID. Tissue pack. The shrapnel remains of a hand computer. Several pockets were sealed: emergency gear, stuff you wouldn't want to open by accident; and some of those had survived.

A knife of exquisite sharpness in a built-in holster. Pocket torch. A ration brick. I bit into the brick and chewed while I searched. Mag specs, one lens shattered, but I put them on anyway. Without dark glasses my pink albino eyes would go blind.

Sun block spray, unharmed: good. A pill dispenser, broken, but in a pocket still airtight. Better! Tannin secretion pills!

The boots were shrinking, adapting to my feet. It felt friendly, reassuring. My most intimate friends on this island.

I was still dizzy. Better let the 'doc take care of me now; take the pills afterward. I shook broken ribs out of the jacket. Shook the pants empty. Balled the clothing and tossed it out of the hole. Tried to follow it.

My fingers wouldn't reach the rim.

"After all this, what a stupid way to die," I said to the memory of Sharrol Janss. "What do I do now? Build a ladder out of bones?" If I got out of this hole, I'd think it through before I ever did *anything*.

I knelt; I yelled and jumped. My fingers, palms, forearms gripped rough coral. I pulled myself out and lay panting, sweating, bleeding, crying.

I limped back to the 'doc, wearing boots now, holding the suit spread above me for a parasol. I was feverish with sunburn.

I couldn't take boots into the ICC. *Wait. Think. Wind? Waves?* I tied the clothes in a bundle around the boots, and set it on the 'doc next to the faceplate. I climbed into the intensive care cavity and pulled the lid down.

Sharrol would wait an hour longer, if she was still alive. And the kids. And Carlos.

I did not expect to fall asleep.

Asleep, feverish with sunburn. The Surgery program tickles blocks of nerves, plays me like a complex toy. In my sleep I feel raging thirst, hear a thunderclap, taste cinnamon or coffee, clench a phantom fist.

My skin wakes. Piloerection runs in ripples along my body, then a universal tickle, then pressure ... like that feather-crested snakeskin Sharrol put me into for Carlos's party ...

Sharrol, sliding into her own rainbow-scaled bodysuit, stopped halfway. "You don't really want to do this, do you?"

"I'll tough it out. How do I look?" I'd never developed the least sense of flatlander style. Sharrol picked my clothes.

"Half man, half snake," she said. "Me?"

"Like this snake's fitting mate." She didn't really. No flatlander is as supple as a crashlander. Raised in Earth's gravity, Sharrol was a foot shorter than I, and weighed the same as I did. Stocky.

The apartment was already in child mode: rounded surfaces everywhere, and all storage was locked or raised to eyeball height (mine). Tanya was five and Louis was four and both were agile as monkeys. I scanned for anything that might be dangerous within their reach.

Louis stared at us, solemn, awed. Tanya giggled. We must have looked odder than usual, though given flatlander styles it's a wonder that any kid can recognize its parents. Why do they change their hair and skin color so often? When we hugged them good-bye, Tanya made a game of tugging my hair out of shape and watching it flow back into a feathery crest. We set them down and turned on the Playmate program.

The lobby transfer booth jumped us three time zones east. We stepped out into a vestibule, facing an arc of picture window. A flock of rainbow-hued fish panicked at the awful sight and flicked away. A huge fish passed in some internal dream.

For an instant I felt the weight of all those tons of water.

I looked to see how Sharrol was taking it. She was smiling, admiring.

"Carlos lives near the Great Barrier Reef, you said. You didn't say he lived *in* it."

"It's a great privilege," Sharrol told me. "I spent my first thirty years under water, but not on the Reef. The Reef's too fragile. The UN protects it."

"You never told me that!"

She grinned at my surprise. "My dad had a lobster ranch near Boston. Later I worked for the Epcot-Atlantis police. The ecology isn't so fragile there, but—Bey, I should take you there."

I said, "Maybe it's why we think alike. I grew up underground. You can't build aboveground on We Made It."

"You told me. The winds."

"Sharrol, this isn't *like* Carlos."

She'd known Carlos Wu years longer than I had. "Carlos gets an idea and he follows it as far as it'll go. I don't know what he's onto now. Maybe he's always wanted to share me with you. And he brought a date for, um—"

"Ever met her?"

"—balance. No, Carlos won't even talk about Feather Filip. He just smiles mysteriously. Maybe it's love."

The children! Protect the children! Where are the children? The Surgeon must be tickling my adrenal glands. I'm not awake, but I'm frantic, and a bit randy too. Then the sensations ease off. *The Playmate program. It guards them and teaches them and plays with them. They'll be fine. Can't take them to Carlos's place . . . not tonight.*

Sharrol was their mother and Carlos Wu had been their father. Earth's Fertility Board won't let an albino have children. Carlos's gene pattern they judge perfect; he's one of a hundred and twenty flatlanders who carry an unlimited birthright.

A man can love any child. That's hard-wired into the brain. A man can raise another man's children. And accept their father as a friend . . . but there's a barrier. That's wired in, too.

Sharrol knows. She's afraid I'll turn prickly and uncivilized. And *Carlos* knows. So why . . . ?

Tonight was billed as a foursome, sex and *tapas*. That was a developing custom: dinner strung out as a sequence of small dishes between bouts of recreational sex. Something inherited from the ancient Greeks or Italians, maybe. There's something lovers gain from feeding each other.

Feather—

The memory blurs. I wasn't afraid of her then, but I am now. When I remember Feather, the Surgeon puts me to sleep.

But the children! I've got to remember. We were down. Sharrol was out of the 'doc, but we left Louis and Tanya frozen. We floated their box into the boat. Feather and I disengaged the lift plate and slid it under the 'doc. Beneath that lumpy jacket she moved like a tigress. She spoke my name; I turned ... .

Feather.

Carlos's sleepfield enclosed most of the bedroom. He'd hosted bigger parties than this in here. Tonight we were down to four, and a floating chaos of dishes Carlos said were Mexican.

"She's an ARM," Carlos said.

Feather Filip and I were sharing a tamale too spicy for Sharrol. Feather caught me staring and grinned back. An ARM?

I'd expected Feather to be striking. She wasn't exactly beautiful. She was strong: lean, almost gaunt, with prominent tendons in her neck, lumps flexing at the corners of her jaws. You don't get strength like that without training in illegal martial arts.

The Amalgamated Regional Militia is the United Nations police, and the United Nations took a powerful interest in Carlos Wu. What was she, Carlos's bodyguard? Was that how they'd met?

But whenever one of us spoke of the ARM that afternoon, Feather changed the subject.

I'd have thought Carlos would orchestrate our sleepfield dance. Certified genius that he is, would he not be superb at that, too? But Feather had her own ideas, and Carlos let her lead. Her lovemaking was aggressive and acrobatic. I felt her strength that afternoon. And my own lack, raised as I was in the lower gravity of We Made It.

And three hours passed in that fashion, while the wonderful colors of the reef darkened to light-amplified night.

And then Feather reached far out of the field, limber as a snake . . . reached inside her backpurse, and fiddled, and frowned, and rolled back and said, "We're shielded."

Carlos said, "They'll know."

"They know *me*," Feather said. "They're thinking that I let them use their monitors because I'm showing off, but now we're going to try something a little kinky. Or maybe I'm just putting them on. I've done it before—"

"Then—"

"Find a glitch so I can block their gear with something new. Then they fix it. They'll fix this one too, but not tonight. It's just Feather coming down after a long week."

Carlos accepted that. "Stet. Sharrol, Beowulf, do you want to leave Earth? We'd be traveling as a group, Louis and Tanya and the four of us. This is for keeps."

Sharrol said, "I can't." Carlos *knew* that.

He said, "You can ride in cold sleep. Home's rotation period is fifty minutes shorter than Earth's. Mass the same, air about the same. Tectonic activity is higher, so it'll smell like there's just a trace of smog—"

"Carlos, we talked this to *death* a few years ago." Sharrol was annoyed. "Sure, I could live on Home. I don't like the notion of flying from world to world like a, a corpse, but I'd do it. But the UN doesn't want me emigrating, and Home won't take flat phobes!"

The flatlander phobia is a bone-deep dread of being cut off from Earth. Fear of flying and/or falling is an extreme case, but no flat phobe can travel in space. You find few

flat phobes off Earth; in fact, Earthborn are called flatlanders no matter *how* well they adjust to life elsewhere.

But Feather was grinning at Sharrol. "We go by way of
Fafnir. We'll get to Home as Shashters. Home has already
approved us for immigration—"

"Under the name *Graynor*. We're all married," Carlos
amplified.

I said, "Carlos, you've *been* off Earth. You were on Jinx
for a year."

"Yah. Bey, Sigmund Ausfaller and his gnomes never lost
track of me. The United Nations thinks they own my genes.
I'm supervised wherever I go."

But they keep you in luxury, I thought. And the grass is
always greener. And Feather had her own complaint. "What
do you know about the ARM?" she asked us.

"We listen to the vid," Sharrol said.

"Sharrol, dear, we *vet* that stuff. The ARM decides what
you don't get to know about us. Most of us take psychoac-
tive chemicals to keep us in a properly paranoid mind
frame during working hours. We stay that way four days,
then go sane for the weekend. If it's making us too crazy,
they retire us."

Feather was nervous and trying to restrain it, but now
hard-edged muscles flexed, and her elbows and knees were
pulling in protectively against her torso. "But some of us
are born this way. We go *off* chemicals when we go to
work. The 'doc doses us back to sanity Thursday afternoon.
I've been an ARM schiz for thirty-five years. They're ready
to retire me, but they'd never let me go to some other
world, knowing what I know. And they don't want a schiz
making babies."

I didn't say that I could see their point. I looked at
Sharrol and saw hope in the set of her mouth, ready to
smile but holding off. We were being brought into these
plans *way* late. Rising hackles had pulled me right out of
any postcoital glow.

Feather told me, "They'll never let you go either, Beowulf."

And *that* was nonsense. "Feather, I've been off Earth three times since I got here."

"Don't try for four. You know too much. You know about the Core explosion, and diplomatic matters involving alien races—"

"I've left Earth since—"

"—and Julian Forward's work." She gave it a dramatic pause. "We'll have some advanced weaponry out of that. We would not want the kzinti to know about that, or the trinocs, or certain human domains. That last trip, do you know how much *talking* you did while you were on Gummidgy and Jinx? You're a friendly, talkative guy with great stories, Beowulf!"

I shrugged. "So why trust me with this? Why didn't you and Carlos just go?"

She gestured at Carlos. He grinned and said, "I insisted."

"And we need a pilot," Feather said. "That's you, Beowulf. But I can bust us loose. I've set up something nobody but an ARM would ever dream of."

She told us about it.

To the kzinti the world was only a number. Kzinti don't like ocean sports. The continent was Shasht, 'Burrowing Murder.' Shasht was nearly lifeless, but the air was breathable and the mines were valuable. The kzinti had dredged up megatons of sea bottom to fertilize a hunting jungle, and they got as far as seeding and planting before the Fourth Man-Kzin War.

After the war humankind took Shasht as reparations, and named the world *Fafnir*.

On Fafnir, Feather's investigations found a family of six: two men, two women, two children. The Graynors were ready to emigrate. Local law would cause them to leave most of their wealth behind; but then they'd lost most of it already backing some kind of recreational facilities on the continent.

"I've recorded them twice. The Graynors'll find funding waiting for them at Wunderland. They won't talk. The *other* Graynor family will emigrate to Home—"

"That's us?"

Feather nodded. Carlos said, "But if you and the kids won't come, Feather'll have to find someone else."

I said, "Carlos, *you'll* be watched. I don't suppose Feather can protect you from that."

"No. Feather's taken a much bigger risk—"

"They'll never miss it." She turned to me. "I got hold of a little stealth lander, Fourth War vintage, with a cold sleep box in back for you, Sharrol. We'll take that down to Fafnir. I've got an inflatable boat to take us to the Shasht North spaceport, and we'll get to Home on an Outbound Enterprises iceliner. Sharrol, you'll board the liner already frozen; I know how to bypass that stage." Feather was excited now. She gripped my arm and said, "We have to go get the lander, Beowulf. It's on Mars."

Sharrol said, "Tanya's a flat phobe too."

Feather's fingers closed with bruising force. I sensed that the lady didn't like seeing her plans altered.

"Wait one," Carlos said. "We can fix that. We're taking my 'doc, aren't we? It wouldn't be *plausible*, let alone intelligent, for Carlos Wu to go on vacation without his 'doc. Feather, how big is the lander's freezebox?"

"Yeah. Right. It'll hold Tanya ... better yet, both children. Sharrol can ride in your 'doc."

We talked it around. When we were satisfied, we went home.

Three days out, three days returning, and a week on Mars while the ARM team played with the spacecraft *Boy George*. It had to be Feather and me. I would familiarize myself with *Boy George*, Feather would supervise the ARM crews ... and neither of us were flat phobes.

I bought a dime disk, a tourist's guide to Fafnir system, and I studied it.

Kzinti and human planetologists call Fafnir a typical water world in a system older than Sol. The system didn't actually retain much more water than Earth did; that isn't the problem. But the core is low in radioactives. The lithosphere is thick: no continental drift here. Shallow oceans cover 93 percent of the planet. The oceans seethe with life, five billion years evolved, twice as old as Earth's.

And where the thick crust cracked in early days, magma oozed through to build the world's single continent. Today a wandering line of volcanoes and bare rock stretches from the south pole nearly to the north. The continent's mass has been growing for billions of years.

On the opposite face of a lopsided planet, the ocean has grown shallow. Fafnir's life presently discovered the advantages of coral building. That side of the world is covered with tens of thousands of coral islands. Some stand up to twenty meters tall: relics of a deeper ocean.

The mines are all on Shasht. So also are all the industry, both spaceports, and the seat of government. But the life—recreation, housing, families—is all on the islands.

Finding the old lander had indeed been a stroke of luck. It was an identical backup for the craft that set Sinbad Jabar down on Meerowsk in the Fourth War, where he invaded the harem of the Patriarch's Voice. The disgrace caused the balance of power among the local kzinti to become unstable. The human alliance took Meerowsk and renamed the planet, and it was Jabar's Prize until a later, pacifistic generation took power. Jabar's skin is displayed there still.

Somehow Feather had convinced the ARMs that (1) this twin of Jabar's lander was wanted for the Smithsonian Luna, and (2) the Belt peoples would raise hell if they knew it was to be removed from Mars. The project must be absolutely secret.

Ultimately the ARM crews grew tired of Feather's supervision, or else her company. Rapidly after that, Feather grew tired of watching me read. "We'll only *be* on Fafnir two days, Beowulf. What are you learning? It's a dull, dull, dull place. All the land life is Earth imports—"

"Their lifestyle is strange, Feather. They travel by transfer booths and dirigible balloons and boats, and almost nothing in between. A very laid-back society. Nobody's expected to be anywhere on time—"

"Nobody's watching us here. You don't have to play tourist."

"I know." If the ARM had *Boy George* bugged . . . but Feather would have thought of *that*.

Our ship was in the hands of ARM engineers, and that made for tension. But we were getting on each other's nerves. Not a good sign, with a three-week flight facing us.

Feather said, "You're not playing. You *are* a tourist!"

I admitted it. "And the first law of tourism is: *read everything*." But I switched the screen off and said, in the spirit of compromise, "All right. Show me. What is there to see on Mars?"

She hated to admit it. "Nothing."

We left Mars with the little stealth lander in the fuel tank. The ARM was doing things the ARM didn't know about. And I continued reading . . .

Fafnir's twenty-two-hour day has encouraged an active life. Couch potatoes court insomnia: it's easier to sleep if you're tired. But *hurrying* is something else. There are transfer booths, of course. You can jump instantly from a home on some coral extrusion to the bare rock of Shasht . . . and buy yourself an eleven-hour time lag.

Nobody's in a hurry to go home. They go by dirigible. Ultimately the floatliner companies wised up and began selling round-trip tickets for the same price as one-way.

"I do *know* all this, Beowulf."

"Mph? Oh, good."

"So what's the plan?" Feather asked. "Find an island with nothing near it and put down, right? Get out and dance around on the sand while we blow the boat up and load it and go. How do we hide the lander?"

"Sink it."

"Read about lamplighters," she said, so I did.

After the war and the settlement, UN advance forces landed on Shasht, took over the kzinti structures, then began to explore. Halfway around the planet were myriads of little round coral islands, each with a little peak at the center. At night the peaks glowed with a steady yellow light. Larger islands were chains of peaks, each with its yellow glow in the cup. Lamplighters were named before anyone knew what they were.

Close up . . . well, they've been called piranha ant nests. The bioluminescence attracts scores of varieties of flying fish. Or, lured or just lost, a swimming thing may beach itself, and then the lamplighter horde flows down to the beach and cleans it to the bones.

You can't build a home or beach a boat until the nest has been burned out. *Then* you have to wait another twelve days for the soldiers caught outside the nest to die. *Then* cover the nest. Use it for a basement, put your house on it. Otherwise the sea may carry a queen to you, to use the nest again.

"You're ahead of me on this," I admitted. "What has this lander got for belly rockets?"

"Your basic hydrogen and oxygen," Feather said. "High heat and a water-vapor exhaust. We'll burn the nest out."

"Good."

Yo! Boy, when Carlos's 'doc is finished with you, you know it!

Open.

The sky was a brilliant sprawl of stars, some of them moving—spacecraft, weather eyes, the wheel—and a single lopsided moon. The island was shadow-teeth cutting into the starscape. I slid out carefully, into a blackness like the inside of my empty belly, and yelled as I dropped into seawater.

The water was hip deep, with no current to speak of. I wasn't going to drown, or be washed away, or lost. Fafnir's moon was a little one, close in. Tides would be shallow.

Still I'd been lucky: I could have wakened under water.

How did people feel about nudity here? But my bundle of clothes hadn't washed away. Now the boots clasped my feet like old friends. The sleeves of the dead man's survival jacket trailed way past my hands until I rolled them up, and of course the front and back were in shreds. The pants were better: too big, but with elastic ankle bands that I just pulled up to my knees. I swallowed a tannin secretion dose. I couldn't have done that earlier. The 'doc would have read the albino gene in my DNA and "cured" me of an imposed tendency to tan.

There was nothing on all of Fafnir like Carlos's 'doc. I'd have to hide it before I could ever think about rescue.

"Our medical equipment," Carlos had called it; and Feather had answered, "Hardly ours."

Carlos was patient. "It's all we've got, Feather. Let me show you how to use it. First, the diagnostics—"

The thing was as massive as the inflatable boat that would carry us to Shasht. Carlos had a gravity lift to shove under it. The intensive care cavity was tailored just for Carlos Wu, naturally, but any of us could be served by the tethers and sleeves and hypo-tipped tubes and readouts along one whole face of the thing: the service wall.

"These hookups do your diagnostics and set the chemical feeds going. Feather, it'll rebalance body chemistry, in case I ever go schiz or someone poisons me or something. I've reprogrammed it to take care of you too." I don't think Carlos noticed the way Feather looked at it, and him.

"Now the cavity. It's for the most serious injuries, but I've reprogrammed it for you, Sharrol my dear—"

"But it's exactly Carlos's size," Feather told us pointedly. "The UN thinks a lot of Carlos. We can't use it."

Sharrol said, "It looks small. I don't mean the IC cavity. I can get into that. But there's not much room for trans- plants in that storage space."

"Oh, no. This is advanced stuff. I had a hand in the de- sign. One day we'll be able to use these techniques with everyone." Carlos patted the monster. "There's nothing in here in the way of cloned organs and such. There's the Surgery program, and a reservoir of organic soup, and a googol of self-replicating machines a few hundred atoms long. If I lost a leg or an eye, they'd turn me off and rebuild it onto me. There's even ... here, pay attention. You feed the organics reservoir through here, so the machine doesn't run out of material. You could even feed it Fafnir fish if you can catch them, but they're metal-deficient ..."

When he had us thoroughly familiar with the beast, he helped Sharrol into the cavity, waited to be sure she was hooked up, and closed it. That made me nervous as hell. She climbed out a day later claiming that she hadn't felt a thing, wasn't hungry, didn't even have to use the bathroom.

The 'doc was massive. I had to really heave against it to get it moving, and then it wanted to move along the shore. I forced it to turn inland. The proper place to hide it was in the lamplighter nest, of course.

I was gasping like death itself, and the daylight had almost died, and I just couldn't push that mass uphill.

I left it on the beach. Maybe there was an answer. Let my hindbrain toy with it for a while.

I trudged across sand to rough coral and kept walking to the peak. We'd picked the island partly for its isolation. Two distant yellow lights, eastward, marked two islands I'd noted earlier. I ran my mag specs (the side that worked) up to 20X and scanned the whole horizon, and found nothing but the twin lamplighter glows.

And nothing to do but wait.

I sat with my back against the lip of the dead lamplighter pit. I pictured her: she looked serious, a touch worried, under a feather crest and undyed skin: pink shading to brown, an Anglo tanned as if by Fafnir's yellow-white sun.

I said, "Sharrol."

Like the dead she had slept, her face slack beneath the faceplate, like Sleeping Beauty. I'd taken to talking to her, wondering if some part of her heard. I'd never had the chance to ask.

"I never wondered why you loved me. Egotist, I am. But you must have looked like me when you were younger. Thirty years underwater, no sunlight. Your uncles, your father, they must have looked a *lot* like me. Maybe even with white hair. How old *are* you? I never asked."

Her memory looked at me.

"Tanj that. *Where* are you? Where are Tanya and Louis? Where's Carlos? What happened after I was shot?"

Faint smile, shrug of eyebrows.

"You spent three weeks unconscious in the ICC followed by ten minutes on your feet. Wrong gravity, wrong air mix, wrong smells. We hit you with everything it might take to knock a flat phobe spinning. Then *blam* and your love interest is lying on the sand with a hole through him.

"Maybe you tried to kill her. I don't think you'd give her much trouble, but maybe Feather would kill you anyway. She'd still have the kids. . . ."

I slammed my fist on coral. "What did she *want*? That crazy woman. I never hurt her at all."

Talking to Sharrol: Lifeless as she was, maybe it wasn't quite as *crazy* as talking to myself. I couldn't talk to the others. They— "You remember that night we planned it all? Feather was lucid then. Comparatively. We were there for her as *people*. On the trip to Mars she was a lot wilder. She was a hell of an *active* lover, but I never really got the feeling that I was *there* for her."

We never talked about each other's lovers. In truth, it was easier to say these things to Sharrol when she wasn't here.

"But most of the way to Fafnir, Feather was fine. But she wasn't sleeping with me. Just Carlos. She could hold a conversation, no problem there, but I was *randy*, love, and frustrated. She liked that. I caught a *look* when Carlos wasn't looking. So I didn't want to talk to her. And she was always up against Carlos, and Carlos, he was a bit embarrassed about it all. We talked about plans, but for anything personal there was just you. Sleeping Beauty."

The night was warm and clear. By convention, boats

would show any color except lamplighter yellow. I couldn't miss seeing a boat's lights.

"Then, fifteen hours out from the drop point, that night I found her floating in my sleeping plates. I suppose I could have sent her to her own room, I mean it was within the laws of physics, but I didn't. I acted like conversation was the last thing I'd be interested in. But so did Feather.

"And the next morning it was all business, and a frantic business it was. We came in in devious fashion, and got off behind the moon. *Boy George* went on alone, decelerating. Passed too close to an ARM base on Claim 226 that even Feather wasn't supposed to know about. Turned around and accelerated away in clear and obvious terror, heading off in the general direction of Hrooshpith—pithtcha—of another of those used-to-be-kzinti systems where they've never got the population records straightened out. No doubt the ARM is waiting for us there.

"And of course you missed the ride down . . . but my point is that nothing ever got *said*."

"Okay. This whole scheme was schemed by Feather, carried through by Feather. It—" I stared into the black night. "Oh." I really should have seen this earlier. Why did Feather need Carlos?

Through the ARM spy net Feather Filip had found a family of six Shashters ready to emigrate. Why not look for one or two? Where Carlos insisted on taking his children and Sharrol and me, another man might be more reasonable.

"She doesn't just want to be clear of Sol system. Doesn't just want to make babies. She wants *Carlos*. Carlos of the perfect genes. Hah! Carlos finally saw it. Maybe she told him. He must have let her know he didn't want children by an ARM schiz. Angry and randy, she took it out on me, and then . . ."

Then?

With my eyes open to the dark, entranced, I remembered that final night. *Yellow lights sprinkled on a black ocean. Some are the wrong color, too bright, too blue. Avoid those.*

They're houses. Pick one far from the rest. Hover. Organic matter burns lamplighter yellow below the drive flame, then fades. I sink us in, an egg in an egg cup. Feather blasts the roof loose and we crawl out—

We hadn't wanted to use artificial lights. When dawn gave us enough light, we inflated the boat. Feather and Carlos used the gravity lift to settle the freezebox in the boat. They were arguing in whispers. I didn't want to hear that, I thought.

I turned off the doc's "Maintenance" sequence. A minute later Sharrol sat up, a flat phobe wakened suddenly on an alien world. Sniffed the air. Kissed me and let me lift her out, heavy in Fafnir's gravity. I set her on the sand. Her nerve seemed to be holding. Feather had procured local clothing; I pushed the bundle into her arms.

Feather came toward me towing the gravity lift. She looked shapeless, with bulging pockets fore and aft. We slid the lift into place, and I pushed the 'doc toward Carlos and the boat. Feather called my name. I turned. *Blam.* Agony and scrambled senses, but I saw Carlos leap for the boat, reflexes like a jackrabbit. My head hit the black sand.

Then?

"She wanted hostages. Our children, but *Carlos's* children. They're frozen, they won't give her any trouble. But me, why would she need me? Killing me lets Carlos know she means it. Maybe I told too many stories: maybe she thinks I'm dangerous. Maybe—"

For an instant I saw just *how* superfluous I was, from Feather Filip's psychotic viewpoint. Feather wanted Carlos. Carlos wanted the children. Sharrol came with the children. Beowulf Shaeffer was along because he was with Sharrol. If Feather shot Beowulf, how much would Carlos mind? *Blam.*

Presently I said, "She shot me to prove she would. But it looked to me like Carlos just ran. There weren't any weapons in the boat, we'd only just inflated it. All he could do was start it and go. That takes—" When I thought about it, it was actually a good move. He'd gotten away with himself and Tanya and Louis, with both hostages. Protect them now, negotiate later.

And he'd left Feather in a killing rage, with that horrible tube and one living target. I stopped talking to Sharrol then, because it seemed to me she must be dead.

No! "Feather had you. She *had* to have *you*." It could happen. It could. "What else can she threaten Carlos with? She has to keep you alive." I tried to believe it. "She certainly didn't kill you in the first minute. Somebody had to put me in the 'doc. Feather had no interest in doing that."

But she had no interest in letting Sharrol do that either. "Tanj dammit! Why did Feather let you put me in the 'doc? She even let you . . ." What about the biomass reserve?

My damaged body must have needed some major restructuring. The biomass reserve had been feeding Sharrol, and doing incidental repairs on us all, for the entire three-week trip. Healing me would take another . . . fifty kilograms? More? "She must have let you fill the biomass reserve with . . ." Fish?

Feather showing Carlos how reasonable she could be . . . too reasonable. It felt wrong, wrong. "The other body, the headless one. Why not just push *that* in the hopper? So much easier. Unless—"

Unless material was even closer at hand.

I felt no sudden inspiration. It was a matter of making myself believe. I tried to remember Sharrol . . . pulling her clothes on quickly, shivering and dancing on the sand, in the chilly dawn breeze. Hands brushing back through her hair, hair half grown out. A tiny grimace for the way the survival jacket made her look, bulges everywhere. Patting pockets, opening some of them.

The 'doc had snapped her out of a three week sleep. Like me: awake, alert, ready.

It didn't go away, the answer. It just . . . I still didn't know where Sharrol was, or Carlos, or the children. What if I was wrong? Feather had mapped my route to Home, every step of the way. I knew exactly where Feather was now, if a line of logic could point my way. But—one wrong assumption, and Feather Filip could pop up behind my ear.

I could make myself safer, and Sharrol too, if I mapped out a worst-case scenario.

Feather's Plan B: Kill Shaeffer. Take the rest prisoners, to impose her will on Carlos ... but Carlos flees with the boat. So, Plan B-1: Feather holds Sharrol at gunpoint. (Alive.) Some days later she waves down a boat. *Blam*, and a stolen boat sails toward Shasht. Or stops to stow Sharrol somewhere, maybe on another coral island, maybe imprisoned inside a plastic tent with a live lamplighter horde prowling outside.

And Carlos? He's had four months, now, to find Sharrol and Feather. He's a genius, ask anyone. And Feather wants to get in touch ... unless she's given up on Carlos, decided to kill him.

If I could trace Carlos's path, I would find Louis and Tanya and even Sharrol.

Carlos Plan B-1 follows Plan A as originally conceived by Feather. The kids would be stowed aboard the iceliner as if already registered. Carlos would register and be frozen. Feather could follow him to Home ... maybe on the same ship, if she hustled. But—

No way could Feather get herself frozen with a gun in her hand. That would be the moment to take her, coming out of freeze on Home.

There, I had a target. On Shasht they could tell me who had boarded the *Zombie Queen* for Home. What did I have to do to get to Shasht?

"Feed myself, that's easy. Collect rainwater too. Get off the island ..." That, at least, was not a puzzle. I couldn't build a raft. I couldn't swim to another island. But a sailor lost at sea will die if cast ashore; therefore, local tradition decrees that he *must* be rescued.

"Collect some money. Get to Shasht. Hide myself." Whatever else was lost to me, to *us*—whoever had died, whoever still lived—there was still the mission, and that was to be free of the United Nations and Earth.

And Carlos Wu's 'doc would finger me instantly. It was advanced nanotechnology: it screamed its Earthly origin. It might be the most valuable item on Fafnir, and I had no wealth at all, and I was going to have to abandon it.

Come daylight, I moved the 'doc. I still wanted to hide it in the lamplighter nest. The gravity lift would lift it but not push it uphill. But I solved it.

One of the secrets of life: know when and what to give up.

I waited for low tide and then pushed it out to sea, and turned off the lift. The water came almost to the faceplate. Seven hours later it didn't show at all. And the next emergency might kill me unless it happened at low tide.

The nights were as warm as the days. As the tourist material had promised, it rained just before dawn. I set up my pants to funnel rainwater into a hole I had chopped in the coral.

The tour guide had told me how to feed myself. It isn't that rare for a lamplighter nest to die. Sooner or later an unlit island will be discovered by any of several species of swimming things. Some ride the waves at night and spawn in the sand.

I spent the second night running through the shallows and scooping up sunbunnies in my jacket. Bigger flying fish came gliding off the crests of the breakers. They wanted the sunbunnies. Three or four wanted me, but I was able to dodge. One I had to gut in midair.

The tour guide hadn't told me how to clean sunbunnies. I had to fake that. I poached them in seawater, using my pocket torch on high; and I ate until I was bloated. I fed more of them into the biomass reservoir.

With some distaste, I fed those long human bones in too. Fafnir fish meat was deficient in metals. Ultimately that might kill me; but the 'doc could compensate for a time.

There was nothing to build a boat with. The burnt-out lamplighter nest didn't show by daylight, so any passing boat would be afraid to rescue me. I thought of swimming;

I thought of riding away on the gravity lift, wherever the wind might carry me. But I couldn't feed myself at sea, and how could I approach another island?

On the fourth evening a great winged shape passed over the island, then dived into the sea. Later I heard a slapping sound as that flyer and a companion kicked themselves free of the water, soared, passed over the crater and settled into it. They made a great deal of noise. Presently the big one glided down to the water and was gone.

At dawn I fed myself again, on the clutch of eggs that had been laid in the body of the smaller flyer: male or female, whichever. The dime disk hadn't told me about *this* creature. A pity I wouldn't have the chance to write it up.

At just past sunset on the eighth night I saw a light flicker blue-green-red.

My mag specs showed a boat that wasn't moving.

I fired a flare straight up, and watched it burn blue-white for twenty minutes. I fired another at midnight. Then I stuffed my boots partway into my biggest pockets, inflated my shoulder floats, and walked into the sea until I had to swim.

I couldn't see the boat with my eyes this close to water level. I fired another flare before dawn. One of those had to catch someone awake . . . and if not, I had three more. I kept swimming.

It was peaceful as a dream. Fafnir's ecology is very old, evolved on a placid world not prone to drifting continents and ice ages, where earthquakes and volcanoes know their place.

The sea had teeth, of course, but the carnivores were specialized; they knew the sounds of their prey. There were a few terrifying exceptions. Reason and logic weren't enough to wash out those memories, holograms of creatures the match for any white shark.

I grew tired fast. The air felt warm enough, the water did too, but it was leeching the heat from my flesh and bones. I kept swimming.

A rescuer should have no way of knowing that I had

been on an island. The farther I could get, the better. I did
not want a rescuer to find Carlos Wu's 'doc.

At first I saw nothing more of the boat than the great
white wings of its sails. I set the pocket torch on wide focus and high power, to compete with what was now broad
daylight, and poured vivid green light on the sails.

And I waited for it to turn toward me, but for a long time
it didn't. It came in a zigzag motion, aimed by the wind,
never straight at me. It took forever to pull alongside.

A woman with fluffy golden hair studied me in some curiosity, then stripped in two quick motions and dived in.

I was numb with cold, hardly capable of wiggling a finger. This was the worst moment, and I couldn't muster the
strength to appreciate it. I passively let the woman noose
me under the armpits, watched the man lift me aboard, utterly unable to protect myself.

Feather could have killed me before the 'doc released
me. Why wait? I'd worked out what must have happened
to her; it was almost plausible; but I couldn't shake the notion that Feather was waiting above me, watching me come
aboard.

There was only a brawny golden man with slanted brown
eyes and golden hair bleached nearly as white as mine. *Tor*,
she'd called him, and she was *Wil*. He wrapped me in a silver bubble blanket and pushed a bulb of something hot into
my hands.

My hands shook. A cup would have splashed everything
out. I got the bulb to my lips and sucked. Strange taste,
augmented with a splash of rum. The warmth went to the
core of me like life itself.

The woman climbed up, dripping. She had eyes like his,
a golden tan like his. He handed her a bulb. They looked
me over amiably. I tried to say something; my teeth turned
into castanets. I sucked and listened to them arguing over
who and what I might be, and what could have torn up my
jacket that way.

When I had my teeth under some kind of control, I said,

"I'm Persial January Hebert, and I'm eternally in your debt."

Leaving all our Earthly wealth behind us was a pain. Feather could help: she contrived to divert a stream of ARM funds to Fafnir, replacing it from Carlos's wealth.

Riiight. But Sharrol and I would be sponging off Carlos . . . and maybe it wouldn't be Carlos. Feather controlled that wealth for now, and Feather liked control. She had not said that she expected to keep some for herself. That bothered me. It must have bothered Carlos too, though we never found privacy to talk about it.

I wondered how Carlos would work it. Had he known Feather Filip before he reached Jinx? I could picture him designing something that would be useless on Earth: say, an upgraded version of the mass driver system that runs through the vacuum across Jinx's East Pole, replacing a more normal world's Pinwheel launcher. Design something, copyright it on Jinx under a pseudonym, form a company. Just in case he ever found the means to flee Sol system.

Me, I went to my oldest friend on Earth. General Products owed Elephant a considerable sum, and Elephant— Gregory Pelton—owed me. He got General Products to arrange for credit on Home and Fafnir. Feather wouldn't have approved the breach in secrecy, but the aliens who run General Products don't reveal secrets. We'd never even located their homeworld.

And Feather must have expected to control Carlos's funding and Carlos with it.

And Sharrol . . . was with me.

She'd trusted me. Now she was a flat phobe broke and stranded on an alien world, if she still lived, if she wasn't the prisoner of a homicidal maniac. Four months, going on five. Long enough to drive her crazy, I thought.

How could I hurry to her rescue? The word *hurry* was said to be forgotten on Fafnir; but perhaps I'd thought of a way.

* * *

They let me sleep. When I woke there was soup. I was ravenous. We talked while we ate.

The boat was *Gullfish*. The owners were Wilhelmin and Toranaga, brother and sister, both recently separated from mates and enjoying a certain freedom. Clean air, exercise, celibacy, before they returned to the mating dance, its embarrassments and frustrations and rewards.

There was a curious turn to their accents. I tagged it as Australian at first, then as Plateau softened by speech training, or by a generation or two in other company. This was said to be typical of Fafnir. There was no Fafnir accent. The planet had been settled too recently and from too many directions.

Wil finished her soup, went to a locker, and came back with a jacket. It was not quite like mine, and new, untouched. They helped me into it and let me fish through the pockets of my own ragged garment before they tossed it in the locker.

They had given me my life. By Fafnir custom my response would be a gift expressing my value as perceived by myself . . . but Wil and Tor hadn't told me their full names. I hinted at this; they failed to understand. Hmm.

My dime disk hadn't spoken of this. It might be a new custom: the rescuer conceals data, so that an impoverished rescuee need not be embarrassed. He sends no life gift instead of a cheap one. But I was guessing. I couldn't follow the vibes yet.

As for my own history—

"I just gave up," I blurted. "It was so stupid. I hadn't—hadn't tried everything at all."

Toranaga said, "What kind of everything were you after?"

"I lost my wife four months ago. A rogue wave—you know how waves crossing can build into a mountain of water? It rolled our boat under. A trawler picked me up, the *Triton*." A civil being must be able to name his rescuer. Surely there must be a boat named *Triton*? "There's no record of anyone finding Milcenta. I bought another boat and searched. It's been four months. I was doing more drinking than looking lately, and three nights ago something rammed the boat. A torpedo ray, I think. I didn't sink, but my power was out, even my lights. I got tired of it all and just started swimming."

They looked at each other, then at their soup. Sympathy was there, with a trace of contempt beneath.

"Middle of the night, I was cold as the sea bottom, and it crossed my mind that maybe Mil was rescued under another name. We aren't registered as a partnership. If Mil was in a coma, they'd check her retina prints—"

"Use our caller," Wilhelmin said.

I thanked them. "With your permission, I'll establish some credit too. I've run myself broke, but there's credit at Shasht."

They left me alone in the cabin.

The caller was set into a wall in the cabin table. It was a portable—just a projector plate and a few keys that would get me a display of virtual keys and a screen—but a sailor's portable, with a watertight case and several small cleats. I found the master program unfamiliar but user-friendly.

I set up a search program for Milcenta Adelaide Graynor, in any combination. Milcenta was Sharrol and Adelaide was Feather, as determined by their iceliner tickets and retina prints. Milcenta's name popped up at once.

I bellowed out of the hatch. "They saved her!" Wil and Tor bolted into the cabin to read over my shoulder.

Hand of Allah, a fishing boat. Milcenta but not Adelaide! Sharrol had been picked up alone. I'd been at least half-right: she'd escaped from Feather. I realized I was crying.

And—"No life gift." That was the other side of it: if she sent a proper gift, the embarrassment of needing to be rescued at sea need never become public record. We'd drilled each other on such matters. "She must have been in bad shape."

"Yes, if she didn't call you," Wilhelmin said. "And she didn't go home either?"

I told Martin Graynor's story: "We sold our home. We were on one last cruise before boarding an iceliner. She could be anywhere by now, if she thought the wave killed me. I'll have to check."

I did something about money first. There was nothing aboard *Gullfish* that could read Persial January Hebert's retina prints, but I could at least establish that money was there.

I tried to summon passenger records from the iceliner *Zombie Queen*. This was disallowed. I showed disappointment and some impatience; but of course they wouldn't be shown to Hebert. They'd be opened to Martin Wallace Graynor.

They taught me to sail.

Gullfish was built for sails, not for people. The floors weren't flat. Ropes lay all over every surface. The mast stood upright through the middle of the cabin. You didn't walk in, you climbed. There were no lift plates; you slept in an odd-shaped box small enough to let you brace yourself in storms.

I had to learn a peculiar slang, as if I were learning to fly a spacecraft, and for the same reason. If a sailor hears a yell, he has to know what is meant, instantly.

I was working hard and my body was adjusting to the shorter day. Sure I had insomnia; but nobody sleeps well on a small boat. The idea is to snap awake instantly, where any stimulus could mean trouble. The boat was giving my body time to adjust to Fafnir.

Once I passed a mirror, and froze. I barely knew myself.

That was all to the good. My skin was darkening and, despite sun block, would darken further. But— when we landed, my hair had been cut to Fafnir styles. It had grown during four months in the 'doc. The 'doc had "cured" my depilation treatment: I had a beard too. When we reached civilization I would be far too conspicuous: a pink-eyed, pale-skinned man with long, wild white hair.

My hosts hadn't said anything about my appearance. It was easy to guess what they'd thought. They'd found a neurotic who sailed in search of his dead wife until his love of life left him entirely.

I went to Tor in some embarrassment and asked if they had anything like a styler aboard.

They had scissors. Riiight. Wil tried to shape my hair, laughed at the result, and suggested I finish the job at Booty Island.

So I tried to forget the rest of the world and just sail. It was what Wilhelmin and Toranaga were doing. One day at a time. Islands and boats grew more common as we neared the Central Isles. Another day for Feather to forget me, or lose me. Another day of safety for Sharrol, if Feather followed me to her. I'd have to watch for that.

And peace would have been mine, but that my ragged vest was in a locker that wouldn't open to my fingerprints.

Wil and Tor talked about themselves, a little, but I still didn't know their identities. They slept in a locked cabin. I noticed also an absence. Wil was a lovely woman, not unlike Sharrol herself; but her demeanor and body language showed no sign that she considered herself female, or me male, let alone that she might welcome a pass.

It might mean anything, in an alien culture: that my hair style or shape of nose or skin color was distasteful, or I didn't know the local body language, or I lacked documentation for my gene pattern. But I wondered if they wanted no life gift, in any sense, from a man they might have to give to the police.

What would a police detective think of those holes? Why, he'd think some kinetic weapon had torn a hole through the occupant, killing him instantly, after which someone (the killer?) had stolen the vest for himself. And if Wil and Tor were thinking that way . . . What I did at the caller—might it be saved automatically?

Now *there* was a notion.

I borrowed the caller again. I summoned the encyclopedia and set a search for a creature with boneless arms. There were several on Fafnir, all small. I sought data on the biggest, particularly those local to the North Coral Quadrant. There were stories . . . no hard evidence.

And another day passed, and I learned that I could cook while a kitchen was rolling randomly.

At dinner that night Will got to talking about Fafnir sea life. She'd worked at Pacifica, which I gathered was a kind of underwater zoo; and had I ever heard of a Kdatlyno lifeform like a blind squid?

"No," I said. "Would the kzinti bring one here?"

"I wouldn't think so. The kzinti aren't surfers," Tor said, and we laughed.

Wil didn't. She said, "They meant it for the hunting jungle. On Kdat the damn things can come ashore and drag big animals back into the ocean. But they've pretty well died out around Shasht, and we never managed to get one for Pacifica."

"Well," I said, and hesitated, and, "I think I was attacked by something like that. But huge. And it wasn't around Shasht, it was where you picked me up."

"Jan, you should report it."

"Wil, I can't. I was fast asleep and half dead of cold, lost at sea at midnight. I woke up under water. Something was squeezing my chest and back. I got my knife out and slashed. Slashed something rubbery. It pulled apart. It pulled my *jacket* apart. If it had ripped the shoulder floats I'd still be down there. But I never saw a thing."

Thus are legends born.

Booty Island is several islands merged. I counted eight peaks coming in; there must have been more. We had been sailing for twelve days.

Buildings sat on each of the lamplighter nests. They looked like government buildings or museums. No two were alike. Houses were scattered across the flatlands between. A mile or so of shopping center ran like a suspension bridge between two peaks. On Earth this would have been a park. Here, a center of civilization.

A line of transfer booths in the mall bore the familiar flickering Pelton logo. They were all big cargo booths, and old. I didn't instantly see the significance.

We stopped in a hotel and used a coin caller. The system read my retina prints: Persial January Hebert, sure enough. Wil and Tor waited while I moved some money, collected some cash and a transfer booth card, and registered for a room. I tried again for records of Milcenta Adelaide Graynor. Sharrol's rescue was still there. Nothing for Feather.

Wil said, "Jan, she may have been recovering from a head injury. See if she's tried to find you."

I couldn't be Mart Graynor while Wil and Tor were watching. The net registered no messages for Jan Hebert. Feather didn't know that name. Sharrol did; but Sharrol thought I was dead.

Or maybe she was crazy, incapacitated. With Tor and Wil watching I tried two worst-cases.

First: executions. A public 'doc can cure most varieties of madness. Madness is curable, therefore voluntary. A capital crime committed during a period of madness has carried the death penalty for seven hundred years, on Earth and on every world I knew.

It was true on Fafnir too. But Sharrol had not been executed for any random homicide, and neither, worse luck, had Feather.

Next: There are still centers for the study of madness. The best known is on Jinx. On Earth there are several, plus one secret branch of the ARM. There was only one mental institution to serve all of Fafnir, and that seemed to be half empty. Neither Feather's nor Sharrol's retina prints showed on the records.

The third possibility would have to wait.

We all needed the hotel's styler, though I was the worst off. The device left my hair long at the neck, and theirs too, a local style to protect against sunburn. I let it tame my beard without baring my face. The sun had had its way with me: I looked like an older man.

I took Wil and Tor to lunch. I found "gullfish" on the menu, and tried it. Like much of Fafnir sea life, it tasted like something that had almost managed to become red meat.

I worked some points casually into conversation, just checking. It was their last chance to probe me too, and I had to improvise details of a childhood in the North Sea. Tor found me plausible; Wil was harder to read. Nothing was said of a vest or a great sea monster. In their minds I was already gone.

I was Schrödinger's cat: I had murdered and not murdered the owner of a shredded vest.

At the caller in my room I established myself as Martin Wallace Graynor. That gave me access to my wives' autodoc records. A public 'doc will correct any of the chemical imbalances we lump under the term "crazy," but it also records such service.

Milcenta Graynor—Sharrol—had used a 'doc eight times in four-plus months, starting a week after our disastrous landing. The record showed much improvement over that period, beginning at a startling adrenaline level, acid indigestion and some dangerous lesser symptoms. Eight times within the Central Islands . . . none on Shasht.

If she'd never reached the mainland, then she'd never tried to reach Outbound Enterprises. Never tried to find Carlos, or Louis and Tanya.

Adelaide Graynor—Feather—had no 'doc record on this world. The most obvious conclusion was that wherever she was, she must be mad as a March hare.

Boats named *Gullfish* were everywhere on Fafnir. Fifty-one registries. Twenty-nine had sail. Ten of those would sleep four. I scanned for first names: no Wilhelmin, no Toranaga. Maybe *Gullfish* belonged to a parent, or to one of the departed spouses.

I'd learned a term for *Gullfish*'s sail and mast configuration: "sloop rig."

Every one of the ten candidates was a sloop rig!

Wait, now. Wil had worked at Pacifica?

I did some research. Pacifica wasn't just a zoo. It looked more like an underwater village, with listings for caterers, costume shops, subs, repair work, travel, hotels . . . but Wil had worked with sea life. Might that give me a handle?

I couldn't see how.

It wasn't that I didn't have an answer; I just didn't like it. Wil and Tor *had* to hand my vest to the cops. When Persial January Hebert was reported rescued, I would send them a gift.

Feather didn't know my alternate name. But if she had access to the Fafnir police, she'd tanj sure recognize that vest!

With the rest of the afternoon I bought survival gear: a backpurse, luggage, clothing.

On Earth I could have vanished behind a thousand shades of dyes. Here . . . I settled for a double dose of tannin secretion, an underdose of sun block, a darkened pair of mag specs, my height, and a local beard and hairstyle.

Arming myself was a problem.

The disk hadn't spoken of weapons on Fafnir. My safest guess was that Fafnir was like Earth: they didn't put weapons in the hands of civilians. Handguns, rifles, martial arts training belong to the police.

The good news: everyone on the islands carried knives. Those flying sharks that attacked me during the sunbunny run were one predator out of thousands.

Feather would arm herself somehow. She'd look through a sporting goods store, steal a hunting rifle . . . nope, no hunting rifles. No large prey on Fafnir, unless in the kzinti jungle, or *underwater*.

There were listings for scuba stores. I found a stun gun with a big parabolic reflector, big enough to knock out a one-gulp, too big for a pocket. I took it home, with more

diving gear for versimilitude and a little tool kit for repair-
ing diving equipment. With that I removed the reflector.

Now I couldn't use it underwater; it would knock *me*
out, because water conducts sound very well. But it would
fit my pocket.

I took my time over a sushi dinner, quite strange. Some
time after sunset I stepped into a transfer booth, and
stepped out into a brilliant dawn on Shasht.

Outbound Enterprises was open. I let a Ms. Machti take
Martin Wallace Graynor's retina prints. "Your ticket is still
good, Mr. Graynor," Ms. Machti said. "The service charge
will be eight hundred stars. You're four months late!"

"I was shipwrecked," I told her. "Did my companions
make it?"

Iceliner passengers are in no hurry. The ships keep prices
down by launching when they're full. I learned that the
Zombie Queen had departed a week after our landing, about
as expected. I gave Ms. Machti the names. She set the
phone system searching, and presently said, "Your husband
and the children boarded and departed. Your wives' tickets
are still outstanding."

"Both?"

"Yes." She did a double take. "Oh, good heavens, they
must think you're dead!"

"That's what I'm afraid of. At least, John and Tweena
and Nathan would. They were revived in good shape?"

"Yes, of course. But the women—could they have waited
for you?"

Stet: Carlos, Tanya, and Louis were all safe on Home
and had left the spaceport under their own power. Feather
and Sharrol—"Waited? But they'd have left a message."

She was still looking at her screen. "Not for you, Mr.
Graynor, but Mr. *John* Graynor has recorded a message
for Mrs. Graynor . . . for Mrs. Adelaide Graynor."

For Feather. "But nothing for Milcenta? But they *both*
stayed? How strange." Ms. Machti seemed the type of
person who might wonder about other people's sexual

arrangements. I wanted her curious, because this next question—"Can you show me what John had to say to Adelaide?"

She shook her head firmly. "I don't see how—"

"Now, John wouldn't have said anything someone else couldn't hear. You can watch it yourself—" Her head was still turning left, right, left. "In fact, you should. Then you can at least tell *me* if there's been, if, well. I have to know, don't I? If Milcenta's dead."

That stopped her. She nodded, barely, and tapped in the code to summon Carlos's message to Feather.

She read it all the way through. Her lip curled just a bit; but she showed only solemn pity when she turned the monitor to face me.

It was a posed scene. Carlos looked like a man hiding a sickness. The view behind him could have been a manor garden in England, a tamed wilderness. Tanya and Louis were playing in the distance, hide-and-seek in and out of some Earthly tree that dripped a cage of foliage. Alive. Ever since I had first seen them frozen, I must have been thinking of them as dead.

Carlos looked earnestly out of the monitor screen. "Adelaide, you can see that the children and I arrived safely. I have an income. The plans we made together, half of us have carried out. Your own iceliner slots are still available.

"I know nothing of Mart. I hope you've heard from him, but he should never have gone sailing alone. I fear the worst.

"Addie, I can't pretend to understand how you've changed, how Mil changed, or why. I can only hope you'll both change your mind and come back to me. But understand me, Addie: you are not welcome without Milcenta. Your claim on family funds is void without Milcenta. And whatever relationship we can shape from these ashes, I would prefer to leave the children out of it."

He had the money!

Carlos stood and walked a half circle as he spoke. The

camera followed him on automatic, and now it showed a huge, sprawling house of architectural coral, pink and slightly rounded everywhere. Carlos gestured. "I've waited. The house isn't finished because you and Milcenta will have your own tastes. But come soon.

"I've set credit with Outbound. Messages sent to Home by hyperwave will be charged to me. I'll get the service charges when you and Milcenta board. Call first. We can work this out."

The record began to repeat. I heard it through again, then turned the monitor around.

Ms. Machti asked, "You went sailing alone?"

She thought I'd tried to commit suicide after our wives had changed parity and locked the men out: an implication Carlos had shaped with some skill. I made a brush-off gesture and said, "I've got to tell him I'm still alive."

"The credit he left doesn't apply—"

"I want to send a hyperwave message, my expense. Let's see . . . does Outbound Enterprises keep a camera around?"

"No."

"I'll fax it from the hotel. When's the next flight out?"

"At least two weeks, but we can suspend you any time."

I used a camera at the hotel. The first disk I made would go through Outbound Enterprises. "John, I'm all right. I was on a dead island eating fish for a while." A slightly belligerent tone: "I haven't heard a word from Adelaide or Milcenta. I know Milcenta better than you do, and frankly, I believe they must have separated by now. Home looks like a new life, but I haven't given up on the old one. I'll let you know when I know myself."

So much for the ears of Ms. Machti.

Time lag had me suddenly wiped out. I floated between the sleeping plates . . . exhausted but awake. What should I put in a *real* message?

Carlos's tape was a wonderful lesson in communication. He wants to talk to Feather. The children are not to be put

at risk. Beowulf is presumed dead. *C'est la vie;* Carlos will
not seek vengeance. But he wants Sharrol alive. Feather is
not to come to Home without Sharrol. Carlos can enforce
any agreement. He hadn't said so because it's too obvious.
A frozen Feather, arriving at Home unaccompanied, need
never wake.

And he had the money! Not just his own funds, but the
money Feather knew about, "family funds": he must have
reached civilization ahead of her and somehow sequestered
what Feather had funneled through the ARM. If Feather
was loose on Fafnir, then she was also broke. She owned
nothing but the credit that would get her a hyperwave call
to Home, or herself and Sharrol shipped frozen. Though
Carlos didn't know it, even Sharrol had escaped.

Nearly five months. How was Feather living? Did she
have a job? Something I could track? With her training she
might be better off as a thief.

Yah! I tumbled out of the sleepfield and tapped out my
needs in some haste. She hadn't been caught at any capital
crime, but any jail on Shasht would record Adelaide
Graynor's retina prints. The caller ran its search . . .

Nothing.

Okay, *job.* Feather needed something that would allow
her time to take care of a prisoner. She had to have that if
she had Sharrol, or in case she recaptured Sharrol, or captured *Beowulf.*

So I looked through some job listings, but nothing suggested itself. I turned off the caller and hoped for sleep.
Perhaps I dozed a little.

Sometime in the night I realized that I had nothing more
to say to Carlos.

Even Sharrol's escape wasn't information unless she
stayed loose. Feather was a trained ARM. I was a self-
trained tourist; I couldn't possibly hunt her down. There
was only one way to hunt Feather.

It was still black outside, and I was wide awake. The
caller gave me a listing of all night restaurants.

I ordered an elaborate breakfast, six kinds of fish eggs,

gulper bacon, cappuccino. Five people at a table demanded that I join them, so I did. They were fresh from the coral isles via dirigible, still time-lagged, looking for new jokes. I tried to oblige. And somewhere in there I forgot all about missing ladies.

We broke up at dawn. I walked back to the hotel alone. I had sidetracked my mind, hoping it would come up with something if I left it alone; but my answer hadn't changed. The way to hunt Feather was to pretend to be Feather, and hunt Sharrol.

Stet, I'm Feather Filip. What do I know about Sharrol? Feather must have researched her; she sure as tanj had researched me!

Back up. How did Sharrol get loose?

The simplest possible answer was that Sharrol dove into the water and swam away. Feather could beat her at most things, but a woman who had lived beneath the ocean for thirty years would swim just fine.

Eventually a boat would find her.

Eventually, an island. Penniless. She needs work *now*. What kind of work is that? It has to suit a flat phobe. She's being hunted by a murderer, and the alien planet around her forces itself into her awareness every second. Dirigible stewardness is probably out. Hotel work would be better.

Feather, days behind her, seeks work for herself; but the listings will tell her Sharrol's choices too. And now I was back in the room and scanning through work listings.

Qualifications—I couldn't remember what Milcenta Graynor was supposed to be able to do. Sharrol's skills wouldn't match anyway, any more than mine matched Mart Graynor's. So look for *unskilled*.

Low salaries, of course. Except here: *servant, kzinti embassy*. Was that a joke? No: here was *museum maintenance, must work with kzinti*. Some of them had stayed with the embassy, or even become citizens. Could Sharrol handle that? She got along with strangers ... even near-aliens, like me.

Fishing boats, period of training needed. Hotel work. Underwater porter work, unskilled labor in Pacifica.

Pacifica. Of course.

Briefly I considered putting in for the porter job. Sharrol and/or Feather must have done that, grabbed whatever was to be had . . . but I told myself that Feather thought I had no money. She'd never look for me in Pacifica's second-best . . . ah, *best* hotel.

The truth is, I prefer playing tourist.

I scanned price listings for hotels in Pacifica; called and negotiated for a room at the Pequod. Then I left Shasht in untraditional fashion, via oversized transfer booth, still in early morning.

It was night in Pacifica. I checked in, crawled between sleeping plates and zonked out, my time-lagged body back on track.

I woke late, fully rested for the first time in days. There was a little round window next to my nose. I gazed out, floating half mesmerized, remembering the Great Barrier Reef outside Carlos Wu's apartment.

The strangeness and variety of Earth's sea life had stunned me then. But these oceans were older. Evolution had filled ecological niches not yet dreamed of on Earth.

It was shady out there, under a wonderful variety of seaweed growths, like a forest in fog. Life was everywhere. Here a school of transparent bell jars, nearly invisible, opened and closed to jet themselves along. Quasi-terrestrial fish glowed as if alien graffiti had been scrawled across them in Day-Glo ink to identify them to potential mates. Predators hid in the green treetops: torpedo shapes dived from cover and disappeared back into the foliage with prey wriggling in long jaws.

A boneless arm swept straight down from a floating seaweed island, toward the orange neon fish swimming just above the sandy bottom. Its stinger-armed hand flexed and fell like a net over its wriggling prey . . . and a great mouth flexed wider and closed over the wrist. The killer was dark and massive, shaped like a ray of Earth's sea. The smaller fish was painted on its back; it moved with the motion of the ray. The ray chewed, reeling the arm in, until a one-armed black oyster was ripped out of the seaweed tree and pulled down to death.

One big beast, like a long dolphin with gills and great round eyes, stopped to look me over. Owl rams were said to be no brighter than a good dog, but Fafnir scientists had been hard put to demonstrate that, and Fafnir fishers still didn't believe it.

I waved solemnly. It bowed . . . well, bobbed in place before it flicked away.

My gear was arrayed in a tidy row, with the stunner nearest my hand. I'd put the reflector back on. I could reach it in an instant. Your Honor, *of course* it's for scuba swimming. Why else would I be in possession of a device that can knock Feather Filip into a coma before she can blow a great bloody hole through my torso?

I didn't actually want to go scuba swimming.

Sharrol swam like a fish; she could be out there right now. Still, at a distance and underwater, would I know her? And Feather might know me, and Feather would certainly swim better than me, and I could hardly ignore Feather.

Sharrol had to be living underwater. It was the only way she could stay sane. Life beyond the glass was alien, stet, but the life of Earth's seas seems alien too. My slow wits hadn't seen that at first, but Feather's skills would solve *that* puzzle.

And Beowulf Shaeffer had to be underwater, to avoid sunlight. Feather could find me for the wrong reasons!

And the police of Fafnir, of whom I knew nothing at all, might well be studying me in bemused interest. *He's bought a weapon! But why, if he has the blaster that blew a hole through this vest? And it's a fishing weapon, and he's gone to Pacifica* . . . which might cause them to hold off a few hours longer.

So, with time breathing hot on my neck, I found the hotel restaurant and took my time over fruit, fish eggs in a baked potato, and cappuccino.

My time wasn't wasted. The window overlooked a main street of Pacifica's village-size collection of bubbles. I saw swimsuits, and casually dressed people carrying diving or fishing gear. Almost nobody dressed formally. That would be for Shasht, for going to work. In the breakfast room itself I saw four business tunics in a crowd of a hundred. And two men in dark blue police uniforms that left arms and legs bare: you could swim in them.

And one long table, empty, with huge chairs widely spaced. I wondered how often kzinti came in. It was hard to believe they'd be numerous, forty years after mankind had taken over.

Back in the room I fished out the little repair kit and set to work on my transfer booth card.

We learned this as kids. The idea is to make a bridge of superconductor wire across the central circuits. Transport companies charge citizens a quarterly fee to cover local jumps. The authorities don't get upset if you stay away from the borders of the card. The borders are area codes.

Well, it *looked* like the kind of card we'd used then. Fafnir's booth system served a small population that didn't use booths much. It could well be decades old, long due for replacement. So I'd try it.

I got into casuals. I rolled my wet suit around the rest of my scuba gear and stuffed the stunner into one end where I could grab it fast. Stuffed the bundle into my backpurse—it stuck way out—and left the room.

Elevators led to the roof. Admissions was here, and a line of the big transfer booths, and a transparent roof with an awesome view up into the sea forest. I stepped into a booth and inserted my card. The random walk began.

A shopping mall, high up above a central well. Booths in a line, just inside a big water lock. A restaurant; another; an apartment building. I was jumping every second and a half.

Nobody noticed me flicking in; would they notice how quickly I flicked out? Nobody gets upset at a random walk

unless the kids do it often enough to tie up circuits. But
they might remember an adult. How long before someone
called the police?

A dozen kzinti, lying about in cool half darkness gnaw-
ing oddly shaped bones, rolled to a defensive four-footed
crouch at the sight of me. I couldn't help it: I threw myself
against the back wall. I must have looked crazed with terror
when the random walk popped me into a Solarico Omni
center. I was trying to straighten my face when the jump
came. *Hey*—A travel terminal of some kind; I turned and
saw the dirigible, like an underpressured planet, before the
scene changed—*Her!*

Beyond a thick glass wall, the seaweed forest swarmed
with men and women wearing fins: farmers picking spheres
that glowed softly in oil-slick colors. I waited my moment
and snatched my card out of the slot. *Was it really*—I
tapped quickly to get an instant billing, counted two back
along the booth numbers. I couldn't use the jimmied card
for this, so I'd picked up a handful of coins. *Her?*

Solarico Omni, top floor. I stepped out of the booth, and
saw the gates that would stop a shoplifter, and a stack of
lockers.

For the first time I had second thoughts about the way I
was dressed. Nothing wrong with the clothes, but I couldn't
carry a mucking great package of diving gear into a shopping center, with a stunner so handy. I pushed my
backpurse into a locker and stepped through the gates.

The whole complex was visible from the rim of the central well. It was darker down there than I was used to.
Pacifica citizens must like their underwater gloom, I
thought.

Two floors down, an open fast-food center: wasn't that
where I'd seen her? She was gone now. I'd seen only a
face, and I could have been wrong. At least she'd never
spot *me*, not before I was much closer.

But where was she? Dressed how? Employee or customer? It was midmorning: she couldn't be on lunch break.
Customer, then. Only, Shashters kept poor track of time.

Three floors down, the sports department. Good enough.
I rode down the escalator. I'd buy a spear gun or another
stunner, shove everything into the bag that came with it.
Then I could start window shopping for faces.

The Sports Department aisles were pleasantly wide. Most
of what it sold was fishing gear, a daunting variety. There
was skiing equipment too. And hunting, it looked like: huge
weapons built for hands bigger than a baseball mitt. The
smallest was a fat tube as long as my forearm, with a grip
no bigger than a kzinti kitten's hand. Oh, sure, kzinti just
love going to humans for their weapons. Maybe the display
was there to entertain human customers.

The clerks were leaving me alone to browse. Customs
differ. *What the tanj was that?*

Two kzinti in the aisle, spaced three yards apart, hissing
the Hero's Tongue at each other. A handful of human customers watched in some amusement. There didn't seem to
be danger there. One wore what might be a loose dark blue
swimsuit with a hole for the tail. The other (sleeveless
brown tunic) took down four yards of disassembled fishing
rod. A kzinti *clerk*?

The corner of my eye caught a clerk's hands (human)
opening the case and reaching in for that smaller tube, with
a grip built for a kzin child. Or a man—

My breath froze in my throat. I was looking into Feather's horrible ARM weapon. I looked up into the clerk's
face.

It came out as a whisper. "No, Sharrol, no no no. It's me.
It's Beowulf."

She didn't fire. But she was pale with terror, her jaw set
like rock, and the black tube looked at the bridge of my
nose.

I eased two inches to the right, very slowly, to put myself
between the tube and the kzin cop. That wasn't a swimsuit
he was wearing: it was the same sleeveless, legless police
uniform I'd seen at breakfast.

We were eye to eye. The whites showed wide around her

irises. I said, "My face. Look at my face. Under the beard. It's Bey, love. I'm a foot shorter. Remember?"

She remembered. It terrified her.

"I wouldn't fit. The cavity was built for Carlos. My heart and lungs were shredded, my back was shattered, my brain was dying, and you had to get me into the cavity. But I wouldn't fit, remember? Sharrol, I have to know." I looked around quickly. An aisle over, kzinti noses came up, smelling fear. "Did you kill Feather?"

"Kill Feather." She set the tube down carefully on the display case. Her brow wrinkled. "I was going through my pockets. It was distracting me, keeping me sane. I needed that. The light was wrong, the gravity was wrong, the Earth was so far away—"

"Shh."

"Survival gear, always know what you have, *you* taught me that." She began to tremble. "I heard a sonic boom. I looked up just as you were blown backward. I thought I must be c-crazy. I couldn't have seen that."

It was my back that felt vulnerable now. I felt all those floors behind and above me, all those eyes. The kzin cop had lost interest. If there was a moment for Feather Filip to take us both, this was it.

But the ARM weapon was in *Sharrol*'s hands—

"But Carlos jumped into the boat and roared off, and Feather screamed at him, and you were all blood and sprawled out like—like *dead*—and I, I can't remember."

"Yes, dear." I took her hand, greatly daring. "But I have to know if she's still chasing us."

She shook her head violently. "I jumped on her back and cut her throat. She tried to point that tube at me. I held her arm down, she elbowed me in the ribs, I hung on, she fell down. I cut her head off. But Bey, there you were, and Carlos was gone and the kids were too, and what was I going to *do*?" She came around the counter and put her arms around me and said, "We're the same height. Futz!"

I was starting to relax. Feather was nowhere. We were free of her. "I kept telling myself you *must* have killed her.

A trained ARM psychotic, but she didn't take you seriously. She couldn't have guessed how quick you'd wake up."

"I fed her into the organics reservoir."

"Yah. There was nowhere else all that biomass could have come from. It had to be Feather—"

"And I couldn't lift your body, and you wouldn't fit anyway. I had to cut off your h-h-" She pulled close and tried to push her head under my jaw, but I wasn't tall enough any more. "Head. I cut as low as I could. Tanj, we're the same *height*. Did it work? Are you all right?"

"I'm fine. I'm just short. The 'doc rebuilt me from my DNA, from the throat down, but it built me in Fafnir gravity. Good thing, too, I guess."

"Yah." She was trying to laugh, gripping my arms as if I might disappear. "There wouldn't have been room for your feet. Bey, we shouldn't be talking here. That kzin is a cop, and nobody knows how good their hearing is. Bey, I get off at sixteen hundred."

"I'll shop. We're both overdue on life gifts."

"How do I look? How *should* I look?"

I had posed us on the roof of the Pequod, with the camera looking upward past us into the green seaweed forest. I said, "Just right. Pretty, cheerful, the kind of woman a man might drown himself for. A little bewildered. You didn't contact me because you got a blow to the head. You're only just healing. You ready? Take one, *now*." I keyed the vidcamera.

Me: "Wilhelmin, Toranaga, I hope you're feeling as good as we are. I had no trouble finding Milcenta once I got my head on straight—"

Sharrol (*bubbling*): "Hello! Thank you for Jan's life, and thank you for teaching him to sail. I never could show him how to do that. We're going to buy a boat as soon as we can afford it."

Me: "I'm ready to face the human race again. I hope you are too. This may help." I turned the camera off.

"What are you giving them?" Sharrol asked.

"Silverware, service for a dozen. Now they'll *have* to develope a social life."

"Do you think they turned you in?"

"They had to. They did well by me, love. What bothers me is, they'll *never* be sure I'm not a murderer. Neither will the police. This is a wonderful planet for getting rid of a corpse. I'll be looking over my shoulder for that kzinti cop—"

"No, Bey—"

"He smelled our fear."

"They smell *everyone's* fear. They make wonderful police, but they can't react every time a kzin makes a human nervous. He may have pegged you as an outworlder, though."

"Oop. Why?"

"Bey, the kzinti are everywhere on Fafnir, mostly on the mainland, but they're on site at the fishing sources too. Fafnir sea life feeds the whole Patriarchy, and it's strictly a kzinti operation. Shashters are used to kzin. But kids and wimps and outworlders all get twitchy around them, and they're used to that."

He might have smelled more than our fear, I thought. Our genetic makeup, our diet . . . but we'd been eating Fafnir fish for over a month, and Fafnir's people were every breed of man.

"Stet. Shall we deal with the *Hand of Allah?*"

Now she looked nervous. "I must have driven them half crazy. And worried them sick. It's a good gift, isn't it? Shorfy and Isfahan were constantly complaining about fish, fish, fish—"

"They'll love it. It's about five ounces of red meat per crewman—I suppose that's—"

"Free-range life-forms from the hunting parks."

"And fresh vegetables to match. I bet the kzinti don't grow *those*. Okay, take *one*—"

Sharrol: "Captain Muh'mad, I was a long time recovering my memory. I expect the 'docs did more repair work every time I went under. My husband's found me, we both have jobs, and this is to entertain you and your crew in my absence."

Me: "For my wife's life, blessings and thanks." I turned it off. "Now Carlos."

Her hand stopped me. "I can't leave, you know," Sharrol said. "I'm not a coward—"

"Feather learned that!"

"It's just . . . overkill. I've been through too much."

"It's all right. Carlos has Louis and Tanya for awhile, and that's fine, they love him. We're free of the UN. Everything went just as we planned it, more or less, except from Feather's viewpoint."

"Do you mind? Do you like it here?"

"There are transfer booths if I want to go anywhere. Sharrol, I was raised underground. It feels just like home if I don't look out a window. I wouldn't mind spending the rest of our lives here. Now, this is for Ms. Machti at Outbound, not to mention any watching ARMs. Ready? Take *one*."

Me: "Hi, John! Hello, kids! We've got a more or less happy ending here, brought to you with some effort."

Sharrol: "I'm pregnant. It happened yesterday morning. That's why we waited to call."

I was calling as Martin Wallace Graynor. Carlos/John could reach us the same way. We wanted no connection between Mart Graynor and Jan Hebert.

Visuals were important to the message. The undersea forest was behind us. I stood next to Sharrol, our eyes exactly level. That'd give him a jolt.

Me: "John, I know you were worried about Mil, and so was I, but she's recovered. Mil's a lot tougher than even Addie gave her credit for."

Sharrol: "Still, the situation was sticky at first. Messy." She rubbed her hands. "But that's all over. Mart's got a job working outside in the water orchards—"

Me: "It's just like working in free-fall. I've got a real knack for it."

Sharrol: "We've got some money too, and after the baby's born I'll take Mart's job. It'll be just like I'm back in my teens."

Me: "You did the right thing, protecting the children first. It's worked out very well."

Sharrol: "We're happy here, John. This is a good place to raise a child, or several. Some day we'll come to you, I think, but not now. The changes in my life are too new. I couldn't take it. Mart is willing to indulge me."

Me (sorrowfully): "Addie is gone, John. We never expect to see her again, and we're just as glad, but I feel she'll always be a part of me." I waved the camera off.

Now let's see Carlos figure *that* out. He does like puzzles.

✳

GHOST: SEVEN

"So there you have it," I told Ander. "Carlos is dead. I saw Feather shoot him before she shot me. Sharrol and the children must have gotten away. Feather stayed to put me in the 'doc, then used the other boat.

"She left me marooned on a desert island. I think she'd already given up on catching Sharrol. Otherwise, why would she need me for a hostage? I can't guess where they all are now, but if Feather was holding Sharrol, I think I'd know it."

"How?"

"By now she must know I'm gone. She could advertise on the personals net. There hasn't been anything like that."

Ander held his peace. No point in his telling the poor crashlander that his story leaks like a NASA spacecraft. From the way I'd told it, Ander could only guess that Feather had covered her back trail. Sharrol and the children must be as dead as Carlos, and Beowulf Shaeffer didn't have the courage to face it.

If he bought it, Ander would be hunting Feather, not Carlos.

"And I live in Pacifica because anywhere else I'd need pills to protect me from sunlight. Feather might trace that. Ander, can you do something about Feather? I keep expecting her to pop up behind my ear."

"I'll see what I can do. She's ARM responsibility. Could she be dead?"

"For all I know. Carlos cut her. I don't know how bad, but I saw blood."

"Carlos . . . yah. Sigmund isn't going to like that. What do I give him for proof?"

"You might find traces of him on the island, but I doubt it, Ander. I think Feather dumped him in the hopper for biomass. The closest you'll get to any remains of Carlos Wu is right here." He didn't understand. I stretched my arms, flexing my still not quite familiar body. "Not the fish, Ander. Me."

"Stet. Which island?"

"On another matter," I said. "Carlos Wu's experimental autodoc is a very valuable item. I propose to sell it to you."

Ander studied me, mildly amused. His hands wandered into pockets and came out with a silver match and a box of fat green cigars. He said, "Your bargaining position isn't that terrific."

Was he really going to fire up that thing? Tobacco, it had to be tobacco.

I tore my eyes off his hands. "Cheap," I assured him. "I can't touch it myself, after all, and you can't afford to lose it. *Look* at me! That thing rebuilt me from a severed head!"

"Buying up your trash is not exactly in my job description."

"I'll sell you the location. You collect it and do with it as you will. One hundred thousand stars."

Ander smiled at the number, conveying that it was too high even to be funny. He said, "They wouldn't let me smoke on the ship. Want one?"

"No," I said, watching all my problems solve themselves. Well, half my problems. I could run clear off the planet while Ander worked at getting himself out of a cell. But he'd chosen the wrong restaurant, and I didn't believe it, anyway. He'd delayed too long; his body language was wrong.

I said, "Wait up. Don't light that."

He sat there with the cigar poking out of the center of his grin. "I thought you'd let me do it."

I said, "I toyed with the notion. If it was just a matter of you going to jail, futz, that might improve my leverage. I could make you an offer you couldn't walk away from."

"You used to have the tobacco habit yourself."

"Oh, I gave it up to make Sharrol happy, and tanj if my sense of taste didn't come back. Ander, put those things away. Pacifica *is* a big spaceship."

"Make you nervous?"

"Ander, don't tease the kzinti."

The breath caught in his throat. The match and cigar disappeared with minimal motions of his hands. Then his head turned casually.

They looked at him, three big males with glossy orange coats and carefully closed mouths. Looked away again. They weren't doing anything threatening. Maybe they hadn't even noticed. Riiight. Kzinti living in Pacifica might never have smelled tobacco, but any who had would not forget.

Ander seemed calm, almost sleepy, except that his breathing was a little ragged and there was sweat trickling down his neck. The cigar had been for my benefit, but he really hadn't noticed the kzinti. Mankind had claimed this world, hadn't we? Kzinti didn't belong here, did they?

He sought the thread of conversation. "You don't know where Feather Filip is, and you last saw the magical autodoc a year and a half ago."

"Exactly. I don't know that Feather hasn't been watching for me to come back and get it. There were lamplighter islands in line of sight. She could be watching for me with a pair of mag specs."

"Or she could be anywhere on Fafnir. But if I find her, *she* can take me to the island."

I kept silent.

"I can reach some funds. Tell you what," Ander said. "Take my entire expense credit. Five thousand and change. I'll have to live on credit till Sigmund can send me more."

"No, no, Ander. I want a hundred thousand."

"I'd have to beam Sigmund. I'd have to tell him what it's for. Where does that leave me?"

"Tell him I want two hundred thousand. Keep half yourself."

"Beowulf, what you have to sell is a tool that's been left under seawater. The technology is in records left behind by Carlos Wu."

"*Did* he leave records of his research? You don't know that. Encrypted? You don't know. I don't, either. Could the Fafnir government get the techniques by studying the autodoc itself? We don't know."

Ander laughed at that. "What are you going to *tell* the Fafnir bureaucrats? You stand five ten, maybe, but you can produce records that show you seven feet tall? Records can be faked, Beowulf. I'm your only customer."

This was fun. I had his attention, *finally*. "What if we take a stunted kzinti—there are a few—and skin him, and before he suffers too much trauma, we shove him in Carlos Wu's 'doc. Would it rebuild him into a passable human? A perfect spy?"

He guffawed. "That is *really* ridiculous."

"Oh, maybe. But there are wealthy kzinti families on Fafnir."

"*They* don't know how tall you used to be, either! Anyway, dealing with kzinti is crazy dangerous. Beowulf, I've got nearly six thousand, and you can have it all. Otherwise you'll have to wait while I tell Sigmund Ausfaller what you're selling, and Sigmund makes a counteroffer, and you settle, and he finally sends credit, all by hyperwave across ten light-years. And if I find Feather while you're waiting, you get nothing."

"Good enough. Tell him two hundred thousand stars—"

"One."

"One. Half in advance, half when you've got the 'doc. I'll be here at the Pequod until the money comes in." I stood up. "It's midnight. Pay my consultant's fee at the hotel desk." I walked out, thinking I'd timed that nicely.

* * *

I stopped at the desk to learn my room number. I told them there would be a payment entered against room charges.

My backpurse was hanging in the sleeping plates. I checked through it. Someone might have searched it . . . someone had. Sharrol, looking for what might identify me as a family man. She'd found and removed my two holos of her, one with Tanya and Louis but no Carlos, the other more recent, pregnant, with Jeena at her breast.

Twenty minutes between the plates would do me a world of good, I thought. Four hours would be even better.

No *time*.

I rode an elevator to the roof. There I paused, gazing idly up into the black oceanic night.

Sanity check: Was I being watched? In what fashion?

ARM cameras are little transparent disks you apply with a thumb to a flat surface. They don't cost that much and are impossible to spot. My room would be a good place to scatter a few. So would the lobby doors and the line of transfer booths behind me on the Pequod's roof. But Ander had had no chance to set them . . . had he?

I wished that I'd known Ander Smittarasheed better. I hadn't learned much today. He had the instincts of a cop; he'd treated me as a felon ready to escape. He remembered *me* fairly well. Strong as hell. What else?

He had come here for me, he'd said. More likely he'd come for *us*. For Carlos, the valuable one; Feather, the dangerous one; Beowulf Shaeffer, the talkative one who knows too much; Carlos's children, both United Nations citizens; Sharrol Janss . . . could lead him to the rest. But I could do that for him, too. He didn't need Sharrol.

Ander must have reached Fafnir by tracking a sighting of Carlos's ship. Where had he begun his investigations?

He'd started where he had landed, at the Shasht spaceports, of course. A party of six, three of us flat phobes, would not have come to a weird world like Fafnir to *stay*. He would search through the hotels and spaceports and hiding places on Shasht, try to learn if we'd left, before he faced eleven hours worth of jet lag in the islands.

If he'd gone to Outbound, he'd have found the Graynor family all registered for flight. Those names and a phone file would have brought him to Pacifica.

The public booths in Pacifica are lined along the dome, with a view up into the underwater jungle, for its impact on tourists incoming from Shasht. Ander Smittarasheed must have just arrived from Shasht when he saw me looking down at him.

I didn't like that. It would mean Ander had placed cameras at Outbound. They would have been waiting when Sharrol came in with Jeena. They'd be there now, for me.

But I couldn't be wrong about *this*: Ander had been shocked stupid at the sight of me. If he had found records for the Graynors, he'd have everything: our transplant types, allergies, eye color, *height*.

Ander would have given up then or persuaded himself that Beowulf Shaeffer had made himself shorter. But he *hadn't* known that. He *hadn't*.

No, he hadn't followed a paper trail. He had followed one of six fugitives, the one he knew, through a chain of logic. Beowulf Shaeffer, albino. Track him through the regular purchase of tannin secretion pills. No? Then he must be living like a vampire: working a night shift at Shasht or the Islands, at any business that caters to jet-lagged travelers. No? Then . . . under the sea? Losing hope . . . and *there he is!*

He'd run up a long flight of stairs to catch me. He certainly hadn't phoned anyone on the way. He hadn't let me out of his sight since. Congratulations, Ander! Beowulf Shaeffer has not escaped.

But Ander hadn't had a chance to call for backup.

The curve of glass above me supported kilotons of seawater and a life older than planet Earth. Luminescent angler fish and eels and elaborately shaped jellyfish writhed through the blackness. I sat on a bench and watched. Perhaps something was watching me.

Ander would search in vain for Feather Filip.

That wouldn't stop his search. Using instruments on a ship or satellite, he would pick out every darkened island. Dead lamplighter, no glow of house lights. Choose among those for just two live islands in line of sight; then deep radar for a hollow object more massive than sand offshore. Carlos Wu's 'doc.

In the lamplighter pit: the scorched remains of an antique lander. He'd search out human remains. He'd find bits of my bones and read their DNA. If he found traces of Feather's blood, it would only confirm my story.

If Ander was honest, he'd return the machine to Earth and the UN. If he changed his mind, so much the better. Give him something to hide, to sell.

Meanwhile, Beowulf Shaeffer waits patiently for word. Let him stew long enough, paying hotel rates when he clearly can't afford it, and he'll settle for much less than his hundred thousand. Monitor his phone; we wouldn't want him looking for a better offer from the Shashters, let alone the Patriarchy. At least we know he'll wait.

The thing is, Shaeffer knows too much. A man who has seen Julian Forward's miniature black hole and the tools he used to make it a weapon should not be running loose. (Feather Filip had told me that, but I believed it.) The money is trivial ... well, trivial given that it will never be paid. But Shaeffer needs the money; he won't run away from that.

I watched the eternal show of Fafnir's sea life for a time in case I was being watched myself. I fished my flat portable out—less advanced than Ander's, purchased locally— and tapped at it idly. Addresses popped up, with transfer booth numbers. Some I filed, filling in a map.

People went in and out of the booths. Maybe one was an ARM planting cameras. Maybe not.

So I strolled into the near booth. Got to kill some time— right, Ander?—or the waiting will drive me *nuts*. My card in the slot. Look at the wall, watch the advertisements flow past (discreetly small, by city law), and presently tap out a number.

There were places a single might visit. They advertised on the walls of transfer booths. I'd never been in one—honest, Sharrol! But when the booth flicked me in, I didn't see anything surprising.

It was noisy and close. They were dressed to catch the eye, in those bodysuits with windows, men and women both. The dim light favored them, and holograms of real and fantasy worlds made a distracting magic. Eyes looked me over, judging, not liking what they saw.

On every world some singles nodes welcome the tourist trade; some don't.

How they knew me I can't guess, because Shashters are a varied lot. But I was not welcome here. One or two men were preparing to tell me so. I retrieved my Persial January Hebert card, stepped from the booth, and walked straight to the door faster than they could decide, and then out.

Any flatlander who followed me through might well be delayed.

I was hoping to see a restaurant or juice bar, but I didn't. Around the nearest corner, then, and here was a public booth. I didn't use the card. I used coins.

My ears felt the pressure drop. What I saw as I stepped from the booth was a patchy cityscape. These were the Disneys, a cluster of ten coral peaks linked to another dozen by slidebridges. It was still night. A shadow blocked a patch of stars: a wedge-shaped dirigible just departing from the Flying Island terminal.

You wouldn't find more than one dirigible company to an island. Why risk dirigibles floating into each other when any customer can take a booth to the next island over? There were four terminals in the Disneys, all on outlying islands.

From the Flying Island terminal I began walking.

Daylight would have fried me before I reached my target. But the night was a gorgeous display of stars, and the waves crashed down in spectral blue and yellow flashes of luminous algae. In this light an albino would look no weirder than anyone else.

If I had a trick worth trying, it was unpredictability. Ander might trace me as far as the singles node. What he would learn there might set him to searching hospitals for a battered P. J. Hebert. He couldn't follow coins, I thought, but if somehow he did, he'd find I had reached the Flying Island dirigible terminal, then—

Then? Somewhere else, with the same haste I'd shown up to now. Possibly I'd boarded a dirigible; more likely I was on Shasht via instantaneous booth.

But for most of an hour I rode slidebridges toward Beast Island.

On Aladdin Island I found a tourist section and a hairstyler with a wide range of settings. Nobody but a flatlander would want his hair colored. I turned it sandy and curly and short. I stopped again to buy fresh clothing and a bigger backpurse, again for a steam bath and massage and to ditch my old clothing. Ander could have left any number of cameras on my person. Well before dawn I walked into the Grail Hunt terminal, where I bought my dirigible ticket as Martin Wallace Graynor.

If Ander knew *that* name, he'd have Milcenta Graynor, too: Sharrol. But he didn't have Feather, and Feather was Adelaide Graynor. We weren't caught yet.

I boarded the *Wyvern*. I settled into a hammock chair and fell fast asleep.

✳

GHOST: EIGHT

The Core. Ashes of supernovas: plasma thick and glowing among millions of neutron stars. Lighter stars still glowed, still retained their retinue of planets.

Automated spacecraft streamed out from a pentagon of blue and white worlds. Terraforming began on a vast scale. Would they all be farming worlds to feed one homeworld with a population approaching quintillions? The surface would be lost. A hollow world would form and swell to Jovian size.

Tens of thousands of years away. Would anyone remember the Pierson's puppeteers?

They would, yes. Information is too easy to record, too difficult to destroy. When the Core explosion glared in the night sky, anyone who cared would find the Fleet of Worlds in ancient United Nations records, and the record of their departure, and even Beowulf Shaeffer's opinion, as recorded by Ander Smittarasheed, as to where they'd gone. If our civilization survived, there would be records showing whether I was right.

The easy sway of *Wyvern* had awakened me. I knew before I opened my eyes: we were airborne.

I studied my watch. Four hours I'd slept. Not enough. Dawn must be a long way away, but I ought to do something about it.

The floor jittered under my feet as I made my groggy way to the dispenser wall.

The dispensers were coin-operated. I thanked my luck and bought tannin secretion pills for the first time in a year

271

and a half. I downed four at the fountain, then made my way back to the hammock.

I watched black water and bright islands, their centers marked by white city glow or yellow lamplighter glow, with the electric blue flash of breakers to outline their rims. Presently one crept near. I watched while *Wyvern* descended to a mooring and a spiral stair came snaking up to us.

Passengers were boarding at Thelinda's Island; others were getting off. I got off.

My phone was listed under Graynor, not Hebert. I called Outbound Enterprises.

Ice Trireme would lift for Home in four days, more or less. Milcenta Graynor and a child were frozen solid and doing fine. I was expected; Milcenta had already signed me in. Was I aware that Milcenta was carrying a child? Special techniques had been required, and a surcharge had been added. It had been too long since I'd had my physical. I'd need another before I could board, and that, too, required a surcharge, which Milcenta had paid.

She'd done it! She'd retrieved Jeena; she'd reached the terminal and checked us all in and kept her cool until they cooled her down and had never made a mistake.

My turn now.

The real Martin Wallace Graynor had played the futures market. It had broken him. Feather had made him an offer, and I had become Mart Graynor.

I had taken up his habit. I bought options to buy (or sell) shares of cargoes on outgoing spacecraft, sold the option if the price went up (or down), sometimes exercised the option instead. I'd been doing that for over a year, ever since I had reasoned out how it worked. I was down a few thousand, but that wasn't the point. Mart Graynor held options on cargoes bound for Home.

Ice Trireme was carrying a fertilizer package: cattle dung seeded with minerals, earthworms, and small life-forms including unicellular rock eaters. The stuff would be treated like a concentrate, mixed into rock dust, and used as soil. Mart Graynor owned an option to buy at a set price.

I bought it all.

I would own it when it landed on Home, and there I would sell it. Money moving between stars might be noticed, but fertilizer packages were *supposed* to move.

Next: the apt in Pacifica, in Milcenta Graynor's name. Should I do something about that? But Sharrol had been so efficient. She might well have put it up for sale herself.

Or we could just let the lease lapse. I left it alone.

Twenty minutes gone. Plenty of time to cross the slidebridge to Baker Street Island, put coins in a booth, and be waiting on Landis Island when the dirigible *Wyvern* touched down.

Direct sunlight flamed on my cheeks, forehead, closed eyelids. I thrashed in terror and snapped awake. I'd taken the pills, hadn't I? Pat pockets, find the bottle. Seal broken. Good.

We had left most of the islands behind.

A balcony rimmed the gondola, screened with webbing to discourage fools and jumpers. Several passengers had taken their trays out there. I got my breakfast and went out in time to occupy an inflated chair.

I took my shirt off. My blood was suffused with the antisunburn chemicals, and my skin darkened fast as the morning wore on.

We flew not far above the water. Following the surfaces of enormous swells, *Wyvern* felt a long-period surge and drop. This was the deep ocean. Waves had room to grow out here. So did the sea beasts.

A voice from the control room directed our eyes to where a black shadow was forming in the dark water. It surfaced; water ran from it, a black island. Then a neck rose, and rose farther, dozens of yards into the air. A bar of a head with eyes wide-spaced for binocular vision studied the lights of the flying machine above it.

I felt the heady ecstasy of the discoverer and then a sudden savage guilt.

* * *

We would end on Home.

A flat phobe could live and raise her children there without forcing her body to admit that she had left Earth. In that respect it lacks interest, and that was why we chose it. I would be there, too, marooned beneath the stars . . . at the bottom of a hole, as the Belters say of planets.

I didn't even know if there were alien embassies on Home. "I'm out of the aliens business," I'd said.

I'd been on Fafnir for a year and a half, and I'd spent it beneath the ocean. This was my last chance to see the world. My last spaceflight, in miniature.

It's misdirection, see, Sharrol? The crashlander's hand is more nimble than the eye of the ARM. But I'd known what I was doing all along.

Sanity check—

Ander wouldn't ignore the spaceports; Ander wouldn't forget the iceliners. I had to gamble that he had looked at Outbound Enterprises *first*, and *thoroughly*, before he had come to Pacifica. Sharrol and Jeena and I might get clear before Ander looked again.

Then the records would tell him that a family native to Fafnir had been frozen while, halfway around the planet, Ander was watching water war with Beowulf Shaeffer. He would have no reason at all to connect these Graynors with fleeing flatlanders.

I was *not* burning time at my family's cost. I was confusing my back trail. With luck and ingenuity we'd be clear of Ander Smittarasheed and would stay that way.

Now, what of Sigmund Ausfaller?

They had followed us to Fafnir by following the track of Carlos's ship, but Fafnir wasn't even the best bet. Flat phobes would try to reach Home. My best guess was that Sigmund had sent Ander here and taken Home for himself.

I would wake from the frozen state, and Sigmund Ausfaller would be looking down at me.

If Ausfaller was on Home, then there was not one tanj thing I could do to protect us. Carlos Wu must deal with

him, for I could not. I told myself that Carlos Wu was a
match for a dozen Sigmund Ausfallers.

Night came, and the air grew chilly. I waited until I was
alone and presently pushed my Persial January Hebert iden-
tity through the safety web and watched it fall.

It was very like flying with Nakamura Lines as a passenger. The differences were all to the good: the breeze, the
clean taste of the air, the lesser isolation. In case of disaster,
help was hours away, not weeks or months.

I noticed a "recess" mentality I'd seen during spaceflight.
This was not a real place. Breaks in discipline would not be
paid for. Diets broke down. Couples paired off or split up
for quick liaisons. Children ran wild; distance and the soft
walls absorbed their shrieking. A few adults were trying out
funny chemicals or flying by wire.

The people around me were mostly Shashters eager for
company to while away the hours. Some of us squared off
for computer-game competitions. Our numbers kept changing. Staying with the same people was difficult because jet
lag was hitting us all differently.

I let conversation find me, doing very little of the talking.
I didn't want anyone remembering a pale flatlander or ex-
astronaut on his way to Shasht. I turned down some interesting offers—honest, Sharrol.

The vast reach of Fafnir's ocean passed beneath us. Two
days passed very pleasantly before the long backbone of
Shasht rose from the sea.

And then all the relaxed people around me began acting
like children who have remembered their homework.

The terminal was on the ridge, perched on the spine of
the continent. I had my choice of booths or a magnetic car
or a footpath down through a rocky canyon.

I chose the footpath. Maybe I was being overcautious;
maybe I just wanted the walk, or the tan, or some extra
time before they froze me into something not much like a
living man.

Nobody tried to stop me. An hour's walk brought me to the Outbound Enterprises office at Shasht North Spaceport.

Outbound was a smallish pillbox of a building surrounded by parkland. It reminded me a little too much of a certain park on Earth that had once been a burial ground. Like Forest Lawn, the Outbound building was a pocket of green surrounded by glass slabs of cityscape.

Within the glass wall was a circle of benches and an arc of transfer booths, six, with phones at either end. Ms. Machti ruled at the center. She was a dark, pretty woman guarded by hands-off body language and by the circle of desk that enclosed her like a fortress.

I was glad to see her. She knew me by sight. Her fingers were dancing over her keyboard even as she greeted me. "Mr. Graynor! You've had a busy year and a half."

"Nice and quiet, actually," I said. "Are Milcenta and Jeena all right?"

"Cooled down and ready for shipment. I take it Adelaide never appeared."

"No. Went her own way, I guess."

"Just as well, perhaps," she said primly. I don't think she approved of Mart Graynor having two wives, let alone bent ones. "Well, we have a few formalities to cover, and then you can join them. Did you know that your specs list you at six feet eleven inches?"

My shock must have showed. *Who would have seen that listing?*

I managed a credible laugh. "Did you have an oversized box laid out for me?"

"No, that's not a problem; it was only a matter of rewriting the specs. But *we* couldn't do that. Ms. Graynor doesn't seem to know your exact height. We'll have to measure you."

"Stet."

"So." She waved in a counterclockwise circle. Waving me around the desk? I walked that way and saw the sliding staircase leading down.

Of course. Most of Outbound must be underground.

I started down. Ms. Machti called, "Mr. Graynor? You've a call from a Mr. Ausfaller. He says you can't take off yet."

Ausfaller! How could he know . . . *What* did he know? "He asked for Martin Wallace Graynor?"

"No, he wanted the red-haired man at the desk, and I said, 'Mister Graynor?' and he—"

"Stet. Can you—" I did *not* want the call transferred to my pocket phone. "May I take it on one of those?" I waved at the booths.

"Certainly."

It was half a phone booth, just two black walls and a projection table. It would give me privacy, but I could still see out. I tapped the receiver, and a life-sized bust of Sigmund Ausfaller popped into view.

His rather vicious smile faded a little. He hadn't expected me at eye level. I thought, Sigmund, you're bothering a total stranger, sandy-haired, tanned, a foot shorter than your albino quarry. Could I get away with that?

I didn't feel lucky. I said, "Long story. Ask Ander."

"So your name is Graynor now?"

"*Bray*nard," I said distinctly. "Where are you?" He'd only heard the name over a phone. "Graynor" would give the bastard Sharrol and Jeena, too.

"Where should I be?"

I saw nothing of background, just the head and torso solid projection. He could be anywhere. I suggested, "Retrieving Carlos Wu's autodoc?"

"In due course. It shouldn't be left here. Look outside, Bey. Turn left. Farther. Look up."

He was ten floors up in a glass slab, looking down at me. Doll-sized, he was just big enough to recognize. He waved at me from the window, then turned back to his holovid phone.

"I'm right on top of you. It would take you hours to freeze yourself, perhaps days to be stowed and launched. I need only cross the street to stop you. Let us reason together, Bey."

"You always seem to have an offer I can't refuse. Why are you picking on me, Sigmund? I told Ander everything he wanted to know."

"I haven't heard from Ander."

"Feather. Carlos. Pierson's puppeteers."

"You'll still have to come home with me, Bey. You know too much, and you talk too much. Now, *wait*. Don't go off half-cocked. I can get you a birthright."

"Yah?" It was dawning on me that *he* might not know about Sharrol.

"*One* child. We have that much power if you can do something of clear public benefit. Can you return Carlos Wu to his home?"

"Carlos is *dead*, Sigmund."

"Dead?"

"How did you find me?"

"You can't see it, Bey, but I'm looking at four walls of vidscreens. We scattered cameras everywhere. Then we plastered the screens all over my room. It's been— Wait one. *Pray turn all screens off.*" He waited an instant, looking offstage. Then, "Thank God, I can throw these things away and watch blank walls again. I've been watching three spaceport terminals and the top five restaurants and ten hotel lobbies, and when you finally showed, I couldn't believe it was you."

"You damn well convinced yourself somehow!"

"I couldn't believe it wasn't, either. Sorry about that. Bey, are you sure about Carlos?"

"Feather blew a hole through him. But the nanotech 'doc is his last legacy, and it's UN property, and I might arrange to put that in your hands."

"Very good. We'll have a chance to talk about puppeteers and the like on the way home." A bell pinged. He turned around and shouted, *"Pray open the door!"* He turned back. "And Feather? You know, we never intended to turn her loose on an alien world. We want some weaponry back, too. And the others, Sharrol and the children?"

I set my face for the big lie. "Feather's g—"

Sigmund jumped at me, banged his face on the edge of the field, recoiled, and fell backward and out of sight.

Ander Smittarasheed stepped into view, wading through the table, short ribs deep. He was holding a familiar object. He reached down. Sigmund Ausfaller was pulled into view by his hair. Sigmund's chest was shattered, a huge hole rammed through it.

Ander was holding Feather Filip's horrible ARM weapon, the gun that had blown a hole through my own chest. He pointed it at me. "Recognize this?"

For an instant I thought I was going mad. He couldn't have that. He *couldn't*. It was in the apt, Sharrol's apt, hidden—

Ah. *Sharrol left it for me. She left me a weapon in my backpurse.* Not a bad idea, but Ander must have searched my room, searched by backpurse, found it there. *When?*

After dinner, when I was at the hotel desk getting my key.

Ander said, "Where are you, Beowulf?"

I was still looking through Outbound's huge window. High up in that glass slab I could see a tiny figure where Ausfaller had waved at me. The back of Ander's head and shoulders.

If he turned around and looked down, he would see me. I didn't turn away. The front of me now looked less like Beowulf Shaeffer than the back. And what could Ander see in his phone? The miniature bust of a tanned stranger and nothing behind it.

I said, "I'm in my room at the Pequod. Ander, nothing was said about *killing* the poor flat."

"Beowulf, we can hardly sell our wonderful nanotech machine without Sigmund knowing where we got it. The room isn't registered to anyone, and the punchgun can go with me. You haven't used the punchgun, have you? Like for robbing a droud shop?"

"No."

"Then at worst they'll track it back to the ARM. And then maybe to you."

My head seemed filled with fog. *Did I do this? Did I*

find the temptation that turned Ander Smittarasheed into a thief and killer? Or was he always that?

What do I do now? Play it out— "A dead man can't send us money," I said.

"Sigmund brought local money. It'll be in that case. It may take me a while to break the security programs, and I don't really know how much he brought."

"Show me the case."

"What, you think I'm lying?" He bent out of view, then rose again with a heavy silver briefcase in his fist. "Now is when you tell me where the island is."

I gave him a longitude, the right one. "Latitude when I've got half the money."

"I'll be in touch."

"Wait! Ander, get rid of the punchgun."

Ander laughed. "I think I'll keep it."

He'd seen how I feared it. He'd keep it to intimidate me. I tried anyway. "Ander, I was wearing a v—"

He flicked off.

I waited at the phone until I saw the shape in the hotel room window stand and step out of view. Then I went back to the desk. "Are you ready to freeze me, Ms. Machti?"

White-garbed medics wanted my retina prints and a voice match. I was five feet ten and a half inches tall. The physical exam they put me through seemed perfunctory, but what could they find? Carlos Wu's autodoc had rebuilt me almost from my DNA map. I'd *never* been in better shape.

I wanted to view Sharrol and Jeena. The doctors let me see them. They looked all right . . . well, dead, but otherwise. . . . I was nerving myself to join them.

As if I'd left myself a choice.

What a mess. Poor Sigmund.

What would the local police make of that wound? They'd never seen a corpse like that, but they'd seen a *vest* like that. The punchgun had torn that kind of hole through a survival vest that had belonged to a Persial January Hebert, who'd sunk out of sight a year and a half ago.

Surely they'd make the connection. They'd come looking for the reclusive Persial January Hebert. Hebert had indulged in a sudden flurry of activity: a phone call here, a hotel room at the Pequod Hotel, a dinner with Ander Smittarasheed.

Without the punchgun Ander might bluff his way through.

But the weapon would nail him, would identify him. He couldn't hold on to the gun without using it.

Would he even hesitate? A trained ARM facing colony cops? Fafnir is a "human" world. Ander was unlikely to guess how many police are kzinti.

I wondered how much damage Ander would do before it all caught up with him. There could be one fearful bloodbath if he tried to shoot his way free.

Nice for me. Ander dead was Ander silent. But—

Tens of thousands of years from now nobody would find the old ARM records of a wild hypothesis. Nobody would wonder if a trillion powerful aliens had left known space to take possession of the galactic Core. It might never matter, even if I was right . . . or be all to the good if I was wrong.

Either way, I couldn't think of a way to stop him.

They were spraying my arm. I would be in a coma when they cooled me down and launched me. I wondered whose face would be looking down at me when I woke.

PC SOFTWARE ENTERTAINMENT

DON'T MISS THE SEQUELS TO *RINGWORLD* AND *RINGWORLD ENGINEERS!*

Now that you have completed the literary works of genius story-teller Larry Niven, continue your pursuit of Known Space entertainment on DOS!

TSUNAMI MEDIA presents *RINGWORLD, Revenge of the Patriarch* and *RINGWORLD 2, Within A.R.M.'s Reach.* Larry Niven's beloved characters and intriguing worlds come to life on your DOS PC.

RINGWORLD, *Revenge of the Patriarch*—
A tangled web of intrigue brings together a vengeful Kzin, a kidnapped engineer, and a mercenary—alone against a plot that could plunge all of *Known Space* into total chaos. The Kzinti are on the warpath, the Puppeteers claim innocence, and the Ringworld holds the answer—if only you can find it in time...

RINGWORLD 2, *Within A.R.M.'s Reach*—
You are a fugitive from every society in *Known Space*! With nowhere to go after your first heroic adventure, you and your fellow fugitives decide to return to Ringworld and lay low until you can devise a plan to clear your names. Along the way you crew stumbles upon the great secret of Ringworld that turns out to be the greatest mystery in the history of *Known Space*!

AVAILABLE ON 3.5" HD DISKS OR ON CD-ROM! ORDER THESE PRODUCTS FROM YOUR LOCAL SOFTWARE DEALER.

TSUNAMI™